T0281792

The Bird Cage Theater

The Curtain Rises on Tombstone, Arizona's National Treasure

Michael Paul Mihaljevich

University of North Texas Press
Denton, Texas

10 9 8 7 6 5 4 3 2 1

Permissions:
University of North Texas Press
1155 Union Circle #311336
Denton, TX 76203-5017

The paper used in this book meets the minimum requirements of the
American National Standard for Permanence of Paper for Printed Library
Materials, z39.48.1984. Binding materials have been chosen for durability.

Library of Congress Cataloging-in-Publication Data

Names: Mihaljevich, Michael Paul, 1981- author.
Title: The Bird Cage Theater : the curtain rises on Tombstone, Arizona's
   national treasure / Michael Paul Mihaljevich.
Description: Denton, Texas : University of North Texas Press, [2024] |
   Includes bibliographical references and index.
Identifiers: LCCN 2024038177 (print) | LCCN 2024038178 (ebook) |
   ISBN 9781574419481 (cloth) | ISBN 9781574419573 (ebook)
Subjects: LCSH: Bird Cage Theater (Tombstone, Ariz.)--History. |
   Theaters--Arizona--Tombstone--History. | Music-halls (Variety-theaters,
   cabarets, etc.)--Arizona--Tombstone--History. | Frontier and pioneer
   life--Arizona--Tombstone. | BISAC: HISTORY / United States / State &
   Local / Southwest (AZ, NM, OK, TX) | PERFORMING ARTS / Theater /
   History & Criticism
Classification: LCC NA6835.T66 M54 2024 (print) | LCC NA6835.T66
   (ebook) | DDC 725/.8220979153--dc23/eng/20240919
LC record available at https://lccn.loc.gov/2024038177
LC ebook record available at https://lccn.loc.gov/2024038178

The electronic edition of this book was made possible by the support of the
Vick Family Foundation. Typeset by vPrompt eServices.

For Jen, Mom, Dad, and Michelle—the purest
love possible on earth.

Contents

Illustrations

Preface

Near the corner of Sixth and Allen Streets in Tombstone, Arizona, stands an unassuming building measuring just 30 feet wide and 120 feet long. In late summer of 1881, builders constructed it from the very ground it sits on, molding desert dirt and bear grass into sun-hardened bricks stacked 18 feet high to form its outside walls. They reinforced the roof and frame with lumber that local suppliers procured from wood camps in the neighboring Dragoon and Huachuca Mountains. The building materials may be unimpressive, but they were assembled to create a world inside that is undeniably special. The building is small, covering just 3,600 square feet of Arizona's expansive desert. Yet its true story is the product of a previously unknown international cast that spanned the globe. A teenage runaway from California, a refugee from war-riddled Germany, the son of a working-class miner in England, and many more all helped make it a legendary building. Every year tens of thousands of people are welcomed through its doors to experience an atmosphere that begs wonder and imagination. For over one hundred years, private and public tours of its interior have inspired questions, evolving lore, and conflicting stories.

Those stories began a quest for me, but it didn't start out as a book. More than a decade ago I gathered a small file of period clippings related to the Bird Cage that generated a few basic questions. The search for answers took me deep into city, county, and territorial records and other repositories across the country. This led to the discovery of many revealing and previously unused period resources. The trail of evidence provided answers about how the Bird Cage came to be and how it was run, and unveiled unknown people who contributed to its story. A book became a natural consequence of these findings. In light of these newly discovered documents and resources, the reader should be prepared to depart from the easily found and often contradicting Bird Cage lore that is told in absence of fact. Like Wyatt Earp, Doc Holliday, or other notable Old West icons, the Bird Cage has become a victim of its own popularity by having attracted the kind of attention that has made it susceptible to identity-altering stories. Sadly, these stories actually disconnect people from the fascinating truth of the Bird Cage and at times defame those involved with its operation. My goal in writing the book is to give a voice to these unused records without interference of my own ideas or the modern myths and to bring long overdue attention to truth that has been avalanched under fiction. By doing so, these pages will put readers in direct contact with the real identity of the Bird Cage, its performers, and its proprietors for the very first time—a reality that needs no embellishments.

The Bird Cage stands today as Tombstone's most iconic original building, calling back to the town's most storied era, but it represents more than that. It's a lasting monument for the several hundred performers who spent part of their careers there. Even bigger than that, it calls back to an era in American entertainment that included thousands of performers and a network of hundreds of similar venues across the West and the world that don't exist anymore. As the best-preserved example of this piece of American history, it truly is a national treasure. May this effort set the record straight where all previous attempts have given in to myth and fallen short.

Who This Book Is For

I've written this book with a number of people in mind. For people who find academic research and truth more stimulating than fiction, this book is for you. For those that care enough about the Bird Cage to truly know what it is, this book is for you. For those that are deeply fascinated by the Bird Cage and have wondered what was it actually like, this book is for you. For those that aren't able to visit the Bird Cage in person but want to feel connected, this book is for you. For that rare individual who may come along wanting to advance the research of the Bird Cage even further, this book is for you. For those living today who are descendants of the several hundred previously unidentified Bird Cage performers, employees, and proprietors who added color and vitality to the history of the building, this book is most definitely written for you. And for generations of people in the future who may see the day when the Bird Cage no longer stands, consider this book a permanent opportunity to walk inside its doors forever.

Acknowledgments

As I look back, I see how this project grew beyond my imagination and took many wild, unpredictable turns. As it progressed I met many people who not only aided my progress but also became instrumental in making this book a reality. Among those to be acknowledged are fellow researchers, librarians, custodians of records, descendants and family members of people important to the body of work, and my own family and friends who offered encouragement and guidance at key times. Without them this project likely would have been less complete or perhaps unfinished altogether. On behalf of myself and all readers who may find this work of value, I am indebted to you all.

Thank you to Greg and Susan Mihaljevich, Michelle Swank, Peter Brand, Michael Lanning, Nancy Sosa, Paul Johnson, Annemarie van Roessel (of the Billy Rose Theatre Division of the New York Public Library), Barbara Lovell (of Kingston's Schoolhouse Museum), Pam Potter, Bob Palmquist, Gary McLelland, Roy B. Young, Marge Elliott, Gail Allan, Susan Twomey (great-granddaughter of Tombstone pioneer businesswoman Mary Twomey), Tom and Pauline Fredericks, Larry and Connie Wittig (descendant of Bird Cage orchestra leader Ed H. A. Wittig), Karen Smith (of the California Eastern Star Chapter 9 of Nevada County, California), Rebekah Tabah Percival (photo archivist and curator at the Arizona Historical Society in Tucson), librarians at the Arizona State Library and Archives, Karen Woodward (descendant of southeastern Arizona pioneer Thomas Dunbar), Gaylene Kennedy (extended family member of Bird Cage performer Millie de Granville), Kari Devere, Ron Woggon, Bill Sudhaus, Jennifer Amodei, Patrick Wells (of the Danbury Museum and Historical Society), Pete Shrake (archivist of the Robert L. Parkinson Library and Research Center in Baraboo, Wisconsin), Rebecca J. Snyder (director for research and publishing at the Dakota County Historical Society), Steve Westlake (custodian of the National Police Gazette archives), Jim and Heidi Doherty, Garner Palenske, Mike Mayberry, and Jeremy Rowe.

Chapter 1

What Is a Variety Theater?

The development of the variety theaters has been about the most
wonderful thing ever known in theatreland.
—Career performer and theatrical manager M. B. Leavitt, 1912

The variety theater . . . is a source of demoralization to young men,
a sink of depravity, and can be regarded in no other sense than
appalling disgust.
—*Seattle Post-Intelligencer*, January 6, 1889

For some the mention of variety theater conjures up images of the Wild West, where cowboys and bandits mingled among high-class actresses, stout businessmen, and timid townsfolk. Imaginations may conjure up high-kicking legs, loud whistling, and liquor-guzzling delight amid an atmosphere filled with smoke, piano music, clacking poker chips, and gratuitous gunfire. We have legends and movies to thank for that. While some of these elements do represent reality, the real world of variety theaters and the array of classes they attracted in both the audience and on the stage is far more compelling. Examining their reality is not only a fascinating journey into history but also necessary to understanding exactly what the Bird Cage was and is.

When the Bird Cage swung its doors open in December 1881, it became part of a network of hundreds of variety theaters operating across the country and around the globe. What began as a new entertainment business model in large eastern cities decades earlier quickly caught on and became an international craze. Peaking from the Civil War until roughly 1900, variety theaters were found in Europe, Australia, the United States, Russia and even Africa— from the biggest cities in the world to the remote canvas-and-frame boomtowns that popped up in the West.

Prior to variety theaters, society coveted large and formal opera houses and refined plays that obeyed Victorian standards. Despite their generally negative stigma, variety theaters should be recognized for revolutionizing entertainment by making it available on a daily basis and at prices more suitable to a larger portion of the population. Many forms of entertainment we enjoy today were supplemented by these venues in their height of popularity. Their less formal acts and quick-change format appealed to audiences that "preferred to be amused rather than educated," according to one theater owner.[1] Acts included singing, dancing, acrobatics, feats of strength, illusions, comedy, oration, impersonations, and often several of these in combination. The written, spoken, and sung material would often play off of current events or common life experiences that would engage audience members the same way media (movies, television, and music) does today. Variety theaters also featured popular plays and productions seen in larger theaters (in whole or in part), as well as original productions written in-house by capable career writers/actors. Sporting exhibitions were also common—walking matches, wrestling, boxing, and other competitions. While these kinds of entertainment remained most popular, they were also shunned by polite society, which saw them as unsophisticated and at times immoral. This was similar to twentieth-century resistance to rock music or other fashionable trends that bucked society's standards. Some of that attitude was justified, given the blatant disregard for decency displayed by many theater owners who looked the other way while their venues harbored crime and vice of all kinds. Aside from indecency, some owners resorted to inhumane forms of entertainment. One Leadville, Colorado, theater in 1879 featured a "fight between a cinnamon bear and Arkansas dogs" in front of a packed crowd—on the Sabbath, no less.[2] Such features contributed to the backlash and stereotyping of less formal venues.

In addition to entertainment, variety theaters also provided a social center where one could let loose in a sea of diversions described by one theatergoer: "It is a place to go and be free and easy, to drink, smoke, chew tobacco and spit all over your neighbor (and take the chance of getting whaled), laugh, watch frailty in every style and form. . . . You can talk spiritualism, gas with pretty waiter girls, listen to latter day saint expositions, hear a political clique argue for or against [current issues], learn how to put an engine to work, [or] ascertain the whole scandal of the separation of Mr. and Mrs. B, and how C did it."[3]

While variety theaters became popular around the globe, their designs were as widespread as their locations. A Deadwood, Dakota Territory, newspaper described its first theater, which opened in 1876. "The building was enclosed on the sides but had only a canvas roof. The floor was dirt covered with saw dust. During the first performance a heavy rain fell drenching everything; part of the audience [left] and part sat through it while some of the actors went through their parts under an umbrella."[4] In 1882 Albuquerque had a variety theater housed in a canvas tent. One evening a storm blew in that "demolished poles on two sides . . . which caused a cutting of the play."[5] It wasn't uncommon for new western settlements to lack proper buildings for various civic meetings and social activities. Those circumstances forced political gatherings and church services into the same space reserved for variety performances. In 1879 Leadville had a variety performance tent where "artists of questionable character performed acts of still more questionable decency." One visitor recalled that same tent was rented for religious services every Sunday morning.[6] Another man recalled local church services were held inside a variety theater where "whiskey barrels made the pulpit."[7]

By contrast, other variety theaters were large stately buildings that featured ornate architecture, extravagant interiors, and a host of visual and physical amenities on par with the finest venues in the world. In 1885

This 1881 view of Glendive, Montana, shows L. B. Mixter's Music Hall in the foreground and Jim's Opera House farther down the row. Both were crudely constructed in whole or in part with canvas. Photo by L. A. Huffman, from author's collection.

two Bird Cage performers worked at San Antonio's Fashion Theatre. It featured walls covered with fine art, a six-foot chandelier suspended in the auditorium, a well-appointed kitchen, and a bar with "magnificently large mirrors and artistically stained glass panels." In all it was called an "elegant and recherché resort . . . equal to any in the South and entirely [above] anything of a like character in San Antonio."[8] In 1877 Deadwood's booming main street was lined with rows of wooden frame buildings. By contrast, the costly stone facade of the Bella Union theater was a real standout. Local press insisted it "adds much to the appearance of Main Street and speaks well to the enterprise of our citizens."[9] A Leadville venue that employed several Bird Cage performers had seating for five hundred people

Miles City, Montana's, Cosmopolitan Theatre (*top*) and Georgetown, Colorado's, Comique (*bottom*) speak to the basic nature of some frontier venues. Comique was such a common variety theater name that it was often used to describe other venues that had proper names. Top photo by L. A. Huffman, 1883. Bottom photo, date and photographer unknown. Author's collection.

with "elegantly fitted boxes" on either side that sat four hundred more. One visitor said it had "a style of elegance surpassing anything ever before seen amid the cloud capped Rocky Mountains."[10] Butte, Montana's, Comique also saw many Bird Cage performers throughout the late 1880s. When it opened in 1885, its three-story brick architecture was called "a credit to the city . . . which presents a very imposing appearance." The interior had every modern convenience, including "private boxes cosily [sic] and elegantly fitted up in the latest and most approved style." Residents couldn't miss its illuminated entrance—a real novelty at a time when electricity was cutting edge.[11] Even the *Butte Miner* newspaper broke away from its antitheater bias and called it "the coziest and handsomest in the West."[12] Likewise, San Francisco's Adelphi theater saw a number of Bird Cage performers in the late 1870s and 1880s. Its $15,000 construction cost exceeded what Tombstone spent on its own city hall in 1882. When it opened, a local reporter gushed over its opulent interior.

> The upholstery is in blue cloth leather and hangings. Elegant lace curtains and heavy blue damask cloth are used in the boxes. The celling and walls have been frescoed in the Pompeiian style. The painting is white throughout, set off with gold leaf gilding. The papering is blue, figured, and is very pleasant and tasteful in design. The gas fixtures are in crystal, silver and gold of elegant design. The general effect of the interior of the auditorium is at once cool, rich and pleasant. In the rear of the circle is a handsome parlor, in which is located a [bar] where refreshments can be obtained. This is connected by electric bells with the boxes.[13]

Although physical forms of variety theaters differed greatly, the controversies they triggered were almost universal. For many reasons they were very difficult to run well and very easy to run poorly. In contrast to their formal opera house counterparts, their intimate and informal settings attracted less refined attendees and sometimes crude behavior. And it wasn't always men. One variety theater visitor saw two women in a balcony box that "swallowed so much beer that one of them . . . threw something at the actors on the stage."[14] An early Montana pioneer recalled a performance in Virginia City

St. Louis's Olympic (*left*, in 1870) was originally built as a variety theater in 1866. Its formal design is a great example of how substantial some venues were. Photo courtesy of the Missouri Historical Society. Deadwood's Bella Union (*right*) featured an ornate stone facade that stood out against every other building clad with locally procured lumber. Photo by F. J. Hayes, 1877. Courtesy of the Montana Historical Society.

that was interrupted by a local bad man named Slade. As the performance began, he barked vulgar orders at a dancer to take her dress off. Mortified fathers and husbands immediately ushered out their wives and children, and the show ended right there.[15]

Presenting fresh daily entertainment meant cycling through performers and changing acts weekly. Such a routine presented yet another difficulty of the business. The constant need to recruit reliable and capable entertainers was a challenge, particularly when the country's transportation infrastructure was in its infancy. Some theater owners made half-hearted attempts to acquire quality entertainers, while others made no effort at all. Many communities also fought hard to eliminate variety theaters, which were blamed for encouraging local crime and for corrupting young men and women. These and other factors discussed ahead also made it exhausting to run them for long periods of time. Consequently, most variety theaters had very short lifespans.

FASHION THEATRE
The Finest Amusement Palace in the South.

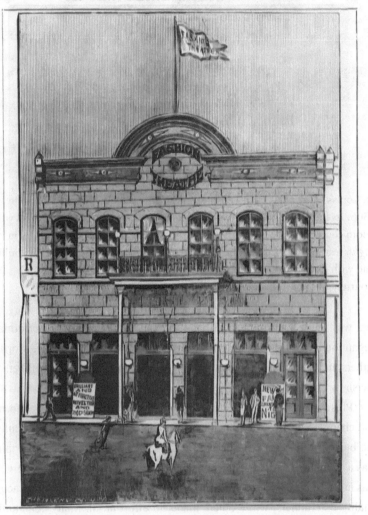

At least eighteen Bird Cage performers appeared at San Antonio's Fashion
Theatre between 1885 and 1891. Its owners worked hard to maintain
an atmosphere on par with the building's appearance and performers.
San Antonio Light, June 13, 1885.

Yet all of these difficulties were overcome because of one main factor: variety theaters had incredible profit potential. A visitor to Leadville, Colorado, in 1879 estimated a crowd of seven hundred packed in the Comique at $1 a head, while the wine room took in another $300. In an era that saw most Americans earning between $1 and $3 a day, that was enormous revenue. The frenzy was repeated seven nights a week.[16] Deadwood's notable Gem theater was operated by savvy and notorious Al Swearingen in 1876. On opening night he took in $1,512.50 (roughly $40,000 today), even after refunding money to many who couldn't fit inside.[17] While not necessarily typical, that kind of potential tempted entertainers and non-entertainers alike to try their hand at navigating the business. Even several Tombstone, Arizona, notables got in on the action. Thomas Fitch, lawyer for the Earps in the post-gunfight inquest operated theaters in Tucson and Prescott, Arizona.[18] Bat Masterson operated theaters in Dodge City and Denver and eventually married one of the performers.[19] Leslie Blackburn, a deputy US marshal for Arizona Territory in 1882 and foreman of Tombstone's Engine Company No. 1, was the proprietor of a variety theater in Virginia City, Nevada, before coming to Arizona.[20] Even Wyatt Earp's brother Virgil got in on the action. In the winter of 1885–1886, he took a brick building on the corner of Third and C Street in San Bernardino, California, and opened it as the Bijou Theatre. He even hired former notable Bird Cage comedian John Mulligan.[21]

Today's concept of variety theaters consists of scantily clad women, gambling, and drunkenness all jammed together in a boisterous, smoky, and virtually lawless environment without reserve or inhibitions. Gunplay, fighting, harassment of performers, and general indecency is assumed to be the norm. These elements are irresistibly highlighted in movies and writings based on the period. Many of the cliches aren't necessarily untrue. In their day, variety theaters and gambling houses alike represented lawless elements that civilized communities fought hard to suppress. Through reality or rumor, they became associated with problems that plagued growing communities, such as drunkenness, fighting, prostitution, general nuisances, and the moral decay of young men and women—all of which were repugnant to decent society. These attitudes found their way into many period newspapers:

> The glare of light, the glitter of the stage, the smiles of the sirens, the dizziness caused by the tobacco fumes, the intoxication of liquors— each and all of them are at work to cause the downfall of every man that enters within the precincts of a variety theater and strong he is if he withstands them.
>
> —*Butte Weekly Miner*, March 20, 1886

> The Cremorne [theater] is a big net of nastiness into which thousands of girls, now happy in school and home, will be caught unless it is destroyed. I have witnessed sights in and about that vile dive that would make any decent person sick to look upon.
>
> —*San Francisco Call*, May 22, 1892

> We believe that the [variety theater] is a place of infamy and vice, where youth are beguiled, and where they take their first lessons that lead them to crimes of all grades.
>
> —*Leavenworth* (KS) *Bulletin*, August 8, 1863

> The variety theater may have its place in the economy of city life, but surely the principle [sic] streets of the city should not be devoted to such amusements.
>
> —*Fort Worth Daily Gazette*, August 23, 1890

> The brunette and the blonde at the Park theatre are dangerous institutions.
>
> —*Arizona Daily Star* (Tucson), August 30, 1883

> The Theatre Comique, a rough frame box, seats about 700 people, though they crowd in a thousand a night—sardines in a box are comparatively comfortable. The wine room alone, the attraction being a lot of beefy women with few clothes and very aggressive legs, takes in $300 a night for liquors. It is the loosest show, with no merit but its outrageous indecency.
>
> —Letter from an *Indianapolis News* correspondent in Leadville published in the *Coffeyville* (KS) *Journal*, March 22, 1879

> If a young man studies art exclusively at the variety theater, he is an exceedingly unlucky artist.
>
> —*Black Range*, December 14, 1883

Now that our city is crowded with roughs it would be well to look at some of the causes, and especially one that affords them shelter for half the night for ten or fifteen cents. This is the cheap variety theaters.

—*St. Louis Post Dispatch*, December 28, 1890

Tom Wade . . . opened a theater [in Santa Fe] one night last week and the next morning the legislature was too sleepy to do any work. Some New Mexicans say that the territory would be as well off if Wade and his pretty actresses kept the legislature from doing any more business this session.[22]

—*Western Liberal* (Lordsburg, NM), February 3, 1893

Many parents shared fears of their children being lured into the forbidden variety theater atmosphere and irreversibly corrupted. One man in 1881 conveyed a story that proved the fear was legitimate.

One night . . . a poor woman with whom I am acquainted came to me and said her son, a lad of 14 years, had formed the habit of attending variety shows. On the night in question the boy had stolen the mother's bed quilts and pawned it for fifteen cents. She feared he had used the proceeds to pay his way into the varieties. We went . . . and found him in the gallery. But this is not the worst of it. While I stood in the corridor, I counted seven girls, none of whom were more than 14 years of age, who came in, bought tickets and went upstairs. I was much shocked at that, for I had never known that children of such a tender age, especially girls, were admitted to the place. I went in on the ground floor and looked up into the first gallery, and there I saw each one of those seven little girls with a glass of beer in front of her! I looked into the upper gallery and I think I am safe in saying that I saw there 200 boys from 10 to 15 years of age.[23]

Many communities went beyond the war of words and actively legislated against variety theaters. Some took a subtle approach, hoping vital blows to operations would take care of the problem indirectly. The city council of Denison, Texas, passed an ordinance prohibiting "indecent performances" in 1885, making sure to select wording that left plenty of room for interpretation.[24] Butte, Montana, passed a law in 1887 that prohibited alcohol from being consumed in a variety theater (which was a major revenue source) and another that prohibited women and children from being employed in them.[25] San Francisco added what was called the Dive Ordinance to its penal code in 1877, which declared it "unlawful for any female to play any musical instrument or exhibit herself in any place where liquor is sold."[26] In 1891 the mayor of Columbus, Ohio, ordered all "low variety theaters" with bars where women were admitted to be closed. After a noncompliant theater continued business, local police crashed a performance and attempted to shut it down. Backlash ensued. Employees attacked the police, and shots were fired by the owner, who "refused to be taken alive."[27] California passed a statute in 1892 prohibiting the sale of liquor in theaters across the entire state.[28] Taking a more direct approach, Seattle flat-out banned all variety theaters in 1889.[29] That law impacted several former Bird Cage performers who were employed there at the time.

San Francisco clamped down on variety theaters again in 1893. Former Bird Cage performer Ned Nestell addressed the Health and Police Committee who were about to close them down. As a family man and career entertainer, he pleaded for the cause of his industry brethren. "I represent the variety profession in which there are between 600 and 700 men and 1,500 and 2,000 women earning a living today," he told them. With his young family beside him he asked, "Must we submit to have the bread taken from our mouths and from the mouths of our wives and children? Further than this there are hundreds of us who are supporting our fathers and mothers and sisters and brothers by the work we do on the variety stage. Are we entitled to no consideration?"[30] His pleas fell on deaf ears that only heard complaints of the worst run venues in town.

It wasn't just moral decay that concerned communities. All types of crimes were attributed to gambling houses and variety theaters alike. At the heart of these crimes was the concern for lethal violence. While rare, that fear was at times justified. In 1878 John Lanham killed actress Georgia Drake in a San Antonio variety theater and was sentenced to death.[31] It was nationwide news when actress Effie Moore was brazenly shot to death in Denver's Palace Theater in 1887.[32] One-time Bird Cage actress Ruby Grant had her own narrow escape while performing in El Paso, Texas. The testimony of the accused speaks for itself:

Yes, I have heard of Ruby Grant. I believe I did present a pistol at her at the theater. I did it to shoot at her feet to make her dance on the stage. I did not throw a bundle containing $53 on the stage while [she] was dancing. Don't know how much money I spent at the theater, nor how much I threw on the stage. Don't think I got as much as 50 bottles of wine [but] for all I know I may have got 100 bottles. I may have spent $500 all together, but don't see how I could have spent more than that.[33]

Such occurrences weren't common, but they were high-impact ammunition for anti–variety theater initiatives. These stories also created a negative identity for all variety theaters, no matter how well they were run. More common crimes included petty theft and fighting, which are still found among certain bar scenes today. In 1882 Chicago experienced a rash of crimes along a four-block stretch of State Street where ten variety theaters ran full-tilt. Local press named the area Chicago's Black Hole and declared it to be a "burning disgrace to the city where thousands of young men are yearly ruined and millions in money [is] annually wasted."[34] Even where crime didn't occur, bad reputations and wild rumors were enough to embolden anti–variety theater movements. One account from a visitor of an early Leadville venue provides an example:

A violin and viola furnish the music. Six girls are employed in the hall, and are on the floor from dark until midnight, their partners varying in social standing from dignitaries to the dirtiest and coarsest of bullwhackers. The men dance with their hats on. [This is a suggestion that they were unrefined.] Decorum is unknown to audiences. Great clouds of smoke fill the room, while many girls, dressed in the loudest fashion peddle drinks through the audience. The performance continues until the last auditor leaves. The amount of money nightly squandered here upon wine, women and gambling is simply enormous. Yet there are many excellent people here.[35]

On the Other Hand

The modern concept of variety theaters is at times accurate, but another side of them is overlooked. While movies and writers focus on their most salacious elements, the reality has gotten lost in the shuffle. Upscale, well-run, and high-level variety theaters not only existed but also were prevalent. Some towns saw them as a sign of permanence, growth, and prosperity, as not all communities had a strong enough economy to sustain them. Towns without variety theaters often called for their development and celebrated their arrival when finally established. Many were run very respectably, and some even offered entertainment tastefully arranged specifically for women, families, and children. Cheyenne, Wyoming's, McDaniel's variety theater hosted a number of Bird Cage performers in the 1870s and had separate admission prices established for children to attend daily performances.[36] Thousands upon thousands of refined, respectable career performers lived their lives and built families around life in variety theater circuits. Many celebrated stars of the nineteenth and early twentieth century, including legendary icons Buffalo Bill Cody and Annie Oakley, started their career in them.[37] The existence of quality variety theaters and a positive attitude toward them was also reflected in daily press.

> The variety theater, honestly and cleanly conducted, is as legitimate as grand opera or the best drama. Nearly everyone will enjoy a specialty performance—even the most cultured and refined. It is only when such places decline in to dives and gin-mills . . . that they lose caste and become dangerous.
> —*Butte Miner*, March 18, 1886

> While variety theaters of the ordinary type are to be deprecated and should be discouraged, it is fair to presume [the owner] proposes to conduct a thoroughly respectable and high-toned show.
> —*Bismarck Weekly Tribune*, December 31, 1886

> It is a standing advertisement to the public spirit . . . that such a [variety theater] could be profitably maintained.
> —*Tombstone Epitaph*, June 20, 1882

> The International Hotel . . . in the very heart and center of the city . . . is in every way one of the finest family hotels in San Francisco. It contains 180 rooms all elegantly furnished and with the modern appliances to comfort . . . with the best variety theater directly in front.
> —*Arizona Weekly Star* (Tucson), November 29, 1877

> I consider both Mr. Kernan and his brother gentlemen, who are doing their best to run a good variety theater, and, as such, it is a credit to the city.
> —*National Republican* (Washington, DC), November 16, 1887

The Odeon variety theater—guaranteed to be refined and edifying and not a rip, tear or run down at the heel—will be opened with a sounding of trumpets and rattle of drums.

—*Bismarck Weekly Tribune*, January 7, 1887

It is not surprising that [San Antonio's Fashion Theatre] should be patronized so liberally, a high class variety performance being given and this standard of excellence is never allowed to sink below par. All parties visiting can rest assured that the best of order shall be maintained, and any one shouting, whistling, loudly stamping, or otherwise disorderly, will be placed under arrest and prosecuted to the full extent of the law. A special officer is employed by the management and is in constant attendance to secure the enforcement of these rules.

—*San Antonio Light*, April 15 and June 29, 1885

The performances [at Tucson's Fashion Theater] will be chaste and witty, and no vulgarity will be permitted. Threadbare and worn out jokes which have become decrepit by being knocked around in every variety show over the world will not gain admittance, and anything which would be repulsive to decency will not be permitted there.

—*Arizona Daily Star*, January 6, 1883

The variety show seems to be an essential to every live and prosperous community. Well conducted variety shows are not only harmless but delightful places.

—*Butte Weekly Miner*, June 3, 1885

Many owners went to lengths to make variety theaters truly viable centers of entertainment in the eyes of respectable people. Management of San Antonio's Fashion Theatre posted its high drink prices as a method to repel unwanted low-class customers.[38] In Globe, Arizona, one owner placed an ad requesting "six intelligent and respectable girls to wait upon customers," offering ten dollars a week plus expenses.[39] Dallas, Texas, had a venue in 1881 called Antoine's Bird Cage family resort that was conducted in an "excellent manner" and advertised that "none but respectable characters [were] allowed."[40] As much as variety-theater detractors spoke out against drinking that took place within them, career entertainer Eddie Foy, who traveled coast to coast for over fifty years, recalled, "Why, even in the highest class theaters and opera houses the elite had champagne sent into their boxes from the bar which was a part of every theatre building."[41]

Although variety theaters ranged in design and level of decency, they were all the same in the minds of the high-minded and conservative. In many cases rumors and politics overruled reality. Many assumed all variety theaters were public nuisances, regardless of how well they were run. In some communities theaters became a hot topic of debate, much like today's controversial and contentious subjects. Public interest in the issue prompted newspapers in various cities to send correspondents inside them to report on the conditions and expose racy details that could sway public opinion. In 1881 a reporter for the *Detroit Free Press* visited three venues in one night and reported his findings to the anxious public. The first was located across from city hall and was the "most pretentious and respectable of the three." The performances were "quite as respectable and fully as good as [those] on the legitimate stage, and none the more vulgar or indecent." The second theater was filled with "drunken besotted men . . . smoking pipes filled with vile tobacco and uttering obscene language whenever anything on the stage displeased them." One was even "too drunk to know where he was." They were served by "shabbily dressed" women whose beauty was "buried under many a sinful year." The performance was no better having been comprised of acts that were "simply third rate." The last theater was nothing more than a bar with a hole cut in the front window to serve as a box office and a stage in the back. Instead of a full orchestra, it had only a broken-down piano. On the night the reporter visited, performances had been stopped after a fight broke out among the crowd, which he described as being "about the wildest [I] ever gazed upon [that had] scarred and battered faces with crime written all over them." He went so far as to call them "the lowest classes in the city." Aside from being a dive, it was also running without a valid city license. The reporter's experience in the three venues exemplifies just how different variety theaters could be and how much interest the general public had in knowing what was going on inside them.[42]

Defining variety theaters is difficult because they were extremely controversial and widely dissimilar in design, and their spectrum of morality and overall quality was extremely broad. In the end it was all up to the proprietor—how virtuous he or she was and how unwilling they were to compromise those virtues as public opinion, local politics, customers, and finances applied pressure to them. Generally speaking, better stage talent translated to a more respectable theater all around. A theater owner who invested more into performers generally upheld higher standards for everything else, which made it a quality venue. The same Butte, Montana, newspaper that staunchly supported antitheater laws in the late nineteenth century conceded that "where a higher class of performers [exists], a more wholesome atmosphere prevails."[43] It's not uncommon to find venues that transitioned from good to bad in the eyes of the judgmental public just by a change of management. Such was the case in Tucson in 1884 when the local paper declared, "The Park [theater] was once the pride of Tucson, the resort of the most respectable, now it is the stink of drunkenness, vice and debauchery."[44]

The big question to be asked, then, is where on this spectrum was Tombstone's Bird Cage?

Chapter 2

Tombstone's Early Venues

Tombstone is still expanding, and business though slightly overdone in the whiskey line, is good. Come and see us, and if we cannot amuse you with our big mines, mills and hoisting works, our daily stage lines, newspaper, dance houses or theaters, we will get up a fracas for you that will suit the most aesthetic taste, and don't you forget it.

— *Tucson Citizen*, November 13, 1879

By the spring of 1878, determined prospector Ed Schieffelin located the mines that were key to Tombstone's beginning. Although the region's mineral wealth had been explored by Spain, Mexico, Native Americans, and other independent organizations dating back to the 1700s, it was Schieffelin's strikes that set the wheels of Tombstone's future in motion.[1] As word slowly leaked out, opportunists descended on the area forming a series of small settlements such as Merrimack, Watervale (locally called Gouge-Eye), Richmond, Hogem, and Pick-Em-Up.[2] For more than a year these early settlements battled to become the district's main hub. In early 1879 one visitor recognized, "There is already the beginnings of strife as to where shall be located the future city whose magnificent proportions are already confidently predicted."³ Even as late as June 1879, another newcomer observed, "Instead of one concentrated, prosperous town, there are three distinct town locations, all having hope of being the great town."⁴ Ultimately it was proximity to the most productive mines surrounding present-day Tombstone that lured miners and the merchants that catered to them away from competing locations.

However, through early 1879 Tombstone was not located where it is today. On a narrow flat behind its present location sat a scattering of temporary canvas tents and crudely constructed dwellings that came to be known as the "old Tombstone townsite." One early resident remembered it and the resourceful building materials that were used. "In the 'old town' there were . . . about 40 buildings, at least four adobe, several [made of] frames, tents and brush. Ocotillo [limbs] made good walls and bear grass let in the light but would shed water."⁵ People early on the scene were well-versed rovers of western mining camps, and they wasted no time in establishing various enterprises. A single street was fronted by a supply stores, a stage office, blacksmith shop, saloons, restaurants and dwellings—everything that was needed in a male-dominated mining camp environment.

When the passing months of 1878 and 1879 proved the long-term productivity of area mines, newcomers overwhelmed and strained the awkward location of the old townsite. A much larger flat plateau at the base of Tombstone's hills became a natural overflow, and a new townsite was surveyed there in March 1879.⁶ According to early miner Robert Lewis, it was an area called Goose Flatts by a group of miners, but since the mining district had officially been filed by Ed Schieffelin and other founders as the Tombstone Mining District eleven months prior, it was referred to simply as Tombstone.⁷ Thus began the "new" Tombstone we know today.

Throughout the summer of 1879, many transitioned from the old townsite to the new. Joining them were outsiders drawn in by news of Tombstone's promising future as published in newspapers, written about in outgoing letters, and spread through word of mouth across the country. While several mining camps saw a lot of empty hope and unfulfilled hype, Tombstone was the real deal. The new Tombstone took rapid form and offered that which could be found in large cities. In October 1879 it got its first newspaper, the *Weekly Nugget*, quickly followed by a second, the *Tombstone Epitaph* six months later. By 1880 Episcopalian, Methodist, Catholic, and Presbyterian congregations were formed. Within two years they all erected formal churches.[8] Temporary canvas tents gave way to more permanent adobe buildings, some reaching two stories as early as April 1880.[9] Tombstone established a local government, city hall, fire department, city police court, and various ordinances to maintain public health and safety. Such improvements welcomed the arrival of women, wives, and families that brought about public schools and an array of social clubs. The US Postal Service also established mail service. Continuously improved roads brought all the goods available in San Francisco to the streets of Tombstone. Residents saw shipments of everything from massive industrial mining machinery to fine foods, rubber soled boots, Singer sewing machines, and periodicals from around the country.[10] Two stage lines brought in upward of fifty passengers a day in addition to the many who came in their own conveyances.[11]

Its growth was so abrupt, one newspaper humorously observed, "Tombstone is growing so rapidly that they soon expect to be big enough to change [their] name to Sarcophagus."[12] In February 1881 the territorial legislature upgraded its status from a village to a city by officially approving the Tombstone City Charter.[13] Yet with all this growth, advancement, and civic improvement, the Bird Cage was still nowhere to be found. The reason behind this is a part of the exciting beginning of the Bird Cage discussed ahead, but in the meantime Tombstone turned to a number of other venues to break the monotony of life in a distant mining camp that lacked a proper variety theater.

Some of the earliest venues were too crude and short-lived to have formal names. An early resident recalled one unnamed location that was nothing more than a "bear grass thatched bowery and bar on Allen between Sixth and Seventh [that] would accommodate 200 people."[14] In January 1880 a traveler from Chicago remembered a one-hundred-foot-long dank tent identified only by an illuminated sign that read "varieties." Inside he witnessed a mixed crowd of Mexicans and whites who were "mostly dirty, ill-dressed and half drunk." Some were gambling and few others were dancing with women who were no better. He described them as being "homely, with the evidences of worthlessness . . . [who] form a ghastly picture of immorality."[15] The Chicago correspondent's limited experience with frontier life may have contributed to his shock. Nevertheless, these makeshift venues were quickly brushed aside by the surge of money that brought refinement and civility to Tombstone. The improved venues defined the town in its early stages of growth.

Danner and Owens: Tombstone's First Major Venue

Named after owners Sam Danner and Sylvester Owens, the town's first gathering place began as a tent saloon in the old Tombstone townsite. There it became the scene of the town's first death by gunshot when John Hicks fell dead within a few feet of the doorway.[16] One local recalled going to the sound of gunfire where he found Hicks "shot through the head and instantly killed." He was placed on a strip of canvas, taken inside Danner and Owens's, and covered. His burial was the first at the old Tombstone townsite, and it's likely his body is still there.[17]

Two months later Danner and Owens were a part of the wave that moved to the new townsite, setting up shop on the southwest corner of Fifth and Allen directly across from the present-day Crystal Palace.[18] One local recalled the crude accommodations of their saloon and gathering hall, which was nothing more than a large tent. "A string of planks laid on top of empty whiskey barrels formed the original front bar of this saloon. Lighting for the tent saloon was furnished by kerosene oil lamps hung from the ridge pole of the tent . . . which had nothing but a dirt floor . . . [and] was general head-quarters [in Tombstone]."[19]

After enduring ten months in their tent, Danner and Owens replaced it with an adobe building that covered the entirety of their 30 x 120–foot lot. In a dramatic upgrade, the Tombstone *Nugget* described it as having "elegant club rooms" where "everything is first-class."[20] It featured a beautifully lighted hall with grand chandeliers, making it desirable for various gatherings.[21] Tombstone's first high society organization, the Tombstone Social Club, was formed there.[22] The hall hosted political club meetings and three denominations of church services, and was the polling place for the town's elections in 1880.[23] Tombstone's first fire department, Engine Company No. 1 was formed there in a meeting held September 9, 1880, in which Wyatt Earp was elected secretary.[24]

What appears to be two separate buildings indicated by the arrows is actually the Danner and Owens hall and saloon on the corner of Fifth and Allen in April 1880. This newly constructed building replaced the crude tent they had been using for ten months. Stereoview by Carleton Watkins, from author's collection.

A month later the hall was leased and converted into gambling rooms by Bob Winders and Charlie Smith, who employed notable gamblers Dick Clark and Johnny Tyler.[25] Smith and Winders were described by the *Nugget* as being "well known in this community, where they have many friends." Included in this list of friends were the Earp brothers, Winders having worked with Wyatt and James Earp at James's Cattle Exchange Saloon in Fort Worth, Texas, before coming to Arizona.[26] The Earp-Winders relationship also included a partnership in several Tombstone mining claims.[27] A week after the gambling

hall opened in October 1880, Tombstone's Marshal Fred White was mortally
wounded by "Curly Bill" Brocius one block away. As the events leading up
to the shooting unfolded, Wyatt was inside Danner and Owens's hall, likely
due to his friendship with Winders and Smith. In the resulting trial against
Brocius, Wyatt testified, "I was in . . . Owens's saloon and heard three or four
shots fired; upon hearing the first shot I ran out in the street and I saw the
flash of a pistol up the street about a block from where I was; several shots
were fired in quick succession; ran up as quick as I could."[28] Two weeks after
White was killed, Danner and Owens's hall hosted the special election to fill
his vacancy—an election narrowly lost by Virgil Earp.[29]

Danner and Owens sold out in July 1881, but in two and a half years
of operation, their hall hosted many socials and entertainments that saw
nearly every notable and important person in early Tombstone pass through
its doors.[30]

Sixth Street Opera House

The Sixth Street Opera House was Tombstone's first permanent dedicated
gathering and entertainment venue. It was located on the east side of Sixth
Street, midway between Allen and Fremont, just a half block away from
where the Bird Cage stands today. Enterprising 33-year-old Italian immigrant
Giuseppe Fontana operated the hall that was opened no later than April 1880.[31]
It was a completely wooden structure with a narrow and long interior that
housed a bar, stove, and "an elevated stage and abundant standing room."[32]
At various times it featured variety theater actors, several of whom eventually performed at the Bird Cage, including Joe Bignon, who became its
longest tenured proprietor.[33] By virtue of its size and accommodations, it was
also used for wrestling matches, various association meetings, and even a
hosted a church fair.[34]

In June 1881 the Sixth Street Opera House and Tombstone's entire east
business district was gutted by a massive fire. Fontana's loss was reported at
$3,000, offset by only $1,000 worth of insurance.[35] Instead of rebuilding he
sold the lot, marking the end of the Sixth Street Opera House.[36] As for Fontana,
he remained in Tombstone, dabbled in mining interests, bought property, and
fell back on the watchmaking business he had known previously.[37] On the

The Sixth Street Opera House is the elongated building in the center.
Cropped from a much larger photograph of town, this is the only known view
of the building. Photo by Carleton Watkins, April 1880, author's collection.

southwest corner of Sixth and Allen he erected a building with a striking
stone facade directly next to the Bird Cage.[38] Unfortunately, Fontana's building was razed in 1924, but a portion of its facade can still be seen clinging to
the left side of the Bird Cage today.[39]

Ritchie's Hall

Tombstone's busiest early venue was Ritchie's hall, located on the west side
of Fifth Street between Allen and Fremont. The lot now sits empty just sixty
feet from the present day *Epitaph* office, but in Tombstone's early growth, that
section of town was referred to as "one of the important business streets."[40]
Its construction and operation was headed by William Ritchie, a 39-year-old
Tennessean who arrived in Tombstone fully intent on prospecting mines.[41]
When the building was completed in May 1880, it became the town's second
two-story building, with each floor serving a unique purpose.[42]

Unhindered by being only twenty feet wide (ten feet narrower than the
Bird Cage), the first floor hall saw much of the same activity as Danner
and Owens's hall but was used much more frequently. It hosted nearly
every early Tombstone organization, including the Miners Union, the elite

Tombstone Social Club, social balls, meetings for both political parties, and Sunday school and church services for all of Tombstone's religious congregations.[43] On many occasions multiple groups used Ritchie's in the same day.[44] It was a very busy place. Unlike Danner and Owens's hall, Richie's featured a stage and hosted performances both professional and amateur.[45]

Five months after opening the hall, William Ritchie partnered with William J. "Billy" Hutchinson—the future founder, owner, and operator of the Bird Cage. They turned the second story into a gambling resort that was run "in grand style."[46] The interior was colorfully described by the *Tombstone Nugget*:

> The front room is open to the public, in which there is a black walnut, marble top side-board, ladened with the choicest wines and cigars, and other luxuries, in the mid of which King Faro holds sway. [This roughly translates to mean the popular gambling game of faro was a main feature of the room.] A hall leads in to a private room adjoining, elegantly carpeted with Brussels, furniture to match, which is visited by those only who have private keys, and each key-holder can, of course, invite his friends. The parlors were well filled last evening, and it was a happy gathering indeed of gentlemen until the wee sma' hours.[47]

In the gambling rooms said to be "elegantly fitted up," Billy Hutchinson operated a faro bank where he dealt to many of Tombstone's notable gamblers, who followed him there from other tables.[48] Such was noted a week before the club rooms opened when "Scotty" lost $1,550 and won $2,050 (roughly $60,000 in today's money) within four deals at Billy's faro table. One has to imagine the unique combination on a Sunday that saw church services in the first-floor hall while gamblers vied for ill-gotten gains right above them.

Ritchie's hall was unfortunately destroyed by Tombstone's second massive fire, which occurred on May 26, 1882.[49] Within a month Ritchie rebuilt a near replica, but the ground floor was rented business space, as Tombstone's need for a hall had been satisfied elsewhere.[50] By that time Billy Hutchinson had established the Bird Cage, and the second story opened as headquarters of the Tombstone Club. Like the gambling resort before the

William Ritchie (pictured in 1894) partnered with future Bird Cage founder Billy Hutchinson in the club rooms on the second floor of his two-story hall on Fifth Street. When the original burned down in May 1882, he immediately built a near replica at the same location. That building is seen here shortly before it was dismantled in the 1940s. Author's collection.

fire, it was elegantly appointed, as described by a newspaper correspondent before the exterior of the building had been finished:

> The elegant rooms of the Tombstone Club in the second story of Ritchie's building were thrown open to the members last evening. A casual glance at the rough, unplastered walls and crude stairway on the exterior, would not lead one to believe that such taste and elegance reigned within. The floor is carpeted with rich Brussels carpet, large pattern, and yellow the predominating color. The unity of color in the furnishing of the room immediately attracts attention. The chairs, cuspadores [sic] and curtains are of the same general color as the carpet, which as the effect of making the appearance more pleasing to the eye than a heterogeneous blending of hues. A magnificent sideboard, well laden with choice liquors and cigars is no the least attractive portion of the furniture. A spacious apartment in the rear of the reading room will be subdivided into card, store, and wash rooms in a few days. The Club has about sixty members and is a very flourishing condition. More than seventy publications, comprising all the leading American and foreign newspapers, magazine and periodicals are received.[51]

William Ritchie is a fascinating character of early Tombstone. His hall, which hosted virtually every major group in early Tombstone, made him extremely well-known. In later years he became involved in town politics, ran for mayor in 1886, and remained loyal to Tombstone through its bleakest days of the mid-1890s.[52] He remained in Tombstone until his death on September 12, 1906, and is buried in the city cemetery just west of town.[53] The hall he rebuilt in 1882 remained a landmark on Fifth Street until it was razed in the 1940s.

Turnverein Hall

Located near the corner of Fourth and Safford, the Turnverein Hall was farther from the beehive of Allen Street activity than the other general-use halls.[54] Its construction was entirely sponsored by members of Tombstone's Turnverein. The Turnverein society is an active global organization comprised of primarily Germans who, in the nineteenth century, emphasized physical fitness and the general betterment of individuals and the community. The Tombstone Turnverein was established on September 23, 1880, making them the town's second formal social club. Unlike other chapters they allowed non-German members.[55] This allowed in many of Tombstone's notable early business leaders. Among them were Albert Bilicke, who owned the Cosmopolitan, Tombstone's largest hotel; Ben Wehrfritz, owner of the Golden Eagle (later known as the Crystal Palace); and John Clum, editor of the *Tombstone Epitaph* and future mayor.

One of their first orders of business was to erect a formal building. A month after forming, they pooled member finances and purchased a lot where the eventual hall would be built.[56] In the meantime they took temporary occupancy in a building on Fremont between Fifth and Sixth.[57] On March 10, 1881, the hall was finished and was inaugurated with a grand opening ball. A *Tombstone Epitaph* employee attended and took readers on a descriptive tour of the new building.

The new home of the Turn-Verein is a most creditable one. The hall . . .
is so arranged that every foot of space is available. On the left hand side
of the main entrance a small room has been elegantly fitted up 'for the

ladies', while on the right is a refreshment room. Above these rooms and the hallway a gallery has been erected with a seating capacity for about 70 persons. In honor of the occasion the Turners had decorated their hall in a very tasteful manner, the walls being hung with paintings, surrounded with flags, while festoons of red, white and blue made careful curves to the sides and ends of the room and robbed the ceiling of its bareness. The unwonted sight of flowers also greeted the eye.[58]

The local newspaper reported on the opening ball, which included a dinner "fit for the gods," and dancing, which created a picturesque scene: "During the dancing the scene from the galleries was a most enjoyable one. 'Brave men and fair women' there were in plenty and the handsome toilettes of the ladies, as they were whirled through the various dances did much to make up a picture which no pioneer of this ambitious little city would have dared predict a year ago. An Eastern gentleman present expressed the utmost astonishment at the beautiful and elegant costumes of the ladies present, and it was indeed hard to realize at time that the bright scene was really in Tombstone."[59]

Such balls were held regularly. Attendees included Johnny Behan, Billy Hutchinson (shortly before opening the Bird Cage), and "the very best of Tombstone's people."[60] In addition to the routine socials, the hall featured exercise equipment for use by members. The equipment was offered to outsiders on Tuesdays and Fridays for the monthly price of one dollar—a sort of modern gym membership equivalent.[61] The hall hosted many of the same groups and organizations as Danner and Owens's and Ritchie's hall. The hall was also used as a secondary classroom at one point when the public schoolhouse became overwhelmed.[62]

A notable attempted stagecoach robbery on March 15, 1881, outside Tombstone (a key event leading up to the OK Corral gunfight) resulted in the death of the driver, Eli "Budd" Philpot, who left behind a wife and four kids.[63] A benefit was hosted at the Turnverein hall that netted more than $330 for his family—roughly $9,300 in today's money.[64] One of the volunteers who performed at the benefit was Billy Hutchinson's wife, Lottie Hutchinson.[65] Another special event was held in the wake of President James A. Garfield's assassination.[66] Eventually a stage was erected and several notable professional performers discussed ahead were booked.[67]

Other Notable Venues

Tombstone's growing population demanded many additional venues and entertainments. One of Tombstone's founders, Richard Gird, built a hall on the northeast corner of Fourth and Allen. Below second-story offices, the hall saw many social gatherings, amateur performances, and special events like the funeral of Fred White, who was shot and killed by "Curly Bill" Brocius.[68] In the late 1880s it hosted weekly social dances put on by one-time Bird Cage proprietor Oliver Trevillian.[69] Socials and entertainments were held there into the twentieth century.[70] Unfortunately, like Ritchie's second building, it was also razed in the 1940s.

Another unique venue was the Tivoli, located on Allen Street in between Danner and Owens's hall and the Grand Hotel in the heart of Tombstone. Tombstoners could indulge at the bar, but as an adult entertainment hall and recreation grounds, it also offered bowling, a shooting gallery, a popular ring toss game called quoit, and card tables, all backdropped by nightly musical concerts.[71] German owner J. D. Ahlers also hired fellow German and future leader of the Bird Cage orchestra Ed Wittig to conduct a formal musical performance there.[72]

Tombstone's many saloons were also viable options for entertainment. The Oriental at the corner of Firth and Allen is famous as a saloon and the location of Wyatt Earp's one-time gambling concessions. But it also featured singers and piano players, several of whom were imported from Sacramento.[73] According to the *Epitaph*, the regular music and singing added "largely to the attractions of the [Oriental]."[74] One such act was described favorably: "The nightingale who presides at the piano at the Oriental saloon was unusually melodious last evening, and drew forth rounds of applause from her enraptured audience. Her [singing] was exceptionally fine, and extracted well-merited applause from the attentive hearers."[75] Among its many performers was the wife of Wyatt Earp's gambling partner, Lou Rickabaugh. Even Tombstone's brass band made an appearance.[76] It was also the scene of a wrestling match won by one-time Bird Cage proprietor Frank Broad.[77] A local woman described the Oriental shortly after it opened: "The Oriental is simply gorgeous and is pronounced the finest place of the kind this side of San Francisco. The bar is a marvel of beauty; the side boards were made for the Baldwin Hotel; the gaming room connected is carpeted with Bussels, brilliantly lighted and furnished with reading matter and writing materials for its patrons. Every evening music from a piano or violin attracts a crowd; and the scene is really a gay one—but all for men."[78]

Across the street from the Oriental stood the Golden Eagle Brewery, known today as the Crystal Palace saloon.[79] Like the Oriental it featured musical entertainers such as Mendel Meyer, one of Tombstone's most notable musicians.[80] For a period between spring of 1883 and at least until 1889, it was a full-blown variety theater complete with elevated boxes, a stage, and an orchestra pit.[81] A number of Bird Cage performers operated it and performed on its stage. When Arizona prohibition took effect in 1918, the Crystal Palace became a movie theater. Among the feature films shown were those that glamorized the frontier life that once played out inside its walls. Musical entertainment is still being offered there to this day. In 2018 Dennis Quaid, who famously portrayed Doc Holliday in Kevin Costner's 1994 film *Wyatt Earp*, performed at the Crystal Palace with his band Dennis Quaid and the Sharks. From Mendel Meyer to former Bird Cage performers, and early motion pictures to modern performances, no location has hosted more entertainment in Tombstone's history than the Crystal Palace.

Several of Tombstone's highly skilled musicians also opened saloons that featured regular entertainment. Thomas Vincent had his Music Hall Saloon, which was also the headquarters for the Tombstone Brass Band.[82] Miles Kellogg owned the Diana Hall, where he offered continuous live music and other social events such as a Grand Masque Ball.[83] A number of other saloons featured music, such as the Alhambra, where it was reported "every evening an artist peels forth sweet music."[84] Other venues included the short-lived Sportsman's Hall on Fifth between Allen and Toughnut.[85] In September 1880 enterprising Jennie Forrest turned the San Diego restaurant into a public dance house called Our Opera.[86] She quickly added a variety stage and booked nightly performances from local artists.[87] Unfortunately, Jennie was chloroformed and robbed of a considerable amount of money less than four weeks after opening and was forced to close.[88] Even Tombstone's streets were the scene of musical entertainment, speeches, foot races, and boxing matches.

Tombstone had access to other outdoor venues as well. A little more than a mile outside town on Charleston Road, Tombstone residents patronized J. C. Brady's Neptune Wells Hall. It was a saloon and general-purpose hall advertised as "the finest summer resort in the Territory . . . a short and pleasant drive from town." [89] Brady made a habit of hosting grand picnic socials in the summer that coincided with the full moon, allowing the festivities to go deep into the night.[90] Future Bird Cage proprietor Oliver Trevillian furnished music for several of the gatherings.[91] The festive atmosphere might have been therapeutic for Brady, who lost two sons in a drowning accident shortly before he opened the hall.[92] Another outdoor venue was Doling's saloon and racetrack, located two miles outside town straight down Allen Street. Horses owned by the Earps, Johnny Behan, and many other Tombstone notables competed on its oval, which opened in May 1880.[93] But it would be used for so much more: wrestling, prize fights, foot races, glass ball shooting, baseball games, track-and-field style competitions, holiday celebrations, political gatherings, and more. While Doling's buildings no longer stand, a faint outline of the racetrack can still be seen today.

Many of the earliest venues became somewhat obsolete when Tombstone's crowning civic building, Schieffelin Hall, opened in June 1881. More than 140 years later it still serves the community by hosting city council meetings, theatrical productions, and other social gatherings. As a true piece of living history, Schieffelin Hall has a story as rich as any original building in Tombstone. Yet the wave of original venues that preceded it included many that were important to Tombstone's beginning. Although Tombstone didn't have "a man for breakfast" every day as the legend suggests, it did have a song for dinner every night. Most importantly, many of these venues were responsible for hosting a number of international stars. Their presence validated Tombstone's prominence, and the crowds they drew proved how desperately Tombstone needed a genuine variety theater like the Bird Cage.

Chapter 3

Early Performers Prove the Concept

*All who have left their homes in the large cities and cast their lots
in the new camps of the border for the purpose of building fortunes
sadly miss the delight [of] witnessing the operatic and dramatic
performances, which, in the days of old, did much to lighten the daily
routine of weary toil.*
—*Tombstone Daily Nugget*, November 30, 1880

How funny it sounds . . . opera amongst the Tombstones!
—*Arizona Daily Star*, December 2, 1879

Before the Bird Cage opened its doors, Tombstone was visited by a number of significant nineteenth-century performers. A case could be made that several were the most famous stage entertainers to ever visit the town. Their appearances in Tombstone are important because their consistent financial success and draw of large audiences proved how prosperous a dedicated variety theater in Tombstone could be. This directly paved the way for the Bird Cage. Their visits also confirmed and emboldened the notion that Tombstone was on the rise and worthy of all the intense publicity it was getting. To appreciate their arrival, one has to imagine a time and place where entertainment was only available when a living, breathing person was in front of you singing, dancing, playing an instrument, and delivering dialogue. Where that didn't exist, overseeing a gambling game, reading the newspaper, waiting on a letter from home, or another creative diversion had to suffice. By the time the first notable performers came to Tombstone, many residents were eager to see a performer no matter how good or bad they were. As you will see, entertainment-starved Tombstone was eager for them to come, frenzied when they got there, and longed for their return.

Pauline Markham: Tombstone's First Star

Many resources give credit to Nellie Boyd as Tombstone's first notable performer. In truth, Pauline Markham predated her by a full year. Pauline was born in 1847 in the heart of London and began performing while still a teenager.[1] After several trips back and forth to the States, she experienced such strong success that it warranted the publication of an autobiography when she was just 23 years old. A few years later the widely popular *Police Gazette* featured her on the front cover.[2] She became so recognized that her likeness was used to market a whole array of consumer products, from cough syrup and mattresses to cigarettes and a number of small businesses.[3] One newspaper insisted, "the whole nation worshipped her and rang with praises of her beauty," and it wasn't far from the truth.[4] Her aura, skill, and beauty aroused interests from many men. One committed suicide when Pauline declined his long-shot marriage proposal.[5] Many others vied for her attention with gifts of money and jewelry that she claimed to have totaled $100,000 in one ten-year stretch.[6] Her responses were always self-preserving. "I told them that I never sold my favors—not even for charity."[7]

On the back of that success and notoriety, her troupe was touring the southwest in 1879. Their main feature was a highly praised rendition of *HMS Pinafore*—one of the most popular plays of the nineteenth century.[8] In the lead role, Pauline received rave reviews. "[Pauline] sustained the character of Josephine in a manner perfectly in accord with her exalted reputation.

Beautiful and talented Pauline Markham was the first notable entertainer to test Tombstone's thirst for entertainment. She arrived in Tombstone on December 1, 1879—the same day as Wyatt, Virgil, and James Earp. Original carte de visite (CDV) from author's collection.

Her notes are always sweet from the highest to the lowest, and she passes from strain to strain with an exquisite modulation of tone. . . . This is one of the surest indications of true artistic merit."[9]

While Pauline was thriving onstage, the company met serious trouble in Tucson. Performances were held up when the overland stagecoach transporting their scenery and stage necessities went missing.[10] Worse yet, the company's manager ran them into the ground financially, leaving behind a trail of debts and unpaid salaries to company members. With their welfare at stake, the fed-up performers united, exiled the manager, and reorganized the company, taking on all previous debts.[11] They attempted several performances in Tucson, but the vengeful former manager hired a lawyer and did everything in his power to make it difficult for them.[12]

The bold decision was then made to gamble on Tombstone. It was a risky move for several reasons. In late 1879 the only way to reach Tombstone from Tucson was by a hazardous and unrelenting twelve-hour stagecoach ride. More importantly, as the first performance troupe to attempt it, there was no precedent that playing Tombstone would be profitable—a daunting possibility for a group of people with no money and a mountain of debts. They needed a sure thing, and Tombstone was not it. With more hope than options, Pauline and her company loaded on to Ohnesorgen and Walker's stagecoach bound for Tombstone and pulled into town on December 1, 1879—the very same day that Wyatt, Virgil, and James Earp arrived with their wives.[13] Much to their relief, Tombstone responded well. For three days performances met capacity crowds.[14] There's no record of exactly how much money they made, but it was reported they were "well patronized" and "took in money enough to pay bills and declare a dividend."[15]

Tombstone's enthusiasm and prospects made such an impression on the troupe's talented tenor Frank Roraback that he left for San Francisco with a plan to assemble his own performance company and return.[16] That's exactly what he did, but instead of Pauline Markham headlining, he recruited a woman of equal talent and celebrity—Patti Rosa.[17]

Patti Rosa

Upon returning to Arizona, former Pauline Markham troupe member Frank Roraback introduced his newly formed performance company to Tucson on April 17, 1880.[18] Crowds at the Park Theater—a venue that would see dozens of Bird Cage performers in following years—instantly took to them. None got more praise than his star, Patti Rosa. Tucson papers called her a "first class" performer with "few equals on stage [who] completely captivated her audience."[19]

Although Patti was just a teenager, her stage presence was instilled by her mother, who was a notable English performer. Together they were brought to America by renowned talent agent Thomas Allston Brown—a man who also represented high-profile Bird Cage performers Millie De Granville and Pearl Ardine early in their careers.[20] Like Pauline Markham, Patti created a reputation across the country but did it with a wider array of talents: singing, clog dancing, and instrument playing. Perhaps her greatest asset was her playful demeanor that drew crowds in and made long-lasting impressions. This effect was typified by the review of one journalist months after she left Arizona:

> So unique, merry and picturesque is Miss Rosa that it is impossible to consider her from a serious standpoint. As to her talent there can be no question. She is so thoroughly clever, so graceful and charming, and at the same time endowed with such an inexhaustible spirit of true humor. . . . Her voice is a sweet mezzo-soprano, and her natural step a waltz paz. Sentiment or pathos are strangers to her, and her voice and actions are only harmonious when she is 'cutting up'. Every turn seems tame unless rounded off with a kick or a wink. Rosa's capers and caprices were . . . endless, and her versatility presented a new turn or a new twist at the most unexpected moment. Her banjo solos, songs and dances were among the chief features of the evening. Such is Patti Rosa, the impish mischief-maker—a veritable Lotta.[21]

After a run of performances in Tucson, Roraback took Patti and the troupe to Tombstone. It had been a few months since he made the trip with Pauline Markham. In that time twenty-five miles of Southern Pacific track had been laid east of Tucson, making the journey less daunting. Patti and the company became some of the first passengers transported by rail to the small town called Pantano at the end of the track, thirty-six miles northwest of Tombstone. Its crude canvas-and-frame buildings provided services for travelers— boarding, restaurants, provisions, and stagecoach offices. Anticipating their arrival, stagecoach operator J. D. Kinnear reserved a Concord coach specially for Patti Rosa and company.[22] All fifteen souls crammed into the coach and endured the four-hour journey through the San Pedro Valley's intolerably dusty roads.[23] After their wheels stopped on bustling Allen Street, they checked into the commodious Cosmopolitan Hotel, rested a day, and went to work.[24]

Petite and charming Patti Rosa had quite an effect on Tombstone miners, including founder Ed Schieffelin, who was "badly gone on her" according to local diarist George Parsons. Original cabinet card from author's collection.

For eleven days and nights they performed in front of "an overflowing house" filled with "large audiences [that were] enraptured with the superbly selected program."[25] In addition to performing every night, they added a 3:00 p.m. matinee that gave miners who worked night shifts and children a chance to attend.[26] Another one of their performances raised $61.50 ($1,750 in modern money) for the local school fund.[27] Tombstone's population was so thankful for the entertainment and contributions that they threw Patti and the company a benefit in return.[28]

Throughout their run of performances, the *Tombstone Nugget* agreed with the reputation that had proceeded young Patti. "Our people have never before been visited by so talented a company. Patti Rosa . . . was received cordially by the immense audience before her, as her singing and dancing was superb. She is a talented lady, and deserves the celebrity she has won."[29] After a few days of performances the *Nugget* was even more impressed. "The Little Favorite, Patti Rosa, has been a great attraction. . . . As an artist of rare merit, a lady of refinement and culture, she has been received nightly before the foot lights with great enthusiasm by an admiring audience."[30]

The local paper wasn't the only one that noticed Patti. Local diarist George Parsons attended a performance with Tombstone founder Ed Schieffelin. In his journal after the show he noted that Ed "seems to be badly gone on her."[31] Ed wasn't the only victim of her charms. Three days after Patti left, two young miners were so impressed by her they located a mine near Tombstone and officially recorded it as the "Great Patti Rosa" mine.[32] Her popularity also prompted a single night's performance in the infamous cowboy stronghold of Charleston nine miles away after leaving Tombstone.[33]

Praise aside, Patti Rosa's appearance in Tombstone is important to highlight because it drew the success and packed houses of Pauline Markham, but instead of three nights, she did it for a week and a half. It was further proof of Tombstone's eagerness for entertainment—and yet there were more.

Henry Willio

April of 1881 saw a trio of male performers visit Tombstone in quick succession. The first was successful and highly respected career magician Henry Willio. He was internationally celebrated, having performed in "nearly every civilized country on the globe" since he was ten years old.[34] While he performed at the Turnverein Hall for only three days, the reason why reads like fiction.[35]

In 1874 Willio was traveling with his pregnant wife and two young daughters on a performance tour throughout the Caribbean. During the tour he accepted an engagement in Panama and left his family behind. Upon arrival in Panama he was hit hard by yellow fever. After months of hospitalization and several bouts with death, he recovered only to find out his wife had died

TURN-VEREIN HALL!
Three Nights Only:
WEDNESDAY, THURSDAY, FRIDAY, APRIL 6, 7, 8.
PROFESSOR WILLIO,

The Man Mystery!
And PROF. BLUMAN, in their wonderful entertainments of MAGIC, MIRTH, AND MYS-
TERY, VENTRILOQUISM, IMITATIONS OF BIRDS AND ANIMALS, THE FIRE-KING,
SWORD SWALLOWE., FEATS OF STRENGTH, CONTORTIONS AND ACROBATIC EXER-
CISES, ETC., ETC.   WILLIAM A. CUDDY, Manager.
☞ For Particulars See Small Bills.

This advertisement appeared in the April 6, 1881, *Epitaph*. Henry Willio's short performance run in Tombstone helped fund the ongoing search for his daughters. Author's collection.

giving birth to their third child. Rushing back from Panama he met further horror when his two daughters, aged 3 and 5, were missing. Following leads from locals he discovered that the girls were given to a notable traveling American female performer with the understanding that Henry had died. Believing them to be orphans, she took the girls under her wing and trained them as performers.

In the fifteen years that followed, Henry took on the role of traveling magician and detective. Using his performances to pay his way, Henry traveled as far and wide as the West Indies, Australia, South America, Mexico, and coast to coast in the United States endlessly following leads and looking for his daughters. At one point his travels put such strain on finances he had to leave personal possessions to pay for room and board.[36] His short stint in Tombstone was a paying stop in his relentless search that didn't end until 1887. His tenacity paid off, and through contacts he found both daughters alive and well—one having married in San Francisco, the other in Rochester, New York.

Henry's youngest daughter, Mabel, thought she had been orphaned long ago, destined for a life without knowing a loving home. Before reconnecting in person they exchanged letters. Mabel's neat round hand gave Henry hope she had been educated and cared for. She wrote, "My dear papa: Is it possible that my dear father lives? This is indeed a resurrection to me. It seems like a dream from which I will awake only to find myself again desolate and an orphan. I can hardly wait to see you and my darling sister. I will close with a thousand kisses and my best love for you and dear sister. Your daughter, Mabel Lillian Willio."[37]

For three days in Tombstone crowds at the Turnverein Hall, completely unaware of Henry's plight, supported his performances. His mixture of illusions, ventriloquism, fire-king sword swallowing, feats of strength, and acrobatics were billed as "magic, mirth and mystery." His combination of talents earned him praise as "the world's greatest wonder [who] accomplished the greatest feats that can be done by living man."[38] Every dollar helped get him closer to his daughters, and every performance gave Tombstone a reason to be truly wowed.[39]

Robert McWade

Ten days later Tombstone was visited by career entertainer Robert McWade. As a young man he left the stage to join the Union Army in the Civil War and honorably rose from private to lieutenant. He saw combat in numerous battles such as Williamsburg and the Second Bull Run and was awarded the Kearny

This postcard-sized lithograph advertised McWade's 1874 performance of
Rip Van Winkle in Milwaukee, Wisconsin. He continued the role until his
death in 1913. Original lithograph from author's collection.

Cross—a medal given to Union soldiers who had displayed meritorious,
heroic, or distinguished acts in battle.[40] After a near fatal illness and an
honorable discharge, McWade began a forty-five-year run of performing
Washington Irving's classic *Rip Van Winkle* across the country. In April 1881
he brought his revered success to Tombstone.

With Schieffelin Hall still two months from completion, McWade secured the Sixth Street Opera House. His thorough preparations included a complete renovation before his arrival. They gutted out the old bar, stove, and anything that detracted from an upstanding appearance. The hall was refitted with a stage, new scenery and 150 chairs, assuring the "comfort and convenience of the patrons."[41] Performance reviews noted that McWade "excels in [Rip Van Winkle] . . . as his renown has everywhere preceded him."[42] His weeklong performances starting April 14, 1881, were so well received that attendees threw a benefit in his honor and publicly announced it in an open letter printed in the *Epitaph*. Among those that signed the letter was Mayor John Clum, future lawyer of the Earps, Thomas Fitch, Tombstone Chief of Police Ben Sippy, Cochise County Sheriff John Behan, and many others.[43]

McWade continued the *Rip Van Winkle* production he had shown in Tombstone until his death in 1913.[44] Shortly before passing, early movie giant Vitagraph produced a film titled *Rip Van Winkle* with McWade in the lead role reprising his lifelong character. The movie continued to be shown in theaters well after his passing.[45]

Edward Cooper Taylor

A week and a half after Robert McWade left Tombstone, the Turnverein built a stage in anticipation of a highly successful magician. He was 29, a brash dresser, stoic and confident, and his eventual fifty-year career earned a place in the American Magician's Hall of Fame with the likes of David Copperfield and Harry Houdini. His name was Edward Cooper Taylor. [46]

Arriving on April 29, 1881, Taylor and his wife (who also performed in the act) lodged at the Grand Hotel on Allen Street.[47] Throughout his week of performances, word of mouth and favorable press promoting his skill and reputation swelled crowds. Even big-time eastern critics called him "a worthy successor of Houdini."[48] For Tombstone's children Taylor featured an Italian marionette troupe brought to life by his own hands. His wife also performed an aerial suspension act. In another she danced blindfolded on a stage covered with dozens of eggs. With "unapproachable

E. C. Taylor poses in 1876 with several medals awarded to him by communities that celebrated his performances. From E. C. Taylor III.

ease and grace" she "went through all the intricate steps of a mazy waltz . . . never touching one [egg] until the conclusion when she tipped them one by one with the toe of her gaiter spinning them across the stage." The audience was astonished.[49]

Among other illusions Taylor's act also included the Phantom Bird Cage, in which he made a cage and the real live canary inside vanish. While standing in the middle of the audience, he took off his coat and vest to show the cage wasn't hidden and then effortlessly made it reappear.[50] Audience members also saw him "fill a hat with gold and silver coins by picking [them] from the air, from the hair of the heads of his audience, from the soles of his boots, picking it from the mouth of his wife, and even caused a shower of it to fall when he sneezed."[51]

The crown jewel of his act was called the Turkish Mystery Box. In this illusion Taylor invited two audience members to examine a large wooden box, making sure it contained no trick modifications, and then instructed them to lock it with a padlock. The keyhole was sealed with wax, and the key was placed in one of the volunteer's pockets. The volunteers were then instructed to bind the box with netting and rope until everyone present was satisfied it was completely impenetrable. Next Taylor was seated and shackled by the ankles and wrists to a platform and tied up by the two audience members in similar fashion to the box. He was then covered by a sack, which was also secured by lock and chain to the platform he was chained to. Once Taylor and the box were secure, a curtain was drawn in front of both. Tense minutes passed until a pistol shot rang out and the curtain was dropped. Upon inspection nothing was left in the bag that once held Taylor aside from the chains and rope that bound him. The box, appearing completely untouched with the same knots and ropes as before, was untied and unlocked. Inside was Taylor, free from any former restraints. The illusion was electrifying.[52]

From April 30 to May 7 Taylor and his wife presented shows at the Turnverein Hall every night in this manner, bringing new acts to each one. Patronage was large despite the hall's location outside of Tombstone's bustling business district. Audiences were further enticed by a raffle in which Taylor gave away one hundred gifts he had purchased from local Tombstone merchants. One was a cash prize of twenty-five dollars—a substantial sum at a time when local miners earned four dollars a day.[53] One performance was reviewed by the *Epitaph* under the heading, "A Night of Mirth and Magic."

Prof E. C. Taylor's performance of refined illusions, magic and sleight-of-hand last night was witnessed by an audience composed mainly of the best people in Tombstone. The ladies graced the entertainment with their presence, and seemed to enjoy the strictly first-class affair. The Professor employs no cheap, clap-trap accessories in the production of his illusions. Every article used by him is exposed to the critical examination of the audience, and astonishment secedes astonishment as inanimate articles are made to take themselves wings and fly from place to place on command. There is no attempt at concealment in anything he does, and one is almost forced to believe in the truth of the "black art."[54]

Taylor's lasting legacy in Tombstone came as a contributor to the Engine Company No. 1 building, which still stands on Toughnut Street. As an important part of fire-prone Tombstone's preservation, erection of this proper firehouse was aided by funds generated from Taylor's last performance. Among those that volunteered to perform with Taylor was Lottie Hutchinson, the wife of Bird Cage founder Billy Hutchinson.[55] Like those before him, Taylor's performances proved that everyone from children to miners to "the best people in Tombstone" were hungry for entertainment.

Other Notables

Shortly before Schieffelin Hall opened in June 1881, the Turnverein Hall hosted yet another performance group, the Mitchell Dramatic Company, headlined by Millie Willard. Not as widely known as Pauline Markham or Patti Rosa, Millie was still "a lady of commanding presence" who had the kind of talent, popularity and respect that made her death in 1908 a newsworthy event.[56] Tombstone was also visited by the Ryland Circus in September 1880. Ryland's was a large production, taking up much of undeveloped block 17— the very ground that eventually became the OK Corral passageway. It featured an international cast of gymnasts, trick bronco riders, high-wire acts, feats of strength exhibitors, a troupe of performing dogs, and a menagerie of monkeys, ponies, trained camels, and trick mules. Tombstone supported it well and became a popular stopping point for many circuses throughout the nineteenth century.[57] However, among all the notables that came to early Tombstone, none emphasized the need of a variety theater more than Nellie Boyd.

Nellie Boyd

Of all performers and companies to play early Tombstone, none exceeded the length of run, success, and impact of Nellie Boyd. What was scheduled to be a short visit to Tombstone turned out to be a seventeen-day run urged on

Nellie Boyd.

Nellie Boyd is seen here in one of the few photographs of her known to exist. Original CDV, from author's collection.

by the demands of insatiable crowds. From November 29 to December 15, 1880, her company drew crowds that overwhelmed Ritchie's Hall directly underneath Billy Hutchinson's gambling rooms on the second floor. Both the *Epitaph* and *Nugget* newspapers reported daily reviews of the previous day's performances and reviewed that day's upcoming shows. Her press was so energetic, it nearly outweighed daily mine reports, which were the heartbeat of Tombstone's very existence.[58] No one received as much column space and praise as Nellie herself.

After spending her teens and 20s in traditional eastern theater scene, Nellie migrated west and headlined her own company. By the time she came to Tombstone, Nellie was 32 years old and in the midst of a decade-long run of traveling performances that covered every state and territory of the West from Canada to Mexico. Although she was exposed to rough travels and environments, Nellie remained unchanged. Her one-time musical director remembered, "She did not have Sunday manners and week-day manners. It was Sunday manners with her all the time." Although publicly known as a skilled and versatile actress, she was known by those closest to her for her kind heart and passion for "giving pleasure and comfort to others."[59] Many stories throughout her life support that. Yet this polite and soft-hearted woman was also able to thrive in harsh western towns and the volatile events that so often accompanied them.

During her seventeen-day run, Tombstone experienced a modest surge in violence. One afternoon the Tombstone to Charleston stage was robbed at gunpoint.[60] Another night saw two men revive a personal rivalry by exchanging gunfire on Sixth Street.[61] Events like this became more numerous, prompting one local to observe, "Shooting now about every night. Strange no one is killed."[62]

Tombstone was also in the midst of a property war between lot owners and a townsite company that both claimed rights to lots. During Nellie's run, bad blood stirred when townsite officials physically moved a man's home off its foundation and into the street. Swarms of fellow property owners came and made a stand. Only by the efforts of Police Chief Ben Sippy "being compelled to take off his coat and show he meant business" was further incident prevented. The property feud found its way into Ritchie's Hall the next night when one attendee of Nellie Boyd's performance recalled, "at the theater . . . 10 men had shotguns loaded and ready in case the signal for help came and . . . they had brought some rope to stretch [townsite official's] necks with in case they were not shot."[63]

Amid such chaos Nellie and her troupe remained professional and poised, if not comfortable. If they took special notice of these events, energetic crowds easily distracted them. Patrons came to see the company's array of dramas and comedies, such as *East Lynne*, *Lady of the Lyons*, *Two Orphans*, *Ticket of Leave Man*, *Octaroon*, *Rose Michel*, and others. In perhaps Nellie's best lead role, the company performed *Fanchon the Cricket*, in which Nellie "won the hearts of her auditors." Throngs of Tombstone's citizens gathered outside Ritchie's entrance, spilling across Fifth Street every evening. Opening night experienced a "crowded house [with] standing room being at a premium and many being turned away from the door."[64] A full week later things hadn't changed when the *Epitaph* reported "another crowded house. Audience enthusiastic. [Nellie Boyd] has become a prime favorite of Tombstone."[65] The *Nugget* agreed. "The troupe [was] able to present in a manner that held the audience spell bound until the curtain dropped upon the last thrilling tableau."[66] With demand that consistently outsold available seating in Ritchie's Hall, the *Epitaph* concluded, "It is greatly to be regretted that Tombstone has not a hall or opera house sufficiently large to accommodate the people who desire to witness such first-class entertainments."[67] Even in Nellie's last performances Tombstone's thirst for entertainment hadn't been quenched, with "many people turned away on account of not being able to get in."[68]

The demand was so potent that Nellie returned and played Tombstone three times by 1883—further evidence of how unaffected she was by the streak of lawlessness during her initial appearance.[69] Evidence of her Tombstone popularity went beyond the rush of patrons. A saloon one block away from Ritchie's advertised and served "Nellie Boyd cocktails."[70] Stagecoach operator J. D. Kinnear (who arranged the private coach that brought Patti Rosa to town) named one of his coaches "Nellie Boyd" and painted her name on its side.[71] Miners in the audience were also taken by her. The day after her very first performance, four young miners lucky enough to fit into Ritchie's Hall recorded their mine outside Tombstone as the "Nellie Boyd" mine.[72] The same thing happened on her second visit to Tombstone a year later when two miners located a claim in the Dragoon Mountains and recorded it as the "Nellie Boyd."[73]

Nellie's success in 1880 was noticed by yet another individual. Directly above the frenzied activity of Richie's Hall sat Billy Hutchinson, dealing faro in the club rooms on the second floor. He heard every round of applause and chorus of laughter through the floor. Some at his table may have been those unable to get into the show. As a partner of the hall's owner, Billy was acutely aware of the show's financial success. In the middle of Nellie's great run, the *Nugget* determined "an Opera House in Tombstone would be a paying investment."[74] Sitting mere feet from the action, Billy Hutchinson likely came to the same conclusion and decided to give Tombstone the variety theater it so obviously needed.

Chapter 4

Bird Cage Founders
William and
Lottie Hutchinson

No two people imparted greater influence on Bird Cage history than Billy and Lottie Hutchinson. It was their vision, ambition, and efforts that gave rise to its walls, ensured its early success, and created lasting notoriety celebrated more than a 140 years later. Understanding who they were is therefore important to understanding the Bird Cage. Their will became the cornerstone of the business, and it dictated the pattern of events that took place there under their watch.

Like many, the Hutchinsons were drawn to Tombstone from Tucson, where they were bombarded with irresistible reports and rumors of wealthy mining strikes. As it turned out, many of the rumors were true. After returning from a full tour of Tombstone's mines early in 1879, one skeptical Tucson newspaper correspondent wrote that he "became an ardent convert and [was] strongly tempted to remain and prospect."[1] Such reports would have aroused Billy's curiosity, and in March 1879 he made his first Tombstone area mining claim.[2] It was relatively early in the area's development. The town itself wasn't really a town at all but a scattering of canvas-and-frame buildings split between the old and new townsites and other nearby locations competing to be the center of the district. Billy and Lottie, both in their late 20s, were on the scene early with determination to work it every way possible.

Billy was born very near the legendary battlefield of San Jacinto, Texas, to Minerva and William D. Hutchinson in 1849.[3] His parents came from different backgrounds and geographic locations but were brought together by the events that shaped the growing country and put its population in motion. Billy's father was a southerner, born and raised in Columbia County, Georgia. Several prior generations of Hutchinsons lived in Virginia, but that all changed in the 1780s when the family acquired land grants in Georgia for service in the Revolutionary War.[4] Thus Billy's father and grandfather were both born and raised amid the towering pines of Augusta, Georgia. The family's military legacy was carried on by Billy's grandfather, who fought in the War of 1812. As a private in the cavalry of the Georgia militia, his allegiance to Georgia and the country was tested when he became a prisoner of war. Surviving the experience, he continued his military career until at least 1830.[5]

For several generations the Hutchinsons sank deep roots in the social and political structure of Augusta. The family was supported in part by their high-volume liquor and grocery store that sold everything from Jamaican and Indian rum to crockery, produce, and gunpowder.[6] Billy's grandfather continued to acquire land throughout Georgia in the land lotteries of the 1820s and '30s. He also acquired several thousand acres in southeast Texas through land grants as the Texas Revolution raged. However, after defeat at the Alamo and the subsequent victory over the Mexican Army at San Jacinto in 1836, Texas became an enticing frontier. With a keen sense of the opportunity there, Billy's grandfather uprooted the family from Georgia to "engage in mercantile pursuits" in the newly founded community of Houston.[7] Sadly, Billy's grandfather died less than two years after arriving in Texas, which left his father and his father's five siblings—all in their teens and early adulthood—to take on Texas by themselves.[8]

After his grandfather's untimely death, Billy's father claimed several large tracts of land outside San Antonio. He could have easily moved there or returned to Georgia where many of his family members remained, but he didn't.[9] Ultimately he remained in southeast Texas, and it may have been a woman that made up his mind. Her name was Minerva Bloodgood—the daughter of one of the earliest families to settle in southeast Texas. For generations predating the Revolutionary War, her family lived in colonial America. Fate intervened when her father received a land grant in the first Texas colony directly from Stephen F. Austin—the man known as "the father of Texas. In 1824 the family acquired a tract of land twenty miles northeast of Houston that favorably straddled the natural resources of Cedar Bayou (present-day Trinity River).[10] For a while Minerva's father farmed and worked as a carpenter. Eventually he built a successful mercantile near San Jacinto and achieved relative wealth.[11]

Solid family backgrounds and community standing made William D. Hutchinson and Minerva Bloodgood a good match, and on January 15, 1846, they were married.[12] Three years later Minerva gave birth to William James Hutchinson, the future founder of the Bird Cage. Four years later they gave him a brother, although lack of records moving forward suggest he may have died in childhood.[13] In 1857 they had their third and final child—a girl named Ella.[14]

Ella lived her entire life in Texas, sixty years of which was spent in Fort Worth. Her first child, William Gideon (possibly named after her big brother), would be remembered in the history books as "Kid Nance," the first Detroit Tiger to collect six hits in a Major League Baseball game—a feat he accomplished on July 13, 1901.[15]

Early in Billy and Ella's life their father supported the family as a farmer.[16] By 1860 he owned and operated the area's largest producing sawmill, where he employed five men and churned out $28,000 of lumber annually. Records indicate one of his employees may have been Minerva's brother.[17] What appeared to be a comfortable upbringing ended in 1867 when Billy's father died. Records revealing his cause of death have remained elusive, but at 44 years old, he left behind a family too young to be fatherless. Billy was 17 and Ella was only 10. Minerva became a 37-year-old widow, yet she stepped up, took responsibility for William's estate, and held the family together. It's unknown what became of his sawmill.[18]

Details of Billy's early adulthood and early 20s remain a mystery. In 1870 his mother and sister lived with family in Galveston. However, those

Billy Hutchinson's nephew, William Gideon (*front left, leaning on his elbow*), in the 1901 Detroit Tigers team photo. Author's collection.

same records that place them there show no sign of Billy.[19] Five years later, in 1875, Ella married and moved to Fort Worth shortly thereafter.[20] That same year Billy reappeared in the city directory, which noted he and his mother were living together. The same was true in 1876, at which time Billy's mother was operating a boardinghouse in Galveston's central neighborhoods. But by December of that year, Billy's mother remarried and moved to Fort Worth to be near Ella.[21]

After 1876 the evidence trail runs cold on Billy, and there's no sign of him until he resurfaced in Arizona in 1879. While these small hints reveal Billy's whereabouts in the mid-1870s, what he was doing with himself is unclear. In 1882 one Bird Cage customer noted Billy was an "old a hand at the [theater] business," providing a strong suggestion he had been in or around theater circuits for a substantial amount of time.[22] His management style of the Bird Cage discussed ahead strongly supports that. If so, Galveston provided plenty of variety theater opportunities. While Billy was living with his mother in 1875 and 1876, there were seven theaters operating throughout the city. Interestingly, four performers whom Billy hired at the Bird Cage in 1882 were at Galveston's Grand Central theater in the fall of 1878.[23] Another one of his Bird Cage hires was at Galveston's Comique in December of 1877.[24] These are either coincidences or pieces of evidence that Billy was there forming industry relationships that served him in Tombstone. At the same time, Galveston had a very popular Bird Cage saloon mere blocks away from where he was living. It may have inspired the name Billy chose for his legendary Tombstone theater.[25]

An even greater mystery is the background of Billy's wife, Lottie Hutchinson. Records kept during her residence in Tombstone indicate she was born in Pennsylvania or New Jersey in 1851 or 1852.[26] While it seems likely she and Billy were married between 1876 and 1879, no marriage record or evidence of her maiden name has been located. Marrying within the entertainment industry was extremely common. As will be discussed ahead, 22 percent of all Bird Cage performers were married to one another, and the vast majority of them married fellow entertainment industry professionals. Lottie proved she was a very skilled singer while performing at the Bird Cage and other high-profile public gatherings in Tombstone. Such performances solidified her reputation as a "popular lady [with] many admirers."[27] The *Nugget* even called her "an actress of many years' experience."[28] It's very possible she had the same variety theater experience as Billy. It's also very possible she and Billy met in theater circuits as so many others in the industry had.

Like any modern business, knowing who built, owned, and operated it suggests much about the nature of its operations. The quality of a business's product is largely a reflection of who's in command. Knowing who Billy and Lottie were is thus an important component to understanding the Bird Cage and its first years of activity. The unknown periods of their life make that difficult, particularly in the case of Lottie. Fortunately, they were both extremely active and highly visible in their five years in Tombstone. Examining their many associations and activities leaves little doubt about the kind of people they were. They connected with everyone from pickaxe-swinging miners and gamblers to church groups and the political and business elite. From the moment they arrived in Tombstone, they built relationships, participated in the growth of the town itself, and purchased what they believed to be key lots and mines. Like everyone else in Tombstone's early rush, they were positioning themselves to have the best chance to get their share of the wealth.

Before opening the Bird Cage in December 1881, Billy owned eleven different mines in whole or in part. Several were located within walking distance of Tombstone's most profitable mines, and for a time several were assumed to have great potential.[29] One was recorded with the notable outlaw Pete Spence as a witness.[30] Among his partners was Artemus Fay, a journalist from Pennsylvania who became a figurehead in the community when he established Tombstone's first newspaper, the *Weekly Nugget*.[31] Together they located a mine Billy lovingly named "Lottie" after his wife.[32] With apparent fondness for his home town, Billy named another mine the "City of Galveston." Fittingly, that mine appears to have been his most successful and was the only mine he kept until he and Lottie left Tombstone in 1884.[33] Billy also acquired a number of town lots. Aside from the long and arduous struggle to secure the Bird Cage lot, discussed ahead, he bought several on Fremont Street, including one between First and Second that served as his residence. There he became neighbors of Wyatt, Virgil, and James Earp.[34]

At the same time, Billy formed many business relationships. One notable was Billy Allen Le Van, whose granddaughter Robin Andrews recalled he was "one of [Billy's] closest friends and business partners."[35] Hard records back this up, as both men operated businesses across the street from one another and were involved in back-and-forth property and financial transactions.[36]

Billy was also operating several faro banks, where some of the highest wins and losses ever reported on Tombstone gambling tables took place. One deal yielded a win of $2,050 (or roughly $60,000 at the time of publication).[37] In the fall of 1880, he teamed up with William Ritchie, who built one of Tombstone's earliest gathering halls on Fifth Street, as discussed earlier. It was the second two-story building in Tombstone and the most heavily used multipurpose venue that hosted everything from church services and Sunday school to formal performances by the likes of Nellie Boyd.[38] Billy partnered with Ritchie in the second-story club rooms where he continued to mix with Tombstone's gambling fraternity so frequently they simply called him "Hutch."[39]

Among the Hutchinsons' strong network of relationships, perhaps none is more curious than Billy's relationship with John Henry "Doc" Holliday. Evidence of their friendship surfaced in the wake of the gunfight near the OK Corral. Days after the smoke cleared, Judge Wells Spicer, who oversaw the court proceedings, determined Wyatt Earp and Doc Holliday were to be detained. When Spicer allowed bail, a number of supporters contributed money to keep them out of jail. Eight men came forward with money on behalf of Doc Holliday. Among them were Wyatt and James Earp and Billy Hutchinson.[40] Because he put up the least, Billy's contributions are typically overlooked. In reality Billy was in financial hot water. He sank significant amounts of money into the development of the Bird Cage, which included paying for the lot three times, procuring legal representation in the process of securing it, and erecting the building itself. More importantly, as he handed over $500 for Doc Holliday's bond, he was nine months overdue in repaying a $315 loan to Ben Goodrich—the same Ben Goodrich who was prosecuting the Earps and Doc Holliday after the gunfight. Goodrich must have been furious when he found out Billy gave $500 to keep Doc out of jail while refusing to pay back the loan.

One former resident remembered that while many Tombstone lawyers were "pickled in alcohol," Goodrich wasn't. Unlike many, he didn't drink, gamble, or carouse with different women.[41] This kind of straight-lined man would not have tolerated Hutchinson's handling of his loan, and he may have seen it as disrespectful. Within days of Billy offering money to bond Doc, Goodrich took him to court.[42] Billy faced a choice to either repay his defaulted loan or help Doc. He chose Doc. So the question remains, why was Billy so supportive of Doc that he'd expose himself to legal troubles with one of the town's leading lawyers? Could Doc and Billy have become friends across the faro tables? Perhaps their friendship grew out of their many hours spent in the Tombstone gambling scene. If so, conversations would have revealed their shared southern heritage, Georgia roots, and family military background, which would have led to deeper bonds. The reason is speculation, but one thing is certain: Billy extended himself in Doc's aid when he had little to give, and he did it surely knowing he would face the wrath of Ben Goodrich, one of Tombstone's most respected lawyers.

Billy Hutchinson had a curious friendship with Doc Holliday (pictured here in 1879) that likely stemmed from their shared Georgia heritage, which they may have discovered while sitting together at Tombstone gambling tables. Copy author's collection.

Outside the likes of Doc Holliday, Billy's networking gained him entry to Tombstone's first elite organization, dubbed the Tombstone Social Club. Its membership was a who's who of early Tombstone business and political leaders. Among them was Oriental Saloon proprietor and future County Supervisor Milt Joyce; Tombstone's eventual mayor and editor of the *Epitaph*, John Clum; notable judge in the OK Corral gunfight inquest Wells Spicer; future

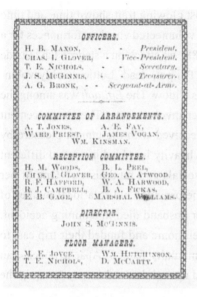

This original dance card for the Tombstone Social Club promoted the elite group's Thanksgiving Day party two and a half months after Billy Hutchinson was elected a member in 1880. Billy is listed on the bottom as one of the floor managers. Heritage Auctions.

county treasurer and journalist John O. Dunbar; and more than seventy-five others that represented Tombstone's best.[43] Several of Billy's partners, Artemus Fay, and Billy Allen Le Van were also club members. Less than a week after the organization was created in September 1880, Billy was voted in as a member.[44] The club enjoyed lavish dances hosted at Tombstone's best facilities such as the Grand Hotel and Gird's Hall on Fremont.[45] The gatherings were backdropped by the stylings of preeminent Tombstone musicians like Miles Kellogg. Billy served as the floor manager for several of the events, and Lottie gave vocal performances. Local newspapers praised Lottie's singing and her "very fine mezzo soprano voice and soubrette qualities of no mean order." One of her performances received glowing poetic praise from the *Epitaph*. "Bright, sparkling, and vivacious [Lottie] and the song held the audience captive, and rapturous applause greeted the fair [songstress] at its close."[46]

Like thousands of others, the Hutchinsons were there for the financial opportunities. But the cash-grab culture of booming Tombstone didn't sour their values. On the contrary, their most glowing trait shown time and time again was their sense of charity. Lottie volunteered vocal performances for a number of notable causes. In March 1881 an attack on a stagecoach outside Tombstone left the driver, Eli "Bud" Philpot, dead. Lottie quickly volunteered to sing at a benefit put on for his widow. The *Epitaph* was among the many who were pleased to hear of her involvement. "The announcement of that popular lady's name will be received with the utmost pleasure by her many admirers."[47] Lottie was also heavily involved in several different churches, often helping to organize socials and fundraisers.[48] One of her last acts in Tombstone came when she provided aid to a local mother of seven who was left penniless after her husband died in a mining accident. With Lottie's help, the family sold their home and funded their trip east to be in the safety of family.[49] When community fears of Apache attacks ran high in 1882, Billy and Lottie stepped up and donated money to equip the Arizona Rangers.[50]

While Billy was building business relationships, Lottie was also networking with many notable women in town. She became connected with strong-willed and highly active women like Carrie Hanson, Clara Spalding Brown, and Tombstone's most famous woman, Nellie Cashman. This group of women ran businesses, catered to the welfare of those in need, and were among the town's most respected citizens. The Hutchinsons were also invited to the close-knit wedding of local businesswoman Samantha Fallon.[51] Through her public visibility and charitable acts, Lottie became a highly recognizable and celebrated member of the community. These excerpts from local newspapers attest:

> Mrs. Wm. Hutchinson [is] a lady well known to our citizens, and one who has never been known to decline to serve the Tombstone public when benefits have been given for the churches or charitable purposes.
> —*Tombstone Epitaph*, December 22, 1881

> Mrs. Lottie Hutchinson . . . has been a resident of Tombstone almost from the inception of the operations in this camp, and has at all times, when occasion offered, been foremost to volunteer her services to advance the interests of any worthy object. She has appeared at the

numerous benefits which have been given from time to time, and has
contributed in no small degree to their success.

—*Nugget*, December 22, 1881

Mrs. Hutchinson has always been a liberal giver to deserving charity,
and her kindness of heart is [obvious] to all who ever came in contact
with her. Hence the people of Tombstone filled the large hall on the
occasion of her benefit, glad to show their appreciation of her many
sterling qualities.

—Harry K. Morton Scrapbook, p. 12, New York Public Library

Billy and Lottie were also exceedingly loyal to the local fire department.
After it was formed in September of 1880, plans were made to erect a suitable
firehouse. As she had done many times before, Lottie volunteered to sing at
a benefit performance to generate necessary funds. Appropriately one of the
songs she chose was "Boston Fire."[52] She continued to perform at a number
of fire department balls and gatherings, which helped ease the constant need
for funding.[53] Her contributions were so significant she became the first and
only known woman granted an honorary membership to Engine Company
No. 1. A certificate "of superior excellence and beauty" handmade in red
ink was awarded to her "as a token of gratitude for the many past favors she
has bestowed on [Engine Company No. 1]."[54] In doing so she joined other
notable honorary members such as OK Corral gunfight judge Wells Spicer
and Wyatt Earp.[55]

Billy invested a lot into the town's fire department as well.
He volunteered as the floor manager for their annual ball at Schieffelin
Hall.[56] Several of his friends were also involved, including his mining
partner Alfred McAllister, who was one of the men directly responsible for
establishing Tombstone's fire department.[57] Even during financial hardships
Billy continued his support. In May of 1882, the fire department may have
saved the Bird Cage building when an illuminated advertisement sign in
front of the building caught fire. It was "quite a lively blaze" when the fire
alarm was sounded, but it was put out quickly.[58] In 1883 Billy served as the
foreman of Engine Company No. 1, which was housed in the very building Lottie's performances helped fund. It still stands as one of Tombstone's
prized landmarks on Toughnut Street.[59]

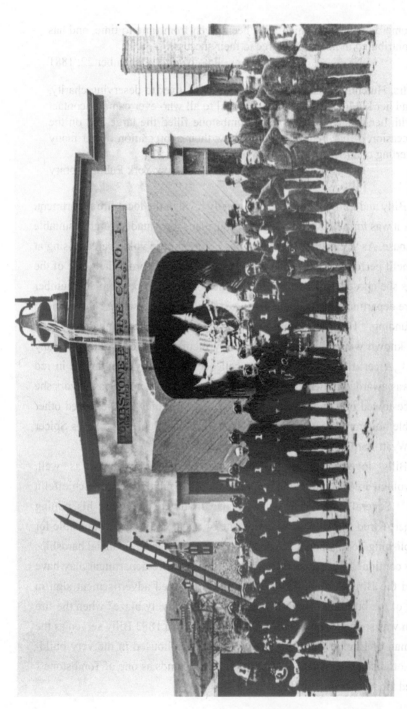

The Engine Company No. 1 building is seen here shortly after it was built in 1881. Billy and Lottie Hutchinson played roles in helping fund its construction and continued operation. Billy eventually became the foreman in 1883. The building still stands on Toughnut Street. Copy from author's collection.

In another act of kindness, the Hutchinsons helped a friend from Texas who was laid up fifty miles away at Fort Bowie with an accidental gunshot wound. The military doctors refused him treatment, and nearly a month went by before Billy heard of his critical, declining health. Immediately Billy made the long trip under the hot August sun to bring him back to his home in Tombstone. Although the wound and lack of medical attention ultimately resulted in the friend's death, the local newspaper reported that Billy and Lottie "nursed and tended to him assiduously" and enlisted three of Tombstone's best doctors to try to save him. Billy hosted the funeral at his residence and memorialized his friend's generosity and compassion by insisting that "no heart beat quicker [and] no hand was extended sooner to relieve suffering humanity [than his]."[60] Perhaps it was this same compassion and generosity that inspired Billy and Lottie. Their charitable ways continued throughout the operation of the Bird Cage, where many individuals, groups, and causes became the focus of numerous benefit performances.

It may have been an understatement when local newspapers said Billy was "well and favorably known" and Lottie was "popular [with] many admirers."[61] Their relationships spanned the entire cross-section of Tombstone's society, and they won warm favor through selfless charity work and civic contributions. These factors likely had much to do with the early success of the Bird Cage, discussed ahead. They had legions of friends, associates, and supporters eager to patronize their business no matter what kind of business it was. Many of them were the town's financial, political, and social leaders. Billy and Lottie's many strengths and ambitions served them well and contributed to their relative rise in blossoming Tombstone, and they were positioned very well for success. But they had one dominant weakness: financial choices. This one weakness would jeopardize all they had established in Tombstone and would ultimately control their destiny with the Bird Cage. But their first challenge was establishing it. That proved to be more daunting that they could have imagined.

Chapter 5

How the Bird Cage Came to Be

The performance era of the Bird Cage lasted just ten years, starting in December 1881. In that relatively short time, a legend was created that contains many alluring and engaging elements. Its performers, customers, and nightly activity figure into the most colorful period of Tombstone's history. By the time its construction commenced in early September 1881, Tombstone had nearly every comfort, convenience, and amenity it would have in its early years. In that sense the Bird Cage was somewhat late to the game. The reason why and the story of how it came to be is as provocative as its legend.

As discussed previously, Tombstone itself had a long road to becoming a consolidated town. After the first wave of mining strikes in 1878, word of the area's potential leaked out, and soon many combed the hills to claim their piece of it. The mining district was widespread, ranging more than ten miles wide, which gave rise to a number of small settlements that competed to be the main hub. However, many of the mines were never worked, and many that were quickly proved to be worthless. Some were bought and sold on overzealous intuition or the idea that they contained the same valuable ore as a neighboring mine that was producing. One miner recalled, "So much was spent for worthless claims in Tombstone that it is safe to say that more money was put in the ground there than was ever taken out."[1]

As the wealthiest mines rose to the top, miners and other mine employees were drawn to their vicinity. Right behind them were the merchants who supplied their wants and needs. Then came the transportation companies, lawyers, gamblers, and eventually families. As this natural progression sorted itself out, Tombstone became the natural gathering point over less conveniently located early settlements such as Watervale, Merrimack, Richmond, Pick-Em-Up, Hogem, and others. By late 1878 a small townsite was perched on a narrow flat behind the current Tombstone location. In less than a year, the surging population overwhelmed the slanted single street, and many began to relocate to the larger and more level plateau where Tombstone sits today.

Between the exodus from the old Tombstone location and the constant arrival of outsiders congregating at new Tombstone, an official village townsite was surveyed, mapped, and claimed by a consortium of speculators known as the Tombstone Townsite Company in early 1879.[2] The Townsite Company assumed rights to sell deeds, but there was one major problem. Many people were already occupying lots when the survey took place. Furthermore, the Townsite Company held no legal townsite patent. At that time, claiming a lot was as simple as finding desirable space and occupying it. One old timer recalled, "The new town grew fast. One camped back off the street. First one on the ground held it; no one recognized the Townsite Company. Possession was the only title, but it was orderly. There was no serious trouble until after the gamblers and politicians got ahold. If you left your property unguarded you were likely to find [it] in the street."[3] The question then was who had rights, the lot occupants already there or the Townsite Company without a legal patent that came after them? It was a question that became the source of serious problems for the entirety of Tombstone's boom. What resulted was a longstanding legal battle that often edged on physical and lethal violence, with both sides wanting to protect their stakes. Nearly every early resident was drawn in and took a side on what became to be known as "the townsite issue." The lot on which the Bird Cage would eventually be built was caught right in the middle of it.

The first occupants of the eventual Bird Cage lot were Jerry Ackerson and Henry Fry. Ackerson was a 40-year-old foreman of the Head Center mine and part-time stock raiser who had ties to the loosely associated Cowboy faction that famously figured into local controversies and crimes.[4] Fry was a 36-year-old Bavarian native who ran a cigar and liquor distributorship at Fourth and Allen Streets.[5] Both dabbled in mines and lived on the future site of the Bird Cage. Their dwelling was a modest frame cabin with an adobe chimney that sat on the middle of the lot, which was enclosed by a fence made from crude ocotillo limbs.[6] Like many early on the scene, they appear to have simply claimed the lot by "holding the ground," as no deed was recorded. So it was a good deal when Billy Hutchinson paid them $600 for the lot and cabin on July 28, 1880.[7] Market values for lots were determined by how desirable the location was, how close it was to Tombstone's developing business center, how developed the lot was, and how much faith a buyer had in the future of the mines. It was a risky proposition with no real guidelines for success. By the fall of 1880, Billy purchased four lots in different areas of Tombstone, but $600 was by far the most he paid for any of them. That suggests the degree of faith he had in the area of Sixth and Allen, and it hints at his intent to develop the lot for business purposes.[8]

Exactly three months after purchasing it, Hutchinson's cabin became linked with one of Tombstone's notable events. On the night of October 28, 1880, Marshal Fred White was shot by "Curly Bill" Brocius directly behind the cabin. Wyatt Earp's longtime friend Fred Dodge claimed he and Morgan Earp were living in the cabin and that they were both present at the time of the shooting. Years later he recalled, "The killing took place right at the rear end close by the chimney of a cabin occupied by Morgan Earp and myself."[9] He expanded in letters to Wyatt Earp's biographer Stuart Lake in 1928 and 1929:

First I will give you a description and location of the cabin occupied by Morgan and myself. The lot faced on Allen St. with a lot intervening . . . between that and Sixth St on the south side of Allen. The cabin was about eighteen feet long by twelve wide. At the south end was built in a very large and heavy adobe fireplace and chimney. There was an

Cropped from a much larger photograph, this image shows the back side of
the cabin Henry Fry and Jerome Ackerson sold to Billy Hutchinson on the
eventual Bird Cage lot (indicated by the white arrow) as it appeared in
April 1880. Clearly visible is the chimney and ocotillo-limb fence on the
lot's perimeter. Photo by Carleton Watkins, from author's collection.

open space on each side of this cabin that gave back from Allen St. This
is the cabin that held the lot upon which the celebrated and notorious
Birdcage Theater was afterward built. Fred White, the City Marshal,
was killed by Curley Bill . . . at the back end of [this] cabin occupied by
Morgan Earp and myself.[10]

In the moments before White was shot, Wyatt Earp descended on the
scene behind the cabin; he gave his own account.

I was in . . . Owen's saloon and heard three or four shots fired; upon
hearing the first shot I ran out in the street and I saw the flash of a
pistol up the street about a block from where I was. Several shots were
fired in quick succession; [so I] ran up as quick as I could, and when
I got there I met my brother, Morgan Earp, and a man by the name of
Dodge. I asked my brother who it was that did that shooting. He said
he didn't know—some fellows who ran behind that building. I asked
him for his six shooter and he sent me to Dodge. After I got the pistol,
I [ran] around the building and as I turned the corner I ran past this
man Johnson, who was standing near the corner of the building. I ran

between him and the corner of the building, but before I got there I heard White say: "I am an officer, give me your pistol."[11]

As Wyatt reached the scene, Fred Dodge looked on: "When Morgan and I and several others reached Wyatt who was by the chimney of the cabin, the shooting was lively and the balls were hitting the chimney."[12] From there, Morgan, Wyatt, and Dodge witnessed the gun of Curly Bill discharge into Fred White's lower abdomen. Despite the removal of the bullet and a hopeful prognosis, White's condition worsened over the next thirty-six hours.[13]

Ironically, Jerry Ackerson and Henry Fry, who sold Billy Hutchinson the lot and cabin, were part of the Fred White shooting storyline in very different ways. Ackerson was actually with Curly Bill and the group of men who were firing guns, which started the whole series of unfortunate events. He was arrested, but unlike the other participants, he was not prosecuted and left Tombstone the night after White was shot.[14] The next day Ackerson was found dead thirty-five miles outside Tombstone. His body was found in the open desert "covered with blood and brains" with a fatal wound to the head, a cut across his face, and his hands firmly clutching his rifle, which was cocked and ready to fire.[15] One newspaper called it "a clear case of murder" by the Cowboys, whom Ackerson was associated with. His death was never resolved.[16] Henry Fry also made it into the storyline, but in a very different capacity. As White's condition worsened, he was informed by his attending physicians of his imminent death. Upon this news, White requested the presence of his father and his friend Henry Fry at his bedside. White's state of agony passed into quiet peace, and he died shortly after.[17]

As for Hutchinson's cabin, Fred Dodge's recollections didn't stop at the Fred White shooting. He claimed that he and Morgan Earp were still living there the following March and that Wyatt Earp shacked up with them for a period. "Morgan Earp and I were still living in the cabin on the lot that the Bird Cage Theater was later built. Wyatt was with us most of the time, but he was desirous that we give up living there for the reason that we were too much exposed to assassination. And I feel sure that was the main reason that Wyatt stayed with us so much."[18] Throughout his memoirs and letters to Stuart Lake, Dodge remained consistent about living in the cabin with

Morgan and Wyatt. These recollections were repeated in Wyatt Earp's biography written by Lake. He wrote, "Across Allen Street, later site of the Bird
Cage Theater . . . was the cabin shared by Wyatt, Morgan Earp and Fred
Dodge."[19] If true, it adds a decided layer of historical significance to the cabin
and the lot even before the Bird Cage was built. This would also mean that
Billy Hutchinson was a landlord to Fred Dodge, Morgan Earp, and, for a
short period, Wyatt Earp.

Meanwhile, the property rights of Billy Hutchinson and many other
citizens hung in the balance. By the time Fred White was killed, the townsite
issue had done much to disrupt Tombstone's growth, and it created real
concerns for safety among many otherwise peaceable citizens. Townsite
officials battled lot owners for years in varying levels of courts. Property
cases became so prevalent that one newspaper noted, "Lawyers are flocking
in at an alarming rate—not only one of a firm, but whole firms and three or
four of them at a time, each seeking his share as the coyote seeks a dying
ox."[20] One lawyer wrote home to Sacramento and told his family, "I believe
that any damned fool of a lawyer could make money in Tombstone."[21]

Beyond courtrooms, the Townsite Company made it very clear they
were willing to use force. The fact that they held no legal townsite patent
did little to soften their stance. With personal fortunes at stake, citizens
were not dissuaded by threats of violence. In one episode the Townsite
Company henchmen pulled a man's fence down and literally lifted his house
and moved it into the street. Never mind the man had paid the previous
owner for the lot and held a deed. Things escalated when citizens banded
together to stop them. One local man observed, "Much artillery was on
hand and I expected shooting at one time." The situation was diffused by
Police Chief Ben Sippy, who was "compelled to take off his coat and show
he meant business," which gave citizens the clear to move the house back.[22]
In another scenario a man purchased a deed from the Townsite Company
for a lot that was already occupied. He confronted the occupant, whom he
considered a squatter, and attempted to remove him. The situation ended
when the occupant backed him down with a shotgun.[23] Such confrontations
became so prevalent, the *Epitaph* spoke of it in a "business as usual" tone
in a short report on November 15, 1880. "One man built a house yesterday

and another took an axe and knocked it down. Then they consulted lawyers. Such is life in Tombstone."[24]

Many similar tense and violent incidents were recorded, but the Hutchinsons weren't a part of them. Unlike many that engaged in the physical and legal tug-of-war over lot ownership, they took an unorthodox way out and paid for the lot a second time. On November 13, 1880, three and a half months after buying the lot from Jerome Ackerson and Henry Fry for $600, Billy secured a $315 loan from notable Tombstone lawyer Ben Goodrich. Pooling the loan with his own funds, he handed over $465 to the Townsite Company to avoid trouble.[25] Of the four lots the Hutchinsons owned at that time, it was the only one they exercised this option for. It seems clear they were taking special measures to protect it.

Interestingly, the loan from Goodrich was to be paid back in ninety days, but Billy failed to do so. Even after selling a mine to Goodrich's brother for $500, Billy didn't make good on the debt.[26] A year later (and nine months overdue) Billy still hadn't repaid the loan. Perhaps Goodrich would have been more patient if not for an ironic series of events. In the wake of the OK Corral gunfight, Wyatt Earp and Doc Holliday were to be detained. With bail granted by Judge Wells Spicer, several supporters came up with the money needed to keep them out of jail. Billy was one of eight men to put up money for Doc Holliday, offering $500 on October 30, 1881. But he was still in default of the loan from Ben Goodrich. It just so happened Goodrich was hired to prosecute the Earps and Doc Holliday, which gave him a front row seat to Billy's insulting financial move. It must have been incomprehensible and infuriating for Goodrich to watch Hutchinson put up $500 to bond the man he was prosecuting instead of paying him back. Goodrich, who had been patient up until then, was patient no longer, and he immediately sent Billy a summons and took him to court.[27] Sharing Georgia roots with Doc apparently went deeper than financial obligations to Goodrich. This questionable financial decision was a sign of bad things to come for Billy.

With the lot paid for twice, it would seem that Billy's ownership of the Bird Cage lot was secure and undisputed. But it wasn't. Unbelievably there was a third party claiming rights to lots in Tombstone's townsite.

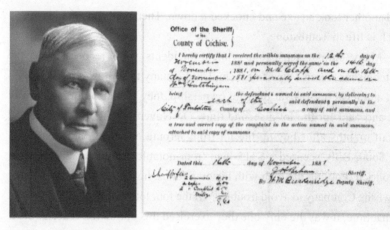

Ben Goodrich (*left*) had this summons served to Billy Hutchinson after he defaulted on his loan. While Goodrich was prosecuting Doc Holliday for his role in the gunfight near the OK Corral, Billy took the money he should have used to repay the overdue loan and used it to keep Doc out of jail. Arizona State Library and Archives.

Months before the illicit Tombstone Townsite Company was formed, several mining claims covered the layout of the village.[28] A large section of Tombstone's eastern portion was established on top of one of those claims. It was called the Gilded Age mine, and the owner wasn't backing down from asserting his rights to every lot on its surface. He was a jovial but unrelenting bulldog. The local newspaper called him "a man of true grit" who was "courageous as a lion."[29] His name was Ed Field. One local man remembered him well.

> [Field] was a rather small, stocky-built man, bald headed, always smooth shaven, and always nattily dressed. In fact, he was by far the best dressed man who ever walked the dusty streets of Tombstone. Without fail, he always appeared in the mornings in a well tailored, dark business suit. In midday, the Duke's form would be clothed in an immaculate white coat and trousers, and he would be wearing a straw hat. His evening attire was the regulation dark blue or black cutaway and striped pants. "Make way for his Royal Highness, the Duke!" was often heard on Tombstone streets, but he was always good natured.[30]

Good nature aside, Ed Field was attacking lot owners whether they arrived there first, bought from previous owners, or bought from the Townsite Company. His first target was the Townsite Company itself, whom he battled for two years in all levels of Arizona's territorial courts. The issue wasn't black and white. Although Field located his mine before the townsite was created, US mining law stated that a mine within a townsite must produce ore in order for it to claim surface rights.[31] Field made foolhardy attempts to create the illusion his Gilded Age was producing, but it never did. The ruse was obvious to one newspaper that sarcastically pointed out it yielded nothing but "large quantities of lime cement."[32]

As the tug-of-war between Field and the Townsite Company raged on, money was being lost by both sides. Courts jammed up with other cases did little to sort it out, and soon impatience produced violence. A surveyor hired by Field arrived at the Gilded Age mine and was confronted by Townsite Company crony Mike Gray. Gray attempted to intimidate him by pulling a gun and announcing, "You can't survey here except at the point of a gun."[33] Townsite officials also had a warrant sworn out for Field's arrest as a trespasser on his own mine.[34] Field had another run-in with Townsite Company partner James Clark at the Maison Dorée restaurant. After heated words they lunged after each other. As they were pried apart by onlookers, they grasped anything within reach—a sugar bowl and a pitcher of water—and desperately launched them at each other in a tirade.[35] In another altercation Field was forced off his mine "by the persuasive argument of a shotgun." In Field's absence the Townsite Company's henchmen constructed a cabin right over his mine shaft. When Field won early victories in lower courts, he was increasingly threatened with "harsh words [and] fists shaken in his face."[36] The Townsite Company ignored early court rulings and "urged inhabitants on to violence by their acts."[37]

As their two-year legal battle advanced, many townsfolk avoided investing in the east end of Tombstone. One Tucson newspaper put it well: "As a controversy it has done no little damage in retarding building improvements in that locality, as those who purchase ground don't care to buy a law suit also."[38] The *Tombstone Epitaph* agreed, calling the Townsite Company and Gilded Age battle a "fruitful source of turmoil to the people

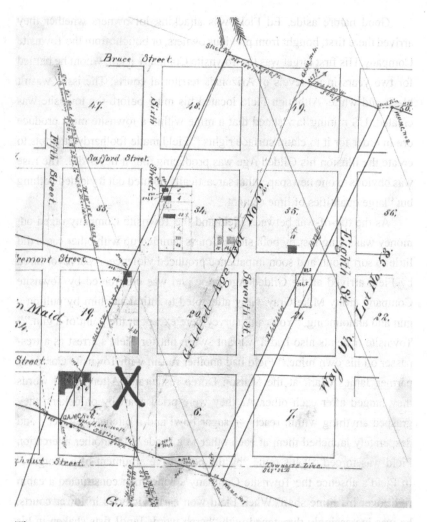

This 1883 survey map shows the city blocks of Tombstone's eastern townsite inconveniently laying on top of the Gilded Age mine. The "X" (*lower left*) marks the location of the Bird Cage. US Department of the Interior, Bureau of Land Management field survey notes, Gilded Age, Lot 52, Arizona Mineral Surveys, General Land Office Records.

of Tombstone."[39] The detrimental affair resonated all the way to Boston, where it was reported, "The uncertainty . . . gave [Tombstone] a black eye and discouraged business."[40] Unfortunately Billy Hutchinson (who had already paid for the lot twice) and more than one hundred other occupants on the Gilded Age mine were caught in the middle. Many people had developed businesses and established homes after purchasing what they believed to be legal titles to the lots.

It all came to a head in mid-April 1881. In a decision handed down by the Territorial Supreme Court, Ed Field was granted surface rights. He swaggered into Tombstone the next day intent on enforcing the judgment backed by the highest court in the territory. Reactions among the lot owners were split. Approximately 40 percent of them agreed to pay Field for lots they already owned. Successful merchants McKean and Knight, future lawyer of the Earps Thomas Fitch, enterprising prostitute Emma Parker, even town mayor John Clum all lined up with dozens of others to square their bill with Field. One onlooker observed, "[the occupants] are compelled to call upon Fields . . . who has been named the 'Duke of Tombstone' and come to his terms. A steady stream of crestfallen squatters throng to his rooms—where he sits in state, guarded by the City Marshal—all day long, paying tribute to this might man."[41] Taking advantage of those who had established homes and successful businesses, Field charged prices as high as $3,000 for lots the occupants thought they already owned.[42] Meanwhile, Field was seen in Wells Spicer's office guiltlessly submitting paperwork with "money just pouring in upon him."[43]

However, the other 60 percent of Gilded Age occupants refused to settle. Each one was subjected to forceful removal by Johnny Behan.[44] Behan's allegiance may have been questionable, as Ed Field became Behan's surety for Cochise County sheriff. He also leased residential property from Field on the northeast corner of Seventh and Safford—the likely location of his residence.[45] Nevertheless, his actions brought about strong reactions. Local diarist George Parsons recorded the tensions as Behan ejected the holdouts:

April 25: "Quite a time dispossessing Gilded Age occupants. Much Trouble feared."

April 26: "Field threatened with pictures of coffins, bloody hands, gallows, etc. Nearly shot this afternoon and shot at I believe tonight."

April 27: "Field . . . keeps close; goes out for air once in a while with his body guard."[46]

Parson's observations are backed by another tense account from a Boston newspaper man who visited Tombstone during the conflict. He noted, "Some men paid [Field] to save lawsuits, but others declared their purpose of clearing up the cloud of their titles by filling Mr. Field with cold lead. [Field] enlisted a number of good fighters, garrisoned his cabin and proclaimed his intention of fighting out on that line. The citizens laid for him, but he always appeared on the street with a shotgun body guard."[47]

Every lot owner had to make the difficult choice between paying Field to avoid trouble or fighting him by legal or physical force. What path did Billy Hutchinson take? He had already paid for the lot a second time to avoid conflict with the Townsite Company. It would make sense that he would do the same with Ed Field. But he didn't. In late April 1881, he defiantly stood up to Field, filed a lawsuit, and banded together with sixty other lot owners in an association they called the Gilded Age Protective League.[48] To protect the lot he had already paid for twice, Hutchinson not only offered support and leadership but also poured in $100 of his own money—a figure equal to a full month's wages for a working miner in Tombstone who made $4 a day.[49] More than sixty back-and-forth lawsuits overwhelmed courts well in to the spring of 1882, which kept many occupants in a year-long holding pattern of uncertainty—an undesirable position in a boomtown where time is money.

After nearly three months of deadlock and growing impatience, Field saw an opportunity to offer out of court settlement in mid-July 1881. With time and money slipping away, an impatient Billy Hutchinson gave up the fight and paid for the lot a third time. On July 22, 1881, Billy secured a loan and handed over $650 to Field. Punctuating the ridiculousness of the situation, original records show Billy actually mortgaged the very lot he was buying to secure the funds needed to buy it from Field.[50]

Billy couldn't have known it at the time, but he had done the right thing. Even after reaching the US Supreme Court, the Gilded Age saga plagued Tombstone for years to come.[51] Ed Field finally sold out to original Townsite Company member John D. Rouse in October 1883. Rouse promised the town he would end the surface rights controversy when he told the public, "I purchased the Gilded Age in order to unite our townsite title with its mining title, and so remove all question about the title to that portion of the townsite."[52] But he didn't make good on that promise, and occupants continued to be pressed for payments into the latter half of the decade. Billy's decision was expensive, but it may have been the right move. By avoiding conflict that ultimately went unresolved for years, he was finally freed up to move forward with his plans to establish a business. In all, he spent $1,715 for the lot, not counting what he invested in legal representation and donations to the Gilded Age Protective League. (Much of this money was invested while the loan from Ben Goodrich went unpaid.) While Hutchinson put it all behind him, Ed Field would haunt him again. Looming Gilded Age issues would factor into the end of Hutchinson's operation of the Bird Cage just as it had dictated its beginning.

On a positive note, Hutchinson's three-month battle with Field in the summer of 1881 may have saved him from disaster. On June 22, 1881, one month before giving up the fight and paying Ed Field, a massive fire gutted Tombstone's east business district. The historic cabin that saw Fred White's shooting and sheltered Fred Dodge and Morgan and Wyatt Earp burned to the ground in a blaze that resulted in nearly $250,000 in total losses (equivalent to $7 million at the time of publication).[53] Among the victims were dozens of Gilded Age occupants who paid two and three times for their lots. Some never recovered and watched their Tombstone dreams—along with their businesses, homes, and possessions—go up in flames. Without the legal hangups with Field, it's a distinct possibility Billy Hutchinson would have established the Bird Cage in the spring of 1881 only to see it swept away in the June 22 fire along with everyone else.

Within days of the fire, the *Epitaph* noted Hutchinson rebuilt a "neat little frame building" on the lot.[54] It's possible he built it as a temporary placeholder to deter Field from seizing the lot or to dissuade other lot jumpers. The *Epitaph* recognized a similar strategy by one property owner who built a small cabin "to hold the lot from any further attempts to jump it until the permanent building is commenced."[55] That's exactly what Hutchinson did. A month later he approached the town council with a request to move his new cabin into the street. The reason he gave the mayor and council was for the purpose of "completing an adobe dwelling."[56] On August 30, 1881, the council approved his request, and so began the construction of the Bird Cage.

Early construction reports were favorable. Adobe bricks were made on-site, and throughout September they were in abundance. The *Epitaph* reported, "Mexican adobe-makers . . . have been unusually active of late, and there seems to be a lively demand."[57] These adobe makers accelerated production of bricks by damming a wash during late summer rains. Doing so not only sped up production but also alleviated the considerable cost of procuring water required to produce the bricks—music to Hutchinson's ears after paying for the lot three times. By mid-September it was reported Hutchinson's "elegant fire proof building near the corner of Sixth and Allen is fast approaching completion [and] judging from present indications will be second to none in the Territory."[58] The building was completed in the first week of October, and it was reported that Hutchinson opened it up as a "first class saloon."[59] This opening date figures important when considering the famed OK Corral gunfight took place on October 26, 1881. While the Bird Cage building was not a functioning theater at that time, it was completed, and it possibly served customers that debated the gunfight's outcome.[60]

In the lead-up to opening Tombstone's first full-time variety theater, Billy Hutchinson made many preparations. Choosing a name for the business was one of them. There are several stories that attempt to explain how the name "Bird Cage" came to be. One popular version involves the theater's name being changed after songwriter Arthur Lamb wrote the song "A Bird in a Gilded Cage." However Lamb was eleven when the Bird Cage opened, and his popular song was written almost twenty years after the Bird Cage closed. The more popular explanation insists the name was inspired by the boxes that surround the auditorium. This story is an impossibility because Billy opened it without boxes, and it was called the Bird Cage before he installed them.[61] Boxes were also common features in every venue, from variety theaters to the most refined opera houses in Europe, and in themselves weren't unique and did not inspire venue's names any more than its doors or windows.

Misunderstanding the name's origin is the very beginning of the building's misrepresented identity. In the 1880s bird cages were incredibly common items in homes, hotel lobbies, and businesses. Bird cages were even sold at Spangenberg's gun shop, the store where the Clantons and McLaurys were seen filling their guns right before the gunfight near the OK Corral.[62] In period speak "bird cage" was a phrase commonly used to describe a woman's dress, hats, bustles, a prisoner in a cell, a person's home, and a number of other things that drew obvious or witty comparisons in print and conversation. The phrase was even used in the *Tombstone Epitaph* on October 20, 1880, to describe the town's makeshift schoolhouse. "The public school of Tombstone is at present held in a little bird-cage on Allen street, about large enough to accommodate a man and his wife, if they hadn't been married long." The suggestion here is that the building was small like a bird cage.

"Bird Cage" was not an uncommon name for businesses. There were Bird Cage Saloons in Louisiana, Texas, and Kansas.[63] In 1881 Dallas also had a theater named Antione's Bird Cage Family Resort that advertised "none but respectable characters will be allowed."[64] Geneva, Ohio, also had a Bird Cage Theater.[65] Mississippi and Maine offered Bird Cage Cottages.[66] Cincinnati had a Bird Cage Cafeteria.[67] There was even a small barbershop down the road from Tombstone in Bisbee called the Bird Cage Barber Shop.[68] Even today you can get coffee at the Birdcage Coffee House in Long Beach, California. The common trait among all of these businesses is their modest size. One hundred years ago, before Bird Cage fiction had spun out of control, local Arizona newspapers agreed that the Bird Cage "got its name from its rather small size."[69] The *Santa Ana* (CA) *Register* of October 22, 1929, agreed, saying, "The Bird Cage [was] so named because it was very small and intimate." When traveling performer Annie Ashley arrived in 1882, its modest size struck her. She called it "a little affair, like the one in El Paso" that was unlike the larger venues she commonly saw throughout her fifty-year career.[70] Simply put, Billy Hutchinson attempted to re-create a full-scale theater in the small space of one Tombstone lot that measured thirty feet wide, thus he named it the Bird Cage. It's very possible he borrowed the name from the very popular Bird Cage Saloon that was just blocks away from his home in Galveston, Texas, shortly before relocating to Tombstone.[71]

With a name chosen, preparations continued into December 1881 for the opening of the theater.[72] Meanwhile, Billy took a three-week, two-thousand-mile round trip to recruit performers from San Francisco's thriving variety

THE "BIRD CAGE,"
DIRMEYER & STEELE, Propr's.

Lunch from 10 to 1 o'clock. Red Fish Chowder
every day. The choicest Liquors. Corner Market
and Twenty-second street.

This ad is for the popular Bird Cage saloon in Galveston, Texas, which was just blocks away from Billy Hutchinson's home in 1875 and 1876. It may have inspired the name he chose for his famous theater. *Galveston Daily News*, June 6, 1872.

theater circuit.[73] He scouted two of the city's top venues, the Bella Union and Woodward's Gardens. Amazingly, he was able to secure commitments from several feature performers who were staples in San Francisco's proven venues, though it's not clear how he was able to pull it off.[74] It may have been through industry connections or simply promises of bountiful wages. Years later, former Tombstone resident and Bird Cage patron Billy Breakenridge recalled Hutchinson's performers "were attracted first by the adventure, but principally because of the large salaries."[75] For a performer in the early 1880s, there was no better place to be in the West than San Francisco. The number of venue choices, the work opportunities, the money, the connections—there was no place like it. It would have been hard to trade it for an isolated border town like Tombstone that had one unproven venue. However Billy did it, he began the return journey on December 18, 1881, with sixteen performers—eight women, eight men, and one toddler. Among them was a strongwoman who had performed coast to coast in the United States, South America, and Australia. There was also a husband and wife who gained acclaim in the mining towns of California and Nevada and traveled with their young daughter. And there was a comedic duo who would go on to operate theaters up and down the coast from Southern California to Seattle well into the twentieth century.[76] Representing more than one hundred years of combined experience, the talented crew was about to open the Bird Cage in grand style.

For two and a half days, the motley group traveled south by train through Colton, California, and east into Arizona.[77] On December 20 they reached Benson, Arizona, amid cold and miserable weather and piled into and on top of a stagecoach for the last twenty-five miles of the journey. A drive that takes thirty-five minutes today took three hours by stage-coach along the now-abandoned road on the banks of the San Pedro River. As they rolled along in relative discomfort, a snowstorm bore down on them.[78] The newspaper called it "a cold disagreeable day with . . . enough snow falling to preserve the proper consistency of mud on the streets." Pulling up to the stage office at Fourth and Allen, the newcomers stepped out of the coach amid a circle of gathered onlookers and sank their feet into the slushy mud, perhaps wondering why they had left San Francisco. Their arrival was surely one that inspired the *Nugget* to report, "The incoming stages [on December 20] were loaded with passengers."[79]

Positive press preceded their first performance. Billy Hutchinson confidently advertised them as "the greatest array of talent and beauty that ever appeared in Tombstone." Given their broad talents and experience, every word of it was true. The *Epitaph* added, "This is no snide company [that has] come here for a few days to pick up the floating change to take away with them, but people who have come here to stay and make their living and spend money among us."[80] For a time several of them did. As the finishing touches were being applied to the Bird Cage, Billy scheduled a performance for his new troupe at Schieffelin Hall.[81] After arriving on December 20, they thawed out and rehearsed a formal program the next day. On December 22 they presented their first performances in Tombstone to an eager crowd in Schieffelin Hall.

Billy leveraged the popularity of his wife, Lottie, by naming her as the beneficiary of the evening's entertainment. Doing so gave the Tombstone public even more reason to attend. The *Nugget* validated Billy's strategy. "[Lottie] has at all times . . . been the foremost to volunteer her services to advance the interests of any worthy object. She has appeared at the numerous benefits . . . and has contributed in no small degree to their success.

HUTCHINSON'S
Variety Combination
—WILL OPEN AT—
SCHIEFFELIN HALL,
THURSDAY EVEN'G NEXT.

The greatest array of Talent
and Beauty that ever ap-
peared in Tombstone,
inaugurating a New
Era in popular
Amusements.

Billy Hutchinson placed this ad boldly touting his hand-picked performers for their first performance at Schieffelin Hall on December 22, 1881. *Epitaph*, December 21, 1881.

In consideration of these facts it is to be hoped [she] will be greeted with a crowded house."[82] And she was. Performances included singing, dancing, comedy acts, physical exhibitions, and "side splitting" after a piece called "The Ash Box Inspector" that left everyone with "tears in their eyes."[83] One attendee noted encores were "numerous and prolonged."[84] Every act gave

Tombstone residents the thrill of seeing big city entertainment that was featured in San Francisco just days earlier.

Billy did it. He battled through the financial, legal, and violent gauntlet to build the Bird Cage. He traveled thousands of miles to extract top performers from San Francisco's leading venues. With a successful first performance at Schieffelin Hall, the era of the Bird Cage was set to begin, and its legend was about to be written.

Chapter 6

Hutchinson's Bird Cage Success

The Bird Cage, under the management of Hutchinson, is gradually becoming one of the best variety theaters in the country, and it is a standing advertisement to the public spirit of Tombstone that such a resort could be properly maintained.
—Tombstone Epitaph, June 20, 1882

In the days and hours leading up to the grand opening, improvements to the Bird Cage were being urgently completed.[1] Billy Hutchinson boldly advertised the event, and after all the struggles of the past, he wasn't about to let slow hammers and paintbrushes hold up business. On December 24, 1881, two days after Lottie Hutchinson's benefit at Schieffelin Hall, the doors swung open for the first time.[2] Throngs of customers filled the bar and auditorium amid the smells of new construction on an eventful Christmas Eve.

Everything was prepared for an enormous wave of business, and opening night did not disappoint. That early success was unfortunately overshadowed by an untimely tragedy. On Christmas morning, just hours after the first performances ended the night before, Billy's stage manager, Harry Lorraine, whom he had just recruited from San Francisco, passed away. Still in

THEATRE !

Hutchison's Varieties !

WM. HUTCHINSON · · Proprietor.
HARRY LORAINE · Stage Manager.

Grand Opening !

This Evening, December 24.
Entire Change of Programme.

Fun ! Fun ! Fun !

Great Joy !

COME ONE !   COME ALL !

Admission—50 Cents,

Billy Hutchinson placed ads announcing the December 24, 1881, grand opening of the Bird Cage. He also received publicity through his mining partner, A. E. Fay, who was the former editor of the *Nugget*. *Nugget*, December 24, 1881.

his 30s, Lorraine had more than a decade of experience managing western variety theaters as a proven musician, comedian, and actor.[3] Those skills and character traits earned him a considerable reputation in San Francisco, where he was regarded not just as a skilled entertainer but also as "a kind friend and genial gentleman."[4]

Sadly, the cause of Harry's death remains unconfirmed. With his death certificate and other hard records undiscovered, we look to local reports. One newspaper called it "an unfortunate illness," which may have stemmed from the miserable stagecoach ride through the winter storm on December 20. That possibility is supported by the fact that he suffered poor health while attempting to perform at Lottie Hutchinson's benefit at Schieffelin Hall three days prior. Another newspaper speculated his asthma was to blame.[5] Whatever the cause, Harry was gone less than five days after arriving in Tombstone. Making the trip with him from San Francisco was his actress wife, Clara, and their young daughter. Clara forged on and continued to perform at the Bird Cage through the spring while maintaining her motherly duties. Fortunately she received "substantial aid" from Tombstone's theater-goers and citizens alike, possibly resulting from the favor her husband had won.[6] Those same people may have made up the "large cortege of friends and acquaintances" who attended Harry's funeral the next day.[7] He is one of only three Bird Cage performers buried in Tombstone.[8]

The tragedy of Harry's death did little to slow the fortunes of the Bird Cage. While the bar remained open all day, shows were put on nightly starting between 8:00 and 8:30.[9] Merely a week after opening, the *Nugget* proclaimed the Bird Cage "has now become a fixed institution and is nightly thronged by large and appreciative audiences."[10] For months local newspapers consistently reported the building was packed for performances. How packed was it exactly? Forty-five days after opening, the Hutchinsons hosted a benefit for a local man in poor health. After insufficient local care, he was directed to seek specialized treatment in Hot Springs, Arkansas—a trip he was unable to afford. Extending their generosity once again, Billy and Lottie donated all of the money collected at the door on the night of February 8 to fund his travel. The take amounted to an impressive $170.[11] Advertisements for the Bird Cage in February note general admission was set at $0.50 and $2.50 for boxes.[12] Given a reasonable number of box admissions, roughly 160–200 individuals came into the Bird Cage that night. It's a shocking figure given the original Bird Cage dimensions were smaller than what is seen today. The back third of the building was not added on until eight months after the benefit.[13] The event's attendance provides great evidence of how busy and profitable the Bird Cage was early on, especially when considering the substantial revenue from drink sales that wasn't figured in their door receipts.

Tombstone's intense demand for live entertainment, proven by the town's early performers and venues, was fully unleashed inside the Bird Cage. The opening surge of business was so great that Billy installed extra seating "in order to satisfy . . . [his] numerous customers." He also added twelve boxes surrounding the auditorium.[14] Today the Bird Cage boxes have become easy targets for loose stories and salacious assumptions that they were designed to facilitate prostitution. Modern claims also state boxes went for $25 a night. Neither of these statements are true. In fact, Billy cut the price of admission in half seven months after opening from $0.50 to $0.25, and box admission never went for more than $2.50.[15] These prices were extremely common among period theaters, especially those in the West. Billy also made a habit of letting certain people in for free because, as one customer insisted, he knew "which side his bread is buttered on."[16] As for prostitution, Tombstone regulated it through a series of ordinances that determined where it could be conducted and solicited legally. As Billy battled the Townsite Company and Ed Field for outright ownership of the lot, Ordinances 10 and 14 were passed, which outlined the legal boundaries for prostitution. Both ordinances placed the lot Hutchinson fought so hard for outside of that legal boundary. It was part of neither his business model nor that of any of the proprietors that came after him. Likewise, prostitution was regulated by the city's licensing code. No license had ever been issued to the Bird Cage or anyone employed at the Bird Cage.[17]

From a business standpoint, particularly in the case of the cramped interior of the Bird Cage, boxes not only increased seating capacity but also presented an opportunity to charge significantly higher admission rates. Box prices in variety theaters were often two to three times that of general admission. At $2.50 for box admission, Hutchinson was able to charge customers five times general admission.[18] Several Bird Cage performers migrated to Tucson's Fashion Theater in 1883 where they changed an almost unheard of $5.00 for box admission, which was twenty times general admission.[19] Drink prices followed the same price hike when served in boxes. One former Bird Cage customer recalled drinks were four bits in the boxes ($0.50) and two bits ($0.25) everywhere else.[20] Two of Hutchinson's performers relocated to Butte, Montana, in 1885 and worked a venue that had private boxes. The local newspaper stated they were for "the accommodation of the more stylishly inclined people who may happen to be present."[21] That same theater also had a "private entrance to boxes from the rear of the theater for ladies and families."[22]

For attendees, boxes provided an improved and unobstructed view of the performances. At the same time it allowed occupants to attend without public judgment, particularly in cities where variety theaters where highly controversial. In October 1882 several Bird Cage performers appeared at Tucson's Park Theater, which had just added its own boxes. They were said to "increase the appearance of the auditorium [and] give seclusion to such visitors as would be free from public gaze."[23] One reluctant and judgmental attendee recalled the boxes at the Bird Cage:

> In front of these boxes . . . curtains hung, and if the occupants had even a little pride left they of course did not want to be seen, the curtains would be down. If the man had still a small spark of self-respect left, he might draw back the edge of the curtain nearest the stage, so that he could witness the performance, while at the same time running the risk of being seen himself. But if he did not care for his reputation, or had none to care for . . . the curtain was drawn entirely back.[24]

There is no doubt that boxes in some theaters became places of questionable behavior, particularly in those run by immoral owners who condoned and attracted equally immoral customers. However, balcony boxes were also aesthetic and functional features found in many of the world's most respectable venues, and their inclusion in variety theaters should not automatically be associated with sexual acts. As for Hutchinson, the *Nugget* conceded the Bird Cage boxes were simply meant to "add to the seating capacity of the theater."[25] By adding them Billy Hutchinson not only packed in more people, but he also charged those additional people higher prices for admissions and made more money on drinks they bought. People wanting a box paid five times as much for admission and twice as much for drinks. Adding two rows of boxes likely doubled nightly revenue while giving the interior an aesthetic boost. The Bird Cage boxes seen today are a testament to the fury of sustained business and the business savvy of Billy to include them. Based on newspaper reports of the hall being packed to capacity every night, it was clear his tiny venue needed them badly.

In addition to boxes, Hutchinson added afternoon matinee performances.[26] Two months after opening Billy began conducting highly successful Grand Masquerades every Wednesday night. These became signature

This advertisement promoted a Wednesday night masquerade ball at the
Bird Cage on July 26, 1882. In tune with his management standards, Billy
noted they were "conducted strictly first class." *Epitaph*, July 26, 1882.

events that were well-known throughout town during his years of ownership.[27] He advertised them as "elegant [and] refined" socials that were
"conducted strictly first-class." Accommodations were provided for men as
well as dressing rooms for ladies.[28] The *Nugget* applauded the masquerades.
"These weekly gatherings have become one of the main features of this

popular resort . . . and the proprietor's efforts are evidently appreciated by the public judging by the goodly number of people who nightly attend."[29] One attendee agreed, calling them "an advent in town that couldn't be missed [that was] taken advantage of by a large number. Amusements were indulged in til [the sun] rose . . . in the east."[30] The masquerades kept customers spending money deeper into the night, and the inclusion of masks provided anonymity for those concerned about judgment and gossip, similar to the effect of box curtains. Hutchinson advertised that masks were raised at midnight, with fifteen minutes' notice given for those wanting to leave before revealing themselves.[31] Former Bird Cage customer and future building owner Charles Cummings remembered the events. "The chairs were stacked back and everyone danced and drank until daylight, which didn't much stop the drinking even at that."[32]

Continued success throughout 1882 prompted Hutchinson to make more improvements on the building. In February he made $600 of upgrades, and in October he added on more than twenty feet to the rear of the building, bringing it to its present-day dimensions. With that addition, what was once a rear entrance to the boxes became the present-day stage. One visitor noted, "Twenty feet has been added to the seating capacity of the room and a large stage built."[33] It was a necessary change. In the weeks leading up to the addition, performances were so packed the *Epitaph* said, "It was impossible to find standing room in the house."[34]

Billy also attempted to elevate the status of the business by renaming it. In July 1882 he formally changed the name from Bird Cage Theater to Bird Cage Opera House.[35] What might seem like a small change is quite significant. Negative stigma was often associated with variety theaters. By contrast, opera houses were presumed to be of a higher class. In her analysis of western Victorian theaters, author Carolyn Grattan Eichin wrote, "The greatest levels of respectable entertainment were reserved for opera, as a cultured, lettered art form. Unsurprisingly, a theater dubbed an Opera House found attendees driven by the name alone as a purveyor of respectable culture."[36] Changing the name was a conscious move in step with everything else the Hutchinsons did to elevate the status of the Bird Cage and maintain it as a respectable venue.

To keep customers interested, Billy circulated talent frequently, as was customary in variety theaters. Some were engaged for a week, others stayed several months. Nightly programs were changed at least once a week to further encourage regulars. Keeping that routine up while maintaining high performance standards was exhausting. To maintain quantity and quality of entertainment, Billy made repeated trips to San Francisco to handpick performers, just as he had for the grand opening.[37] In August 1882 he made a recruiting trip to Denver. While there he stopped at the National Mining and Industrial Exposition, where Tombstone representatives displayed local minerals and promoted the area's wealth. He grabbed a drink at the bar and penned a letter back to Tombstone to report on what he saw. Having secured a number of noteworthy performers he wrote, "[I] will start home Tuesday morning, with some good people to make Tombstoners laugh."[38] Research efforts for this book have identified seventy-two performers hired by Billy. Throughout their careers many ran their own theaters, became stage managers of other venues, and managed performance troupes well into the twentieth century.[39]

As a complete businessman, Billy Hutchinson aggressively advertised and proudly promoted his theater and performers. Ad campaigns were consistently printed in multiple papers but were more prevalent in the *Nugget*. This may be explained by the fact that the former editor of the *Nugget*, Artemus Fay, was one of Billy's mining partners.[40] Even the front of the Bird Cage brilliantly advertised performances by making use of an eye-catching illuminated transparent sign.[41] He also orchestrated promotional parades that were can't-miss spectacles around the streets of Tombstone. One such parade took place on the afternoon of July 16, 1882, and was described by the *Epitaph* as it passed their office: "Bird Cage parade through the principal streets was the most comical turnout yet witnessed in Tombstone. 'Hutch' and a band occupied the leading carriage, next came Neal Price and Harry Morton, in charge of the [women] and the procession terminated with that prince and princess of Irish comedy, Mulligan and Annie Duncan, in a car drawn by a donkey. Of course they were dressed up to kill, and made no effort to hide the glory of their appeal. The Epitaph acknowledges a salute from the procession, with thanks."[42]

The scrapbook of one of Hutchinson's performers, career entertainer Harry K. Morton, included an account of another promotional parade one month later: "The parade of the Bird Cage company [this] afternoon was a brilliant affair. Field Marshal W. J. Hutchinson, K. C. B., mounted on a dashing charger, led the van, and was followed by three cabriolets, bearing the band and the man folks of the Cage. Next came the [ladies] in two double carriages, while three handsome equestriennes brought up the rear. The Epitaph acknowledges a serenade from the band and a salute from the boys as the procession passed the office."[43]

Through all of the demands, adventures, and difficulties of operating the Bird Cage, Billy and Lottie were unwavering in their charitable ways. Numerous performances and events were held to financially benefit various citizens, town causes, and performers who contributed to the theater's success. One of their leading causes was the local fire department, which they remained devoted to throughout their time in Tombstone.[44]

In an era when Tombstone's local newspapers disagreed on nearly every issue and many theaters in the West were being suppressed by their communities, there was unwavering praise and support for Hutchinson and the Bird Cage. The following excerpts from Tombstone's newspapers attest to their endorsement of the Bird Cage:

> The attractions now offered at the Bird Cage would reflect credit upon the management of even a metropolitan theater. That the efforts of the proprietor are appreciated is evinced by the fact that the theater is nightly crowded by our amusement loving people. New people are constantly being engaged, and all the latest Eastern successes will be presented in quick succession. In addition to the regular olio and sketches the program is strengthened by living pictures, which are models of live grace and beauty.
>
> —*Nugget*, January 31, 1882

> Attractions now being offered at the Bird Cage Theatre are second to no variety show on the coast, and as new specialties are constantly being added, its popularity is sure to increase with each succeeding week.
>
> —*Nugget*, February 4, 1882

The Bird Cage, under the management of Hutchinson, is gradually
becoming one of the best variety theaters in the country, and it is a
standing advertisement to the public spirit of Tombstone that such
a resort could be properly maintained.

—*Tombstone Epitaph*, June 20, 1882

On par with this praise, one San Francisco theatergoer visited the
Bird Cage in October 1882 and offered his reactions: "The Bird Cage still
ranks as the only regular place of amusement in the city, and a person can
spend several hours in an enjoyable manner. Billy adds new talent almost
daily, and the house to-day stands peer over any south of San Francisco for
elegant, beautiful and accomplished artists. [It] is run nearly on the same
style as Buckley's [Adelphi Theatre], in San Francisco, and is a paying
institution."[45] Buckley's Adelphi was called "the leading theater of San
Francisco" by the *Stockton Mail* newspaper just months before the Bird
Cage opened.[46] Comparisons to the Adelphi take on a greater meaning with
the account of one performer who worked there in 1882: "I played at the
Adelphi Theatre . . . where Ed Buckley was running a high-class variety
show. The program, like that of the commoner concert halls, lasted several
hours. It opened with the inevitable minstrel first par, then came the olio and
finally the full-length play. Drinks were of course served on the floor. For its
play the Adelphi had no cheap, risqué affair written on the spot by one of the
actors or house staff, but a melodrama selected from what has then classed
as the legitimate."[47]

The local newspapers insisted Billy Hutchinson ran the Bird Cage
in a "strictly first class" manner and maintained performances with a
"high order of merit."[48] In later years former Bird Cage patrons recalled it
the same way. In 1924 Johnny Behan's former deputy Billy Breakenridge
wrote, "The artists were attracted first by the adventure, but principally
because of the large salaries. Hutchinson ran the place in first class style
and no disorderly conduct was allowed."[49] A few years later he remembered more. "It was the only resort of the kind in town, and was well
patronized. The place was filled every night . . . the bar did a rushing
business. No one had been killed there, and the Hutchinsons ran it in an
orderly manner."[50]

In 1926 several old-timers were consulted by the *Tucson Citizen* for a feature article on the Bird Cage. They, too, remembered Hutchinson's high standards. "Not withstanding the rough element with which he had to deal, Hutchinson ran the place in first-class style and no fighting or disorderly conduct was permitted on the premises."[51] These memories are supported by the Tombstone City Police court records, which chronicle several arrests of those fighting or engaging in disorderly conduct at the Bird Cage, one of which was specifically noted as being made "on Mr. Hutchinson's complaint."[52]

All of Billy and Lottie's efforts added up to an unbroken run of performances in the background of Tombstone's most notable events. On the evening of March 18, 1882, Morgan Earp was mortally wounded and laid out on a couch in the back room of Campbell and Hatch's billiard saloon. As Wyatt leaned over him and whispered an exchange in his last moments of life, audiences a block and a half away at the Bird Cage were enjoying the singing of Civil War veteran and San Francisco favorite Ned Nestell and his 16-year-old wife, Annie Ashley. Clara Lorraine, the widow of Billy's deceased stage manager, Harry Lorraine, also continued her performances.[53] In the following weeks, Wyatt Earp, Warren Earp, Doc Holliday, and five hand-picked confidants roved the countryside hunting the murderers of Morgan Earp on what became known as the vendetta ride. On March 20 they killed Frank Stilwell at the Tucson train station. As he laid on the tracks riddled with bullets, the Bird Cage was hosting a crowded benefit for two of Billy Hutchinson's celebrated comedians.[54] That same night Billy's star, world-renowned strongwoman Millie De Granville, was given a bad prescription medication that put her on the brink of death and bedridden for a month.[55] While Wyatt killed "Curly Bill" Brocius in the foothills of the Whetstone Mountains days later, the Bird Cage prepared for another packed masquerade ball.[56] In mid-July 1882 freighters found the lifeless, sun-blackened body of Johnny Ringo under a tree at the foot of the Chiricahua Mountains with part of his skull blown off.[57] As news reached Tombstone and the gory details made the rounds, Bird Cage customers raved over performances arranged by Billy's new stage manager—the young and talented songwriter Neal Price. They laughed at the clever original comedic skits and clog dancing of Harry Morton and loved the singing of his wife, whom they dubbed "the Tombstone nightingale." The highly popular nineteenth-century play *Muldoon's Picnic* filled the smoky hall with laughter, and patrons raved over the new actors Billy Hutchinson had just brought in from Leadville, Colorado.[58] Whatever was going on in Tombstone, the Bird Cage was always running in the background.

The success of Tombstone's earliest performers and performances halls were proven right. The Bird Cage was an immense success, and it received none of the backlash many variety theaters in countless other communities were subjected to. That says a lot about Billy and Lottie's standing in the community and the standards they kept. Having endured all of the troubles to get it going, they experienced an unbroken run of enormous Bird Cage successes and were clearly taking in mountains of money. Yet somehow in the midst of the rushing business, packed houses, and cash flow, Billy made an inexplicable financial move that put the future of the Bird Cage into an uncontrolled tailspin.

Chapter 7

Hutchinson's Downfall

Business in the opening months of the Bird Cage was incredible. Few days passed without glowing reports of performances and packed houses. Just weeks after its opening, the *Epitaph* proclaimed the Bird Cage was "in the full tide of popularity, and is nightly crowded by appreciative audiences."[1] Even after adding seating and building boxes to increase capacity, the theater was still taking in more people every week eager to see performances called "second to no variety show on the coast."[2] A benefit performance on February 8, 1882, in which upward of two hundred people visited the theater, yielded $170 in admissions in addition to drink sales. With business that brisk night after night, week after week, Billy's long struggle to secure the lot and attract talent was paying off.

Yet right in the middle of the opening fury of income, Billy Hutchinson mortgaged the Bird Cage and the lot for $2,500 on March 13, 1882. At that point the business had taken in tens of thousands of dollars since its opening, and Billy should have been well on his way to financial security. It was a level of revenue not achieved by many other local businesses. Yet he sought a personal loan from two unlikely men, 55-year-old John Sroufe and 45-year-old Hugh McCrum.[3] They were highly successful liquor distributors with a towering building in the belly of San Francisco's business district. As self-made American success stories, they took the rags of their beginnings and found riches in the West despite very different backgrounds.

John Sroufe was home-grown stock born in the farmlands of Buford, Ohio, in 1827. After marrying his wife, Zelda, they made the overland crossing to California with many other gold rushers around 1850. They settled, as much as could be expected, in the crude gold fields of El Dorado in the Sierra Nevada Mountains before seeking more civilized climes in Petaluma, California.[4] Petaluma was an important commerce center in the California Gold Rush, and Sroufe took advantage by starting one of the first general merchandise stores there in 1857.[5] He rode the store's success for twelve years before relocating to booming Virginia City, Nevada, followed by a move to more stable San Francisco. Sroufe came to California with little to his name; however, by 1870 he had not only four children but also a $16,000 home and a thriving business estate worth $30,000.[6] His success was attributed to his motivation, business savvy, and family support system. But he was also said to be "well liked because of his straightforward business methods and his generosity."[7] In 1875 he took all of these glowing assets and transitioned to the liquor distribution business. The man selected to be his partner was the irascible and resoundingly ambitious Hugh McCrum.[8]

They had a lot in common. With similar business prowess, Hugh McCrum also rose out of a modest background and achieved financial prominence in California. Born in 1836 or 1837 in Carnmoney, Northern Ireland, his family fled the devastation and unrest in the wake of the Irish Potato Famine.[9] They arrived in the United States aboard the *Aberdeen* on March 3, 1850.[10] Following nearly identical footsteps as John Sroufe, he was eventually lured to the California gold fields of the Sierra Nevadas before engaging in business in Virginia City, Nevada, and at last San Francisco.[11] Not without a cantankerous side, he was also known as a "large hearted, generous and genial man."[12]

When they began their partnership, John Sroufe had twenty solid years of business success behind him. Although McCrum was ten years younger and had less experience, he had been in the liquor distribution business going back to his time in Virginia City. More importantly he served as the traveling agent for the established San Francisco firm of J. M. Goewey and Company—the same firm Sroufe and McCrum would eventually take over.[13] As their representative, McCrum traveled thousands of miles to countless boomtowns acquiring customers, selling untold amounts of liquor, and forming a strong network of relationships in the process. His travels brought him to Arizona for the first time in the spring of 1872, years before Tombstone's existence. The *Los Angeles Star* conveyed his harrowing experience: "He reports that the Apaches . . . rally and carry on their murderous attacks against peaceful citizens. Mr. McCrum [says] that traveling in the Territory, except with a strong and well armed escort, is exceedingly hazardous, and he was compelled to do most of his traveling under the cover of night to prevent being waylaid by the Apaches. The enemy [has] every advantage over the traveler, as they are thoroughly familiar with every portion of the country, and are liable to spring upon you at any time from their concealments behind the rocks and in the mountain gorges."[14]

McCrum was unimpressed with the military presence that was supposed to protect travelers, noting "they are looking more to their own comforts and pecuniary interests than to the protection of the lives and property of the people of Arizona."[15] His rigorous western travels presented other threats, such as highway men who preyed on travel routes. There were also dangers presented by long, empty stretches where horses and transportation equipment could fail. Many stage roads were crudely built, sometimes hugging mountainsides on narrow passes and claustrophobic canyons. When danger wasn't looming, coach passengers were assaulted by the elements—heat, cold, snow, rain, and dust. None of it stopped Hugh McCrum. While many travelers hated stage travel or were afraid of it, he loved it. His willingness to hit the dusty, dirty, and dangerous road made him a perfect business counterpart to a grounded family man like John Sroufe.

What's more, McCrum had an equal passion for the liquor he sold. On one trip to Arizona, he traveled from Superior to Globe on horseback through the arduous terrain of Devil Canyon. A gallon demijohn bottle of whiskey lashed to his saddle horn came loose and fell a hundred feet into the canyon, shattering to pieces. One travel companion equally reliant on alcohol exclaimed in horror, "We're 25 miles from Globe, and we'll all perish for something to drink." With dry sarcasm McCrum pointed out the river in the canyon below declaring, "There's lots of water to drink." Not in the mood for jokes, his companion snarked back, "This is no time for joking. What good in the world will water do us?"[16]

For Hugh McCrum there was more to traveling than just selling liquor. Boom-town environments also presented irresistible opportunities to scout for mines, properties, and other investments. The potential for making money on all of it was irresistible for a man who fled an impoverished and disease-threatened childhood in Northern Ireland. Traveling and speculating became his passionate addictions, lasting thirty-five years and ending only when he died in 1902.[17] It was a fixation that may have even cost him his first marriage, which ended when his wife filed for divorce on the grounds of "willful desertion."[18] He covered Washington, Oregon, Idaho, California, Nevada, and nearly every community in Arizona. His unrelenting travels and business dealings abroad made him well-known in boom-town circles. In Nevada it was said he was known "as well as sagebrush, and as popular as the [liquor] he sells."[19] The first fifteen years of his travels predated railroads in many areas and was done almost exclusively by stagecoach. One newspaper observed he "went through experiences in traveling for his firm that would have worn out an ordinary man."[20] Arguably no one traveled more miles by stagecoach to more boomtowns across the West in the nineteenth century than Hugh McCrum. What tales he must have taken to the grave.

Under the apt firm name of Sroufe and McCrum, their combined backgrounds and abilities made them a real business force. They began their partnership in the summer of 1875 representing dozens of well-known brands of fine wine and Kentucky whiskies such as Slater's Premium Bourbon.[21] While their liquor distribution partnership ended sixteen years later, their investment partnership endured even after Hugh McCrum's death in 1902, at which time his estate was taken over by his second wife.[22] Through years of travel McCrum expanded the partners' portfolio, handling real estate, mines, reduction mills, cattle farms, and other businesses, including general

John Sroufe and Hugh McCrum's success is evident in their substantial headquarters, seen here in 1880. Located near the intersection of Market and Pine, they had a prime location in San Francisco's bustling business district. Courtesy of Open SF History.

merchandise, hotels, saloons, and even barber shops. Their holdings covered every state and territory west of the Rocky Mountains, but no place captured McCrum's attention like Arizona. His dangerous first encounter among the Apache in 1872 hardly scared him off. Over a thirty-year period, McCrum covered thousands of miles in Arizona alone and became "well known all over the territory" according to the *Prescott Weekly Miner*.[23] Throughout those travels he invested Sroufe and McCrum capital in towns such as Tombstone,

Tucson, Prescott, Fairbank (near Tombstone), Dos Cabezas, Douglas, and many more. Their portfolio of businesses included the Fort Bowie trading post (which they owned while Geronimo was held there in 1886), Tucson's Fashion (or Pierson) Block, and the historic Palace Saloon in Prescott, which is still one of the great Old West saloons in the country.[24] Their investments were so substantial they were among the thirty highest taxpayers in Cochise and Pima Counties through the turn of the century—despite operating out of San Francisco.[25]

With special interest in southeastern Arizona, Hugh McCrum made at least thirteen documented trips to Tombstone between 1879 and 1891.[26] Even as early as the spring of 1880 the *Nugget* called him "the well-known liquor man from San Francisco."[27] No doubt he had acquired many liquor customers as Tombstone grew and changed. It's very possible Billy Hutchinson was one of them. On March 11, 1882, McCrum arrived in Tombstone by stagecoach, dusted off his clothes, and checked into Brown's hotel at the corner of Fourth and Allen.[28] His purpose in town was likely to service and acquire accounts as well as scout for investment opportunities. Two days after McCrum arrived, Hutchinson secured a $2,500 loan from him in the name of the Sroufe and McCrum firm. As security Billy borrowed against his most valuable asset—the Bird Cage and the lot that brought so much difficulty to secure.[29]

The loan terms were simple. Billy was to repay $2,500 in six months with 1 percent interest. However, six months went by and Billy made only one token payment of $162.50, despite considerable nightly revenue continuously taken in at the Bird Cage.[30] With bigger business matters at hand, Sroufe and McCrum took no immediate action when the loan term expired. Months continued to pass without payments, and cracks in Hutchinson's finances began to emerge. Three weeks before the mortgage deadline, Billy signed a letter to the mayor and council asking for relief from city taxes, which were outlined as "hard and unjust."[31] The Hutchinsons' 1882 county tax bill of $156.15, which included the Bird Cage and their residence on Fremont, was not only delinquent, but records show it was never paid even though they remained in Tombstone until 1884.[32] At this same time, more than a dozen performers left the Bird Cage for the mini theatre boom that was underway in Tucson. There's no direct financial documentation, but their mass exodus

Billy Hutchinson initiated this original mortgage agreement in 1882 with Hugh McCrum, who had arrived in Tombstone two days earlier to service client accounts. The $2,500 loan was borrowed against the Bird Cage and lot and was to be paid back in six months. Billy and Lottie's individual signatures appear on the bottom of the agreement. This single document changed the course of Bird Cage history. Arizona State Library and Archives.

Local diarist, miner, and businessman George Parsons followed his financially irresponsible partner to the Bird Cage, where he witnessed him spending money on "champagne and women" until two in the morning. Copy from author's collection.

may simply be explained by an inability to pay salaries. Even the *Epitaph* noticed the "departure of several leading performers."[33]

Strangely, business at the Bird Cage appeared to hold strong, which made the entire need for the loan and inability to pay it back hard to understand. Local diarist George Parsons complained that his business partner, Joseph Redfern, was dodging creditors while spending money freely at the Bird Cage.[34] Overwhelmed with frustration, he followed Redfern to the Bird Cage only to witness him blowing money on "champagne and women" until 2:00 a.m.[35] At the same time, the *Epitaph* reported the theater was "crowded nightly," suggesting many others were doing the same. Yet Billy made no payments on the loan and his county tax

Office of the Sheriff
OF THE
COUNTY OF COCHISE.

I hereby certify that I received the within summons on the Sixteenth *day of* April *1883, and personally served the same on the* Sixteenth *day of* April *, 1883, on* W. J. Hutchinson *&* Mrs Lottie Hutchinson, they *being* all of *the defendants named in said summons, by delivering to* each of *said defendants personally in the* City of Tombstone *County of* Cochise *a copy of said summons, and a true and correct copy of the complaint in the action named in said summous, attached to said copy of summons* and a copy of mortgage attached to said copy of complaint and Summons

Dated this 16th *day of* April *1883.*

J. L. Ward *Sheriff.*

By A. O. Wallace *Deputy Sheriff.*

After being seven months overdue on repaying Sroufe and McCrum, Billy Hutchinson was sent this summons on April 16, 1883, to resolve the matter in court. Arizona State Library and Archives.

bill remained delinquent.[36] Though it remains a mystery where Billy's money was going, it certainly wasn't going toward bills.

It got worse from there. Thirteen months after procuring the loan from Sroufe and McCrum (which was then seven months past due), Billy had made only two payments totaling $262.50—well short of the $2,500 plus interest he owed.[37] With their generous patience gone, Sroufe and McCrum finally took legal action. On April 16, 1883, Cochise County Sheriff J. L. Ward served Billy Hutchinson with a summons and a foreclosure notice on the Bird Cage to recover the funds.[38]

It seems obvious Billy simply didn't have the money. With the May 14, 1883, court date approaching, he got desperate and mortgaged all of the contents of the Bird Cage—the bar, bar fixtures, $100 of glasses, $25 of silverware, six decanters, five chandeliers, five dozen chairs, twelve tables, stage scenery, "furniture of every description, kind and character," and, with apparently no money left to put inside of it, the iron safe.[39] With the theater still open every night, it was a desperate and bold move to risk items necessary for its operation, and it was a confusing move given that money was still coming in. Nevertheless, the mortgage put $500 in his hands, but it wasn't enough. On May 14 Billy was scheduled to appear in district court to answer for the unpaid loan from Sroufe and McCrum, but he never showed.[40] Ironically, on the same day, he was arrested for carrying concealed weapons in Tombstone and fined $10—a fine he couldn't pay. He was forced to make an arrangement with the court to defer payment of the small fine for five weeks.[41] Worse yet, Billy failed to repay the $500 he got by mortgaging all of the Bird Cage contents and lost every item outlined in the agreement.[42] Money was clearly an issue.

With unpaid bills and legal troubles mounting, Billy had no other options but to continue operating the Bird Cage as best he could while the clock ticked. Even in those grim times he still kept it together—a fact recognized and praised by the local newspaper. "The Bird Cage performances are far superior to what they were two months ago. Billy's motto is excelsior, and he leaves no stone unturned to get there."[43] As late as July 1883 Billy continued to recruit and import performers to restock his lineup, and he scheduled promotional parades.[44] But Tombstone itself was in trouble. One resident reported early signs of economic instability in late 1882. She wrote, "The town is certainly dull, and has been since the [May 25, 1882] fire. Property sells, if it sells at all, at a ridiculously low figure. . . . Quite a number of people are leaving."[45] Tombstone continued downward thorough 1883, as Billy also lost his financial footing. The effects were ominously laid out by the *Arizona Daily Star*: "[Tombstone] is now undergoing one of those trying vicissitudes through which all mining camps, at some stage in their history, must pass. Complete stagnation prevails in all branches of business, and if the present situation continues for six months or longer—and many predict that it will—it will inevitably end in general bankruptcy."[46]

Tombstone wasn't done by a long shot, but Billy Hutchinson's financial state on the brink of disaster made him vulnerable to the slowing economy. He battled other factors too. During one of his final performance attempts, a massive storm hit Tombstone that "unroofed buildings, carried away signs, tore down outbuildings and threatened at one time general destruction [that] was a spectacle of grandeur as well as fear." It was hardly the kind of night that encouraged theatergoers. His last promotional parade was also canceled as a series of storms shook the town.[47] In late May, with time running out, the Hutchinsons attempted a ladies' night, as was common practice among variety theaters. That too failed.[48] The clock had run short on Billy Hutchinson's time with the Bird Cage. Out of options and money, he was forced to sell the building and lot to Sroufe and McCrum for $4,350.[49] To this day it is the highest amount paid for the building.[50] Unbelievably for Sroufe and McCrum, what was supposed to be a simple six-month loan resulted in what became a twenty-year era of owning the Bird Cage that extended into the twentieth century and outlasted McCrum's own lifetime.

On August 16, 1883, Billy publicly announced he was closing the Bird Cage, blaming it on what he called "dull times."[51] In reality his financial irresponsibility was the problem. He took in tens of thousands of dollars at the Bird Cage in the seventeen months after securing the loan from Sroufe and McCrum, yet he only repaid $262.50. As a final financial blow, Billy was arrested for public drunkenness on the same day he made the announcement to close. Charges resulted in a guilty verdict and an option to pay a fine of $5 or spend five days in jail. Unable or unwilling to pay the fine, Billy took the five days in jail, indicating how broke he may have been.[52] Despite rushing business and massive crowds early on, he never appeared to gain financial ground. It's unknown if his entire Bird Cage saga yielded a single dollar of profit.

There is little direct evidence to suggest where all the money went. One possibility exists in the mines he retained until leaving in 1884, but there is no indication they were significantly developed. As a man deeply integrated into the gambling circles of Tombstone, it's possible he continuously patronized gambling banks and lost money there. As far as hard evidence goes, the most likely cause of his money troubles comes from his old nemesis, Ed Field of the Gilded Age mine. Even after Billy gave up the fight and paid him for the lot outright, Ed sought damages for legal fees and rents that went unpaid while occupants resisted and battled him in court. It was a secondary court victory that awarded him several judgments totaling more than $12,000. That bill fell in the lap of Billy Hutchinson and others who were part of the organized resistance.[53] Ed Field directly factored into the beginning of the Bird Cage, and he very likely played a role in its demise under Billy Hutchinson.

As Tombstone's economy waned in 1883 and faltered further in 1884, many residents moved on, and a number of businesses closed. On the back end of so many struggles and so much effort to produce a quality venue, Billy Hutchinson's Bird Cage went dark along with them . . . but only for a while.

Chapter 8

The Bird Cage Era History Forgot, 1884–1885

One hundred and forty laughs in one hundred and forty minutes, at
the Bird Cage tonight.
—Daily Tombstone, July 3, 1885

Because of poor and confusing financial decisions, Billy Hutchinson was unable to endure Tombstone's downturn in 1883. As the town's economy continued to wane in 1884, financial strains forced a cut in miners' pay, from four dollars a day to three dollars, giving rise to heated labor disputes.[1] A month later Tombstone's largest bank closed its doors, disrupting local business and shaking local confidence.[2] Tombstone also suffered an alarming number of fires throughout the city. They were so frequent, some speculated there was an arsonist running loose. At the same time, storms washed out roads, paralyzing transportation.[3] All of these factors painted a grim picture. For the sake of simplicity, some history books suggest Tombstone's story ended when the initial boom was over and the Earps left. But it was far from dead. In reality mining and the businesses that survived off mining continued to flourish. A pattern of momentary strikes and setbacks maintained Tombstone's intermittent pulse throughout the 1880s. After Billy officially closed the Bird Cage in August of 1883, it sat silent for a period. He and Lottie left Tombstone for good in the early months of 1884. But eventually others came along who saw it as an opportunity and revived it in the same enthusiastic spirit as its vivacious founders.

The first was likable 31-year-old Billy Sprague. He was born in Cornwall, England, and grew up with four siblings near the tin and copper mines that employed his father. Such surroundings made him familiar and perhaps comfortable with mining town life, thus he spent his early adulthood in and around the fast and furious mining communities of Virginia City and Eureka, Nevada, after immigrating to America. Like his father he worked as a miner but eventually sought a livelihood as a saloon proprietor—a relative rise in life that was less strenuous if not more profitable.[4] Those who roamed Old West boomtowns followed rumors or gut instinct to what they believed to be the most prosperous locations. Such factors may have driven Sprague to leave Nevada and come to southeastern Arizona. He spent much of his time alternating business ventures between Tombstone and Bisbee, where he quickly acquired many friends and was recognized as a diligent worker.[5] One Tombstone newspaper stated, "There are few men in this city that have such a host of friends as old boy Billy."[6]

San Francisco liquor distributors John Sroufe and Hugh McCrum still owned the Bird Cage, but it's possible Sprague coordinated a lease arrangement with them while being a customer of theirs in his previous saloon ventures.[7] By late April 1884, Billy was advertising Bird Cage performances, but he may have opened even earlier.[8] In mid-March boxing celebrity and heavyweight champion of the world John L. Sullivan visited Tombstone while touring with an exhibition sparring company he had assembled.[9] Tombstone had seen its share of celebrity visitors before. William Tecumseh Sherman, the highest-ranking officer of the United States military known for his Civil War and Indian Wars exploits, came to Tombstone with huge fanfare in 1882. Such overblown planning had gone on for weeks that it was joked "half the male citizens of Tombstone have been placed on the Committee of Arrangements."[10] Billy Hutchinson was one of them.[11] Upon arrival Sherman was greeted by the mayor, city council, and a full band in front of the Grand Hotel, which was completely cloaked in red, white, and blue. Townsfolk rolled out the red

BIRD CAGE
OPERA HOUSE.

WM. SPRAGUE.   Proprietor,
FRANK RICE.   Manager.

Variety, Minstrelsy and Burlesque.

Programme Changed Every Monday and Thursday.

Billy Sprague ran this ad in the *Epitaph* in April 1884.

carpet with specially prepared meals, meticulously appointed private apartments, and a grand reception at Schieffelin Hall.[12]

Yet even Sherman's status didn't overshadow that of heavyweight boxing champion John L. Sullivan, according to former local resident James Wolf. Wolf was living near Charleston, a notorious town nine miles from Tombstone that once harbored many Cowboy clansmen. During Sprague's management of the Bird Cage, Wolf recalled seeing Sullivan inside the building, where he received attention from several of the female employees, and hinted that he may have even performed there.

> Many famous European princes and other celebrities came to see the camp, but none of these visitors created any particular stir. It was decidedly different, however, when John L. Sullivan, Champion of the World, came to town. Every man in Charleston found he had important business in Tombstone that day. All the mines and mills had to practically shut down. . . .

When John L. unloaded from his conveyance, all the men formed in line to shake his hand and say a few words of welcome. For many a year afterward, you could have heard and seen our citizens on occasions exhibit their right hand and proudly announce you were gazing at a hand that had clasped that of the great champion. . . .

A self-appointed reception committee surrounded him all the time as it was feared some ignorant rascal might try to make the front pages and win world-wide notice by mortally plugging our guest with a forty-five. . . .

I do not remember whether the champion had been engaged as a stage actor for the Bird Cage or not. I never saw him on the stage. He simply stood inside the door, but his mere presence packed the house, and the proprietor [Billy Sprague] put on many extra bartenders. . . .

The Champ stayed some days in Tombstone. He went underground and saw how the boys mined the ore. . . .

He was the most wonderfully built man I ever saw. Small feet for such a big man, but beautifully muscled arms and shoulders with hands like hams that could knock a horse down. Of course the hostesses of the Bird Cage did their damn best, or worst, to attract his attention. Different ones of them tried to display her speed or naughtiness by high kicking at the chandeliers or wall bracket lamps, but the big boy would merely turn to the bar and call for a drink. Either he was not a ladies man or he disapproved of their profession. He had undoubtedly been worked on by experts of that kind in the casinos of Paris, London and New York long before he came to Tombstone. When he left, the whole town urged him to come again, an invitation that many more highly educated and polished visitors, before and since never received. Thus ended the visit of our Greatest Guest.[13]

The *Tucson Citizen* announced that Sullivan left for Tombstone on March 22, 1884, which gives credibility to Wolf's claim. While his account implies the Bird Cage was open earlier than that, Sullivan's appearance is the first undisputed evidence of its reopening in 1884.[14] Regardless of the exact date, ambitious and well-liked Billy Sprague had reopened the Bird Cage under its well-known original name.[15] Unlike Billy Hutchinson, there's nothing in Sprague's past that suggests any involvement in theaters or the entertainment industry. To supplement his apparent inexperience, he hired the very capable career entertainer Frank Rice as stage manager.[16] Frank's connections gained him access to a range of capable entertainers such as Ed Moncrief,

Dashing and strong, 26-year-old heavyweight champion boxer John L. Sullivan left a lasting impression on Tombstone when he visited the Bird Cage in March 1884. Author's collection.

a man who went on to act in several Charlie Chaplin films decades later.[17] Before his death Moncrief also claimed to have been a personal friend of Wyatt Earp, Doc Holliday, and Bat Masterson.[18] After six decades in entertainment and many noteworthy accomplishments, Moncrief's death notices proudly highlighted he was once a Bird Cage performer.[19] Rotating in such performers as Ed allowed for changes in the program every Monday and Thursday. For a time the Bird Cage appeared to thrive despite Tombstone's slumping economy.[20]

In the latter half of 1884, Sprague may have also introduced his own creative feature. In November the *National Police Gazette* ran a short story about a manager of a "prosperous theater" in Tombstone. "He has built a platform on top of the orchestra circle, and on this twenty amazons go in

WALKING INTO THEIR AFFECTIONS.
HOW A MANAGER AT TOMBSTONE, ARIZONA, UTILIZED HIS PRETTY WAITER GIRLS AS MARCHING AMAZONS.

This engraving accompanied the *National Police Gazette* story in November 1884 about Sprague's creative feature at the Bird Cage. It's likely an artist's concept. *Police Gazette* archives.

procession from the stage. This act of intermingling with the audience he calls, on the program, the Amazon March."[21]

By the summer of 1885, Billy Sprague took on two business partners. While the reasons are unclear, his unstable health likely had something to do with it. Billy was battling tuberculosis, and it wasn't going well. One newspaper reported, "He has had more than his share of ill health during the last two years," suggesting his management of the Bird Cage was being disrupted.[22] Worse yet, the travel and treatment he required left him nearly broke. He traveled thousands of miles for treatment and often had to rely on friends to help finance both the travel and the medical expenses.[23] Yet he remained optimistic about the Bird Cage, which may have been his main hope for income.[24] With this in mind, financial reasons and his need to travel may have forced the need to take on partners. He chose two young and well-liked local saloon men, Oliver Trevillian and Frank Broad.

His choice of partners seems obvious when considering their similarities. Aside from being similar in age, Sprague, Broad, and Trevillian were all born in Cornwall, England, within fifty miles of one another and were brought up in mining families. The unity they felt from shared heritage was only strengthened by their experiences thereafter. All three immigrated to the United States while they were young and experienced life in famous mining boomtowns of the West prior to arriving in Tombstone and were extremely well-liked once they got there. All three also transitioned from being mining laborers to businessmen who owned saloons. In the year leading up to the Bird Cage partnership, Frank and Oliver were partners in a saloon near Fourth and Allen. Evidence suggests they operated it in conjunction with their joint Bird Cage venture.[25]

Oliver Trevillian was born in the mining community of Camborne, Cornwall, England.[26] His father left the copper mining fields of Cornwall for better mining work in the United States when Oliver was a teenager. Older brother James followed their father to the United States shortly thereafter in 1868, and Oliver may have joined him at that time. A year later his father was killed in a tragic nitroglycerin explosion, and his mother back in Cornwall died shortly thereafter, reportedly due to uncontrollable grief.[27] After their father's death, Oliver and James went westward to Colorado and eventually Virginia City, Nevada, where they remained for the better part of six years. They had both been active miners since childhood, and it continued to dictate their lives the same way it did their father's death.

Older brother James gained quite a reputation as a bruising pugilist who took on several high-profile opponents. Word of his victories spread, and he became "well known in the western part of [Nevada]" for his "great courage and endurance."[28] In one open-air match he sent his opponent spinning to the ground flat on his back with blood gushing from his mouth and nose in one punch. Even after a pause between rounds, his rival returned to the ring "staggering and stupid." With a smile on his face James continued to pummel him effortlessly. At last he landed a blow that dropped his opponent "like an ox." James walked away without a scratch while his bloody adversary had to be carried to the train depot and supported by two men en route to his boardinghouse.[29] A year later James was in a saloon in Eureka, Nevada, and began to shake uncontrollably. Within moments he got up, staggered to the rear of the saloon, and fell dead. Oliver was telegraphed of the news, and just like that he was on his own. He drifted into Tombstone several years later, where he got out of mining and became a saloon owner.[30]

Eventually Oliver was joined in Tombstone by younger brother Frederick. Together they formed a musical combination that catered to dozens of social events. Newspapers routinely urged people to attend their gatherings. "Those boys are worthy of being patronized as their sweet music has enlivened many social entertainments in the city."[31] For years Oliver held weekly soirées and even conducted dancing classes in the same building that held the inquest after the OK Corral gunfight.[32] Nearly every socially active person in Tombstone knew Oliver. His growing popularity and reputation culminated in an election victory for Tombstone city treasurer.[33]

Frank Broad's story followed a similar path. He was the middle sibling of three that grew up around the mines of St. Austel, Cornwall, England. Like William Sprague and Oliver Trevillian, he traveled to the United States and spent time as a miner in Colorado and Nevada. In 1878 he followed opportunity to Pioche, Nevada, where several Tombstone notables laid footprints, including Nellie Cashman, Doc Holliday's nemesis Johnny Tyler, and Billy Hutchinson's first stage manager Harry Lorraine.[34] By 1881 Frank arrived in Tombstone, perhaps on the advice of his older brother John, who had been there since 1879. Both carried on as miners.[35] The community quickly took to Frank. In 1882 he married Kate Bannon, locally known as an "estimable young lady." At the same time his legion of friends urged him to run for chief of police while the Earps were still in town.[36] He gained additional popularity as a member of the Tombstone city band and as a staunch supporter of the fire department.[37]

With a growing army of friends and supporters, Frank won the nomination for Tombstone constable along with Fred Dodge, confidante of Wyatt Earp and former resident of the Bird Cage lot.[38] In 1890 Broad won the election and served the community to great effect.[39] He was athletic and eagerly participated in everything from foot races on Allen Street to wrestling matches at the Oriental and bare-knuckle prize fights.[40] Those physical gifts paired with his bravery and dedication made him a very effective constable. It may be argued that he was everything the golden image of Wyatt Earp was made out to be in many mid-twentieth-century television shows, books, and movies that glorified him.

In one instance he came to the rescue of a local prostitute. She was pulled into a gulch on the edge of town by a Mexican man who stoned her and viciously bit her ear off. Frank was made aware of the situation and immediately grabbed his pistol and rushed to the scene. In a dead sprint he chased the man, firing his pistol in the air and threatening to shoot him if he didn't stop. After the man bailed into an alley, Frank caught him and arrested him amid desperate resistance that required the help of three others.[41] The *Epitaph* celebrated his years as constable. "[Frank] has done many meritorious acts and has rounded up many a criminal. He is never [hesitant] when called upon to perform an official duty, whether it be to serve a paper or chase a lawbreaker. He is always at the front in cases of emergency and has made one of the best all round officers this precinct ever had."[42] His popularity and support was justified.

Broad and Trevillian's background, experience, entrepreneurial energies, and standing in the community made them both great partners for Billy Sprague. In 1885 they made preparations to reopen the Bird Cage in time for the Fourth of July weekend, but the holiday alone wasn't reason enough to open for business. After enduring all the economic hardships and disarray of 1884, there was a resurgence of hope in 1885.

For months optimism grew as massive pump engines were paraded through town and assembled in newly erected buildings near Tombstone's most productive mines. Piece by piece the fifty-thousand-pound apparatuses took shape on the hill visible from town. Once completed, the pumps, called "the largest of their kind ever built," would extract water that flooded the mines and stalled the town's progress. They literally represented hope for everyone who continued to stick out tough times in Tombstone. Once the water was removed, the valuable ores that gave Tombstone its heartbeat would be within reach. As the Bird Cage preparations were almost complete, locals predicted a boom bigger than Tombstone had experienced at its inception. Caught up in the excitement, the local newspaper reported, "A happy smile is seen on the faces of all our citizens, for they know in a few weeks the water will be drained . . . and work will be resumed . . . and hundreds of men will be working the mines, and our streets will be lined with visitors and capitalists seeking investment. Inside of two years our city will contain a population of 10,000 people, and the noble band of business men who have

FRANK BROAD,

AS CONSTABLE AT TOMBSTONE HE HAS PROVED HIM-
SELF A TERROR TO THE CRIMINAL CLASS.

Frank Broad's career in law enforcement was so prominent that he made the
pages of the nationally distributed *Police Gazette*, September 23, 1893.

stayed with it in its adversity will reap a harvest in its prosperity."[43] Not even
in Tombstone's prime did the population reach 10,000, but like many western
fortune seekers, dreams of prosperity often overshadowed fear and reason.
Word of Tombstone's potential even drew many newcomers to the area.
Like days of old, incoming stages came in loaded down with passengers.[44]
Caught up in this hope and hype, the three likable boys from Cornwall moved
forward with their plans to breathe life into the Bird Cage.

They opened on June 27, 1885, with a program slightly different from
that of Billy Hutchinson. In addition to variety acts and dancing, sparring

and wrestling were introduced.[45] They were well organized and regulated matches with official timekeepers, referees, and judges. One evening the contests lasted nine hours.[46] The stock of variety performers received a significant upgrade when veteran performer Mark Grayson arrived. Grayson was connected to many Bird Cage performers throughout his career and like many of them, he also married one. He had been involved with major venues throughout the West and had traveled as far as Alaska.[47] He was skilled in theater management and performance techniques and was also adept at writing music, skits, and scripts. One of his contemporaries called him "an hireling genius."[48] In the summer of 1885 he created a circuit of stops between major cities in Arizona, Texas, Colorado, and New Mexico.[49] Thanks to Grayson and his circuit, a number of noteworthy performers that Sprague, Broad, and Trevillian could not have procured themselves came through the Bird Cage. Like Billy Hutchinson, they also concluded each nightly performance with grand balls and hired "a number of beautiful girls . . . to wait upon the guests."[50] It was a true revival of the old days when Tombstone's population was at its peak. With renewed optimism for Tombstone's mines, a remodeled interior, a stock of worthy performers, and three likable and popular owners, the Bird Cage thrived.

Before they opened, the three Cornwall comrades invested in an extensive renovation of the Bird Cage. This suggests they had long-term plans. Unfortunately, it didn't last. Billy Sprague's health continued to decline, and by September their endeavor was over. Even as they reopened for the Fourth of July, Billy was in Hot Springs, Arkansas, receiving medical treatment.[51] Throughout the remainder of 1885 he continued to seek remedies in California and Nevada, which not only kept him away from managerial tasks but also drained his finances. He was still sick and penniless when he returned to Arizona, and his Bird Cage endeavor did little to reverse his fortunes.[52] After walking away, he spent most of his years thereafter running saloons in Bisbee.[53] He persisted through years of health struggles and was remembered as "the popular manager of the Bird Cage" who was "a giant."[54]

With Billy Sprague's exit from the Bird Cage, Frank Broad and Oliver Trevillian also left the business behind to open their own music saloons. Several of those run by Frank were very close to the Bird Cage. One of them

Sprague, Broad, and Trevillian placed this ad in the local newspaper ahead of
their Fourth of July festivities. *Tombstone*, July 3, 1885.

even shared a wall with the theater.[55] At night sounds of music, dancing, and the harmonious notes of a Mexican band continuously spilled out of his saloon on to the darkness of Allen Street.[56] Likewise, Oliver Trevillian ran a saloon across the street from the Bird Cage that featured music, singing, and dancing. While Sprague, Broad, and Trevillian experienced mild success in their saloon ventures, they did not achieve financial success at the Bird Cage, and never again made efforts to reopen it.

As 1885 came to a close, the Bird Cage once again sat silent, with one notable exception. On Christmas Day 1885, Lucien Marc Christol, who was called "one of the most expert wrestlers on the Pacific Coast," took on Tombstone local and Arizona's champion wrestler Peter Schumacher at Schieffelin Hall.[57] Heralded as the "champion light wrestler of the world" Christol's presence in Tombstone was a notable event reflected by the admission price, which was set at $1 a head. With $200 at stake and lively side betting, trustworthy sporting aficionado Dr. George Goodfellow was appointed as referee.[58] The match took a shocking turn when Christol's collarbone, which had been weakened by two prior breaks, snapped. He gritted through the injury but lost the match and vowed to give up wrestling. Recognizing his inability to wrestle, the sympathetic and appreciative Tombstone public threw him a benefit to recoup the money he lost in the match. The venue of choice was the Bird Cage. On New Year's Eve a crowd packed the auditorium. The event featured a boxing match and several variety performers, including George A. Bird, a man who would perform at a Bird Cage reproduction in Tucson fifty years later.[59] Even Peter Schumacher, the man who broke Christol's collarbone, performed. In a feat of strength he climbed onstage and lifted a 150-pound iron bar with "three average sized men" hanging off the ends and carried them about the stage with apparent ease.[60]

Christol was so impressed with the Bird Cage, community support, and prospects of the town that he expressed interest in staying in Tombstone and "opening the Bird Cage theater as a first-class sporting house."[61] After all, he did have years of experience wrestling and performing in variety theaters. To a broken wrestler intent on retiring, the idea must have sounded good. But it became an afterthought as Christol recovered and ultimately returned to wrestling. And so the Bird Cage remained dark.

After his wrestling match defeat in December 1885, Lucien Marc Christol received such a warm benefit at the Bird Cage that he considered reopening it as a sporting hall. *National Police Gazette*, May 26, 1883.

As Tombstone's fortunes continued with uncertainty in 1886 and beyond, many businesses and buildings were intermittently abandoned. The same easily could have been true for the Bird Cage. The industrial pumps that gave hope to Tombstone in the summer of 1885 had failed by year's end, causing a stoppage of work for several months. One local grimly predicted, "Camp will be idle till spring. Won't be much left of the town I'm afraid by that time."[62] There was little reason to think the Bird Cage would ever open again. Christol's benefit could have been its last glimmer of activity. With the mines faltering, a dedicated variety theater had little if any income potential. It would have taken a very daring, energetic, and experienced individual to gamble on a revival. Then, as if delivered by fate, a man came along who fit that exact description.

Chapter 9

A Rise from the Ashes
The Joe Bignon Era

There are few . . . who are more enterprising and successful than
Joe Bignon, and the fallacy of saying that "a rolling stone gathers no
moss" was never better shown than in his case.
—*Weekly Tombstone Prospector*, January 15, 1889

By 1886 Tombstone's economy was undeniably past its prime. In the five years that followed, considerable money continued to be pulled from the mines, but slumping silver prices and the increased cost of machinery and resources required to extract it narrowed profit margins. Some economic support came from the growth of area ranches and the offices of the county seat that remained in town. Still many businesses struggled, even those that provided essential goods and services. It took very little convincing for some to leave, and word of promising strikes throughout the West motivated many of the holdouts to leave. So it seemed certain that an expendable business like a variety theater could not survive. Attempting a revival would have been a high-risk gamble that may have bordered on financial suicide. Frank Broad and Oliver Trevillian wanted nothing more to do with it. Aside from industry savvy and ambition, it would have taken all the luck Tombstone silver could buy to make it work. In all probability the story of the Bird Cage should have ended in 1885. And it probably would have ended if not for one uniquely energetic and enterprising individual. His name was Joseph U. Bignon.

Joe had several instantly recognizable traits. He was a dashing dresser, spoke with a charming French accent, and was slight in stature. He stood five feet, three inches with a twenty-nine-inch waist and weighed 116 pounds—most of which was muscle.[1] A face-to-face meeting would have also revealed the positive aura of energy in his eyes and mannerisms. Disproportionate to his stature, he lived life large, unyielding to challenges, and was addicted to the pursuit of new endeavors. Risks that made most feel uneasy were the same that enticed and excited him. His life was defined by his willingness to take on challenges and the manner in which he handled them.

Bird Cage legend is forever intertwined with Joe's life. Unfortunately, very few factual details about him have found their way into print. Biographical information has been printed, reprinted, and pushed farther from the truth over the decades. Tracing it back to its origins, almost all of it comes from two sources: a spotlight article written in 1888 and the memoirs of a Tombstone saloon man named Billy King. King's recollections were published in 1942, and despite a fair attempt by author C. L. Sonnichsen, much of it doesn't measure up to primary period sources. In recent years Joe and his wife have been turned into cartoon characters that add flavor to the increasingly unrealistic Bird Cage narratives. Virtually none of it is true. Some of it is even slanderous.

Joe was born in Montreal, Quebec, Canada, to French migrant parents in 1851.[2] There's very little that documents his childhood. One account claims he left home at age 12 and joined several notable traveling performance groups.[3] Whatever experience he gained in those early years paid off. He spent his early 20s in and around the port towns along Lake Michigan. By that time he displayed experience as a singer, acrobatic dancer, and a specialty clog dancer—all skills he eventually showcased to Arizona crowds in coming years. Exercising his young entrepreneurial ambitions, he opened and operated several performance venues in Sheboygan, Wisconsin, and across the lake in Michigan. He got in on the ground floor of towns like Luddington. Incorporated in 1873, it quickly became the county seat of Mason County, Michigan, thanks to the thriving

This undated full-length portrait of Joe Bignon offers a great sense of his elevated style and presence. Copy from author's collection.

lumber industry.[4] There Joe became a naturalized citizen of the United States, suggesting long-term intentions to remain in the country.[5] He also spent time in Manistee, a lumber- and salt-mining community twenty-five miles north of Luddington. These early prospering towns taught Joe the excitement of boom-town life and the immense potential they had. Those lessons shaped his life, and he ran with them.

Joe continued his fearless travels with two separate circuses out of eastern Michigan managed by con man William H. Dwyer. They were financially shaky at best, and the 1878 season proved disastrous.[6] That year Joe set out with Doc Hager's Great Paris Circus (which had nothing to do with Paris) along the Northern Pacific Railroad en route to Winnipeg. As the season rolled on, it became evident Dwyer had charmed his way into the managerial role for his own devious gains. He was the kind of man who constantly philandered with other women even though he brought his wife on the trip. His criminal handling of the finances was even worse. Performers were forced to survive off food scraps and river water while going weeks without salaries. At one point locals at their performance stops were solicited for money to fund their transportation to the next town.[7] The circus was headed for imminent failure while deep in a desolate region of present-day North Dakota. Dwyer ultimately abandoned the performers and made off with their salaries. Several performers bailed along the way, but many ended up dire and desperate in Winnipeg.[8]

That experience didn't sour Joe's feelings about the upper plains. In fact, it may have lured him farther west. Just months later he became engrossed in the variety-theater scene in Bismarck, Dakota Territory, and took work under theater manager Charles A. Keene. Charles was a 32-year-old Civil War veteran who, like Joe, was highly adept in both business and performance entertainment.[9] Charles's management in Bismarck produced "crowded houses every night." He was praised for having "developed a versatility of talent surprising to the most ardent of admirers."[10] Sharing on-stage chemistry, Joe and Charles performed together so often they became "too well known to need special mention" by the local newspaper.[11] Though Joe moved on from Bismarck in 1879, he and Charles built a trusting friendship—one that resurfaced years later in Arizona and became crucial to the Bird Cage revival.

In 1879 Joe made it to the mecca of western show towns—San Francisco. But not even its vast opportunities and desirable venues kept him from wandering. After meeting young and like-minded showman Billy Brewster, they decided to head for adventure in the expanding frontier of the Southwest. It was a decision that changed Joe's life.[12] The next four years he crisscrossed Arizona and New Mexico. Virtually every town he saw boomed with activity from mining strikes or the advancement of railroads.

After nearly a full tour of Arizona by stagecoach, Joe crossed the New Mexico border. Late in 1879 he performed in Las Vegas, New Mexico, just after Doc Holliday ended his tumultuous run there.[13] Shortly after that he visited Santa Fe, where he performed at the Comique and got well acquainted with its colorful proprietor Joe Fowler. Bignon and Fowler hit it off and formed an eight-person performance company that traveled by private stagecoach throughout New Mexico. Their success peaked in Silver City when they scooped up an unprecedented $380 in one night.[14] An equal to Joe in business ambition, Fowler was not afraid of the ruffians that frequented variety theaters. One night in Santa Fe a local bad man on a bender entered the theater and agitated him. According to the local newspaper, something was said that set Fowler off and "in less than ten minutes [the bad man] was unrecognizable about the face as last year's corpse." The melee prompted the bummer to leave town.[15] Throughout these adventures Joe made connections with many entertainers he would eventually hire at the Bird Cage.[16]

Joe's Southwest travels naturally brought him to Tombstone several times. His initial visit came in August 1879, and it was obvious the fury of activity was underway. Urgent and widespread construction in the new townsite suggested how significant the mines were. "The sound of the axe and the hammer makes merry music," one newspaper reported. Adobe buildings and thirteen saloons went up amid a rapidly growing population. On the roads to and from Tombstone, Joe saw "freight teams loaded with merchandise, household goods, etc."[17] To an experienced traveler like Joe, all of these were obvious signs of the area's potential. That impression may have been why he returned to Tombstone a year later.[18]

On his second trip, Tombstone still had many canvas-and-frame buildings and miners were still living in tents, but it had grown beyond imagination. There were permanent buildings, two banks, telegraph service, US mail, and a multitude of civic improvements and conveniences not found in lesser camps. The Cosmopolitan Hotel even had a freshly laid cement sidewalk.[19] Every day there were reports of incoming stagecoaches loaded down with passengers. The *Epitaph* announced, "The streets are thronged with new faces," and Joe was among them.[20] A half block from the eventual location of the Bird Cage, he put on his nightly energetic clog and song act at the Sixth Street Opera House. During his performance run, Joe was certainly a standout, and not just for his onstage antics. French immigrants accounted for less than 2 percent of Tombstone's population, which made his heritage and accent a real novelty.[21] Audiences were so enamored with him they threw Joe a benefit before his departure.[22] As the coach took him north to his next adventure, he left with a real sense that Tombstone's growth and potential was well beyond what he'd seen elsewhere.

Still his wanderings continued. From Prescott in northern Arizona he toured the mountain mining communities outside San Francisco, then to New Mexico and back to Arizona again. In November 1882 he secured steady work in Tucson at Levin's Park, Arizona's longest running and most successful variety theater of the nineteenth century. It was also a virtual sister venue to the Bird Cage that shared dozens of performers and employees. Joe was hired on as stage manager and was instantly praised. One local newspaper said, "[Joe] is doing all he can to make the theater attractive and succeeds very well."[23] He also made nightly stage appearances "in his excellent clog, which in itself would attract numbers."[24] One performance shocked a local reporter. "It is a wonder that Joe does not break his neck at some of his reckless jumps."[25] Improvements to the orchestra, performances, and the theater itself were all hallmarks of Joe's tenure as stage manager—a job that one local said "he fills to perfection."[26] His run was so successful, he remained for more than four months and became the theater's proprietor. During his time in Tucson, there is evidence that Joe made yet another trip to Tombstone.[27] Through many associations with performers who worked for the Hutchinsons, he likely knew Billy and Lottie and possibly even performed for them at the Bird Cage in 1882.[28]

Ever restless, Joe left Arizona yet again. After managing San Francisco's Comique, he toured with Harry Leavitt through the mining camps of Nevada, as far north as Tuscarora, and California.[29] Leavitt was a newcomer to California who arrived with a young and dashing clog dancer from New York named Harry K. Morton. Morton would not only become a Bird Cage performer, but he also appeared onstage with Joe Bignon in a clog duo at Tucson's Park Theater in 1882.[30] This connection with Morton is likely how Joe became partners with Harry Leavitt. Such connections proved valuable throughout Joe's career.

Nearly six years removed from his disastrous circus experience of the Dakota plains, Joe connected with another circus in 1885 that toured through Nevada and Idaho.[31] Like his previous circuses, it was a modest organization that trucked along in a nine-wagon convoy.[32] And like his previous circuses, they were also plagued by corruption and serious money problems. Financial attachments, failure to pay local licenses, and dubious practices for collecting admission fees pointed to the growing problem.[33] More than two months and seven hundred miles into their journey, they trudged through southwest Idaho. Horses and performers alike became visibly exhausted.[34] Once again employees were not being paid, and many refused to perform out of frustration. Resulting show stoppages disrupted the advance schedule of the tour, and the whole system broke down.[35] It all came to a head in August as they sluggishly emerged from the Sawtooth Mountains in central Idaho.[36] The circus organizer and his brother were arrested on a list of charges that included defrauding investors. This left thousands of dollars of employee salaries unpaid.[37] For Joe it must have brought back bad memories of the Dakota plains in 1878.

Among the company was 35-year-old Taylor Frush. His wife, a talented equestrienne, and their two young children were among the performers living the nightmare. Taylor was personally owed $320 in unpaid wages.[38] He became the top candidate to "assume control of the circus and start to fulfill overdue contracts of the former management."[39] Taylor was a hard-working midwestern farmer and freighter who emerged from the 1870s with a wife and a family.[40] For him the circus wasn't a wild west adventure; it secured his family's welfare. For several years he toured circuses through Idaho's interior, where for a time he had resided.[41] His experience, background, and motivation made him the perfect candidate to lead the circus out of trouble.

After resetting in late September 1885, Frush led Joe and the rest of the circus south with cold autumn air on their heels.[42] Continued performances over the following three months saw them through Utah and eventually Arizona, where Frush had set up winter camp for his Idaho circuses in years past.[43] Sandbagged by former debts, they arrived with little financial cushion. While in Tucson the newspaper noted, "It is vaguely hinted that the only thing of any value left is the clown."[44] As 1885 came to a close, they left Tucson and headed for Tombstone, still in need of work.

It's unclear if Joe's influence had anything to do with the circus's trip to Tombstone. However it is clear that Joe had everything to do with keeping them there despite Frush's intentions to spend winter in Tucson.[45] By the time Joe returned to Tombstone in December 1885, he had covered thousands of miles of the West and had seen hundreds of communities of all kinds. None of them lured him in—not the logging communities of Michigan, the commercial center of Bismarck, the entertainment mecca of San Francisco, or the mining communities of California, Nevada, or New Mexico. It was Tombstone and southeastern Arizona that drew him in.

On New Year's Day 1886, the benefit for the broken lightweight champion wrestler Lucien Marc Christol was held at the Bird Cage, as described in the previous chapter. With intentions of retiring from competition, Christol entertained the idea of staying in Tombstone and "opening the Bird Cage theater as a first-class sporting house."[46] At the same time, Joe Bignon, fresh off the road with Frush's circus, had the same idea. As he had done so many times before, he quickly developed plans for the new enterprise and went to work. It happened so quickly that he likely had little time to realize the extent of Tombstone's lagging economy. By then Joe was 34 years old with more than twenty years of performance and variety-theater experience as an owner, stage manager, and performer. He had experienced difficulties and failures, but none of it kept him from moving forward. The Bird Cage became the object of his biggest efforts yet.

Bird Cage Resurrection

Within days Joe arranged an overhaul of the building, which was "thoroughly renovated, reseated and artistically decorated." The extent of the renovation suggested he had long-term plans to stay. He announced full-scale operations of the Bird Cage as a complete variety theater with new performers every week. Joe also made it known he intended "to run a strictly legitimate variety show of the highest standard."[47] Renovating the theater on short notice was one thing. Securing performers was another. That problem was solved when he hired Taylor Frush and his family to be his featured opening act. Remaining members of Frush's circus set up quarters near the towering county courthouse on Toughnut and remained in Tombstone for the winter.[48] The man who guided Joe and dozens of performers out of the Idaho mountains was now going to bring the Bird Cage to life again. In less than two weeks, Joe's vision and energies came together, and the Bird Cage was opened on January 16, 1886.[49] Putting his own stamp on the Bird Cage, he renamed it the Elite Theater. (For continuity, Joe's Elite will be referred to as the Bird Cage throughout the remainder of the text.)[50]

A local man recalled Joe's reopening. "This was the early part of 1886, the very year in which Tombstone began to slip, but the Bird Cage felt no depression for several years. Night after night the place was crowded. Usually there was a show, but the bar did a good business even when the stage was empty."[51] It sounded like the days of the Hutchinsons were back, and in many ways they were. Booming business got even busier in the summers, when many wives left for the California coast and other parts abroad to avoid high seasonal temperatures. According to the local newspaper, it was a "noticeable fact that since the wives of a number of citizens have gone to California . . . the attendance at the [Bird Cage] has increased wonderfully."[52]

Like the Hutchinsons, Joe made great efforts to constantly locate and import talent, often leveraging the connections he had made during his decades of travels. He made routine trips to San Francisco to recruit performers, just as Billy Hutchinson had.[53] The majority of his performers were acquired from El Paso, Texas, where a number of variety theaters were supported despite local controversy over their existence. Joe's efforts brought in performers like the Heeley Brothers, who were sons of a Civil War veteran who grew up in the shadows of downtown Chicago. Just two years after leaving Tombstone, the Heeleys toured the world and "gained a worldwide reputation as variety performers, having appeared in the largest cities of every land except Australia."[54] There were others like Dan Creelan, a Texas league baseball player with a troubled past. After finding his way in the entertainment industry, he went on to manage several venues in Seattle before tragically dying of consumption at 32.[55] Joe also brought in his friend and stage partner from Bismarck, Charles Keene. In the years that followed, Joe attempted to open up a number of venues in cities abroad. Charles then became the trusted manager to oversee the Bird Cage and several others when Joe was traveling. Charles's allegiance to Joe and his industry know-how earned him the distinction of being the longest tenured employee in Bird Cage history.[56] To date, research has identified more than 150 performers hired by Joe, proving how persistent his efforts were to bring entertainment to Tombstone. Several were even European and Australian natives.

Similar to the Hutchinsons, Joe was also very invested in the community. He was a staunch supporter of the fire department, was a founding member of Tombstone's Liquor Dealers Protection Association, and even ran for city council.[57] Just like Billy and Lottie Hutchinson, Joe hosted a number of benefit performances to support local causes. In 1888 he orchestrated one that netted $249.75 for the local cemetery fund.[58] Many of the benefits were so heavily patronized that he had to rent Schieffelin Hall for its increased capacity. Between 1886 and 1891 he made fourteen appearances at Schieffelin Hall and brought dozens of his Bird Cage performers to its stage. This speaks to the popularity of Joe and his performers, who were financial beneficiaries of a number of performances. Like Billy Hutchinson, Joe also organized promotional parades to entice theatergoers. One in 1889 was an illuminated nighttime parade right down Allen Street, where "different colored lights were burned and all the small boy spectator was in his glory."[59]

There were many similarities to Billy Hutchinson's management of the Bird Cage, but there were a number of notable differences. The entertainment remained a classic combination of variety theater acts—singers, comedians, actors, song writers, skit writers, acrobats, strength exhibitors, magicians, and dancers. However Joe branched out and brought in more creative features to entice customers and to fill performance gaps. He added wrestling and boxing matches. One of them was even refereed by Dr. George E. Goodfellow, the physician who attended to Virgil Earp's wounds after his assassination attempt in December 1881.[60] He was not a surprising choice. Goodfellow loved sporting endeavors—boxing, wrestling, horse racing, betting—it didn't

This original Bird Cage handbill from October 1887 is one of only a few known to survive. These small printings were produced and distributed around Tombstone to promote performances and attract customers. Note Joe's good friend Charles A. Keene listed as stage manager on top and as a performer near the bottom. Author's collection.

matter. One local recalled, "Nothing happened in the sporting society of Tombstone that [Goodfellow] wasn't in on, and nine times out of ten he had a hand in starting it. He was a good fighter himself . . . and would smack the miners around occasionally, sending a suit of clothes or something else of value to his victims if he thought they had it coming."[61] If true, Joe made a wise choice in selecting him as referee.

Reaching even further for fresh ideas, Joe featured walking matches. Surprisingly, such events were popular in the late nineteenth century. One of Joe's recruited performers even got her start in entertainment as a 9-year-old who exhibited in walking matches.[62] Tombstone had seen its share of walking matches before, but not at the Bird Cage. In May 1886 Joe arranged a match between two local men who each wagered fifty dollars. The competition took place on a specially built track inside the Bird Cage auditorium and was to commence at the same time as the evening's stage performance, at 8:00. Almost comically this was by design "so the audience [could have] the opportunity of witnessing two performances at the same time."[63] In another walking exhibition, a local man made a one hundred dollar wager with Joe that he could walk on hundred miles in twenty-four hours inside the Bird Cage. On the bare floor covered in sawdust, he hustled 44 laps to the mile around the perimeter of the auditorium. Amazingly he completed the necessary 4,400 laps in twenty-three hours and twenty minutes. Joe handed over one hundred dollars and the door receipts, per the terms of the bet. Hopefully he sold enough drinks in that twenty-four hours to cover the steep loss.[64]

Joe also featured a group of "performing monkeys, ringtails, apes, orangutans, and gorillas," which he secured on one trip to San Francisco in 1888. According to information Joe provided the newspaper, he "expended a great deal of money and lost considerable valuable time" in procuring them.[65] There was no report of how the spectacle played out, but the event shows how determined he was to bring features that would keep people coming.

Amazingly, Joe did all of this amid Tombstone's incredible economic rollercoaster. The fate of the Bird Cage ultimately remained tied to the fortunes of Tombstone's mines. Those fortunes ranged from hopeful and optimistic to downright abysmal. The mines still produced throughout the late 1880s, but every up was followed by an even bigger down. Many residents held on, but the population slowly declined with every misfortune. This unstable pattern was exemplified by the local newspapers. There were plenty of moments that lent encouragement:

The prospects of Tombstone were never better than they are to-day.
—*Prospector*, April 27, 1887

The streets of Tombstone presented a livelier appearance this week than they have in three years. The boom is fast approaching.
—*Tombstone Epitaph*, October 8, 1887

Mining is assuming much of its old time activity in Tombstone . . . and it is said that 150 men could find employment at the present time. Tombstone has a promising future before her.
—*Tombstone Epitaph*, November 19, 1887

Prospectors are busy upon their assessment work, and cheering blasts are heard in all the hills and mountains.
—*Tombstone Epitaph*, December 7, 1887

These positive moments were rare and were generally based more on hope than reality. Bad fortunes rained on Tombstone. The pumps for one of Tombstone's most productive mines, the Grand Central, went up in flames in May 1886. One local newspaper called it "the most disastrous fire" in Tombstone's history, which was saying a lot, considering the fires that gutted the business district in 1881 and 1882.[66] At the same time, the price of silver sank below one dollar. People left Tombstone in such numbers that the city council passed an ordinance making it unlawful to remove buildings.[67] Even the generally optimistic tone of the newspapers turned sour when they reported, "Rather a dual week in mining circles. A crisis is approaching in Tombstone [and] something will have to be done."[68] One resident summarized the many problems on the minds of locals: "Indians, drought, depreciation of silver, etc have brought us down."[69] A drought in one season was accompanied by torrential floods the next. Storms and flooding knocked out miles of roads and bridges, which kept trains, news, and goods from arriving. At one point Tombstone was said to be "isolated from the outside world."[70] The Bird Cage narrowly avoided further disaster when a violent storm ripped the roof off a nearby building and sent it crashing into the building right next door. Ironically, the damaged building next door was the saloon owned by former Bird Cage proprietor Frank Broad.[71]

And the hits kept coming. In May 1887 Tombstone was rocked by a massive 7.2-magnitude earthquake that originated 150 miles away in Mexico. It changed the flow of the San Pedro River, killed more than fifty people, and caused havoc to Tombstone and many other communities. Schieffelin Hall's north wall cracked, clocks stopped, chandeliers at the Crystal Palace crashed to the floor, and chimneys were turned to rubble. Scared citizens rushed to the streets, and it was reported that several schoolgirls fainted—all in the span of forty seconds.[72] News reverberated 2,400 miles away in New York, where it was reported, "The earthquake shook the [Bird Cage] and audiences up badly."[73] Three years later Tombstone was hit hard by severe winter storms that contributed to a lethal pneumonia outbreak. One of the deaths, discussed ahead, hit the Bird Cage family hard.

In spite of these misfortunes, Joe pushed through. Tombstone's tug-of-war between hope and reality made operating the Bird Cage a much tougher job than during the Billy Hutchinson era. Joe remained confident enough in Tombstone to pour money into at least four renovations of the building. In some cases he closed to redo seating, improve scenery, install new curtains, and to "artistically redecorate."[74] Renovations were so extensive in 1888 that he closed for a whole month to "renovate and enlarge" the auditorium.[75] Somehow the Bird Cage stayed afloat. Word was sent to the nation's leading entertainment journal in New York that "in spite of so-called hard times, the Elite [Bird Cage] Theatre continues to do a good business."[76] Local newspapers agreed, noting that "despite dull times, the Elite [Bird Cage] is still supported and Joe stocks the theater with a good company making it a pleasant place to spend a few hours."[77] But Joe was still a wanderer at heart. Even those who knew him in Tombstone recognized it. The local newspaper said what everyone knew to be true. "Joe has ever been of a restless nature and no matter how well he is prospering, when the desire to satisfy his roving disposition comes on everything is sacrificed to that end."[78] Something had to give.

Expanding Portfolio

Between the faltering economy and constant news of outside opportunities, many people bailed on Tombstone. These same factors put great pressure on Joe's restlessness. As rough times hit in the summer of 1886, a local noted that "an exodus to Kingston, New Mexico" was underway.[79] Kingston was a little brother to Tombstone, fresh in an upward cycle of mining and prosperity. Located just 230 miles away, it was well within reach of the abled roamer Joe Bignon. He couldn't resist.

Joe left Tombstone in early August 1886 and put Charles Keene in charge of Bird Cage operations. He arrived in Kingston amid a fury of activity that must have reminded him of Tombstone the first time he saw it. It buzzed with anticipation and life that Tombstone in 1886 lacked, and he quickly determined Kingston was "a good place for business."[80] Within days Joe bought a twenty-five by one-hundred-foot lot in the heart of town. In less than two weeks he erected a wood-frame building he called the Kingston Opera House and opened it on August 29, 1886.[81] It was a small venue, even narrower and shorter than the Bird Cage. Although it was an unassuming wood false front building with two modest windows, Joe bought it to life using all the big ideas and resources he had at his disposal. Along with performers he recruited in El Paso, Texas, he brought a handful of his Bird Cage crew, a full-scale band, and eventually his trusted friend Charles Keene to manage stage operations. Talent was circulated quickly, just as it had been in Tombstone. To keep nightly performances fresh, he continued to make trips to scout for new performers. As Tombstone came out of its lull in 1887, Joe temporarily closed the Kingston Opera House, but not before he gave the secluded mining town eight months of continuous, spirited entertainment. For years he returned to Kingston to open the opera house as Tombstone's highs and lows dictated. He owned the building in whole or in part as late as 1899.[82]

Opening the Kingston Opera House was the beginning of a pattern throughout the remainder of Joe's years with the Bird Cage. Whenever Tombstone mines and population waned, he stayed true to his nature and pursued other locations. Each venture was approached with the same

Joe's Bignon's Kingston Opera House is visible in the center behind a group of citizens gathered on Kingston's main street. Photo dated 1886–1890. Original J. C. Burge cabinet card, courtesy of Barbara Lovell, Kingston Schoolhouse Museum.

urgency and tenacity as everything else he did. In all, Joe opened five different theaters in six years—one in Kingston, two in Phoenix, one in Albuquerque, and the Crystal Palace in Tombstone, which he leased and operated as a genuine variety theater for two years.[83] He often ran several at the same time, shifting scenery, performers, and other resources to whatever venue made sense financially. Operating multiple venues also gave him leverage in securing performers, who could be offered more work at multiple locations. He proudly promoted this selling point on daily advertising handbills for the Bird Cage, which read, "Performers opening at this house can have the privilege of playing at the Kingston Opera House."[84]

Several of his venues were modestly successful. Others fell victim to the same economic stagnation and wrath of Mother Nature that plagued Tombstone. In January 1891 Joe opened the Elite theater in Phoenix with "25 artists from San Francisco and Denver" whom he employed at the Bird Cage.[85] Solid performances and positive press helped pack the theater every night.[86]

But it all came to a screeching halt four and a half weeks later when the Salt River that peacefully flowed through Phoenix was turned into a "roaring torrent."[87] Fed by melting snow and exaggerated seasonal rain, the river swelled to unprecedented levels that devastated many communities along its banks. Early flooding started on February 19 and swept away countless businesses and homes in young Phoenix. When those immediately along the river fell victim, Joe hosted a benefit performance and donated all $115.50 it generated to the sufferers.[88] But the river kept rising. Many who were thought to be safe from the rising waters became the next victims. Soon Joe's theater, which was several blocks away, was consumed. Four of his performers who were featured in the benefit for the early victims became stranded and victims themselves. They sought the safety of the theater, where they witnessed nature's epic wrath. One wrote of their dire situation,

> Our house, the Elite closed owing to the severe floods which rendered so many families destitute. At one time we were expecting the whole city would be washed away, [and] when the worst came . . . my wife and myself hurriedly [went] to the theatre, which was the highest point and the safest place. At the time of the closing we had sufficient [money] to get out, but could not do so, and now that we can get away by stage, we have not the means. I hope something will turn up for us soon, as we are in poor shape, I can assure you.[89]

In all the river rose eighteen feet above normal levels and flooded an area three miles wide across the Phoenix valley. It became the largest recorded flood in Arizona history.[90] Two months later Joe sold the theater, or what was left of it, for $100, which was exactly $15.50 less than he had donated to the flood's initial victims.[91]

Such events helped Joe maintain faith in Tombstone. He remained invested in local affairs and executed at least four renovations of the Bird Cage while pursuing other theaters. Considering all of his activity, it is obvious Joe remained confident that Tombstone would boom again. He remained so confident, in fact, that he purchased three adjoining lots on the southeast corner of Sixth and Bruce Streets in March of 1889 and built a home.[92] This is the first known record of Joe, who was now 39 years old, owning a home anywhere in his years of roaming.

The year 1889 proved to be pivotal for other reasons as well. In January he acquired his first mine in southeastern Arizona. Joe eventually gave up on theaters, and the second half of his life would be dominated by a fury of mining activity. His first mine in 1889 then became a real landmark that foreshadowed the second act of his life yet to come.[93] But there was an even bigger event in 1889. Joe got married.

Bird Cage legend includes a lot of salacious and spurious information about Joe's wife. The legend would have you believe she was a performer and a prostitute named Big Minnie who bought the Bird Cage with Joe in 1886. In reality, following their movements around the country reveals they were never in the same state until the fall of 1888, when they met in California. Joe's wife was never in Tombstone until late in 1888—almost three years after he reopened the Bird Cage. And of course when Joe did reopen the Bird Cage, San Francisco liquor distributors John Sroufe and Hugh McCrum still owned the building. Joe and his wife never owned it. Furthermore, there's no evidence she was a prostitute or involved in prostitution at any point in her life. Virtually none of the commonly recited script about her is true.

She was born Matilda Quigley in 1852 in England.[94] Her adult life was almost entirely spent as a traveling singer and dancer.[95] In the early 1870s she toured the United States with her then husband, Charles Bouton, a talented piano player. Professionally she was advertised as Tillie Bouton, a name she retained throughout her career, even after meeting Joe.[96] Charles and Tillie lived in the St. Louis area but traveled frequently through the central United States, ranging from Ohio and Tennessee all the way to the Rocky Mountains.[97] But Charles fell suddenly ill and was taken to the St. Louis city hospital, where he died on September 28, 1876.[98]

Tillie became a widow at 24 and continued to perform as a means to provide for herself. From Pensacola, Florida, to Cheyenne, Wyoming, and many places in between, she kept up a rhythm of travels over the next twelve years.[99] In the late 1870s she became a feature in Leadville, Colorado, at a time when many future Bird Cage performers were there. She arrived when Leadville was a rough-hewn mining camp with "but a few log cabins" and saw it grow to a "bustling, roaring, crowded town with the usual accompaniments of theaters, dance-halls [and] gambling rooms." One theatergoer who saw her perform at the newly built Coliseum noted it was "the coziest little theater in Colorado . . . and its appointments would do credit to many an Eastern provincial."[100] It was one of many Leadville venues she played. After repeated engagements over a nine-year stretch, local papers referred to her as "an old time favorite in this city."[101]

In the summer of 1888 Tillie's travels took her to Sacramento, California, where she played the Mascot Music Hall through early fall.[102] At the same time, Joe was northbound to San Francisco from Tombstone on one of his numerous performer recruiting trips.[103] There's no record of their first meeting or what Joe said to lure her to Tombstone, but shortly thereafter they arrived in Arizona and Tillie made her Bird Cage debut.[104] Their relationship moved fast. A few months later, Joe bought three lots on the southeast corner of Sixth and Bruce on the north edge of Tombstone and built a home.[105] Plans for their future may have been the motivating factor for a restless wanderer like Joe to finally own a home after decades of unattached roaming. Less than two months later, on May 5, 1889, Joe and Tillie were married in that very home. Right at his side as a signed witness was his good friend Charles Keene.[106]

Tillie continued to perform at the Bird Cage and the other venues Joe had opened.[107] One Tombstone resident recalled they performed together on occasion. "Joe and [Tillie] frequently presented an act themselves and got as much applause as any."[108]

Modern legend insists Tillie was a prostitute at the Bird Cage. As discussed in chapter 10, prostitution was regulated, licensed, and legally enforced in Tombstone during this time. City records define where prostitution was conducted throughout Tombstone, yet there are zero records that support the Bird Cage was one of them. Such claims are a recent invention meant to add a perceived intrigue to the building. Likewise, there is no evidence Tillie was in any way involved in prostitution at any point in her life.

Legend also says she was a bouncer at the Bird Cage as if it was an ongoing role. This comes from a single incident that has been misrepresented to make her persona seem more interesting. The incident involved an alter-cation with a furious Bird Cage patron on the night of May 10, 1889—just five days after Joe and Tillie's wedding. Hours after reciting their wedding vows, Joe rounded up a number of his performers and hopped on a stage bound for Phoenix to open his newly established theater.[109] As he had done before, he left his trusted friend Charles Keene behind to oversee the business. On the night of May 10, Charles decided to organize a show with the few performers left behind. During the performances he stationed himself behind the bar to serve drinks. At midnight a Mexican woodchopper from the Dragoon Mountains came in and asked Charles for a drink but refused to pay full price for it. When Charles refused to fill his order until he paid in full, the man drew his gun, which sent a shockwave of terror across the crowded theater.[110]

Longtime Bird Cage musician Ed Wittig came to Charles's aid. Ed and Charles may have had a deeper bond, as both were Civil War veterans and members of the fire department. With the courage of a man who had seen Civil War battlefields, 47-year-old Wittig went after the woodchopper and grappled with him, trying to gain control of the gun. The gun went off as they wrestled in the doorway and Wittig "came back like a shot." After their separation, the woodchopper fired several rounds at Wittig, which brought on a crowd "from all directions." Among the crowd that descended on the action were two law officers who pursued the woodchopper into the gulch behind the Bird Cage. One of the law officers was Bob Hatch—the man who was present when Morgan Earp was assassinated at his billiard hall in March of 1882. The *Prospector* described the shooting match that ensued: "The fun began. Bang! Bang! went the shots at the form of the Mexican as he went over a dump near the engine house."[111] One shot hit the man in the knee and exited near his hip. Incapacitated by the wound, he was arrested and thrown in jail.[112]

Two separate newspapers thoroughly reported the incident. One did state that Tillie "put the objectionable visitor out the front door, he in the meanwhile flourishing the pistol at close proximity to her person" just as Wittig intervened.[113] Both newspapers universally agreed it was Wittig who tried to take control of the situation. In fact, the *Epitaph* reported that Tillie "was frightened a little" by the incident.[114] Another local recalled Tillie's involvement: "It was one of the few times she got tough with anyone. Mostly she went her placid way leaving the arguments and worries to Joe, who was well able to bear the load."[115] At the time, Joe was opening his theater in Phoenix, which explains why Tillie felt compelled to get involved at all. Claims that Tillie was a bouncer/prostitute misrepresent and defame her. In reality she was a gentle woman. A local man who knew her said she was "a simple, childlike soul [who] enjoyed applause and laughter, sympathized with the down and out, and had pleasant heart throbs when she made somebody else happy."[116] It's no wonder why Joe fell in love with her.

Beginning of the End

Joe's resilience, energy, and determination overcame Tombstone's many ups and downs, but at a certain point they took their toll. In January 1890 he rolled back into town with two stagecoaches full of performers and baggage "and [was] welcomed by a large crowd of friends" on Allen Street. Among the passengers were "several new stars" Joe had recruited.[117] Locals praised him for the entertainment he brought to struggling Tombstone. "[Joe] continues to give meritorious performances every night. [He] is always devising something new to please our public and a few pleasant hours can always be spent in his popular house."[118] That wasn't just polite talk. According to the *Epitaph*, the Bird Cage was booming. "The Elite [Bird Cage] Theater is in full blast again under the management of Joe Bignon. The familiar sound of 'X four' can now be heard every night and causes remembrance of flush times in this city."[119] But money struggles forced him to ask town officials for a reduction in his required licensing fees.[120] Worse yet, a devastating tragedy struck the Bird Cage family.

Just as Joe was reopening the Bird Cage in early 1890, Tombstone was visited by severe winter weather that killed local livestock and produced a deadly pneumonia outbreak. The *Tombstone Prospector* reported on the widespread problem. "Allen street resembled a graveyard in motion this morning. Every man who had been laid up with [pneumonia] was out sunning himself."[121] Among the sufferers was Mollie Fly, wife of Tombstone's notable photographer C. S. Fly.[122] Sadly, another victim was Joe's good friend and trusted confidante, Charles Keene. He came down with a severe case of pneumonia, which he battled for several weeks. At one point he was said to have been "at death's door."[123] He battled back, showing some signs of improvement, but died on January 31, 1890. After four years in Tombstone, Keene had become well known, not just as a Bird Cage employee and performer but also as a member of the fire department and the Grand Army of the Republic for his service in the Civil War. Joe remembered him as "a genial, whole souled fellow and was esteemed by all who knew him."[124] His funeral at Schieffelin Hall was followed by a burial in the city cemetery (not Boothill) attended by his many friends. Seasonal pneumonia contributed to ten other deaths in Tombstone by the time Charles died.[125]

Unfortunately, with money woes and perhaps a heavy heart from the loss of his friend, Joe closed the Bird Cage in late February to contemplate his next move. Like Billy Hutchinson seven years earlier, he cited "dull times" as the cause. Not willing to concede defeat, he promised it was only temporary and publicly announced the closure was only for "a short season."[126]

Joe still refused to give up, and revived Tombstone's theater scene again by leasing the Crystal Palace. He also took control of the bar by purchasing all of its stock and fixtures.[127] Running it much like the Bird Cage, he featured a continuous stream of performers in tandem with the saloon. One local remembered that "Joe and [Tillie] . . . were good managers. They cut down the overhead, put on an occasional show themselves, and made the old white elephant pay."[128] One of their regulars was sporting aficionado Dr. Goodfellow—the same man Joe selected to referee a wrestling match at the Bird Cage in 1886. The same former resident recalled that Joe's Crystal Palace was Goodfellow's favorite hangout: "[Goodfellow] preferred the barroom to the bazaar any day, and . . . the Crystal Palace was his favorite hangout, especially when Joe Bignon took it over after the Bird Cage. Nobody thought of looking for Doc at his office if the Crystal Palace was open. When he could not be located at either his bar or his office, it was only necessary to find out where a bet or contest of some kind was being settled."[129]

From July 1890 to June 1892, Joe served Goodfellow and hundreds of others at the Crystal Palace. Interestingly, he may have also tried to revive the Bird Cage during this time. In mid-December 1891 notice was published in the *Epitaph* that the Bird Cage was reopening under a new name—the Olympic.[130] There's no indication that Joe was behind it, nor are there continuing reports of how long it lasted. If Joe was the driving force behind the

Olympic, it lasted no longer than June of 1892. At that time his Crystal Palace lease ran out, and once again he looked elsewhere for business opportunities. Calling back to his early days roaming New Mexico by stagecoach, he made plans to open a venue in Albuquerque. But after years of patience and persistence reviving the Bird Cage, Joe was no better off financially. Like Billy Hutchinson, he failed to pay his taxes and requested a reduction in local licensing fees, suggesting money was becoming thin.[131] In 1892 he also deeded the house he built to Tillie, perhaps to protect the property against seizure.[132] Joe needed money to fund his next move, so he got creative, if not desperate. Three days after his Crystal Palace lease ended, he mortgaged his and Tillie's personal possessions for $500. The list included many items that suggested how desperate they were: a rocking chair, bed, bed pillows, quilts, personal photographs, a coffeepot, baking pans, kitchen utensils, a washboard, a lamp, a sewing machine, and dozens of additional incidental personal items of modest value.[133] With that $500 he left for Albuquerque, promising friends in Tombstone that "he would not go so far away but that he can get back here on short notice when the resurrection comes."[134] He still believed Tombstone would rise.

On August 7, 1892, he opened his venue in Albuquerque, which he called the Horse Shoe Club. It was a first-class theater that featured "a gallery facing the stage . . . fourteen private boxes . . . a stage of good proportions, with ample dressing rooms, and all the necessary scenery for the production of first-class variety acts." Much like his preparations of the Bird Cage in 1886, everything Joe did suggested he had "come to Albuquerque to stay."[135] Early indicators were good, and he stocked numerous performers who had "a large number of admirers in the early days of Tombstone."[136] Joe even shipped in the scenery he had used at Bird Cage and the Crystal Palace.[137] Then in late November, on a fifteen-dollar licensing fee technicality, Joe was arrested and thrown in jail, and his theater was "closed up tight as beeswax" by the police.[138] It was all a ruse. Local reports noted that Joe had paid "enormous rent and license [fees] for months."[139] His arrest likely had to do with community division on the issue of variety theaters. In any event, Joe knew Albuquerque didn't want him, and after his release from jail, he returned to Tombstone to "wait for the next boom."[140] He made it known he had intentions to "reengage in show business in Tombstone," but he never reopened a theater.[141] With that, the Bird Cage era ended forever. If Joe couldn't do it, no one could, and no one after him tried.

For six years Joe had harnessed his experience, ambition, and connections from twenty years of western travels to bring quality entertainment to Tombstone. He battled the plummeting price of silver, flooded mines, mining pumps burning, loss of hundreds of local jobs, a pneumonia outbreak, an earthquake, and the general downturn in population and business. His efforts gave life and spirit to Tombstone and simultaneously doubled the performance era of the Bird Cage. Without him the story of the Bird Cage would have likely ended in 1885. His contributions were recognized by many fellow Tombstone citizens who threw him three separate benefits to show their appreciation and encourage him to continue.[142] The local newspaper often sang his praises: "Joe has been [relentless] in his efforts to cater to the amusement loving public, and his energy in this line should meet with fitting reward."[143] Much like Billy Hutchinson, Frank Broad, William Sprague, and Oliver Trevillian, there is no evidence Joe received financial rewards from the Bird Cage. But he was rewarded with friendships, community warmth, and now with an eternal place in the history of Tombstone's most iconic original building.

Chapter 10

Bird Cage Mayhem?

E ven before the Bird Cage ended its operational era it was attracting sensationalized stories. Eye-grabbing anecdotes written to meet the wild perceptions of a border town called Tombstone were printed and reprinted across the country, regardless of their authenticity. Today those journalistic practices may be called irresponsible or worse. Nevertheless, they planted the seed of wild legend. While Joe Bignon was still serving customers in 1888, the *Omaha Daily Bee* ran a story about a gunfight at the Bird Cage between the Earps and Johnny Behan, Curly Bill, "Jack" [sic] Ringo, and a host of others. Firing at one another from boxes on opposite sides of the auditorium, it was reported twelve bodies laid dead when the smoke cleared.[1] Six years later the story was still being printed, and it spun even further out of control when a random, made-up brother, Julian Earp, was inserted. It also added a stunning conclusion that claimed Wyatt and Ike Clanton met years later in Phoenix to settle the score. Rekindling their Bird Cage feud, they engaged in a gunfight in which Clanton was killed and Wyatt was "so badly wounded . . . his career as a fighter ended then and there."[2] One account insisted the gunfight resulted from Ike becoming romantically involved with Jessie Earp—yet another made-up Earp sibling.

In that version Ike not only survived but also won the duel.[3] Of course nothing of the sort ever occurred. Increasingly wild versions of this story persisted into the early 1900s, with details that grew ever more fanciful with each retelling.[4]

Today's version is no more factual. A classic line in the current Bird Cage legend says that in the 1880s, the *New York Times* reported it as being "the wildest, wickedest night spot between Basin Street and the Barbary Coast."[5] Without being questioned, this colorful tagline is repeated countless times in magazines, books, and internet articles. The *New York Times* retains an archive of every page it has printed dating back to 1851. A search of their archives with the help of their staff shows that the quote (or any vague version of the quote) was never printed.[6] But it only starts there.

During its decade of operation, the Bird Cage existed solely as a theater, saloon, and after-performance dance hall.[7] In the last several decades, groundless claims that it was a gambling hall, brothel, and even barber shop have been added to its identity. Modern lore also includes a great number of deaths from gun and knife fights. Depending on the age of the story and who tells it, the number fluctuates from a dozen to upward of thirty.[8]

As a chartered city in a county of a United States territory, deaths in Tombstone left a paper trail not unlike what one finds in their community today. There were arrest records, indictments, summonses, coroner's inquests, coroner's logs, death certificates, burial records, incarceration records, court transcripts, probate records, newspaper accounts, and on and on. These records are preserved at the city, county, and state level, and each one has been thoroughly consulted in an effort to arrive at an accurate body count. The result is that no deaths have been recorded inside the Bird Cage. Without knowledge of the surviving records, countless books, articles, and blogs comprised of thinly scanned internet information repeat racy stories of individuals killed inside the Bird Cage. None of those claims are backed by a single one of the above-mentioned records that document actual deaths and crimes. The names of those allegedly killed are almost never mentioned, and when they are, there are no records to prove the person existed or the event occurred. Yet these stories are often believed unconditionally, and contrary to their intent, they actually distance people from the building's real story. Like other modern Bird

Cage lore, the creation of this myth is used to entertain tourists in place of diligent research and the intrigue of truth. Billy Breakenridge, county deputy under Sheriff Johnny Behan in the early 1880s, agreed when he said, "No one had been killed there, and the Hutchinsons ran it in an orderly manner."[9]

As you will read, gunfire at the Bird Cage was very rare, though it did happen. Many assume it was general practice for men in Tombstone to carry guns in holsters as part of their daily attire. So did one Boston native who relocated to Tombstone in 1882. He arrived just five weeks after the Bird Cage opened and wrote a letter home admitting he had expected to see men walking the streets "with at least two pistols stuck in their belt." Instead he was shocked to find none in sight.[10] Despite what movies show, gunfire in Tombstone was not overlooked like car horns honking in big cities today. There was little tolerance for it by the public, and a single gunshot would bring strong reactions from those in the area, local law enforcement, and the newspaper the next day.

Tombstone's gun laws began on April 12, 1880, when the village council first passed Ordinance 9 restricting the carrying of concealed weapons.[11] When incidents of gun violence occurred, there was often a push for stricter enforcement, not unlike public reactions to similar acts of gun violence in the twenty-first century. The shooting of Marshal Fred White in October 1880 and the famed OK Corral gunfight a year later are both examples of events that emboldened local gun laws.[12] Gunfire not only was dangerous but also discouraged advancement and outside interest that town leaders hoped to attract. These attitudes are reflected in the following series of newspaper excerpts taken as they happened. Each account creates a better understanding of Tombstone's attitude toward guns going off.

> A couple of pistol shots in the rear of the Sixth street dance house yesterday afternoon . . . and the crowd was soon surging toward the point indicated.
> —*Tombstone Epitaph*, September 15, 1880

> A succession of pistol shots about nine o'clock last night on Allen Street between Sixth and Seventh started our community and soon attracted a large crowd.
> —*Nugget*, December 5, 1880

A random shot last night on the corner of Firth and Allen streets brought out a large crowd.

—*Tombstone Epitaph*, December 16, 1880

A man standing on the south side of Allen between Fourth and Fifth took out his pistol and fired a shot downward into the ground. Officers Kirkpatrick and Magee were on the spot almost instantly and took the gentleman to the city prison where he will have a chance to sober up before morning when he will be compelled to settle with the Recorder to the tune of about $25 for carrying a concealed weapon and another $25 for target practice in the streets.

—*Tombstone Epitaph*, April 14, 1881

Officer Kirkpatrick arrested a man for firing off his pistol . . . at the moon on Allen Street below Fourth last evening and raked him in to Judge Wallace who paroled him upon a payment of $25. This kind of treatment will have the effect to stop shooting on public thoroughfares.

—*Tombstone Epitaph*, May 4, 1881

A bad man from Bodie drew his little gun on Scottie [a well-known gambling man] in the Alhambra last evening. The officers promptly raked him in and took him to the cooler [jail], where he spent the night to appear before his Honor Judge Wallace this morning.

—*Tombstone Epitaph*, June 26, 1881

Three shots fired in the lower part of the city last night . . . were the result of an unknown drunk who was riding on horseback out of town. When the officers arrived on the spot . . . he was not there.

—*Tombstone Epitaph*, September 29, 1881

The stillness of Sunday night was rudely broken by the sharp crack of the pistol, four shots being fired in rapid succession . . . on Third street between Allen and Fremont. Many citizens living in the vicinity [were] awakened by the noise [and] officers were promptly at the spot where the shots were fired.

—*Nugget*, December 13, 1881

Last evening a pistol shot was heard in front of the Grand hotel which, for a moment, caused a silence of suspense, when a crowd broke for the spot.

—*Tombstone Epitaph*, February 16, 1882

A young society man was observed by a group of city and county officials who happened to be standing on the edge of the sidewalk at [Colonel Hafford's saloon] in top boots with spurs clanking, he evidently having just come in from a ride. As he passed the group it was observed that the skirt of his coat was thrown back over the handle of a large revolver, leaving the whole weapon exposed upon his right hip. The aspect of the young man was so perfectly self-assured and unsuspecting of any infraction of Ordinance No 9 that the event caused considerable [amusement].

—*Tombstone Epitaph*, February 18, 1882

Some damphool [sic] fired off a pistol on Allen street between Third and Fourth last night. If the police and reporters caught him when they got through running they would make it decidedly warm for him.

—*Tombstone Epitaph*, June 27, 1882

The sharp report of a revolver was heard near the corner of Fifth and Toughnut. Officer James Coyle . . . ran immediately . . . to the spot.

—*Weekly Epitaph*, November 2, 1882

Last evening a man [near] Allen street near Seventh fired his pistol in the air. Immediately after the street [was] filled with an excited crowd.

—*Weekly Epitaph*, December 9, 1882

Some of these incidents resulted in arrests, charges, and fines entered in the original handwritten City Recorder's Docket preserved in the city archives. The idea that bullet holes are riddled throughout the Bird Cage is not supported by early twentieth-century photographs. Detailed photographs taken by Pomona, California, photographer Burton Frasher in 1934 show a nearly pristine ceiling before the "bullet holes" visible today were added. During the ten years of Bird Cage theatrical operations, the building was renovated at least six times, bringing into question why the alleged bullet holes would have been preserved through each of them.[13]

In equally sensational fashion to gunfire and murders is the claim that the Bird Cage was a brothel. However, just as local laws regulated firearms, there were also those that regulated prostitution. The mayor and city council created strictly defined boundaries where prostitution and solicitation of prostitution was legal. They also established a licensing system that was a requirement for those operating prostitution houses and for prostitutes themselves.[14] While Billy Hutchinson was arm wrestling with Ed Field over rights to the eventual Bird Cage lot in 1881, the lot was outside the legalized boundary for prostitution.

This photograph, circa 1934, provides a clear view of the ceiling before many of the holes visible today were added. Author's collection.

If a prostitute was found soliciting her services outside the boundary, she was removed and often fined. In fact this very law was enforced by one-time Bird Cage proprietor Frank Broad, who also served as one of Tombstone's constables.[15] One local recalled, "If one of the girls from the [prostitution] cribs strolled up towards the Crystal Palace and seemed to be meditating a business deal, Frank Broad hustled her back where she came from."[16]

When the prostitution boundaries were eventually changed, no license or license log exists to prove the Bird Cage or anyone at the Bird Cage was conducting prostitution there. In fact no prostitution related business activities can be associated with any of the five Bird Cage proprietors. Tombstone's original recorder's docket (which logged arrests, charges, pleas, and fines for city infractions) includes dozens of arrests for prostitution and licensing violations across town, yet none were made at the Bird Cage.[17] Firsthand accounts provided ahead substantiate this.

As a means to legitimize the legend, the rooms below the stage today are presented to tourists as prostitution cribs. Throughout the early 1900s, former customer and building owner Charles Cummings stated the rooms were actually dressing rooms. Several references to them being dressing rooms were made after the turn of the century, including a report made when the building's east wall collapsed in 1931. The gaping hole was said to have exposed "one dressing room."[18] As a matter of practical necessity, the building would have required them when it was an active theater. Billy Hutchinson advertised the availability of dressing rooms in formal ads for his masquerade balls in 1882.[19] In the late 1920s, there were several accounts of visitors who toured the building and saw performer autographs on the room's walls. Author Walter Noble Burns saw them and transcribed more than twenty of the names in his 1927 book *Tombstone: An Iliad of the Southwest*. Although he transcribed the signatures with misspellings, research shows they were the cast members hired by Joe Bignon in 1889—further proof that the rooms were in fact dressing rooms.[20] Today the Bird Cage distributes pamphlets with a summary of the building's lore that plainly states, "Directly below the stage are . . . the dressing rooms."[21] This small detail in the pamphlet, which has been published since the 1970s, appears to have been overlooked when the brothel room legend was created. Claims of prostitution at the Bird Cage, like those of murders and gunfights, are a modern invention entirely contradicted by period resources.

Gambling was also regulated by the same licensing system all Tombstone businesses were subject to. Modern Bird Cage legend includes an eight-year poker game in which $10 million passed hands with the house taking 10 percent (which is $1 million, or roughly $30 million in today's money). In reality no license or license log shows any gambling was ever conducted at the Bird Cage. Furthermore, all five of the building's proprietors left the business in a weak financial state. Billy Hutchinson lost the entire business because of a defaulted mortgage and was forced to sell the chandeliers, chairs, scenery, and bar glasses in a last-ditch effort to keep the business going.[22] The same day he closed the theater in the summer of 1883, he was arrested for drunkenness. The court gave him the option to pay a $5 fine or take five days in jail. He took the jail time, showing how little money he may have had.[23] Joe Bignon fared no better. After five years at the Bird Cage, he mortgaged his personal possessions, including personal photographs, rugs, kitchen utensils, his bed, and the pillows he sept on to fund his next business venture in Albuquerque, New Mexico.[24] He and Billy Hutchinson both struggled to pay the city license fees and petitioned the council to lower them. Frank Broad, Oliver Trevillian, and William Sprague each left the Bird Cage for other business ventures in Tombstone and Bisbee and never looked back. Sprague's health problems left him nearly penniless and many of his medical bills and travel expenses were covered by friends in Tombstone.[25]

When considering these outcomes, the idea of the house taking the equivalent of $30 million is beyond fanciful. No owner would have abandoned a business generating the kind of income that would have made them among the West's most wealthy men. As further evidence, it was impossible for a game to have continued for eight years, as the story suggests. The building closed down at least six times for renovations in its first ten years and was shut completely in periods between proprietors—sometimes for many months.[26] Problems arise with the participants of the alleged game as well. Bat Masterson is introduced as a key player, yet he left Tombstone permanently in April 1881—five months before the building's construction began. There is no truth to the story whatsoever.

Tombstone's newspapers liked to report large gambling games and large wins and losses. Big money flowing on gambling tables was an early indicator of how healthy a mining camp's economy was. As the *Epitaph* of October 9, 1880, put it, sizable winnings were "a sure indication of a prosperous camp." A well-traveled journalist who came to Tombstone in 1881 observed, "The man who is familiar with mining towns and the ways of their people can tell within ten minutes after his arrival whether a camp is booming or not. All he need do is to enter the first large saloon, walk back to the faro bank and inspect the layout. The faro game is an infallible barometer and the professional gambler the best authority of the status of a new camp."[27] Large games did occur in Tombstone, and they were eagerly reported in local newspapers to help promote its appearance as a prosperous town. The Alhambra was the scene of the biggest pot in early Tombstone, with hands "as high as $4000 [that became] the center of attention."[28] The game lasted several days and made daily news because of it. The Oriental also saw one of Tombstone's "heaviest poker games" that same summer.[29] Even as late as 1886, a multiday poker game was reported across town.[30] On the same pages that announced these games, respected dealers with good reputations ran ads that attracted customers by guaranteeing fair games.[31] Bird Cage activity was advertised and reported throughout its entire operational era, yet gambling was never once mentioned or even hinted at. Like myths of prostitution and murder, the gambling game story is modern fiction that only covers up and confuses the building's real history.

Real Bird Cage Mayhem

However, this doesn't mean the Bird Cage didn't see its share of wild and colorful events. On the contrary, the following accounts re-create its smoky, boisterous, and vibrant atmosphere the way it really was. They reveal that in spite of their standards, reputation, and good intentions, proprietors Billy Hutchinson, Billy Sprague, Oliver Trevillian, Frank Broad, and Joe Bignon were at odds with the forces of youth, liquor, and unchaperoned spirit of a frontier mining camp.

The least reliable of these accounts come from recollections recorded after the fact—in some cases fifty years later. Through faded memories, irresistible storylines, or possibly more deceptive motives, these recollections must be read with the same consideration given to our own distant memories.

Henrietta Herring was the young daughter of William Herring, one of Tombstone's most prominent lawyers. From their home on Toughnut Street near the county courthouse, she remembered being told to walk on the opposite side of the street from the Bird Cage as she passed it on her way to school.[32] Billy Hutchinson's close friend William Allen Le Van operated a two-story hotel directly across the street from the Bird Cage. From the second story balcony his stepdaughter May recalled peering down at the theater with her younger sister Helena. "Lena and I would go out on the balcony and lay down on our stomachs to try to peer through the doors of the [Bird Cage] theater across the way at the dancing girls. Mama would catch us out there and we would be severely scolded."[33]

Another woman who lived in Tombstone was asked about attending the
Bird Cage years later and vehemently denied it. "I never was there because if
my mother knew I was going there she would have gotten very mad."[34] These
protective measures by local parents reflect the attitude of the time. Many
parents saw variety theaters (along with saloons and gambling houses) as
places that would corrupt children the same way movies, music, and television with mature content could today. Furthermore, they saw the stage as an
undesirable path in life and did what they could to discourage their children's
curiosity the same way parents guide their children today. Some in religious
or high-minded social circles were horrified at the thought of their children
being lured by the variety theater stage or being corrupted by the worst it had
to offer. Few acknowledged the positive world of theater that existed and
naïvely judged the whole industry by its worst.

Charles Cummings was a young man from small-town New York when
he came to Tombstone in 1880. Unlike most, he stayed when the boom was
over, endured Tombstone's darkest times, and in fifty years as a resident
worked his way up from a general laborer to town mayor. He also became one
of the largest volume lot owners, scooping up more than 150 of Tombstone's
most historic properties. As a former Bird Cage customer, he was the proud
owner of the building from 1906 until his death in 1930.[35] Shortly before he
passed he recalled the Bird Cage he knew as a young man:

> The show began about 8:30 with acrobats, singers and dancers taking
> their turns. They came on and off, but between their acts the women
> went down among the audience and sold drinks on commission from
> the bar. Long about 2 or 3 o'clock the actors got tired, and the cowboys
> would want to dance. The chairs were stacked back and everyone
> danced and drank until daylight, which didn't much stop the drinking
> even at that. No, the women didn't dress loud. No sportin' women were
> taken for the theater and you couldn't tell the singers and dancers from
> other women when on the street. No, their dresses weren't short, nor
> too low cut. They were pretty nice girls and several of 'em married and
> made as good wives as any gal.[36]

Adding to the scene's color, Charles told a *Los Angeles Times* reporter
that even as daylight emerged "the regular customers would drape themselves

over the bar out in front, with a toe-hold on the brass rail, while they downed additional 'cheer' and staved off as long as they could that uninteresting period of rest."[37] Loyal customers indeed.

Before the Bird Cage was permanently reopened to the public in 1934, Charles eagerly invited many early tourists inside for a personal tour of the building, complemented by stories he personally experienced there. One of his favorite stories included Frank Leslie shooting the boot heel of a cowboy who was dangling his foot off the balcony. Former Tombstone residents Emil Marks and Dave Adams claimed to have witnessed the event, giving it a degree of credibility.[38] Shortly after Cummings died, the story became immortalized in the 1931 movie *The Cisco Kid*. The scene plays out in a theater where the Kid is leaning back in his balcony seat, making eyes at a young woman performing onstage. An enraged adversary of the Kid sees this, pulls out his gun, and shoots his overhanging boot heel off, sending the theater into a panic. The *Tombstone Epitaph* suggested the scene was inspired by Charles's story.[39]

William Ohnesorgen was a toddler when his parents fled the German Revolutions and came to America in the early 1850s. After growing up in San Antonio, Texas, he became a freighter who worked his way farther west. He eventually settled in southeastern Arizona and operated a successful stagecoach line for early travelers coming to Tombstone.[40] In 1929 he reminisced about his single Bird Cage encounter: "I went to the Bird Cage once—yes just once. That was enough. Even then they dressed better than they do now—didn't show too much. I only saw one scrap. A gambling guy by the name of Rickenbaugh [actually Lou Rickabaugh, a gambling partner of Wyatt Earp at the Oriental] knocked a fellow down with his pistol. The damn thing went off and the bullet struck in a post, just over my head."[41]

It's possible Ohnesorgen confused this incident with another involving Lou Rickabaugh and an accidentally discharged gun. A month before the Bird Cage opened for performances, Rickabaugh got into a heated argument on Allen Street and was clubbed over the head with a revolver. Upon impact the gun discharged and the bullet struck an awning post.[42] If Ohnesorgen did confuse the story, it would be understandable, given five decades had passed.

Billy Breakenridge is best known as a deputy and tax collector who worked under County Sheriff Johnny Behan in the early 1880s. He offered his straightforward Bird Cage memories in 1928: "It was the only resort of the kind in town, and was well patronized. The Hutchinsons brought their talent in from San Francisco, and the place was filled every night. The actresses sold drinks between acts, and when the show was over the seats were moved back and there was dancing. The bar did a rushing business . . . and the Hutchinsons ran it in an orderly manner."[43]

Echoed by other accounts, Breakenridge spoke highly of the female performers who "as a rule, were good women." He also insisted that the Hutchinsons "ran the place in first class style and no disorderly conduct was allowed."[44] However he did mention there was some anticipation that the ongoing feud between the cowboys and Earps or Earp supporters would play out there. "I was told to patrol near the Bird Cage Theatre at night, as the sheriff expected trouble to break out there between the two factions at any time. Although no one had been killed there . . . we looked for trouble between the two factions to come off at any time."[45]

In 1931 (almost fifty years after she left Tombstone) former Bird Cage actress Annie Ashley remembered the same feud and some of the participants by name, such as Johnny Ringo, Curly Bill, Frank Stilwell (who she called "a nice quiet man, though an outlaw"), and the Earps:

> It was a little [venue], like the one in El Paso. I stayed in Tombstone three months . . . and found that a feud was in full swing. Every night the feudists would come to the theatre; sometimes meet each other. The feudists met right in the theatre. After the show was over every night, downstairs would be turned into a dance hall. The tables would be cleared away and we girls would come down to entertain. If the men opened champagne we got one dollar on each bottle. Other drinks we got ten cents on the dollar. Earning money there then was exciting to say the least. After the time, we girls got so accustomed to the over-hanging excitement that we didn't think anything of it. Yet [we] remained morally good women . . . and took care of [our] families. The cowboys treated [us] like children. A woman, no matter who she was, even a street-walker, was respected according to the laws of these outlaws. God help anyone who ever made a slurring remark about a girl.[46]

Cochise County law officer Billy Breakenridge lived in Tombstone during the Earp era and offered numerous consistent recollections about the high standards and orderly manner of the Bird Cage. Author's collection.

Interestingly another local woman recalled similar chivalrous behavior from the Arizona cowboys. "The cow-boys of that country are most of them polished gentlemen. They are exceedingly polite and courteous. They come to town and shop at the best hotels, and, if in walking through the halls, they meet a lady, they invariably take off their hats and hold them in their hands until they are clear past."[47] A Tombstone hotelier in 1882 agreed, calling them "perfect gentlemen."[48]

Annie also recalled local prostitutes attended the theater. "The sights we saw, especially on the outskirts of the red light district were enough to terrify us. Sometimes the women would come to the theatre; and they'd spend their money freely, like the miners."[49] During her engagement at the Bird Cage, the *Epitaph* also suggested prostitutes came to the theater, claiming they "make

Annie Ashley was just a teenager when she performed at the Bird Cage in
1882, but she remembered the adventure fifty years later. National Vaudeville
Artists, 1924. Copy in author's collection.

the place their camping ground."[50] It's possible, if not likely, these women
were fishing for men to buy them drinks or to take back to their abode, but
another performer explained a completely different motive. "The Honkey
Tonks furnished [prostitutes] with [relief] from their professional ordeals.
Here they went for forgetfulness and laughter. Their working day was over;
they could give full attention to the performance . . . as they sat and cried over
a topical ballad or applauded a bit."[51] As one Tombstone resident put it, there
were "degrees of respectability among the nonrespectable."[52]

There are no newspaper accounts that corroborate any feud activity
between the Earps and Cowboys at the Bird Cage, as suggested by Annie
Ashley and Billy Breakenridge. However, there are a number of other
incidents reported in real time, and thus they may be considered more reliable

than potentially faded or scrambled memories. These following newspaper accounts take us inside the Bird Cage when entertainers from across the globe, attention-starved miners, curious family men, alcohol, music, and youth mixed freely. Interestingly, the first two accounts support Annie Ashley's memories of the Cowboys' protective nature of women.

> Quite a little scene occurred at the Bird Cage Tuesday evening. Annie Hines, one of the stars of that genial institution was slightly hissed by some one in the audience and she retired from the stage somewhat disconcerted. She was called on again almost by the united voice of the audience, and cheered to the echo, besides a handsome gift of money being conferred on her. Five and ten dollar pieces were bounding on the stage from every direction, and some San Simon [cow]boys threw their hats and dared any 'galoot' to hiss her while under the protection of a cowman's hat.
>
> —*Tombstone Epitaph*, July 6, 1882

> About 4 o'clock yesterday morning, an international episode occurred at the Bird Cage. It seems that some Mexicans with more money than brains, visited the institution, and were taken in charge by some of the ladies [meaning the ladies got them to buy alcohol]. While the Mexicans spent their money freely, they were 'mucho bueno' but when they asked for some amusement in return, in the shape of dancing, the were called 'damned greasers' and advised to soak their heads. A dispute arose, and some of the cavaliers of the establishment offered their assistance to the ladies, in ejecting the Mexicans. A row ensued, and some lively fist practice was indulged in for some time. The policemen were soon on the scene and three Mexicans and two of the bully boys were taken to the cooler [slang for jail].
>
> —*Tombstone Epitaph*, June 9, 1882

> A couple of waiters at the Bird Cage, one of them [Black] and the other a Frenchman, got into a row about midnight in consequence of some dispute about their work. They started to plug each other in good shape, but were gobbled up by Officers Coyle and Holmes before they could do any damage. They were arrested but subsequently released on bonds, and will have a hearing at 2 o'clock this afternoon.
>
> —*Tombstone Epitaph*, July 19, 1882

Contrary to popular belief, the Bird Cage did employ male waiters. After their fight they were dragged into the city police court where their names were recorded as Tom Turney and Martin Mahoney. They were both charged with fighting and fined fifteen dollars—roughly three days' pay.[53] A similar fight broke out at the Bird Cage on September 15, 1882. In that contest, "John Doe" plugged Dick Roberts in the eye. The fight was completely unacceptable given that it occurred during a benefit the Hutchinsons were putting on for a popular young performer and mother of two who was battling a chronic illness. Intolerant of such behavior, Billy Hutchinson immediately called officers to the scene to arrest "Doe." They hauled him off to city court, where his guilty plea and fine were recorded in the recorder's docket.[54] The immediate response by police in the last three accounts corroborates Deputy Breakenridge's recollections that "no disorderly conduct was allowed."[55]

On the night of February 4, 1882, four members of a traveling performance troupe at Schieffelin Hall decided to take in Tombstone's nightlife. After visiting several saloons they finally settled in at the Bird Cage for a show. While there they met a con man who offered them valuables allegedly lifted from an Indian he claimed to have killed. The troupe members took the bait and followed the man out of the Bird Cage one block away to Fifth and Toughnut, where they were ambushed by masked men who ordered, "Throw up your hands." The attackers struck several of the entertainers over the head and proceeded to steal their watches, studs, and other valuables. One troupe member was shot at and received a wound that required him to "take his meals in a standing position." Police descended on the scene, but the masked men were never caught. Perhaps they continued to use the Bird Cage as a hunting ground.[56] Such an event prompted the nation's premiere entertainment journal, the *New York Clipper*, to publish their negative view of Tombstone just weeks later. "They say that out in Tombstone, Arizona, the residents have fun chasing and shooting bad actors. The sooner our folks [of the entertainment industry] know this the better it will be for them. Until a more peaceful state of society is shown among the Tombstoners, travel in that direction will not be very lively."[57] Meanwhile, local press continued to illustrate the lively atmosphere inside the Bird Cage.

> A well dressed chap wearing a plug hat was arrested at the Bird Cage theater last night by Chief of Police Neagle, and arraigned before Judge Wallace today on the charge of being drunk and disorderly. He being found guilty the court fined him $16 which he paid and proceeded on his way rejoicing.[58]
>
> —*Tombstone Epitaph*, April 18, 1882

Intolerant of disorder, Billy Hutchinson had "Big Jake" Fisher dragged out of the Bird Cage after breaking a chair over a man's head. Jake was brought before local judge A. O. Wallace, who slapped him with a ten-dollar fine and made this entry in his court docket. The *Epitaph* carried the story the next day. Tombstone Recorder's Docket, Tombstone City Archives.

> A party well known in the city as Big Jake, broke a chair over a fellows head at the Bird Cage last night. A [black man] and a "smarty" were playing Jake, which was the cause of the rumpus. On Mr. Hutchinson's complaint, Jake was scooped up by officer Kenney.
> —*Tombstone Epitaph*, July 15, 1882

Big Jake was actually Jake Fisher, a carpenter by day and boisterous personality around Tombstone by night who was arrested numerous times for drunken exploits.[59] On this occasion, two of Tombstone's best officers were required to haul him out of the Bird Cage and into police court where he was fined ten dollars and sent on his way. While it wasn't Jake's first or last episode in Tombstone, Billy Hutchinson didn't tolerate it.[60]

On July 24, 1882, the *Tucson Citizen* reprinted a story from the little-known *Tombstone Independent* newspaper. The report covered an attack on former Under-Sheriff of Pima County, Mr. Coleman, by "Red Dick" Howard at the Bird Cage:

> About midnight last night a tough customer named Howard, but who is better known as Red Dick, requested Mr. Coleman, late Under Sheriff of Pima County, who was at the time sitting in the Bird Cage theatre, to go outside the door with him for a few moments. Coleman though knowing him well, accompanied him outside the door, thinking he might have something to communicate, but no sooner had he reached the outside than Red dealt him a vigorous blow on the head. The attack being unexpected, Mr. Coleman was for the moment stunned, but recovering retaliated on his assailant, and was paying him off in the proper shape when Constable Haggerty put in an appearance and arrested both. Mr. Coleman was bailed out before the jail was reached, and Howard was locked up. It seems that when Mr. Coleman was Sub-Sheriff of Pima County Howard was a prominent and industrious member of the 'top and bottom gang' and was run out of town by Coleman. This was doubtless the cause of the attack. There will be a hearing before Judge Wallace at two o'clock this afternoon.

Tombstone's City Police Court Judge A. O. Wallace recorded that both men were brought in on charges of fighting. Justice seems to have been served as Red was fined five dollars and Coleman was discharged after pleading not guilty.[61] Although their case was settled, Bird Cage mayhem continued to make the columns of the local newspapers:

> W. H. Savage [a Tombstone lawyer] and his old flame were together at the Bird Cage last night, and attracted the attention of everybody in the house by indulging in a fight [which Savage lost]. As a public officer, he should always be exposed when he stoops so low that he will fight with a woman.
> —*Daily Tombstone*, February 16, 1886

> For the past week the Bird Cage has had a burlesque on the boards titled "The Chinese Must Go." The play is full of laughable incidents, the most amusing thing in connection with its production occurred last evening. In the last scene of [the play] the Chinese laundryman is put on a burro [with all his things]. According to the play, the burro is supposed to be led off, carrying his paraphernalia out of town. For some reason he could not be led off or backed off. Like the Rock of Gibraltar, he had come

to stay and stay he did. The language known so well to the army mule had no effect. Budge he would not. The situation was ludicrous in the extreme. His burrowship had evidently joined the pro-Chinese crowd; so far as he was concerned the [laundryman] could stay. The audience convulsed with laughter, screams, cat-calls, etc resounded all over the house. While the excitement was at the highest, the member of the troupe playing the Chinaman raise his head, and after a careful survey of the situation remarked "What for the Chinese no go?" For a bit of side play it was one of the best things ever seen on any stage.

—*Daily Tombstone*, March 9, 1886

It is a noticeable fact that since the wives of a number of citizens have gone to California, that the attendance at the [Bird Cage] has increased wonderfully.

—*Daily Tombstone*, July 1, 1886

A little episode not down on the bills occurred at the close of the program last Saturday night at the Bird Cage. A couple of female attaches had a hair puling match, which but for the promptness of Joe Bignon might have ended in a general row.

—*Tombstone Prospector*, April 25, 1887

Several other incidents involving the Bird Cage were also recorded. In August 1882 two men were arrested for stealing money from a woman in the audience, and they were also suspected of stealing Billy Hutchinson's pistol, which apparently had been kept in an accessible location.[62] In 1888 two men got into a heated dispute in the Bird Cage that resulted in a gunfight in front of the *Epitaph* office the next morning. Both men were fined by Tombstone's recorder and faced the grand jury.[63] Five months later a man was persuaded to loan thirty-five dollars to a woman at the Bird Cage. After she refused to pay him back, he went to police and got a warrant sworn out for her arrest.[64] And finally, during election season late in 1888, a "lady attache" of the Bird Cage was used as political ammunition "in the war of words between two candidates."[65]

As mentioned, there were accounts of gunplay at the Bird Cage. A complete scan of newspapers and city and county records yields three such incidents. The very first occurred a week after the Bird Cage opened during a busy and festive New Year's Eve: "A crowd of boys in the audience ranging from 14–17 were [engaging in] boisterous conduct. Several of them had revolvers which they were flourishing about in a careless manner until one of the dangerous playthings was discharged, the bullet taking effect in the leg of one of the party. Considerable excitement naturally ensued and there was a general stampede for the door."[66]

This event came just weeks after City Recorder and Police Court Judge A. O. Wallace published public notice of strong enforcement of antigun laws in the wake of the gunfight near the OK Corral. Wallace proclaimed, "From this date all persons convicted of carrying weapons and discharging firearms within the city limits will be visited by severe penalties."[67] Like accounts earlier in this chapter, this incident supports the pattern of strong reactions to gunfire. The "general stampede for the door" noted in the article contradicts movies that depict an audience as tolerant of gunfire as they were of applause. Cowboys firing off hundreds of rounds in the auditorium makes good cinema, but it was not reality.

Youth and guns mixed once again for the second documented firearms incident at the Bird Cage. On March 14, 1888, the *Epitaph* reported, "A youth with a gun tried to create a little disturbance at the [Bird Cage] theatre last night, but was quickly disarmed and played the part of a mop for a few seconds." This reiterates that gunplay was not tolerated and was treated as a serious manner.

The third and most notable gun incident at the Bird Cage occurred in the middle of the night on May 10, 1889. A Mexican woodchopper pulled a gun on the bartender who refused to serve him a drink without paying in full. Band leader and Civil War veteran Ed Wittig intervened and attempted to disarm the Mexican. In the scuffle the gun went off and brought on a curious crowd "from all directions." Ultimately the woodchopper was wounded and hauled off to jail, proving again that gunplay in Tombstone and the Bird Cage was not tolerated. While the Bird Cage was still running in 1889, the territorial legislature took bold action passing Act 13, which made carrying weapons inside any town or city in Arizona Territory unlawful. It also required hotels and saloons to post public notice of Act 13.[68] The Wild West was continuously being tamed, and soon the wild days of Bird Cage mayhem passed into legend and the memories of those who lived it.

Chapter 11

Performers,
Performances, and
Employees

*The evening's entertainment [at the Bird Cage] was of that excellence
Tombstone was wont to expect in this home of refined vaudeville.*
—Walter Noble Burns, 1927

*The Bird Cage was . . . a gilded gathering place for Tombstone's elite
[where] some of the nation's best known performers appeared.*
—E. A. Wittig, the son of Bird Cage orchestra leader Ed H. Wittig[1]

mong the most misunderstood elements of the Bird Cage are its
performers. The very people who gave the building its verve and
provided an escape from mining camp life are the people who until now have
gone entirely unnamed and unknown. This vibrant group includes people
from all backgrounds and abilities who performed in hundreds of similar
variety theaters across the West and around the world. Many began as children
and remained onstage until they died. Some made it a family business and
included their children in their acts—children who would go on to have their
own careers. They were a part of a thriving industry and the brotherhood of
those who supported their families and endured difficulties and dangers just

to make a living. Former Bird Cage performer and career entertainer Joe Adams remembered, "There was plenty of action and picturesque incident, and amidst our rough struggles we still had time to make firm friendships, and we playerfolk were a wonderfully happy family."[2] This unheralded group of performers, with their unique skills and personas, prove how hard the proprietors of the Bird Cage worked to showcase quality entertainment. Who they were and the skills they brought with them adds depth and dimension to understanding what the Bird Cage was really like. But performers weren't the only ones to contribute to its operations and legacy.

Structure of employees at the Bird Cage was very similar to other period variety theaters. Entertainment was organized by a stage manager, also known as a director of amusements. Working directly under the business manager or owner, the stage manager was arguably the most important position. They were responsible for creating the nightly program, assigning roles in productions, dictating the order of performances, and ultimately answering for the quality of the show night in and night out. The difference between a good and bad stage manager could make a theater successful over time or break a theater overnight. Because of these demands, the stage manager was generally very experienced and almost always an adept and reputable performer.

Billy Hutchinson had four such managers. Among them was James Holly, a 32-year-old actor, singer, and comedian who had traveled coast to coast throughout the 1870s. His travels gained him experience as the stage manager at venues in Chicago, St. Louis, Memphis, Pueblo, and as far away as Pensacola, Florida.[3] Likewise, Bird Cage stage manager Billy Forrest had more than a dozen years of experience as stage manager in major venues throughout Colorado, including Leadville, Denver, and Pueblo. There he worked with several dozen former Bird Cage performers who flocked to Colorado during the silver boom of the 1880s.[4] Under Joe Bignon there was Charles A. Keene, a decorated Civil War veteran who after the war moved west from Brooklyn and owned his own theater in Helena, Montana.[5] Keene was also the Bird Cage's longest tenured employee, during which time he was heavily involved in the fire department and became a fixture in the community.[6]

Of similar importance to the stage manager was the musical director. No variety theater could operate without competent musical accompaniment. Tombstone was wealthy in silver but also in musicians, much to the benefit of the Bird Cage who employed dozens of them. The Bird Cage house band not only provided a soundtrack for nightly performances, but they also gave street performances, played at community gatherings, and accompanied performers in city-wide parades that promoted the Bird Cage.[7] The most notable musician was Edward Heinrich Augustus Wittig, one of several Bird Cage orchestra leaders. After escaping the deadly German Revolutions of the late 1840s, Ed's parents brought him to America when he was just eight years old. From his youngest days he was taught to play the violin by his father, who was an adept career musician that supported the family by forming bands that served communities in Missouri and southern Illinois. But by no means was music forced on Ed. His son recalled he began composing original music as a young boy and was "passionately devoted to it."[8] After serving in the Civil War and losing a brother on the battlefield, Ed returned to music and used it as a means to support his family, just as his father had. After following the boom to Leadville, he came to Tombstone in 1882 and lived the rest of his life in southeastern Arizona, where to this day members of his family reside. Ed was arguably the most skilled musician in early Tombstone, and he undoubtedly was the most experienced, having led bands in the Civil War and across the west for over twenty years. Nightly performances at the Bird Cage absolutely benefited from his passion, proficiency and leadership.[9]

In addition to musicians, the Bird Cage also employed doormen. Because the theater lacked a box office, a doorkeeper was stationed outside to collect entrance fees and control admittance.[10] Naturally there were bartenders, although to date only one full-time bartender, Hughey Mathews, has been identified by name.[11] Very often performers would fill multiple roles and sell liquor between acts, but the Bird Cage did employ several full-time waiters. The common misconception is that they were all female, but through city arrest records we know some were men, and at least one man was African American.[12] Female waitstaff were very often referred to in the industry as "rustlers." Billy Hutchinson hired a young

Edward Heinrich Augustus Wittig was one of Tombstone's most skilled
musicians and one of several Bird Cage orchestra leaders. Courtesy
Larry and Connie Wittig.

performer, Bessie Harper, who proved to be such an effective rustler that he presented her with a gold pendant with the engraving "Bessie, Bird Cage Opera House Champion Rustler."[13] Some larger variety theaters had scene painters on staff. Others opted for independent professionals who specialized in painting drop curtains and scenery and would ship their work out. While Tombstone had several full-time painters living in town, there's no record of a scenic artist hired at the Bird Cage. However in 1888 Joe Bignon employed a natural physical performer, Frank Heeley, who was also a gifted artist. One of his acts even included a clever and humorous cartoon drawing exhibition.[14] His artistic skill was utilized to paint scenery for the Bird Cage, which earned him praise from the local newspaper as "an artist of more than ordinary ability."[15]

Among the array of employees, none define the Bird Cage as well as its performers. Variety theater owners who sought quality entertainers generally ran more reputable and crime-free venues. Thus, understanding who the Bird Cage performers were is important. Unfortunately their identities and backgrounds have remained a mystery for over a century. In the early 1900s, growing interest in the American West and the story of Tombstone effected several efforts to identify them. In 1927 Tombstone transplant and former theatrical manager Arlington Gardner became so infatuated with the Bird Cage and Schieffelin Hall that he spent several years attempting to compile a roster of performers. He surveyed everyone from local old-timers to the state historian with little effect.[16] Several subsequent authors have employed similar strategies that to date have yielded a short list of uncorroborated names easily ruled out by period sources. Nevertheless, those names are repeated by countless publications as gospel to this day. Among the most common names are Eddie Foy, Lotta Crabtree, Lillian Russell, and Jenny Lind. The Bird Cage itself also promotes additional performers such as Fritzi Scheff, Lillie Langtry, Wyatt's future wife Josephine Marcus, and Fatima—the false identity assigned to the buxom woman immortalized in the painting greeting visitor's in the theater's entrance. None appeared at the Bird Cage.

Fritzi Scheff was born in Austria and didn't come to America until 1900—nearly a decade after the Bird Cage closed as a performance venue.[17] Likewise, Jenny Lind was born in Europe and was not in the United States during the Bird Cage performance era. In 1933 former Tucson attorney John B. Wright studied Lotta Crabtree for years taking sixty-six affidavits from former Tombstone residents and concluded, "Lotta Crabtree never did appear at the Bird Cage, nor any other theater in Tombstone. She never even visited that town."[18] Period newspapers and entertainment journals that recorded her movements agree that Crabtree was never in Tombstone. It's the same story for Lillie Langtry, whose travels and appearances are well-documented around the world in real time, leaving little doubt about where she was at any point in her life. Many authors have sifted through such materials, and no evidence exists that shows Lillie was ever in Arizona. High-profile actress and singer Lillian Russell can be tracked in similar fashion with the same result. She was on the East Coast and in Europe for nearly the entire duration of the Bird Cage era and never was in southeastern Arizona.

One of the most accepted names among commonly listed Bird Cage performers is Eddie Foy. It began in 1903 when Eddie began publicly claiming he appeared at the Bird Cage.[19] It was a story repeated, albeit with a number of changes, in his autobiography, *Clowning through Life*, published just weeks before his death in 1931. His version is clear. After performing in Denver with his stage partner Jim Thompson and their wives, Rose Howland and Millie Thomas, he claimed they accepted an engagement in San Francisco but first detoured to Tombstone "early in 1881" for four weeks.[20] This date was before the Bird Cage was even built. In an attempt to pinpoint exactly when Eddie and the foursome came to Tombstone, period performance reviews, previews, advertisements, and travel notices were consulted. It was then discovered that Foy and his foursome were in Denver continuously throughout the winter, spring, and summer of 1881 and then in San Francisco continuously until they left for Butte, Montana.[21] These notices left no time for a detour to Tombstone. Additionally, the Bird Cage wasn't open when he claimed to have been there, and by the time it was opened, Eddie and his foursome were in San Francisco. Even more damning was the fact that all four were on board a train from Denver to San Francisco on October 26, 1881—the same day the Earps and Doc Holliday shot it out with the Clantons and McLaurys west

There are two versions of C. S. Fly–mounted photographs claiming to be
Eddie Foy in Tombstone (*top row*). While they appear to be the same man,
they are clearly not of Foy (*bottom row*), who was heavily photographed
throughout his career.

of the OK Corral entrance.[22] That conclusively proves they didn't arrive in
San Francisco from Tombstone as Eddie claimed.[23] Armond Fields, author
of Eddie's biography published in 1999, agrees: "There is . . . no evidence
available . . . that Foy and Thompson ever played [Tombstone]. Foy's claim
that he played at the Bird Cage is additionally suspect, because the theater
opened . . . when Foy and Thompson were already playing in San Francisco.
Photos claiming to be of Foy, on display at various locations in Tombstone,
are misidentified."[24]

Among the most fictionalized performer claims is Fatima. Upon entering
the theater today, Bird Cage visitors are greeted by a life-size painting on the
west wall and a fabricated story of its origin. The prevailing story identifies the
woman as Fatima (later known as Little Egypt), a belly dancer who performed
at the Bird Cage in 1881. As a token of appreciation, according to the story, she
gave the painting to the owners, who hung it in its present location where it

has remained since 1882.[25] This myth dates back less than fifty years, and like most parts of Bird Cage lore, was created to spice up the visitor experience and explain the painting's origin, which was unknown to the party responsible for the fictitious story. There is a real story behind the painting, and it's another example of truth being more fascinating than fiction.

In reality it was painted by San Francisco–based artist Charles Marcel Vaccari (whose signature adorns the lower right corner of the painting). Vaccari apprenticed under world-renowned artist Harry Humphrey Moore. The name of the painting is *Almeh, a Dream at the Alhambra*, and it is a copy Moore authorized Vaccari to paint from his original. It depicts a dancer in the Hall of Two Sisters inside the Alhambra Palace in Grenada, Spain. Through Moore's wife's family connection to Spanish aristocracy, he gained privileged access to the Alhambra, enabling him to paint all of the immaculate details straight from real life around 1865. The results were so stunning it won first prize at the 1867 Paris Exposition. All of those details were dutifully rendered by Vaccari, who painted his copy sometime between 1880 and 1881 in San Francisco. He then brought it with him when he relocated to Tombstone in late spring 1882. After a failed attempt to sell his *Almeh* for $350 at Lenoir's furniture shop on Fifth, Vaccari decided to raffle it off.[26] The drawing took place on November 10, 1882, at the Crystal Palace, and the lucky holder of winning ticket number six took it home.[27]

Fast forward to 1906, when long-time Tombstone resident Charles Cummings purchased the Bird Cage. He arrived in Tombstone in 1880 and worked his way up from a young laborer to town mayor and became one of the largest volume lot owners, claiming more than 150 of the town's most historic properties. As he acquired more properties, items dating to Tombstone's past found within them were gathered and stored in the Bird Cage—his most prized property. Among those items was Vaccari's *Almeh* painting. After his death in 1930, Cummings's wife displayed a large part of his collection in a building near Fifth and Allen and opened it for public viewing.[28] Vaccari's *Almeh* was displayed there until being returned to the Bird Cage. For at least twenty years it was displayed in the auditorium, where it was photographed by everyone from tourists and newspaper correspondents to *Life Magazine* and postcard producers. In the early 1950s it was finally

Charles Marcel Vaccari's signature is seen here in the lower right corner of the Bird Cage painting. Author's collection.

The engraving (*left*), published in 1885, shows Harry Humphrey Moore painting in his studio with his original *Almeh* painting, seen in the background. Vaccari's copy of *Almeh* at the Bird Cage is seen on the right. Engraving from *Frank Leslie's Popular Monthly*, May 1885. Modern photo from author's collection.

This 1947 photograph shows *Almeh* hanging in the auditorium, not the front entrance where it is claimed to have hung since the early 1880s. The *Detroit Free Press* published this photograph with a caption indicating the painting once hung in the Oriental, which reflects the changing story assigned to it.

moved to its current position near the entrance, where it was assigned a fictitious identity decades later.[29]

Hanging on the catwalk left of Vaccari's painting are two large lithographs showing the Human Fly and the lady gymnasts claimed to be Bird Cage performers. They depict two young women in matching green performance outfits walking upside down on the ceiling and performing a trapeze act. The story given to tourists is that the lithographs are show bills from the last performance at the Bird Cage before it closed in 1889 in which one of the women fell to her death. (The Bird Cage did not close in 1889.) Yes they are real lithographs, and yes the two women were performers who did such acts, but that's where the truth ends.

The women are Rose and Aimee Austin, two English-born, world-traveling circus and variety theater performers. In early fall 1884 they toured with Cole's Circus, performing in towns along the Southern Pacific Railroad in southeast Arizona. It was fearless 15-year-old Aimee who was the main draw. By the time she arrived in Arizona, she had performed all through Europe and in front of kings, queens, and royalty in Belgium, Austria, Germany,

This 1934 photograph of the Bird Cage interior shows the Human Fly and Lady Gymnasts lithographic posters on either end of the catwalk. They still hang in this location today. Legend insists they are from the last performances in 1889, and that one woman fell to her death. None of those details are true. Original photograph from author's collection.

Hungary, Spain, Russia, and Siberia.[30] But she and her sister never performed for the miners at the Bird Cage.

Headed eastward by train from Tucson, the Austin Sisters and the rest of Cole's Circus stopped for one night in Benson, twenty-six miles north of Tombstone, before moving on to Deming, New Mexico, the next night.[31] Days before arriving in Benson, advance agents covered "every dead wall in town with flaming posters . . . fine lithographs and pamphlets" to advertise the circus's arrival.[32] Bird Cage owner and former customer Charles Cummings recalled after the circus left, "The lithographic work [was] taken by the [Bird Cage] theater manager," who got his hands on two of those left behind and installed them in the Bird Cage "for additional decoration."[33] If Charles's recollections are true, that meant Billy Sprague was responsible for installing them in the Bird Cage in 1884, where they have greeted every visitor since. The Austin sisters did not perform in the Bird Cage, nor did one fall to her death, nor did the Bird Cage close in 1889 as the story suggests. In fact both Rose and Aimee Austin continued to perform into the twentieth century.

Made-up stories explaining the Human Fly lithographs and the *Almeh* "Fatima" painting show exactly how Bird Cage lore has been crafted out of pure imagination and presented as truth. Such stories are damaging to the identity of the Bird Cage and somewhat audacious, considering there're not based on anything truthful.

The common thread among all falsely identified Bird Cage performers is that they include high-profile personalities or highly romantic Old West elements designed to add a level of mystique to the Bird Cage. They were created to fill the void of unknowns under the pretense of truth. Because they've been told so many times, authors, newspapers, and magazines related to western history have given continued life to these tall tales without questioning their background. In reality these false stories are detrimental to the Bird Cage by covering up a significant part of its history. A complete understanding of the Bird Cage can only be achieved by knowing who its performers were. With the overall quality of variety theaters often dictated by the quality of its performers (and the efforts of the owners to seek them out), this element of the Bird Cage has never been revealed. Their backgrounds, refined skills, and personalities add a greatly missed layer of intrigue to the silent sounds that echo throughout the building. Investigating their lives also unlocks colorful details of their performances and provides songs and sheet music actually played at the Bird Cage—thrilling details for truly curious minds. Also missed are the fascinating individual life stories of these people who walked the streets of Tombstone and passed through the front door of the Bird Cage. All of this has been buried beneath a stack of common falsehoods—until now.

Who Were the Bird Cage Performers?

Identifying the Bird Cage performers has been achieved through a variety of resources, including but not limited to local newspapers and entertainment industry journals that reported performer appearances and movements as they happened. Once identified, each individual was examined and researched, revealing their life stories, triumphs, tragedies, failures, successes, family trees, and in some cases their descendants who are alive today. After collecting more than thirty-thousand individual pieces of information on them, the following numbers describe them as a group:

- Total number of performers identified to date: 245[34]
- 44 percent men, 56 percent women
- Average age: 26
- Average length of career: 19 years
- Performers married to one another: 22 percent

Highlights from their life stories describe how diverse and broad reaching they were. Among them was a future US deputy marshal for Arizona Territory, a former Texas League Baseball player, a Fort Huachuca Cavalry deserter, five Civil War veterans, and the inventor of a sport recognized by the International Olympic Committee. One retired in Tombstone and married John O. Dunbar, who was Cochise County Treasurer and a business partner of John Behan. Another relocated to Butte, Montana, and took on one of their most notorious criminals in a knife fight. Four went on to operate the Crystal Palace as a variety theater—complete with elevated boxes and orchestra pit. Three died in Tombstone and are buried there, but only one has a grave marker. One was the stage manager of the theater in Pueblo, Colorado, the night Doc Holliday was confronted by con man Perry Mallon after the vendetta ride with Wyatt Earp.[35] One started a New Jersey yacht club that is still active. Another went on to own "one of the best mining properties in Montana" and one of the most popular theatrical venues in all of New York City by the turn of the century.[36]

Many Bird Cage performers started their careers before the age of 10. One started her career at age 6 and had a New York agent by age 8.[37] The youngestto take the Bird Cage stage was 10. She was sadly also the youngest to die, drowning at age 14. The oldest Bird Cage performer was 57. One performed continuously, with no lapse, from the end of the Civil War until 1923, when he retired at age 83. Another performed continuously until 1933.[38] One lived until 1951. Thirty-three performed up until their deaths. One invented shoes he could walk on water with and successfully walked from the Statue of Liberty to Manhattan, from Oakland to San Francisco, and across the Mississippi, Ohio, and Chicago Rivers. One had a nephew that was a character actor in an episode of the popular television series *The Rifleman*. Two performers had a son that appeared in more than three dozen Laurel and Hardy and Three Stooges films. One starred alongside Buster Keaton and his father, Joe Keaton, in the 1926 blockbuster film *The General*.[39] One acted alongside Charlie Chaplin in several of his early Keystone and Sennett comedies. One performed with Harry Houdini. Sixteen performed at the Palace Theater in Denver while Bat Masterson's owned it. Two performed in Dodge City while Wyatt Earp was there. One was hired by Virgil Earp to perform at his Bijou Theater in San Bernardino, California, in 1886. Four are buried in the same cemetery complex as Wyatt Earp. Many traveled internationally. Collectively they performed in South America, Africa, Australia, New Zealand, Canada, Mexico, Russia, and nearly every country in Europe. Their appearances covered six continents and all fifty states. One even performed for England's King Edward VII and George V.[40]

Their ethnic backgrounds stemmed from France, Chile, England, Australia, and beyond. Many married within the profession and continued to perform until they died. Some led quiet lives hidden behind stage names. Others had run-ins with the law and battled morphine addiction, which plagued many in the entertainment industry. Each and every one of their stories contributes to the legacy of the Bird Cage and provides a better understanding and appreciation for the building itself. They also shed light on the genuine efforts the various Bird Cage proprietors extended to give Tombstone the best performers possible. While their individual stories are dynamically different—sometimes adventurous, heartbreaking, tragic, punishing, and victorious—they all contribute to the true history of the Bird Cage and are all memorialized by the building's existence.

Among them were singers, comedians, actors, songwriters, skit writers, acrobats, strength exhibitors, magicians, and dancers. Every one was expected to perform their "specialty"—a term for the act they were most known for. Specialties varied greatly. Highly touted Charles H. Duncan was brought in to perform his original piano songs. Before digital music downloads, CDs, or records, musical artists wrote and sold sheet music. Duncan's success in that line took him around the globe in a career that yielded "a considerable fortune" by the turn of the century.[41] In early 1883 audiences at the Bird Cage

Charles H. Duncan amassed a small fortune over the course of his career writing comedic and relatable songs, selling sheet music, and performing across the country. He shared his talents with Bird Cage audiences in 1883. *New York Clipper*, September 19, 1903.

were treated to a selection of his songs that featured relatable subjects mixed
with comedic wit. Many were tailored for a male audience. On piano he
performed a song he titled "All on the Quiet," which told the story of a man
courting women in secrecy.[42] In another witty upbeat song titled "I'll Get Rid
of My Mother-in-Law," Duncan formed lyrics that poked fun at the plight of
the married man. The song declared, "Yes, I have had more trouble with that
wife of mine than one mortal can stand. Every time I wish anything done to
suit me, her old woman always sticks in her gab."[43] Male-dominated audiences loved it.

Other specialties included a pedestal clog dance performed by the
husband/wife duo of Billy and Nola Forrest. Billy had formulated the act
in the early 1870s with a male performance partner, but adapted it for his
wife by the time they arrived at the Bird Cage in December 1882.[44] It was so
unique that one newspaper called it "a crowning feature . . . in which they do
what no other [duo] in the world has accomplished."[45] The act included an
acrobatic clog dance on top of two four-foot pedestals with tops that measured just fourteen inches. On those small, elevated platforms they turned a
jolting array of somersaults and dance steps in perfect unison. It was a spectacle that took months of hard and dangerous practice to perfect.[46]

Strongwoman Millie de Granville also offered a specialty act that was
so electric it took her across the continent and abroad to Australia, South
America, and the Caribbean.[47] In an act of pure athleticism and unimaginable strength, she made her "iron jaw" her calling card. She routinely picked
up items that were inconceivably heavy with her mouth and performed
contortions while anchored to a fixed point or hanging on to large objects—
and she made it look effortless. One astonished performance attendee
described it.

[Millie] executes her difficult feats with the greatest ease. She lifts
a common Windsor chain in every conceivable position with the aid
of her teeth alone; lies down and gets up with it, never relinquishing
her hold upon it with her molars, and supporting it in no other way.
She also did a contortion act with the chair in her mouth. She also lifted
a hogshead of water, with a boy twelve years of age seated upon it
several feet from the ground. Her last feat was the most astonishing of

Millie de Granville's unassuming stature made her "iron jaw" act genuinely unbelievable and awe inspiring. Photo dated 1873–1875. Original cabinet card from author's collection.

. all. She raises herself and the boy with her teeth alone, from the stage to the dome of the theater, at least forty feet. This remarkable feat is performed by slipping a rope around the back of her neck, fastening the boy to her, and then with another rope hoisting herself in to mid-air, using her teeth to pull her up instead of the hands. This was perfectly thrilling and astonishing. The audience was electrified, and at last broke forth in cheer after cheer of hearty approval. The lady was repeatedly called back and it was some time before the play could go on.[48]

She was billed as the "female Hercules" and "the woman with the iron jaw" for a reason. In another performance she "closed [her teeth] down on a chair savagely, and, holding it between her teeth, waved it around in a most reckless manner. Not content with this, [she] grasped a barrel of water with her molars and lifted it from the ground on to a chair." An audience member in the performance tent amusingly stated, "We expected to see her take hold of the center pole [of the tent] and walk off with it, but she didn't."[49] Her act was repeated for twenty years in between constant travel and adventure. Through it all she gained international fame and a salary well above the average performer. Tombstone never saw anything like it.[50]

However astonishing they were, Bird Cage performers were required to do far more than just their well-practiced specialties. They had to have the versatility to fill any role dictated by the stage manager on a moment's notice. Decades after the world of variety entertainment had changed, one former Bird Cage performer recalled the versatility required in the old days: "When we played at the honky-tonks we had to act. It made no difference [what] we were playing . . . we had to be there for we never knew what part would be handed us. Whatever the part, that was what we had to play. Those who couldn't play anything that came along were immediately 'canned' on the honkey-tonk circuit."[51]

Performer salaries and bookings were generally made on a weekly basis. A premiere solo performer could draw a salary in upward of $150 a week, with most earning between $20 and $80 a week.[52] Tom Nawn, who appeared at the Bird Cage in 1887, recalled he and his partner made $80 a week.[53] By comparison Tombstone's elementary school teacher made $20 a week in 1886.[54] In 1882 Tombstone's chief of police made $38 a week and the city attorney made $19 a week.[55] Tombstone miners made $3 to $4 a day while most laborers made $1 to $2 a day.

There was money to be made in variety theater circuits as a performer, and some had considerable nest eggs at the end of their careers. Others died penniless. Even for those that achieved financial success, there were hard times along the way. One performer recalled, "In those days [we] didn't have any money . . . and had to live on advances. The only luxury the girls enjoyed occasionally was . . . a personal maid; that is another girl in the company who did slight services like sewing and washing for three or four dollars a week."[56] Another troupe manager remembered taking on performers that were so poor they looked like "poverty-stricken gypsies" and buying them secondhand clothes and shoes to make them presentable.[57] Another performer remembered times when theaters weren't drawing good audiences, and the actors wouldn't get paid at all.[58] Getting paid wasn't always a guarantee. At least five Bird Cage performers engaged in legal disputes over unpaid salaries in their careers.[59] However, many stayed in Tombstone for extended periods, and some made return appearances. This suggests salaries and work conditions were as good or better than other venues. Former Tombstone resident and Bird Cage patron Billy Breakenridge recalled performers under Billy Hutchinson "were attracted first by the adventure, but principally because of the large salaries."[60]

On top of salaries there were additional ways to earn money—and lots of it. Bird Cage performer Annie Ashley remembered how she earned money there.

> My regular salary in the show was $17.50. After the show was over every night, downstairs would be turned into a dance hall. The tables would be cleared away and we girls would come down to entertain. The management charged fifty cents a dance and out of this the girls would get 25 cents apiece. If the men opened champagne we got one dollar on each bottle. On other drinks we got 10 cents on the dollar - our commission. If [patrons] liked the show, they'd sometimes throw us gold. So much that the property man would have to come on the stage with a broom and hat, sweep it up and hand it over to the girl it was thrown to. It was a lot of money. Earning money there then was exciting to say the least.[61]

Drink commissions were a standard among variety theaters, and it often provided considerable additional income. Sale of liquor meant more revenue for the owner, and commissions motivated performers to dispense as much as possible. One journalist in 1884 put it well: "Of the proceeds of their particular sales . . . the girls realize from ten to twenty percent. This together with the price of their charms yields them a considerable income. But to work their man and get the most out of him for the least return, is one of the tricks of the trade and are evidences of skill in the profession."[62] An actress at Denver's highly popular Palace Theater explained the terms of the game blatantly: "When we work at theaters we work on percentages. It is to our interest to have the gentlemen treat us."[63]

As noted earlier in this chapter, females who worked the floor selling alcohol were commonly called rustlers. Decency among rustlers was as broad as variety theaters themselves. Some were virtuous, educated, and self-respecting, while others crossed the line of shameless criminality to meet their financial ends. Flirtatious strategies employed by many of them made it easy for gentle society to label them as prostitutes even if they weren't. One bashful customer recalled an encounter with a Bird Cage rustler. "A dizzy dame . . . seated herself alongside me and playfully threw her arms around my neck [and] coaxingly desired me to 'set me up' [buy drinks]. Hot blood surged through my cheeks [and] I believed I had again returned to my infantile period."[64] Some rustlers were as loose and free as they presented themselves, but in well-run variety theaters that was the exception, not the rule.

Former Bird Cage performer Joe Adams recalled the rustler girls he worked with. "Their occupation was a highly profitable one. A clever singing and dancing girl could draw from $50 to $75 as salary . . . and commissions from wine sales would frequently double that . . . but their morals [were] surprisingly straight."[65] Local laborer and rancher J. C. Hancock was a Bird Cage customer, and he agreed. "Tombstone had the air and personality . . . where everybody had money and demanded the best. The Bird Cage was the principal place of attraction—I speak from actual knowledge—the girls were all good sports. They got a percentage of all the drinks they sold."[66] One female Bird Cage performer who spent forty years onstage recalled,

"[We] remained morally good women . . . upheld responsibilities and took care of [our] families."[67] Career performer Eddie Foy insisted rustlers were better women than most assumed.

> Their profession may not appeal to the reader as having been a very moral one, but I want to say that many of those dance hall girls were personally as straight as a deaconess. Their job was to dance with the men, talk to them, perhaps flirt with them a bit and induce them to buy drinks. If a girl drank with every chap who bought for her, she would have been thoroughly [drunk] and out of commission before the evening was over. I knew a few of these girls who didn't drink at all; but for some such girl a bottle of wine might be sold a thousand times in a year.[68]

One period performer described a method she used to avoid drinking. "While I sat . . . I'd put the bottle in back of me and pour the contents on the floor to drink less and make him buy more. The girls would sometimes order tea in whisky glasses to fool him."[69] Tombstone saloon man Billy King recalled the Bird Cage box rustlers. "They drank champagne with the male patrons . . . [and] took a great deal of pride in their station."[70] Another customer gave a similar account. "Their dresses weren't too short, nor too low cut. You couldn't tell [them] from other women on the street. They were pretty nice girls and several of them married and made as good wives as any gal."[71] In fact Bird Cage performers Emma Budworth and Mabel Deverne did marry respected Tombstone men. *Tombstone Epitaph* editor and local family man C. D. Reppy remembered them. "[They] sang themselves into the hearts of a couple of Arizona's most prominent citizens, and today [1907] they are excellent wives and mothers."[72]

No doubt some young, attractive female rustlers enjoyed prying dollars from the hands of admirers using their charms, looks, and empty promises. One rustler employed by Joe Bignon in Phoenix took money under the pretense that she was sending it to her father in San Francisco. When asked about her swindle she admitted, "I am doing first-rate . . . and find plenty of suckers."[73] Many rustlers knew how to pick out prey and exploit them, even if it meant promising things they had no intention of giving. Employing such strategies could have violent consequences. Male competition and men who felt they

This 1878 lithograph for Harry Hill's New York variety theater features two women rustlers (*top, left and right*). The center vignette shows several women serving male and female patrons during a boxing match with onlookers in elevated boxes. Bird Cage performer Harry K. Morton performed at Harry Hill's the same year as this lithograph. New York Public Library.

were led on encouraged retaliation. In one case a young man in a Los Angeles variety theater bit off a rustler's ear who was reportedly "transferring her affections to another fellow."[74] In San Antonio, Texas, a man the local newspaper reported that a "wild and wooly cowboy with spurs" strutted into a variety theater with a shotgun "and swore he was going to have some gore" after getting the brush-off from a waitress he bought drinks for all night. Luckily he was arrested without incident.[75] Ella Howard, a longtime boomtown performer who crossed paths with many Bird Cage performers, got into an altercation with a customer in Leadville named Robert Gardner. Gardner, who was facing charges for assaulting a man with a knife, threatened to "smash her [and] use a knife" as he had in his assault case.[76] Even worse, actress Effie Moore was shot and killed in a Denver variety theater by 19-year-old Charles Henry after he claimed she made affectionate promises as a means to empty his wallet. The crime was witnessed by several former female Bird Cage performers who attended her funeral days later.[77]

On the other hand, some women loathed selling liquor altogether and did it against their will, out of financial necessity, or simply to keep their jobs. One period performer remembered his wife didn't feel comfortable selling drinks on the floor. As a strategy to avoid it he suggested that she should hang around the dressing room as long as possible. The manager took notice and told him, "I want your wife to hustle more. She must get around." After dodging the task for nearly an entire week, she made only a few dollars in commissions and was fired.[78]

The demands of selling drinks for commissions could complicate relationships and marriages that were already challenged by life on the road and lack of job security. One performer recalled, "Frequently the husbands . . . would be singing or doing a comedy scene while looking on at their wives sitting on the laps of [lovestruck] miners. The girls, alert and mindful of their cues would excuse themselves to the stage, whereupon the miners in adjoining boxes would say: 'look at Brown . . . he's been sitting with an actress.' And the fortunate miner would throw out his chest as if he'd had his way with Diana, goddess of the hunt."[79]

Life spent traveling variety theater circuits had many interesting elements often glossed over by the "cartoonification" of performers in movies, television, and books. It was a reality experienced by all 245 known Bird Cage performers, and it played out nightly inside the building's walls. One thing is certain: the majority were not low-brow performers. They were career entertainers that the proprietors—particularly Billy Hutchinson and Joe Bignon— went to great lengths to recruit. In 1934 *Los Angeles Times* columnist Harry Carr claimed to have been acquainted with one of them. "I know a withered old grandmother who, as a young girl, danced in the Bird Cage Theater in Tombstone and married. She became a heroic sympathetic mother and a grandmother whose advice is sought. But in the bottom of her trunk she keeps one little red dance shoe—worn and scarred and shabby but very dear to her secret heart."[80] He unfortunately omitted her name, but the story brings humanity to performers who are often given no past or future outside of their time onstage.

Butte, Montana, saw more than two dozen Bird Cage performers appear in its numerous variety theaters.[81] The *Butte Miner* newspaper strongly opposed variety theaters and aggressively championed antitheater laws in the late 1880s. However, they still acknowledged the decency of men and women who worked them. "There are bad people in the variety business as in all other walks of life, but there are as honorable men and as virtuous women in that line as are found in any other profession. There are loyal wives and faithful loving and devoted mothers in the ranks of the variety performers who for a 'brief spell' each evening appear to play their parts, and when they have removed the tinsel and the make up, quietly pass into their homes, the peer of any women in the land."[82]

Many communities like Butte battled the variety theater question, wrote laws inhibiting them, and argued over their existence. That trend was intensely prevalent across the country, yet it was not so in Tombstone. Not a single negative stance or action was taken against the Bird Cage in its decade of performances—much to the credit of the performers. It's a significant accomplishment considering Tombstone's various newspapers disagreed on virtually every political and social issue. As one Bird Cage patron noted in 1882, "The house stands peer over any south of San Francisco for elegant, beautiful and accomplished artists."[83] Although there are highly interesting exceptions, that statement certainly holds up after a most thorough examination of their lives. The Bird Cage is a national treasure in part for representing these 245 people and thousands of their industry brethren who have been forgotten in the passage of time and perpetuating myths.

Chapter 12

Post Theater Era
Leading the Charge of Tombstone's Revival

The Bird Cage Theater . . . is one of the most famous buildings now
standing in the Southwest.
—*Los Angeles Times*, January 3, 1926

Its fame has reached from coast to coast. If nothing else is known
about Tombstone, the Bird Cage theater is known.
—*Tombstone Epitaph*, June 7, 1934

After six years of unyielding effort to keep the Bird Cage running (and two years of leasing the Crystal Palace as a variety theater), Joe Bignon had nothing to show for it. In June 1892 he mortgaged everything he and Tillie had—including their furniture, drapes, pillows, rugs, kitchen utensils, and even personal pictures—to gather enough money for a move to Albuquerque, New Mexico.[1] Joe would be back, but his inability to revive the Bird Cage on his return marked a definitive end of its performance era. In ten years of operation, none of its five proprietors saw the kind of financial gains they had hoped for.

Tombstone experienced its toughest years in the 1890s. Owen Wister, author of *The Virginian*, visited Tombstone in 1894 and described its dismal state. "Tombstone is quite the most depressing town I have ever seen. 'The glory is departed' is written on every street and building. Many blocks of buildings stand entirely deserted."[2] This decaying state was reflected in the property value of the Bird Cage, which plummeted from $3,000 to a mere $75 between 1882 and 1900, indicating how dire the community's economy and prospects were.[3] A number of property owners dismantled what would now be considered valuable historic landmarks in an effort to save precious dollars on tax assessments. Other buildings in severe disrepair were deemed public hazards and torn down just the same. Fortunately, financially successful liquor distributors John Sroufe and Hugh McCrum still owned the Bird Cage. Had it not been for their deep pockets (and the financial irresponsibility of Billy Hutchinson that put it in their hands), it too may have been dismantled. But they had no interest in developing the building amid Tombstone's dismal outlook. Selling it was an unlikely proposition, given property values and lack of demand. So it became a distant afterthought among their extensive and profitable business endeavors, and the building sat in decaying silence. However, even before its last performances, events were already in motion that placed the Bird Cage in the very center of Tombstone's second coming.

On April 29, 1889, a seemingly insignificant but amusing article ran on page 2 of the *Kansas City Times* that would impact Tombstone in the coming century. It was penned by a 34-year-old lawyer, Alfred Henry Lewis.[4] Lewis was the son of a carpenter born in Cleveland, Ohio, on January 20, 1853. Out of his humble upbringing, he emerged an intellectual prodigy who was one of the youngest admitted to the bar in Ohio, the first in his class in the bar exam, and became the prosecuting attorney of Cleveland by the time he was 25.[5] In later years he became the editor of *Human Life Magazine* and worked shoulder to shoulder with Bat Masterson during his stint as a writer.

However, Lewis's potential and early success discontented him. After one term in Cleveland he left Ohio for adventures in the West, spending several years in St. Louis, New Mexico, Colorado, Texas, Kansas, and Arizona. Instead of law books and courtrooms, he supported himself as a freighter,

Alfred Henry Lewis's creative writings made the Bird Cage a recognizable icon.
The decades-long success of Wolfville paved the way for twentieth-century
Tombstone tourism, which gave the town a second life. Author's collection.

cowpuncher, and ranch hand. One old-timer recalled Lewis in Dodge City.
"He was a cowboy . . . and his associations were with the cowmen and the
sporting fraternity. He rode the range, bucked the faro banks . . . and danced
in the cowboy dance halls. He was very bright and capable."[6] In later years
Lewis claimed he once lived in Tombstone and worked for one of the newspapers. In his own words, he even insisted he was "a neighbor of the Earp
family."[7] While there's no evidence to directly support that, he was in Arizona
and New Mexico at the time.

After several years of wanderings, Lewis returned to Kansas City and his career in law. In passing moments he humored his friends and acquaintances with tales of his colorful ranch-hand adventures. Newspaperman Jack Nuckles of the *Kansas City Times* found them amusing and encouraged Lewis to put one in writing. His first article, titled "Why Didn't Allison Hang," appeared on April 29, 1889, and it was a sensation.[8] The story was told through a charming main character Lewis called the "old cattleman" whose thick accent and captivating quips gave it a casual campfire story time feel. Positive public response kept Lewis writing. As public acclaim grew, his characters became more developed and their environment more enlivened. It was all set in a southwest border town called Wolfville. Lewis drew from firsthand experiences but continued to look elsewhere for reality-based inspirations. An Arizona rancher, Jim Wolf, provided Lewis with a virtual library of recollections and newspaper clippings that enriched the narratives. Wolf also lived in and around the town of Charleston, which harbored many former legendary Cowboy clansmen nine miles from Tombstone. He recalled one story there.

> On the second day of my arrival [in Charleston], I entered a saloon to get a drink. The faro dealer was having an argument with a customer concerning a bet. The customer went out. The faro dealer sat down at the end of the bar and began to read a newspaper. As I finished my drink, I heard someone outside approaching the doorway to enter. The faro dealer had tilted back his chair and raised his feet to the bar. Suddenly, though sitting in this awkward position, he reached into his belt with his right hand, pulled out a forty-five and dotted the newcomer exactly between the eyes just as that person arrived in front of the open doorway. The dead man was the argumentative customer of only a few minutes before. He had gone to his room for his gun. Without getting out of his chair, the faro dealer calmly went on reading which he had held in his hand as he shot with his right. Past experiences and instinct had told him that that man was coming back ready for trouble. It was simply part of his days work to get in the first shot. The only thing that annoyed him was the smoke from his own gun barrel.[9]

There's little record to directly back up his story, but colorful prose like that makes it is easy to see why Lewis was so drawn to Wolf and why his writings took on such potent flavor. Charleston became a frequently used location in his writings but was referred to as the town of "Red Dog." Wolf's substantial contributions likely resulted in Lewis naming the main town of Wolfville after him. In later years it was speculated that Lewis modeled one of his characters after Wolf as well.[10] Lewis never came out and said it, but Wolfville was modeled directly after Tombstone. It had neighboring towns of Galeyville, Tucson, and Globe. One of the few places in Tombstone named specifically was the "Bird Cage O'pry House," as the old cattleman called it. As far as those around Tombstone were considered, Lewis "drew a vivid and correct picture of the old Bird Cage."[11] Throughout the series it became a recurring location. At times its actors even became side characters.

The popularity of the articles motivated Lewis to consolidate them into a book, which he did in 1897. It was appropriately titled *Wolfville.* After an overwhelmingly positive response, he added five more Wolfville books in the following sixteen years. Several of them featured detailed illustrations from famed artist Frederick Remington. In the last 125 years, continued appeal and demand has resulted in more than two hundred worldwide reprintings of Lewis's various Wolfville books, with many being distributed internationally.[12] Early motion picture giant Vitagraph took notice as well. In 1917 they began producing a series of at least fifteen known films based on Lewis's Wolfville stories and characters. With each additional story and mention of the Bird Cage, it became more obvious Lewis had used Tombstone as a template. The lines of reality became so blurred that some newspapers actually claimed Wolfville businesses, such as the Red Light saloon that Lewis had made up, were real places in Tombstone.[13] People across the country took notice and descended on Tombstone to see where their favorite stories took place.

When they arrived they found a community that still survived on mining. In 1903 the Tombstone Consolidated Mining Company provided the last great surge in mining jobs. That year also brought the long-awaited train service to Tombstone, thus ending the reign of the stagecoach as the primary means of arrival. Quietly in the background, the first signs of Tombstone's future began to emerge: tourism. In following years the automobile industry and auto tourism began to set roots. Over crude dirt roads aided by unsophisticated maps, more and more people found their way to Tombstone, curiously

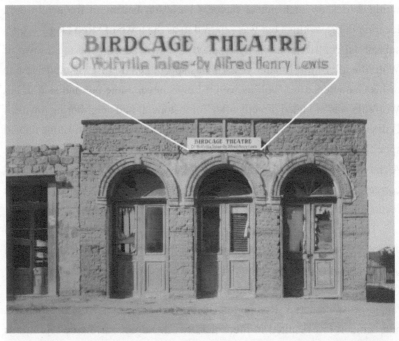

Wolfville brought so many to Tombstone looking for the Bird Cage that a sign was placed on the building on June 6, 1920, to help identify it. As of this writing, that sign is now on display inside the building. Author's collection.

searching for the Bird Cage and the scene of Wolfville's wild stories. As early as 1908 locals recognized the upward trend, declaring, "There would not be another city in the territory that could compare with [Tombstone] in two years."[14] In response to the growing number of visitors and inquiries about the Bird Cage, owner Charles Cummings placed a sign on its facade on June 6, 1920, that read "Birdcage Theatre of Wolfville Tales by Alfred Henry Lewis." The local paper noted the sign on the "famous" theater provided "guidance of tourists and Kodak fans."[15] That original sign, now faded by the last one hundred years, can be seen on display inside the Bird Cage today. In following years, the Tombstone Chamber of Commerce followed the Bird Cage's lead and placed signs at more than a dozen historic locations and points of interest.[16]

Local newspapers routinely reported the presence of visitors and the popular landmarks they came to see, but the Bird Cage was the primary destination. A Phoenix newspaper put it bluntly: "The Bird Cage Theater, which dispensed liquid cheer with its dance and song, is the chief landmark [of] Tombstone."[17] It's hard to imagine now, but many of Tombstone's popular locations today were not yet identified or promoted in the first decades of the 1900s. The OK Corral wasn't a part of popular culture, and the famed gunfight between the Earps, Doc Holliday, and the Clantons and McLaurys hadn't gripped the public's gaze. Tourists visiting in 1908 would have still found the OK Corral operating as a livery and feed stable run by John Montgomery—the same man who owned it the day of the famed gunfight that took place west of its back entrance.[18] No one would have found the OK Corral fascinating anyway, as it wasn't associated with the gunfight until 1927 when the chamber of commerce misidentified it as the location of the gunfight.[19] Initially, visitors stopped to see Schieffelin Monument, the *Epitaph* office, and the Can Can restaurant.[20] But these were incidental landmarks that caught eyes as visitors passed by. The reason they came was the Bird Cage which Lewis exposed the world to in decades of writings.

Wolfville continued to create massive waves of publicity for Tombstone and the Bird Cage for several generations. In 1926, nearly thirty years after Lewis's first book, Tucson's annual rodeo featured a fully reconstructed Wolfville town built by the Tucson Elks. Upon entering, patrons passed through the Wolfville bank and exchanged their money for Wolfville currency redeemable throughout the makeshift town, which included a dance hall, gambling house, saloon, orchestra, news office, jail, and city hall. In recognition of the event, the *Tucson Citizen* also printed its daily edition

Visitors to Tucson Rodeo's Wolfville exchanged their money for Wolfville currency to spend throughout the makeshift town. Wolfville currency from author's collection.

on February 19 as the *Wolfville Citizen*. The inaugural Wolfville in 1926 also featured an operational Bird Cage Theater. The scenery and stage were described as "an actual duplication" of the real thing.[21] Organizers contracted performers for daily entertainment. Among them was a man named George A. Bird (of the Parker Brothers and Frush's Oriental Circus) who was an actual Bird Cage performer hired by Joe Bignon in 1886.[22] It also featured several authentic forty-year-old drop curtains that were used at the Bird Cage and had been saved and donated by Joe. He also donated a punch bowl once used at the Bird Cage for dispensing refreshments to Wolfville visitors, although with prohibition in effect, the drinks were described as being "much weaker than those which formerly excited the [Bird Cage] patrons."[23] Sadly, Joe passed away two months before the event took place, or he may have personally attended.[24] A re-creation of Wolfville continued to be featured during Tucson's rodeo every year until 1934.

Stinging Lizard's grave is seen here (*left*) in Tombstone's Boothill Graveyard, despite being a made-up character from Alfred Henry Lewis's first Wolfville book. In chapter 2 he was stabbed to death (not shot, as the marker suggests) by one of Lewis's main characters, Cherokee Hall, whose illustration (*right*) appeared on page 9 of the book. Author's photograph.

Cody, Wyoming, also jumped on the bandwagon. In 1928 they held a three-day Wild West festival called the Cody Stampede, designed to "bring back the fast-passing characteristics of the old west." Among its many features was a re-created Wolfville town where visitors indulged in "dancing . . . on one of the finest dance floors in the state, [and] where those inclined may roll the little cubes, play the roulette, take a chance at the faro bank, and indulge in any one of a dozen or two old time games of chance."[25] It was all done in the spirit of Lewis's books.

The commercial success of Wolfville paved the way for the explosion of Tombstone-related books, movies, and interest in the decades that followed. In 1922 author Frederick Bechdolt published his highly successful book that featured Tombstone titled *When the West Was Young*. Walter Noble Burns followed in 1927 with *Tombstone: An Iliad of the Southwest*—a book that would be the basis of a major motion picture fifteen years later. Billy Breakenridge, a deputy under Earp adversary Johnny Behan, published his tell-all memoirs titled *Helldorado* in 1928. Even after publication of these successful and influential books, the *Epitaph* still insisted it was Lewis's Wolfville that immortalized the Bird Cage and Tombstone.[26] Evidence of Lewis's influence can still be seen in Tombstone today. A walk around Boothill Graveyard reveals four grave markers for Wolfville characters. One such example is the grave marker of Stinging Lizard, who was killed by Cherokee Hall in chapter two of Lewis's first book. Without knowledge of their origin, these four graves are presented as authentic burials by the city. In reality they are linked to an era in Tombstone history that received an unlikely rebirth thanks in large part to Alfred Henry Lewis and the allure of the Bird Cage promoted in his books. Just as Tombstone's mining economy was coming to a final close, Tombstone embraced early tourists brought by his writings and never looked back.

Chapter 13

From Decaying Building to Western Icon

Cummings, Gardner, Helldorado

> *It is indeed fortunate that today Tombstone can still boast early day*
> *landmarks [that] stand as they did in the early days. Chief among*
> *these is the Bird Cage theater . . . standing as it did when the miners*
> *and cowboys, train robbers and cattle thieves, gamblers and bunco*
> *artists flipped their free-flowing gold at the feet of the highest*
> *priced stage performers that the best theater circuits of the country*
> *could produce.*
> —*Tombstone Epitaph*, February 5, 1922

> *Tombstone is a paradox—a clean, pure, quiet American community which*
> *frowns on wickedness but sells it by the peek in glimpses of the past.*
> —*Richmond* (VA) *Times Dispatch*, April 29, 1941

As time marched into the twentieth century, the West as it once was continued to fade. In 1912 Arizona finally achieved statehood, and within a few short years state officials banned alcohol, prostitution, and gambling.[1] Like cowboy criminals, stagecoach robberies, and Indian attacks, they became things of the past. The harshest realities of life in the

West fell to the wayside, and its most romantic elements became glorified and celebrated. Heroic stories and thrilling western adventures seasoned with drama, vice, and virtue took ahold of the world's interest for much of the twentieth century. While the public became increasingly fascinated by Old West mythology, the Bird Cage itself was slowly decaying. Walter Noble Burns, author of the first book dedicated to Tombstone's story, visited the Bird Cage in the research phase of his book in the mid 1920s and described it as "a building that has died and been embalmed."[2] Passing years took its toll on the fragile adobe walls. Luckily, after changing hands several times, the Bird Cage ended up in the care of one of Tombstone's most proud and unheralded citizens who would save it from a disastrous fate that claimed so many other historic buildings.

John Sroufe and Hugh McCrum maintained ownership of the building through 1902. That year McCrum's life of western traveling and capitalistic adventures came to an end when he died on June 27 at the age of 65.[3] His death resonated in Arizona, especially in Prescott and Tucson, where he had significant holdings and social ties dating back to his years of stagecoaching across the territory.[4] After a bitter divorce from his first wife, he was remarried to Helen Lakeman in 1895—seven years before his death. Thus, his passing put many of his assets in Helen's hands, including the Bird Cage, which she then jointly owned with John Sroufe. Despite Tombstone's plummeting real estate values, they managed to sell the building for $1,000 to Joseph Tasker on February 12, 1903, marking the first time it had been sold since Billy Hutchinson was forced to hand it over twenty years earlier.[5]

Tasker was a local merchant who had been in Tombstone nearly from the beginning. When he bought the Bird Cage, it had been silent for over ten years, with no prospects for breaking that streak. So it was a surprise when he announced that a boxing match and "physical culture contest" (the equivalent to a body-building exhibition) was scheduled there just weeks after he purchased it.[6] If he had plans to host the event at the Bird Cage for profit, it didn't happen. The event was moved to Schieffelin Hall at the last minute for unknown reasons.[7] However, Tasker made a quick $500 profit when he sold the Bird Cage to prominent local rancher Edward Jacklin less than a month

At the turn of the century, the Bird Cage and many other historic structures in Tombstone suffered from years of neglect and the effects of a dying economy. Author's collection.

after buying it.[8] In doing so, he became the first owner or proprietor to walk away with an undisputed profit.

Unlike Tasker, Edward Jacklin held on to the building for several years. There's no record of what he did with it. If he did anything at all, it wasn't significant enough to report in local newspapers. Jacklin owned several other Tombstone properties at the time, and its highly likely it sat idle like many other vacant properties across town. Three years and nine months after buying it, Jacklin sold it to his ranching partner, Charles L. Cummings, in a massive property deal involving thirty-seven lots scattered throughout Tombstone.[9] The sale price of $500 is mixed with other business dealings, giving us no idea what the real value of the building was on its own. Cummings was highly motivated to acquire Tombstone property, and throughout his fifty years as a resident became one of the largest volume lot owners, with more than 150 to his name. They included some of Tombstone's most notable locations, including the OK Corral and its passageway to Fremont Street;

the Gird Block, where the gunfight inquest was held; a part of Schieffelin Hall; the Russ House; and dozens of the most storied lots fronting Allen Street and Fremont Street in the present-day historic district.[10] On December 14, 1906, Charles added the Bird Cage to the list. Unlike many of his other properties, he maintained ownership of it until his death in 1930. His pride in the building stemmed from his early arrival in Tombstone. In a quarter century as owner, he earned a spot on the Mount Rushmore of Bird Cage history for a number of notable reasons.

Charles Cummings is one of Tombstone's unsung legends, with an irresistible rags-to-riches story. He had a major effect on the community and the Bird Cage in the early twentieth century—an effect that resonates to this day. Born in Oxford, New York, in 1855, he arrived in Tombstone in the summer of 1880 a 25-year-old man with just $9.75 in his pocket.[11] Years later he remembered arriving by stagecoach amid "many prospectors, miners and cowboys" and spending his first night at the Cosmopolitan Hotel (where the Earps eventually sought refuge after several attempts to assassinate them).[12] His introduction to the area included a job at the Tombstone Mining and Milling Company just outside the nearby town of Charleston.[13] As a humble laborer he pulled night shifts overlooking the mill's water canal. Quickly he learned to do so without a light because "so many shots were fired from [Charleston] at his lantern" that he became afraid of "being shot by hilarious cowboys."[14]

Out of those modest and dangerous beginnings, Charles found financial stability in Tombstone as an owner/operator of a meat market—a business he continued on and off into the 1920s.[15] He eventually invested in a number of cattle ranches throughout Cochise County where he raised stock that supported his meat market. As he achieved financial success, Charles also climbed the political and social ladder. Through the years he developed a deep love for Tombstone, and he became enthusiastically involved in town matters. In 1910 he helped establish the first chamber of commerce and served as its first secretary.[16] Along with other dedicated citizens, he became instrumental in preserving Tombstone's history and historic assets.[17] In 1911 there was a strong movement to relocate the county seat from Tombstone to Bisbee, which would have been detrimental to the town's already weak

Charles Cummings owned the Bird Cage from 1906 until his death in 1930. He took pride in owning the building he once patronized as a young man in the early 1880s. From *Portrait and Biographical Record of Arizona* (Chicago: Chapman Publishing, 1901).

economy. Charles spearheaded a successful resistance, saving Tombstone from what would have been a heavy blow to its future.[18]

Charles also held a number of high-profile positions at the city, county, and territorial level. He was elected as Tombstone's Third Ward councilman and city treasurer. At the county level he was appointed to the county assembly and as the chairman of the Stock Committee, and served as a deputy under Tombstone's famed photographer C. S. Fly, who was elected county sheriff in 1895.[19] As a businessman Charles tended to his market and ranching business, but he also built and operated an ice house and an electrical plant that provided Tombstone's much-needed utilities. By 1909 he became the president of the First National Bank of Tombstone and served as the vice president of the Border States Oil Company.[20] Charles rose even higher when he was elected to the Eighteenth Territorial Legislature.[21] Socially he was a member of the Tombstone Stags and Odd Fellows.[22] In all he became known as "one of the most esteemed [Tombstone] citizens whose untiring efforts have placed the city on a reliable basis."[23]

It was all capped off when Charles won the election to become Tombstone's mayor in 1920.[24] Unlike most who left during Tombstone's worst years, Charles stuck it out and came out on top. Along with his many positions of power and influence, he owned a large part of the town. Doing so would have been unimaginable when he arrived in 1880. That fact likely added to the thrill of acquiring once highly sought after properties decades later. In 1910 an Arizona newspaper called him the "millionaire banker and butcher."[25] Even if he wasn't a bona fide millionaire, those who knew him humbly insisted he had "amassed considerable wealth."[26] Not bad for a guy who came to Tombstone with $9.75 to his name and dodged bullets working the night shift.

Despite this considerable resume, notices of his death published across the country in 1930 simply stated, "Charles Cummings . . . owner of the Bird Cage Theater, famous during the heyday of [Tombstone's] swashbuckling past, died yesterday."[27] As further evidence of the growing Bird Cage legend, hundreds of newspapers in nearly every state in the country carried the news of Charles's death simply because he owned the building. He may have been okay with that. The Bird Cage was his prized possession, and for decades he eagerly opened it up for curious tourists and dazzled them with his first-person accounts. As a young man he was a customer, partaking in the atmosphere and excitement at the peak of Tombstone's tide. It must have been particularly thrilling to own the building he once patronized.[28] Perhaps in quiet moments alone Charles would sit in the silent auditorium and allow the sights, sounds, and smells of his memory take him back to a time when he and Tombstone were both young.

Most importantly, his love and pride for the building helped ensure steps were taken to properly preserve it. In 1922, after more than thirty years of inactivity, one visitor noted the Bird Cage "is fast going to ruin and in a few more years will be beyond restoration." Recognizing the building's value, many prominent locals felt that "action was necessary" to save it.[29]

Charles Cummings is seen here sitting in a box at the Bird Cage among his growing collection and vivid memories of nights spent there as a young man. Cal Osbon photo postcard from author's collection.

Charles agreed wholeheartedly, and plans were made to restore it "without obliterating its historical value and antique settings."[30]

In 1923 the three-year-old sign Charles had placed above the doors identifying it as the Bird Cage from Alfred Henry Lewis's Wolfville stories was removed, along with the entire adobe facade. Replacing it was a cement-block facade meant to provide indefinite support. At the top of the newly constructed facade "Bird Cage Theatre" was painted in "large black and white" letters, similar to what is seen today. That addition was not meant to reflect its historic appearance. Rather, it was done so that "in the future all pictures of the famous historic building will be properly identified . . . for advertising purposes."[31] Seven months later, the building right next door to the Bird Cage was razed, having been in similar deteriorating condition. Today a section of that building's front wall can be seen clinging to the left side of the Bird Cage. After being deemed a "constant menace to life and limb," that historic Tombstone structure was lost, reinforcing how fortunate it was for the Bird Cage to have fallen into the caring hands of Charles Cummings.[32]

This April 1929 photograph shows the cement-block facade that replaced the original crumbling adobe six years earlier. Upon completion, the sign across the top was added to help identify the building for tourists, not to reflect its historic appearance. A. H. Gardner photo, from author's collection.

Arlington H. Gardner

During his rise in Tombstone's ranks, Charles made a close friend who shared his love for the town's history and its future. His name was Arlington H. Gardner, and he is the father of Tombstone tourism. Unlike Charles, he was a transplant, arriving in Tombstone in 1904. He came from Mississippi, where he had built, owned, and leased several theaters and managed traveling performance companies. That experience earned him the position as booking agent for Schieffelin Hall in 1905.[33] Very quickly Gardner fell in love with southeastern Arizona. In poetic terms he described the impact the area had on him: "It lures one somehow, with its sense of pervading peace; the calm of solitude under the vast vault of azure, bejeweled with stars at night, that is the sky. The sunset and the sunrise are more gorgeous in their colorings than any master's canvas."[34]

Gardner, or "Arlie" as he was called, fell so completely in love with Tombstone and its history that he stayed for thirty-one years. During that

Arlie Gardner on Fifth Street in Tombstone, 1927. Press photograph from author's collection.

time he became the president of the chamber of commerce and championed efforts to preserve and develop Tombstone's historic locations and buildings.[35] In 1927 he pioneered a revolutionary idea to identify and utilize many of the historic landmarks that are must-see locations today. To make them more visible to tourists, he coordinated the placement of diamond-shaped signs indicating their significance.[36]

In February 1927 he had a sign placed at the OK Corral's Fremont Street entrance identifying it as the location of the famous gunfight—a mistake that would have historic implications. The gunfight actually took place seventy-five feet west of the corral entrance, partially in a vacant lot and partially on Fremont Street.[37] Yet this incorrect marker at the corral's back gate remained there for thirty years, where it was visited by writers like Walter Noble Burns, former residents like John Clum, droves of tourists, and movie producers. It was this mistaken sign placement that gave birth to the phrase "gunfight at the OK Corral." The phrase was used in 1946's *My Darling Clementine* and was the title for the 1957 movie *Gunfight at the OK Corral* starring Burt Lancaster and Kirk Douglas. Popular myth states that Hollywood created the phrase because it had a better ring to it than "gunfight in the vacant lot." In reality the gunfight's real location was not known or promoted in the 1940s and '50s when such movies were made. Hollywood latched on to the phrase simply because they were led to believe that it actually happened in the OK Corral. We have Arlie Gardner to thank for that.[38] One has to wonder how the gunfight would be referred to today if Arlie had not misplaced the sign there and promoted the incorrect location.

By virtue of his theater background, Arlie became infatuated with the Bird Cage and for years conducted research about its past. One newspaper journalist who visited with Arlie said he was "thoroughly absorbed with the lore."[39] He chased many leads, communicating with everyone from the state historian in Phoenix to long-time locals like Joe Bignon who was living in nearby Pearce.[40] For years Arlie attempted to compile a roster of performers and even published pleas for help from the public in newspapers.[41] His ultimate goal was to publish "a booklet of the notables who graced the stage in the Bird Cage," but he emerged with mostly names of people who were never in Tombstone. Through foggy and uncertain recollections of those he consulted, nearly all of the 245 performers identified in the research for this book remained unnamed.[42] Arlie also put in more than fifteen years of work into locating Billy and Lottie Hutchinson.[43] Unfortunately, all of his leads were exhausted and provided nothing but dead ends.

This 1931 photograph shows the Fremont Street entrance to the OK Corral and the diamond-shaped sign identifying it as the location of the gunfight. By the time the correct location was identified more than three decades later, writers and movie makers had already latched on to the popular phrase "gunfight at the OK Corral" because they were led to believe it actually happened there. Earp-era Tombstone Mayor John Clum is seen here on his last visit shortly before his death. Author's collection.

While Arlie's efforts to preserve and promote Tombstone were significant, his real impact came as vice president of the Broadway of America Association.[44] The Broadway of America was a 2,800-mile transcontinental road linking New York with San Diego through mostly southern states. In the mid-1920s when it was being connected, automobiles were still relatively new, and the country's roadway infrastructure was undeveloped and crude at best, particularly in the sparsely populated West. The Broadway of America was a massive undertaking, with major economic and social implications for the communities along its route. Arlie was responsible for overseeing the entire stretch from El Paso, Texas, to its end in San Diego.[45] The road was planned to pass through southern Arizona, but it was Arlie who made sure not only that it went through Cochise County but also that it went right down Tombstone's Allen Street and past the Bird Cage. Even as early as 1908 cars were becoming prevalent in the area. The local newspaper observed, "Automobiles are becoming so thick in

Tombstone that one has to step lively to get across the streets nowadays without being run over."[46] The Broadway of America increased that exponentially. It was a major factor in Tombstone's survival as it transitioned to a tourist town in the post–Lewis Wolfville era.

Because of Arlie, Tombstone tapped into the heartbeat of the nation's growing auto tourism craze. Traveling by car was a novelty, and in the 1920s and '30s it caught on in a big way. Many cities had auto clubs and formal auto associations that published papers and magazines.[47] Newspapers across the country catered to the growing trend and published separate automobile sections. These publications were prime advertising space for automobile dealers, services and lodging for travelers, and emerging tourist destinations like Tombstone. Arlie made sure Tombstone was getting its share of the exposure. He was featured in a multipage spotlight on Tombstone's historic landmarks on the front page of the *Los Angeles Times* "Automobile" section in 1927.[48] He eventually became Arizona's highway publicist and a member of Cochise County's Highway Commission.[49] In those roles he was relentless in authoring countless articles promoting Tombstone's attractions as well as the favorable climate and road conditions that appealed to road-weary travelers. His passion for Tombstone was undeniable, and his influence over the town's welfare is immeasurable.

At the same time, books, radio, and movies featuring Tombstone flooded the market and further motivated travelers. What started with Alfred Henry Lewis decades prior grew to unprecedented levels. In the late 1920s, Tombstone got another boost when a lengthy hearing over the significant estate of famed actress Lotta Crabtree made national headlines. Much of the deposition involved details related to early Tombstone. Wyatt Earp himself testified and was asked briefly about the Bird Cage.[50] By virtue of Lotta's fame and the considerable money at stake, newspapers across the country flooded columns with what equated to free advertising for Tombstone.

As the flow of visitors increased, weekly reports tabulating tourism numbers were published in the *Epitaph*.[51] Raw numbers aside, it was obvious to locals that more people were visiting. The *Epitaph* reported on the trend: "America has made up its mind to visit Tombstone. Every month [it] sees more and more tourists and eastern visitors in the larger towns of Arizona asking for proper accommodations in Tombstone so that they can spend from two days to a month visiting these historic landmarks."[52]

Every one of those travelers passed the Bird Cage on the Broadway of America. For many it was an irresistible building unlike any other on the 2,800-mile route. The fact that it was sealed up and cloaked in an aged patina made curious visitors even more interested to know its story and what it looked like inside. Very often they would stop and cup their eyes against the dusty front windows, hoping to get a glance of something interesting. Some property owners may have considered this an annoyance, but Charles Cummings loved it. With pride and enthusiasm he often appeared on the scene to greet people and invite them in for a tour of the building. The *Epitaph* commented on this well-known part of his reputation: "Never is Mr. Cummings too busy to show his Bird Cage theater or his wonderful collection [inside] to any one and every one who is interested. Always he greets them with that whimsical smile that seems to be mirroring thoughts of the days when the Bird Cage theatre was entertaining the rough and ready men of the west. Any time of the day he will unlock his theater . . . and stand stolidly by while the 'tenderfoots' ask inane questions about this or that mark upon the old theater's walls."[53]

Private tours became a routine for Charles, who relished the opportunity to showcase his treasured building and colorful memories. Lucky tourists got to hear enthusiastic stories from the man who lived them, punctuated by engaging winks and puffs of smoke from his pipe. In one week alone he gave fifty tours.[54] Never once did he charge people to come inside. In 1926 he even allowed a local US Army officer to get married in the auditorium.[55] As demand increased, the *Epitaph* reported on the overwhelming interest to see the inside: "All want to see the Bird Cage Theater. If requests to see the interior continue, C. L. Cummings, the owner, will have to stay on the job or place a keeper in charge. People from all over the Union are eager to get a look at this historical building, the interior of which is the Mecca of those who have read 'When the West Was Young' of Bechdolt and 'Wolfville' of Lewis."[56]

Never needing an excuse to be involved with the Bird Cage, Arlie Gardner started accompanying tours and leading them himself.[57] In 1929 he

Thousands of tourists took photographs with the Bird Cage as they crossed the country on the Broadway of America. These examples are not unlike those that visitors continue to take today. Photographs date from 1924 to 1932. Author's collection.

gave a tour to two young blonde flappers road-tripping to Hollywood along the Broadway of America. Arlie couldn't resist asking them how they liked the route. One favorably replied, "It's the berries!"[58] On tours Arlie often repeated Charles's best stories. The most popular one involved Frank Leslie shooting the heel of man's boot heel as he dangled it out from one of the boxes. Charles identified local man Dave Adams as an eyewitness.[59] In 1929 Adams gave his account:

> Frank Leslie and myself were attending a performance at the Bird Cage Opera House one evening when, during an intermission, Leslie took exception to a man across the hall who was hanging one leg over the banister. Leslie hollered at the man to take his leg in and when he failed

to comply within a reasonable time [he] pulled his gun and shot close enough to the man's foot to make him fall over backward in haste to get that leg back where it belonged. Everyone thought there was going to be a shooting scrape, but when nothing happened we lost interest and waited for the show to go on.[60]

In an interview eight years later, former Tombstone barber Emil Marks corroborated the story.[61] The exact scene was reproduced in the 1931 film *The Cisco Kid*. Locals insisted it was inspired by Charles's story, which he had told to countless tourists over several decades.[62]

Along with Charles's stories and the usual question-and-answer sessions that followed, visitors inside the Bird Cage found themselves surrounded by a litany of items related to Tombstone's past. As Charles acquired properties, he collected and stored many items of historical value inside the Bird Cage. But he collected other items as well. For several decades he sought out Native American baskets. The collection was called "the most complete to be found in Arizona . . . representing years of patient collecting at a great expense." Several baskets were acquired from the San Carlos reservation.[63] In 1908 he acquired the entire law library of Allen English, one of Tombstone's famed lawyers who arrived in 1880. He was the same Allen English who gave the glowing graveside eulogy when former Bird Cage proprietor Frank Broad died in 1895.[64] English's collection included legal books, office furniture, and a mountain of local court case records.[65] In 1912 Charles bought a notable restaurant on Allen between Fourth and Fifth called it the American Kitchen, from its owners Ah Lum and Ah Sing. Along with the property, he acquired all of the contents that dated back many years in Tombstone.[66] Charles also acquired many items from John Montgomery, the man who owned the OK Corral from its inception until his death in 1909.[67] All of these items were added to the contents of the Bird Cage, which already included a number of items left behind by Joe Bignon in the early 1890s.

In later years the collection also included valuable firearms such as the rifle of local pioneer A. M. Gideon, early photographs of Tombstone owned by local lawyer Thomas Mitchell, a saddle alleged to be owned by 1884 lynch mob victim John Heath, several large oil paintings that hung in early Tombstone saloons, and a number of pianos, one of which came directly

This early twentieth-century photograph is one of the earliest known of the theater's interior. It shows Charles Cummings's collection in the auditorium and on the stage as it appeared when he led tours through the building. Many of these items are still found inside today. Cal Osbon photograph, from author's collection.

from an old Allen Street business.[68] The collection was massive. Packed inside the Bird Cage, it barely left room for tourists to make their way through the building. Even Charles admitted he "would find stuff in there that he had stored away and forgotten [about]."[69] But the stories behind the items remained fresh in memory. After Charles passed in 1930, his widow, Margaret, honored his collecting legacy and moved a large number of items to a building at Fifth and Allen for public display. It was called the Cummings Curio Shoppe and was advertised as a museum of Tombstone's past.[70] Today many of these items fill the auditorium just as they did when Charles welcomed strangers in more than a hundred years ago.

One of the more unusual items was a miniature mummified mermaid. This handmade novelty, acquired by Charles in 1910, was displayed in the front window of his butcher shop, where it "attracted much attention from passing pedestrians."[71] Charles kept it until his death for unknown reasons. He might be happy to know it is still on display inside the Bird Cage, where it continues to grab people's attention. Along with hundreds of other items, the mermaid overlooks the auditorium where Charles's pipe smoke and colorful stories flowed as freely as music, liquor, and laughter decades earlier.

Helldorado: Tombstone's Fiftieth-Anniversary Celebration

As Tombstone embraced its popularity with tourists and readers abroad, many of the same citizens that were actively preserving local history came together to organize a celebration of the town's past. The festivities were scheduled for four days starting October 24, 1929—fifty years after Tombstone's incorporation. They called it Helldorado. One of the consultants was George Pound, the same man who successfully orchestrated the re-creation of Alfred Henry Lewis's Wolfville town and the Bird Cage replica at the Tucson rodeo in 1926.[72] The goal was to revive Tombstone as it was in the early 1880s and to bring many elements from the period back to life.

The planning committee jammed the event schedule with stagecoach robberies using an authentic stagecoach, full band concerts, outdoor aerialists, boxing and wrestling matches, and a grand parade. Helldorado also marked the first time the gunfight near the OK Corral was reenacted. Although John Clum, former Tombstone mayor, editor of the *Epitaph*, and champion of the

Earps disliked the reenactment and called it a "deplorable number of the Helldorado program . . . which could well have been omitted," he later wrote, "I have always [disliked] the sort of publicity that emphasizes and exaggerates the worst features of the life of any community at any period. Disorder and lawlessness and murder were not the chief occupations of the citizens of Tombstone when I was a resident there in the early 80s—although that impression was emphatically conveyed in the Helldorado program. That is not fair simply because it is not true."[73]

Following Arlie Gardner's misplaced sign installed two years earlier, the reenactment took place in the incorrect location near the back entrance of the corral. The reenactment helped solidify the belief that the gunfight happened in the OK Corral for many authors and filmmakers in the years that followed.

In addition to the itinerary, the committee commissioned a Tucson artist to transform Allen Street into its 1881 appearance using historic photography as reference.[74] In the spirit of the event, many visitors attended in full period costume. Many were former citizens that were located and invited by a special committee. Helldorado organizer and *Epitaph* editor William H. Kelly estimated there were "several hundred former citizens of Tombstone, some of them old-timers who have not visited here for nearly fifty years . . . who made history in Tombstone during the early days."[75]

As part of the preparations, a city of five hundred tents was constructed on the outskirts of town "to solve the housing problem during the celebration."[76] Not unlike the tent city that formed at Tombstone's inception, it added an ironic and unintentional element of authenticity.

The crowning event of Helldorado was the reopening of the Bird Cage, which was enthusiastically offered by Charles Cummings. For the first time since the rumors of being opened as the Olympic in December 1891, it was formally opened to the public. Better than that, it was scheduled to host professional performances. Helldorado organizer William H. Kelly wrote about the plans for reopening the Bird Cage with many details that sounded as though they were straight from Charles Cummings's memories.

> The doors of the Bird Cage Opera House, locked for more than forty years, will swing open to a crowded Allen street. The old time variety performers and dance hall girls will make lively this sole remaining

The east entrance of the inaugural Helldorado was located right in front of the Bird Cage. Author's collection.

> honkey tonk of the old west. The old dumb waiter from the bar on the first floor to the boxes above will once more rattle with the load of drinks [and then] sold by the percentage girls. In the small hours of the morning when the last performer has finished his act the benches on the main floor will be shoved aside and as was the custom fifty years ago, the night will end in an old time dance.[77]

Preparations for performances began on September 18, 1929, when Charles began transforming the Bird Cage. His entire warehouse of collections was removed and improvements were put on to accommodate what was anticipated to be very large crowds. Several out-of-state newspapers got ahold of information that authentic former Bird Cage performer Annie Duncan had agreed to appear onstage twice a day throughout the festival. Annie was in fact a decided favorite when she appeared at the Bird Cage for seven months in 1882. However, she would have been hard-pressed to perform at Helldorado considering she had died in a tragic home fire accident in 1902.[78] While Annie could not appear, the Helldorado planners were very serious about booking professional entertainment that reflected the period.

On October 8, 1929, organizer Kelly began communicating with notable Los Angeles theatrical producers Fanchon and Marco. From their wide array of talent, a group of performers was selected, and the terms of their contracts were negotiated via Western Union telegraph. Four days later fifteen performers were booked. They included a "girl show," comedian, pianist, comedy song-and-dance team, and medicine show headlined by Willard Beeson. A Fanchon and Marco representative described Beeson to Helldorado's committee: "Beeson is an old experienced Medicine Show man and sure looks the part—frock coat and stove pipe hat and a very convincing manner. I am giving you the very best we have for the entertainment of this Medicine Show."[79] In all, $1,115 (or roughly 18 percent of the entire Helldorado budget) was spent to secure performers.[80]

The last three days of Helldorado featured three Bird Cage performances between 3:00 and 9:00 p.m. The show was an undeniable hit. Former mayor and *Epitaph* editor John Clum recalled its success: "The famous old Bird Cage Theater proved to be one of the 'best sellers' within the Helldorado area. In fact, at the first show the full capacity of the house was sold out within ten minutes." Clum also recalled being lured into some of the show's antics. "Mayor Krebs honored my party with seats in the royal box overlooking the footlights—where I was able to indulge in a bit of wide-open flirtation with a fascinating flapper jig-dancer, much to her amusement—as well as that of the audience. That was my wooly-wildest Helldorado stunt."[81]

Success of Bird Cage performances at the inaugural Helldorado in 1929 was repeated in 1930. To promote the event, Tombstone's Mayor Ray Krebs hit the radio airwaves in Philadelphia. He told listeners, "The famous Bird Cage theatre, around which Alfred Henry Lewis wrote his Wolfville Tales is [to be] opened. This theatre has been preserved and is exactly as it was fifty years ago when . . . noted actors of the day played there."[82] A surviving Bird Cage program for 1930's Helldorado notes the Holt Repertory Company's presentation of "Ten Nights in a Barroom," a relatively common production in nineteenth-century variety theaters that was based on Timothy Shay Arthur's 1854 novel of the same name.[83] Among the actors was Cal Cohn, a man advertised as a Bird Cage performer fifty years prior for Billy Hutchinson.[84]

Sadly, 1930's Helldorado was the last for Charles Cummings. A month later he passed away after having been "in poor health for at least ten

Charles Cummings (*left*) and his wife are buried near the front entrance of the Tombstone Cemetery just a few steps away from Bird Cage proprietors Frank Broad and Oliver Trevillian, and longtime stage manager and performer Charles A. Keene. Cummings photo courtesy Gary McLelland. Headstone photo by author.

years."[85] Glowing local obituaries extolled his contributions to Tombstone, his dedication to the community, and his love of the Bird Cage. In nearly every state across the country his death was reported simply because he owned the famous landmark. Honoring Charles's love for the Bird Cage and joy of sharing it with the public, his widow, Margaret, continued to allow organizers to use it for the 1931 and 1932 Helldorado programs. In 1931 the *Epitaph* was excited about the news and reported, "Again the Birdcage Theatre, immortalized by Alfred Henry Lewis in his 'Wolfville' stories, will ring with laughter as in the old days with appropriate entertainment."[86] In 1932 admission was set at 40¢, exactly 10¢ less than Billy Hutchinson charged the day it opened.

Without Charles, the Bird Cage may have been razed just like the neighboring building was in 1924. That seems all but confirmed when other important buildings like the Gird Block (which hosted the court hearing after the gunfight near the OK Corral), the original Epitaph building, Ritchie's Hall (rebuilt in 1882), and many others were all torn down by the 1940s. But thanks to Charles, the Bird Cage remained. Even in bad health, he anxiously opened it up to many wide-eyed strangers and treated them to a private tour and first-person stories. Through shared passion he created a unique friendship with Arlington Gardner, whose love for the Bird Cage brought Broadway of America and hundreds of thousands of tourists to Tombstone for decades after his death. Without Charles and Arlie, Tombstone and the Bird Cage may have had a very different outcome. Their legacies are memorialized by the building's existence where their spirits mingle with those of its performers, rowdy patrons, and dedicated owners of yore. While he took many stories to the grave, one thing is certain: if you're intrigued by the Bird Cage, you would have had an instant friend in Charles Cummings.

Chapter 14

Coffee Shoppe and Beyond

Again the order changeth. The doors of the Bird Cage are to remain
open and the old building which has witnessed cowboys and miners
crazed by sudden wealth or disappointment . . . will continue to be a
Mecca for those who [want to] see something of the past Tombstone.
—*Tombstone Epitaph*, June 7, 1934

Whatever fascination the world had in Tombstone's growing legend, Helldorado took it to another level. Thrilling western events like gunfights and stagecoach robberies only read about in books and seen in films were reenacted in the flesh and promoted in headlines across the country. Such exposure helped make the town a symbol of America's Wild West, and interest grew exponentially. Editors were eager to tell readers about the Bird Cage, which several eastern newspapers called a "bright and shining haven for dusty, dry-throated prospectors from all of Arizona."[1] The Bird Cage continued to see the lion's share of the interest and visitors. The *Epitaph* put it into perspective: "Since 1929 the little theater often called the most colorful building of its kind in the Southwest has been visited by literally thousands of tourists. It's fame has reached from coast to coast. American millionaires,

English playwrights and actors, American screen idols, world travelers, and just folks from all states of the Union and many foreign countries have been guided through the building and told its fascinating history usually by Tombstone's genial secretary of the chamber of commerce."[2]

That "genial secretary of the chamber of commerce" was of course Arlie Gardner, who continued personal tours after Charles Cummings's death in 1930. It wasn't long before Tombstone's local economy and culture shifted to take advantage of the increasing number of visitors. Many business owners were eager to adapt, much like the pioneers that built Tombstone during its boom fifty years prior. Services and amenities that catered to tourists sprang up on Allen Street, which favorably fronted the Broadway of America. The Bird Cage corner became a hotspot when the official highway was rerouted to turn right past it onto Sixth Street. At the same time, an early tourist campground was built across Sixth Street "on account of the desire for tourists to camp closer to the business part of town."[3] More than a few campers walked across the street to gaze through the Bird Cage's front windows with wonder. As a number of such businesses along Allen opened, the Bird Cage was poised to do the same.

Charles Cummings's widow, Margaret, honored her husband by continuing to offer the Bird Cage for Helldorado performances after his death. As dictated by Charles's will, she took on 134 of Tombstone's most historic properties, which made her an influential figure in the community.[4] She also remained well-connected in Tombstone's social scene. Among her friends was Nettie Lavalley. Nettie was a Michigan native born sixteen days after the infamous gunfight near the OK Corral.[5] Her life was turned upside down at the age of fifty when she divorced her first husband of twenty-eight years, with whom she had four children. She remarried Joe Lavalley, a former accountant for the Ford Motor Company, and together they moved to Tombstone in 1932, where they immediately "made a good impression on the people who [were] fortunate to become acquainted with them."[6]

The Lavalleys immediately became immersed in Tombstone's social and business scene. They took over the San Jose House hotel—a historic original building dating to the Earp era that still stands on Fifth and Fremont.[7] Joe began a hardware and lumber store, leased several area mines, was involved with the annual rodeo that replaced Helldorado in 1933, helped incorporate a local sanitarium, became treasurer of the Congregational church, and even ran for town council.[8] Along with running the San Jose House, Nettie became heavily involved in social groups comprised of many of Tombstone's prominent wives, such as Mrs. Walter Cole, the wife of the editor of the *Tombstone Epitaph*, and Margaret Cummings.[9] As a passionate seamstress, she started her own sewing club and displayed her work with the local women's club.[10] As a churchgoer she became chairman of the Sunday school committee.[11]

A strong friendship between Nettie and Margaret Cummings grew as their involvement in mutual organizations deepened. In the comfort of their friendship, Margaret pitched an idea for opening the Bird Cage to Nettie. Margaret wanted to take advantage of Tombstone's increasing tourism and leverage the building's charm by opening a limited menu restaurant and refreshment bar. Nettie agreed to be a part of the enterprise. They called it the Bird Cage Coffee Shoppe. In late spring 1934 they began a series of renovations and upgrades meant to "prolong [the building's] life [and] make it of service to the present generation."[12] Some of these changes ensured long-term preservation of the building, which it still benefits from today, such as underpinning of supporting walls, replastering of exterior and interior surfaces, and cosmetic restorations.[13] The small building that extends off the east wall today was added as part of the renovations. It served as a kitchen to prepare all menu items.

The present-day entrance was turned into a refreshment foyer, which the *Epitaph* noted as being "redecorated and slightly remodeled for a coffee shop, modern in appointments."[14] The prominent bar that stands in the entrance today was reinstalled after having been removed decades earlier.[15] Curtains and lampshades with southwest motifs accented the seating area. Tables were set with silverware modeled after period designs paired with pastel china. All of it was appropriately tied together with a collection of bird cages. In the auditorium the boxes were reinforced and fitted up with balcony tables for food service. This prompted the use of the dumbwaiter to hoist orders to the balconies just as it had fifty years prior. Conveniently located outside the kitchen door, it was a real working relic from the theater's operational era said to have "lifted countless brimming glasses." It can still

Charles Cummings's widow, Margaret (*left*), and Nettie Lavalley (*right*) conceived and executed the plan to establish the Bird Cage Coffee Shoppe in 1934. Ancestry.com.

be seen in the exact same place next to the bar today. All of the renovation work was done in a manner that would not "mar the spirit of the theater nor prevent visitors from seeing it as it has been for the past fifty years."[16] Much of it was completed by Nettie's husband, who not only had extensive home remodeling experience but also was a licensed building contractor.[17] The renovations also marked the first time the Bird Cage was connected by telephone, reachable at phone number 20.[18]

Upon completion, the renovations pleased Margaret. "I am glad my idea has been worked out so faithfully by Mr. and Mrs. Lavalley," she said.[19] Nettie not only helped with the renovations, but she also agreed to run the business as the hostess. With overwhelming local support through her deep network of friends, anticipation grew and "many reservations [were] received for the opening night."[20] The day arrived on June 9, 1934—fifty-two years, five months, and seventeen days after Billy Hutchinson threw the doors open for the first time. Locals and visitors alike crowded the theater and

Exterior renovations included bold signage and the small addition extending off the left side of the building that served as the Coffee Shoppe kitchen. On the interior, the bar was installed in its present-day location and the balconies were reinforced for table service. Library of Congress and author's collection.

felt "honored . . . to make history as the old building entered a new era."[21] Recognizing the significance of the moment and showing further support from local friends, the *Epitaph* printed a full-page card congratulating Tombstone for the long-awaited reopening of the Bird Cage.[22]

This full-page ad in the *Epitaph* boldly announced the grand opening of the Bird Cage Coffee Shoppe on June 9, 1934. Original in author's collection.

The successful opening was followed by a great run of sustained business. Nettie arranged service that included breakfast until 10:00, lunch until 2:00 p.m., and dinner until 8:00 p.m.[23] The menu included hot and cold drinks such as coffee, malted milk, Ovaltine, Coca-Cola, lemonade, iced tea, and more. Customers could order an array of sandwiches, salads, and whole line of breakfast items. As for the coffee, the *El Paso Times* claimed it was "just as good as the wine they used to serve years ago."[24] Alongside food and drink options, the history of the Bird Cage was printed on the menu with a greeting that set the tone of the experience: "Welcome to one of the most colorful buildings of the Great Southwest. This famous building retains all of the romance and historical environment that enveloped it in the early eighties and that is saying much for it was opened as a saloon and variety playhouse. What greater pleasure could one desire than dining in this shrine of yesteryear where the ancient and hoary walls cry aloud with their history and the romance of a past that is here being preserved to future generations!"[25]

In addition to daily food service, Nettie also booked numerous banquets in the auditorium. One such event was hosted by the wife of Jeff Milton—another one of Tombstone's legendary lawmen.[26] With an eye for local goodwill, Nettie also offered tray service to locals who were sick and in need.[27] The Hutchinsons would have approved of the charitable act.

While all was well with the Bird Cage Coffee Shoppe, not all was well with Nettie. Most of her time in Tombstone was plagued with health problems. They even kept her from being present for the Coffee Shoppe's grand opening. After "planning and working for many weeks," she woke up on opening day unable to get out of bed and remained there "for several days."[28] Many of her supportive friends stepped up and helped make the opening a success in her absence.[29] Over several months her health worsened. In the spring of 1935 she was forced to relinquish management of the Bird Cage to make way for surgery and treatment.[30]

To keep the Coffee Shoppe success going, she subleased it to two likable locals, Georgia Ledford and Jeanne Ratzloff, on March, 29, 1935.[31] Jeanne was a 25-year-old nursing school graduate from Michigan who found work with Tombstone's Dr. W. D. Gilmore.[32] Georgia was a 63-year-old widow who had recently moved to Tombstone from nearby Fairbank and reestablished herself as an apartment landlord.[33] The two women arrived in Tombstone under very different circumstances and at very different ages, but they became great friends and roommates bound by the mutual goal of getting ahead and advancing their lives.[34] While maintaining their prior occupations, the duo successfully carried on the Bird Cage Coffee Shoppe

The original Bird Cage Coffee Shoppe breakfast and lunch menu.
Author's collection.

business. But plans changed just five months into their joint venture when
Jeanne was offered an advanced position at Tucson's Southern Pacific
Hospital. With the partnership broken, the very likable Georgia also said
good-bye to Tombstone and moved in with her daughter in nearby Bisbee,
leaving behind "a host of friends that miss[ed] her."[35]

With the lease still ultimately on the shoulders of Nettie Lavalley, she
found another worthy successor, Margaret Ewing. Margaret, the wife of a
local power plant employee, was in her late 20s, personable, and ambitious.[36]
She not only took over the lease of the Coffee Shoppe but also experienced
continued success with it into the next decade, THOUGH the Coffee Shoppe
may have taken a different course if Margaret had her way. Just months after
assuming management, she gave an interview revealing her grandiose plans
to actually revive the Bird Cage as a performance venue.

> We're going to see if we can't make a go of it in the Fall. There is no
> drama around here. People would like to see plays. We might even get

people from as far as Albuquerque. Motor travel is easy down here. The roads are good. A 100 mile drive is nothing at all. Tombstone is well known, and so is the theater, but we'd have to do a lot of advertising. And we will do that if we can get started. We've talked to some Hollywood people. A professional group would be better than a local group. Possibly we might interest somebody in New York in bringing out a company. Anyway we hope to restore the theater to the Bird Cage in the fall.[37]

While the revival plans never materialized, she did draw in one of the Coffee Shoppe's most famous customers. The February 6, 1936, *Tombstone Epitaph* made the announcement under the heading "Amelia Earhart Putnam, famous aviatrix here":

One of the most interesting and distinguished visitors yet to honor the Bird Cage museum and Coffee Shoppe stopped there last Friday in the person of Amelia Earhart Putnam, wife of George Palmer Putnam, New York publisher. Miss Earhart was en route to Tucson where she was engaged to lecture. In the party were, also, Mr. Putnam and Mrs. Noyes, widow of a formerly nationally known flier who was recently killed in a crash. The noted party visited here for a brief time without making their identity known, but they were recognized when preparing to make their departure.

It is recalled that on May 20, 1932, the fifth anniversary of Lindbergh's pioneer adventure Miss Earhart flew the Atlantic from Newfoundland to Ireland. Thus she became the first woman to have flown the Atlantic solo, just as she was the first woman to fly the Atlantic as a passenger. She set a speed record between the two continents and a new distance record for women. Also she became the second person to have crossed the Atlantic by air alone. Miss Earhart is vice-president of the National Aeronautical Association and has been prominently identified with many aviation activities.

Following her flight to Ireland, Miss Earhart was accorded enthusiastic receptions at home and abroad. She received honors from England, France, Italy and Belgium. In Rome she was received by Mussolini; in Brussels by the King and Queen of Belgium. In the United States she was accorded the gold medal of the National Geographic society, and the president by special resolution of Congress bestowed upon her the Distinguished Flying Cross, the first woman to be so honored.

Amelia Earhart visited the Bird Cage Coffee Shoppe in February 1936, sixteen months before she went missing on an attempt to fly around the world. Underwood & Underwood, public domain.

It wasn't the first time Amelia Earhart had been in southeastern Arizona. Eight years prior she landed at the McNeal airport twenty-five miles east of Tombstone. Locals who had the pleasure of speaking with her said she was "a very interesting and likable woman."[38] Just sixteen months after her visit to the Bird Cage, Amelia disappeared between Australia and Hawaii on an attempt to fly around the world. Her many accomplishments coupled with her tragic disappearance have since galvanized her legacy.

Back in Tombstone, the Coffee Shoppe experienced its best success yet as tourism continued to grow stronger by the year. While Margaret Ewing continued the prosperous run of business, the Bird Cage family said good-bye a member of their own. Nettie Lavalley, the woman who helped start it all, passed away on January 16, 1937. Her difficult battle with colitis came to an end after an unsuccessful operation.[39] She was only 55 years old. Even in illness Nettie proved to be the driving force behind the Coffee Shoppe, and her loss was irreplaceable. In September 1941 there was more change in the air. Margaret Ewing decided to leave the Bird Cage Coffee Shoppe when her husband accepted a job offer at a power plant in California.[40] In doing so she ended her six-year run of successful operation. With Nettie gone, Margaret Cummings was unable to find a suitable successor, and the Coffee Shoppe era was over. However, unlike its theater era, it didn't end for want of patronage, economic downturn, or "dull times," as Billy Hutchinson and Joe Bignon both put it. It ran for seven years and three months, which measures just shy of its ten years as a variety theater. All indicators suggest it was financially better to its proprietors during the Coffee Shoppe years than it was as a theater. While the Coffee Shoppe era was over, the Bird Cage itself carried on.

The future of the Bird Cage was hinted at years earlier. Even as the earliest tourist trickled into Tombstone, the value of the Bird Cage was recognized: "This famous relic of tombstone's early days should be converted into a museum, housing the many available exhibits of the days of gold . . . and like the Alamo of San Antonio, Texas, should be for tourists to see and snapshot to their heart's content. It can be made in to a museum that will stand as an everlasting monument to the memory of the time when blood and gold were valued at naught. It is the logical disposition and future of the Bird Cage."[41] Nine years later a Tucson newspaper agreed. "This historic [theater] should be cleaned up, made into a museum, open to the public. It is too valuable a national asset to let fall in decay and its present condition suggests a fire trap."[42]

Margaret Cummings made that vision a reality and reopened the Bird Cage as a tourist museum on October 1, 1941, and lived to see it appreciated.[43] As a nod to Charles, Margaret distributed booklets in the Bird Cage describing its past. The inside cover concisely conveyed her motive. "Presented by Mrs. C. L. Cummings in memory of her husband." In Charles's spirit she also made it known that "[the Bird Cage] will house many of the curios of the famous C. L. Cummings' collection and it will at the same time offer hospitality to all who enter its doors."[44] In the auditorium where the Coffee Shoppe banquets were held and wild cheers for performances bellowed half a century earlier, Margaret reinstalled a litany of Charles's prized collections. They remained that way until her death in 1951, and they continue to grace the theater's interior to this day alongside the echoes of performers and patrons of long ago. Every person who has passed through its doors has participated in this longstanding chapter of Bird Cage history just as Charles would have wanted it. May it continue forever.

Chapter 15

Legacy

*The Bird Cage . . . has been identified with the stirring times and
exciting events of [Tombstone's] palmy days.*
—*Tombstone Prospector*, February 24, 1903

Today the Bird Cage is one of those rare places where myth and reality merge. Western lore lives in books, on movie screens, and in our imaginations. But the Bird Cage offers a real-world portal to experience a piece of it in astonishing reality. Walking into the building is a virtual time-traveling experience that immerses your senses in wonder, and for a moment transports you to the world's circuit of long-gone variety theaters. While there are other period opera houses, there are few period variety theater buildings left. Arguably none of them harness the intimacy and preserved aura of the Bird Cage. In recent years it has become a place where every romantic western element has been packed into its interior—gunfights, gambling, prostitution, dusty miners, dirty cowboys, dirtier women, and a few famous but incorrect performers. Many of the stories have been created from imagination alone, without any consideration for the valuable resources that have survived. In that sense the Bird Cage continues to be an entertainment house that puts a mythologized version of itself onstage. Underneath decades of layered myths is a very real and valuable history. Regardless of how it has been portrayed, the Bird Cage has inspired interest, copycat venues, and countless references in books, movies, and television.

Books

Alfred Henry Lewis broke the barrier with tales of Wolfville, and many more followed. Each one added to Tombstone's legend and depth to the mystique of the Bird Cage. After Lewis came notable author Frederick Bechdolt. His 1922 book *When the West Was Young* is well-known among Tombstone and Wyatt Earp scholars. In his picturesque sketches of Tombstone, he wrote, "Bad men mingled with the sidewalk throngs [and] dropped into the Bird Cage Opera House, where painted women sang in voices that clanged like brazen gongs."[1] Bechdolt made several trips to Tombstone to gather information from long-time residents. Among them was Charles Cummings. Arlington Gardner also assisted by touring Bechdolt around Cochise County on the roads he helped establish to visit key locations relevant to Bechdolt's writings.[2] Both Charles and Arlie were thanked in the book's opening pages.

Walter Noble Burns published his blockbuster book *Tombstone: An Iliad of the Southwest* in 1927. Like Bechdolt, much of his information was acquired through old-time residents such as Charles Cummings, whom Burns credited in the book as one of his sources. How much of his Bird Cage information came from Charles is impossible to know. Burns also visited Wyatt Earp and had ongoing communication with him. At separate times they both had interest in a collaborative effort to write Wyatt's biography, but poor timing kept what surely would have been a landmark book from happening.[3] Wyatt's contributions to the book received criticism by one longtime Tombstone and Galeyville resident, J. C. Hancock who wrote a lengthy page-by-page rebuttal challenging its accuracy. In it he wrote, "Mr. Burns must have well been well paid by Wyatt Earp for writing this book."[4] In truth it was Wyatt who felt he should have been paid for the information he gave Burns. It never happened and their relationship soured.[5]

Criticism and controversies aside, Burns's book was the first that explored Tombstone's range of colorful characters like "Curly Bill" Brocius, Johnny Ringo, and Doc Holliday. Even the Bird Cage Coffee Shoppe sold copies and advertised it in the menu.[6] Among the glorified names and events of Tombstone history, Burns focused on the Bird Cage and apparently had a great fascination with the building. In vivid strokes he conveyed the theater as it once was:

> Nightly the Bird Cage Opera House . . . was packed to the doors. The evening's entertainment was of that excellence Tombstone was wont to expect in this home of refined vaudeville. The audience guzzled whisky and beer and peered through a fog of tobacco smoke at vaudeville performers cutting their capers in the glare of kerosene-lamp footlights. Beautiful painted ladies . . . swelled the receipts of the bar and received a rake-off on every bottle of beer they induced their admirers to buy. When the performance ended, the benches were moved against the walls to clear the floor, and the crowd reeled in drunken dances until the sun peeped over the Dragoon [Mountains].[7]

While Burns's book further promoted the Bird Cage, it also introduced the false story of Russian Bill—a tall tale told to this day. As the story goes, Bill was a regular of the theater who rented a box near the stage for $25 a night. In reality Russian Bill was hanged for cattle rustling in Lordsburg, New Mexico, on November 8, 1881—a month and a half before Billy Hutchinson opened the Bird Cage as a theater.[8] The box price he paid is also made up. We know from period sources that Billy Hutchinson charged no more than $2.50 for boxes. Seven months after opening he cut admission in half, and he even made a habit of letting some in for free.[9] Still, in historical context Burns's book is recognized as being extremely well-written and for bringing Tombstone's legend to a wide audience. Fifteen years after publication it was made into a movie by Paramount called *Tombstone: The Town Too Tough to Die*. The movie's plot revolves very tightly around the Bird Cage, with many scenes taking place in a movie set version of the building's interior.

A year after Burns's book, Johnny Behan's one-time deputy Billy Breakenridge rode the wave of Tombstone interest and published his memoirs titled *Helldorado*. More than two thirds of the book was dedicated to the

Tombstone saga, and for years before his death in 1931, Billy obliged many invitations to talk about it. In 1927 snippets appeared in *Liberty Magazine*, a widespread publication distributed to three million subscribers.[10] In 1924 Billy also provided a series of Tombstone vignettes for the *Tucson Citizen*.[11] In these collective publications Billy provided clear recollections of the Bird Cage as a "well patronized" theater that was "run in an orderly manner." As a law enforcement officer, he also provided a reliable statement that "no one had been killed there," which is backed up by period documentation.[12] His accounts of the Bird Cage align well with period resources and other old-timer recollections, which directly contradict the false version promoted today.

In 1942 one-time Tombstone saloon man Billy King teamed up with author C. L. Sonnichsen in the marginally accurate book *Billy King's Tombstone: The Private Life of an Arizona Boom Town*. King offered many rich anecdotes about daily life in Tombstone, the gambling and saloon underworld, and a hearty dose of Bird Cage information. Although King knew Bird Cage proprietors Frank Broad and Joe Bignon personally, his narratives range from fairly accurate to completely erroneous. This may be expected given fifty years had passed. Still, there are many valuable nuggets and insights. The fact that the book was written at all and that it contained a great deal of Bird Cage material speaks to the interest and demands of the public that was willing to buy such stories by the people who lived them. The book went into several printings throughout the 1940s as the country was sinking its teeth into the legend of the West.

Most of the early books on Tombstone were based on first-person accounts, whereas books today are analytical and fact-gathering exercises. Along the way a number of novels also began to appear. In 1945 actor Lynton Wright Brent took a break from small parts on the big screen to author his first novel titled *The Bird Cage: Tombstone, Arizona Territory*. It was marketed as "the first novel ever written about Tombstone, Arizona."[13] It wasn't Tombstone's first novel. Author Graham Cassidy had published his novel *Tombstone Pistoleers* nine years earlier. Nevertheless, it was the first specifically about the Bird Cage. To craft an interesting storyline, Brent drew from twenty-seven years of experience in motion pictures, which included several parts in Three Stooges movies, although his book wasn't written as a comedy. In an effort to align the plot with reality, Brent moved to Tombstone for six months and talked extensively with long-time residents. Through locals he learned a very blurred version of Tombstone's history. After the book's release, his Philadelphia-based publisher told him the book was "selling heavily throughout the country, especially in New York." With early optimism Brent returned to Hollywood intending to sell movie rights to the book. It's unclear how those prospects panned out, but he did return to Arizona shortly after to begin writing another book about Bisbee.[14] The best evidence suggests his Bird Cage book was only modestly successful. If movie rights were purchased, the film was never pursued.

It's hard to measure the impact that Brent's Bird Cage novel may have had at the time. The only lasting effects are on display at Tombstone's Boothill Graveyard. In row two stands the marker for "Dick Toby" who is listed in the graveyard pamphlet as having been shot dead by Sheriff Johnny Behan.[15] Dick Tobey (misspelled as "Toby" on the grave marker) was in fact shot by Johnny Behan, but it didn't happen in Tombstone. It happened on page 43 of Brent's novel. Tobey was a made-up character, a prospector who engaged in a gunfight in front of the Bird Cage as a crowd rushed the doors to get in. There was no Dick Tobey in real life, and records are clear that Behan killed zero people while Cochise County sheriff. Nevertheless, Tobey "rests" in Boothill alongside the four fictional characters killed in Alfred Henry Lewis's Wolfville stories. They are all thought to be real people by the city and have been promoted as such since the early 1950s.

Movies and Television

With western fever in full swing, twentieth-century filmmakers and television producers climbed on the Tombstone bandwagon. Since that time dozens of productions have been dedicated to its story. Several featured the Bird Cage and its fictionalized performers. Again, Alfred Henry Lewis's Wolfville led the way when early movie giant Vitagraph produced at least fifteen films based on the stories from 1917 to 1919. It was only the beginning.

Dick Tobey (misspelled as "Toby" on the marker) was killed in the pages of Lynton Wright Brent's *Bird Cage* novel. The city has presented his grave in Boothill as genuine since the 1950s. Photo by author, 2022.

The 1931 film called the *Cisco Kid* didn't tell Tombstone's story, but locals argued it was inspired by Tombstone and the Bird Cage. One scene in particular featured a variety theater confrontation in which the Kid, dangling his foot over the edge of his box, had his boot heel shot off. It was precisely as Charles Cummings and Arlington Gardner had been telling tourists for decades. Tombstone residents took notice and instantly identified it as a tribute to the Bird Cage. The *Epitaph* put it in writing: "It was not hard to recognize the interior of the Bird Cage theater, dressed up with curtains at the boxes and other [decorations] that the old theater does not boast at present. There were the same bird cage boxes, the same quaint stage, the same narrow stairs leading from the stage to the floor of the house. Possibly Tombstoners do not know that all visitors piloted through the Bird Cage hear with popping eyes this tale of the cowboy whose heel was shot off in similar fashion."[16] Could Cummings's story have filtered its way to Hollywood?

In 1942, fifteen years after Walter Noble Burns published *Tombstone: An Iliad of the Southwest*, Paramount Pictures released a movie based on the book appropriately titled *Tombstone: The Town Too Tough to Die*. Burns's book was the first to highlight Tombstone's complete cast of characters, and the resulting movie did the same. It brought the whole array of well-known personalities to the screen: Wyatt, Morgan, and Virgil Earp; Doc Holliday; Ike and Phin Clanton; the McLaurys; "Curly Bill" Brocius; Bob Paul; John Clum; and more. It even opened with a scene featuring a grizzled Ed Schieffelin prospecting. The movie plot deviates from Burns's book by providing a fanciful series of events that lead up to the gunfight near the OK Corral. Screenplay writers found the Bird Cage irresistible and placed many of the vital scenes and dialogue inside the theater. Viewers are also treated to several performances that ran nearly uninterrupted.

Four years after Paramount released *Tombstone: The Town Too Tough to Die*, director John Ford produced *My Darling Clementine*. The film gained clout by being loosely based on Wyatt Earp's biography written by Stuart Lake. While it didn't focus on the Bird Cage specifically, John Ford insisted that the film should include music that was once played there, so his research team looked to longtime residents and copies of period newspapers for answers.[17] The director for the 1940 Marx Brothers movie *Go West* also

This lobby card for the 1942 film *Tombstone: The Town Too Tough to Die*
features a scene inside the Bird Cage that borrowed many elements from the
actual building. Original lobby card from author's collection.

recognized the mystique of the Bird Cage. As part of the production he
brazenly made an offer to purchase the building and have it relocated to the
Metro-Goldwyn-Mayer movie lot in California.[18]

Television also got in on the act. From 1957 to 1960, the popular series
Tombstone Territory depicted a variety of real and made-up characters, locations, and events. Among the authentic locations re-created throughout the
series was the Bird Cage. An episode called "The Tin Gunman" featured
the story of a fictitious Bird Cage performer named Billy Denver who was
billed as the fastest gun in the world. It wasn't long before his entertaining gun handling became a nuisance, and the town turned on him after he
gunned down a local man named Johnny Pierce. In an ironic real-world twist,
Johnny Pierce was the name of an actual Bird Cage performer hired by Billy
Hutchinson. He wasn't the fastest gun in the world, but he was billed as "the

greatest comedian that ever visited Tombstone."[19] His name appearing in the television series is a random coincidence. Writers continued to incorporate the Bird Cage and its performers throughout the series.

One of the most influential television series on the popularity of Wyatt Earp and Tombstone was *The Life and Legend of Wyatt Earp* (1955–1961), starring Hugh O'Brian. In its last season it featured an episode titled "Johnny Behan Falls in Love." As the title suggests, Behan became romantically interested in a woman who happened to be a Bird Cage performer. In the process of wooing her, Behan divulged too much information about illegal activities of the Clantons. At one point Wyatt, played by Hugh O'Brian, confronted Behan about the romance. With a tip of his hat and a sarcastically confused look, he zinged Behan with a revelation. "It's too bad. I mean, a whole town of bachelors and she goes out with you. Some women have no taste in men."[20]

A wide array of Old West tales were brought to life in the long-running television series *Death Valley Days*. Among the long list of cast members was Ronald Reagan, who hosted the show and appeared in more than twenty episodes. As a spin-off from the popular 1930s radio show, it retold several chapters of Tombstone's drama. One of the last televised episodes in 1970 titled "The Duke of Tombstone" focused on the Ed Field saga, which put Billy Hutchinson and a hundred other lot owners in a stranglehold in 1881. In real life Ed Field located his Gilded Age mine months before the townsite had been surveyed, causing much debate over who had legal rights to the surface. After several years of legal maneuvering and threats of violence, Field came out on top (temporarily). Ultimately, early court rulings forced lot occupants to submit to Field's demands for high rent and lot purchase prices earning him the nickname "Duke" Field. It was the same storyline in the "Death Valley Days" episode; however, the character "Fields" was a shady gambler who acquired half the Tombstone townsite through a poker game. It's the only known film depiction of this often-overlooked chapter in Tombstone history that dictated how the Bird Cage came to be.

Perhaps no screen or literary portrayal of the Bird Cage is as well-known as the classic scene in 1993's wildly popular movie *Tombstone* starring Kurt Russell. The screenplay mashes a number of the movie's main characters in the auditorium during a smoke-filled and spirited performance. The atmosphere is masterfully captured, despite many misleading elements, which are unfortunately assumed to represent reality by some viewers. Nevertheless, it helped elevate the interest and intrigue in the town and the Bird Cage like many examples before it. With cultlike popularity that seems to have grown with time, *Tombstone* continues to do the same for modern generations.

Bird Cage–Inspired Theaters

Inspiration from Bird Cage lore and legend goes beyond the confines of printed paper, television, and movie screens. Several venues have been constructed around the country that stemmed from the Bird Cage's notoriety. Their existence demonstrates how recognizable it has become by the general public. In these examples the Bird Cage was a symbol of all period venues and the entertainment featured among them.

One of the first came in 1935, when a western-themed town called Gold Gulch opened in San Diego's Balboa Park.[21] The man behind the enterprise was 47-year-old Harry Oliver. With his unique talents as an Academy Award–nominated set director and designer, he created an Old West mining camp that replicated the "rip roaring days of '49."[22] The western town was impossibly large, covering twenty-one acres in "a picturesque canyon . . . chosen for its natural foliage, trees and stream" within the park. It offered an array of western novelties housed in buildings Oliver designed and helped construct that captured the "romance and color" of the period. Guests could order a chuckwagon dinner, ride a stagecoach or burros, engage in dancing in a hall modeled after an old stamp mill, and have their photographs taken in a tintype studio that comically invited visitors to "get shot here." They even had a Kiddy Korral, where "exasperated parents" could drop their kids off to be entertained and sent off with a Tom Mix outfit.[23] Everything was "done to the standard of motion pictures at their very best." Among the attractions was a working Bird Cage Theatre that sat 350 people.[24]

Oliver's expertise and skill made him a perfect consultant for the expanding theme park in Buena Park, California, called Knott's Berry Farm.

The Bird Cage at Knott's Berry Farm opened in 1954 and is still in use today. Author's collection.

What started out as a roadside fruit stand in the 1920s expanded to become a full-on theme park by the 1940s. Today it encompasses more than fifty acres of attractions that sees more than 4 million visitors a year.[25] Among their Ghost Town attractions is an 1880s period western city that includes a steam train, gold panning, and a replica Bird Cage Theatre that not only borrowed the name but also was designed to mirror the original. Opened in 1954, it still features several live shows a year and is a notable landmark within the park.[26]

In staying with the tourist theme, Nevada's Last Frontier hotel opened on what was then the outskirts of the Las Vegas Strip in 1942. It was a western styled hotel that added a mockup western town in the late 1940s called the Last Frontier Village. It included restaurants, a church, a western museum, saloons, a casino, and more. As a part of the growing village, they acquired and moved "one of the first frame buildings in southern Nevada" to the property. It was built in 1905 and served as the headquarters for a freighting and trading company that hauled goods from Las Vegas to numerous mining communities.[27] After being relocated to the Last Frontier Village, the historic building was quickly remodeled to host live performances and was renamed the Bird Cage Theater. Like the Bird Cage in Tombstone, it was a modest venue seating a mere 168 people. Admission was set at $2.50—the same price that Billy Hutchinson charged for box admissions early in 1882.[28] A performance cast was assembled from Hollywood and Broadway for the purpose of reviving "the traditions of rip-roaring 19th century gold boom days when . . . bonanza boom towns guested nearly all the stage greats." Several of the productions were highly popular numbers performed on nineteenth-century stages.[29] Crowded houses were the rule, and a Hollywood newspaper credited it as being "the first legitimate theatre" in Las Vegas that became a "strong cultural and entertainment force in the community."[30]

That same year Newhall, California, put on a western-themed Fourth of July celebration. Among the attractions was an Old West parade and a western theme town called Slippery Gulch. The period styled buildings were faithfully represented and included a boardinghouse, sheriff's office, jail, corral, undertaker's office, blacksmith shop, Wells Fargo office, and "every kind of activity that used to make the walking ring from Abilene, Kansas to Tombstone, Arizona."[31] There was also a Pony Express station, complete with a live mail carrier that raced in "on a dead run," grabbed mail, and exited in dramatic fashion. They also reconstructed a bar called the Palace Saloon, which was a "perfect old time western setting [with a] floor inches deep in suds and sawdust." Among the buildings was a Bird Cage Theatre that showed continuous vaudeville shows where "anybody with a good act got a chance to do his stuff." Sixteen shows were presented throughout the Fourth of July weekend and saw "a surging tide of visitors" that totaled nearly twelve thousand.[32] The event's success prompted organizers to do it all again the following year.[33]

Sixteen years later and fifteen hundred miles away, the children's zoo of Lincoln, Nebraska, joined the Bird Cage craze. In 1965 the zoo opened as a place "where children could get up-close to animals and surround themselves in scenic gardens."[34] The grounds also featured a collection of scaled-down 1880s-styled buildings that they called Zoo Town. Like the Last Frontier Village it included a number of storefronts that epitomized

The Bird Cage Theatre was a part of Lincoln, Nebraska's, Zoo Town for more than forty years. Author's collection.

a classic western town. It included a jail, livery stable, general store, post office, Boothill Graveyard, and Bird Cage Theater said to be "patterned after theaters of pioneer days." As an entertainment venue specifically for children, its construction was financed through significant donations from the *Lincoln Journal Star* newspaper.[35] The theater hosted puppet shows, trained animal acts, and a number of child-appropriate entertainments. It also became a popular venue for hosing birthday parties. The interior was accented by glamorous chandeliers from a local historic home, a black walnut piano, and a dozen bird engravings imported from Arizona. Zoo director Al Bietz said, "The Bird Cage is unique in the zoo world. It's a winner."[36] And it was, having served the zoo and generations of area children for more than forty years.

The 1950s brought about a surge in airline tourism, and Arizona, rich in culture and natural wonders, was poised to take advantage. In an effort to market abroad, a display was set up at the offices of American Airlines in Chicago. The $50,000 spectacle featured several Arizona attractions including "a life-sized replica . . . of the famous Bird Cage theatre." While it wasn't a working replica, it leveraged the building's mystique and fame. Ultimately the display resulted in "very good" advance bookings to the southwest.[37]

These numerous examples reflect how recognizable and intriguing the Bird Cage became throughout the twentieth century. It's the same notoriety that inspired this book and presumably your interest as a reader. The original Bird Cage was an institution that did little to advance the financial situation for its various proprietors, but it proved to be a consistent go-to for writers, filmmakers, and other business folk abroad. The same popularity that has generated so much attention has also encouraged countless myths to be added to its legend. This widespread exposure is an important element to understanding how its identity has become distorted and how it might be better understood moving forward. One thing is certain: fascination with the Bird Cage has resonated across the world and throughout the passing decades. As a unique and enduring connection to Tombstone and American mythology, it has rightfully earned its place among the most storied buildings in all the West. While its performance era ceased more than 130 years ago, its ability to entertain and thrill us rolls on.

Epilogue

T he story of the Bird Cage mostly has a happy ending. The building still exists, which is no small miracle. Every building near the corner of Sixth and Allen built before 1930 (and there were dozens of them) has succumbed to forces of man and nature, some several times over. The Bird Cage had its own narrow misses.

In May 1914 the adjoining building caught on fire. As if guided by fate, the chief of police happened to be walking by and immediately rang the alarm. As strong winds fanned the flames into a rage, firemen raced to the scene and fought them back. If the call had come minutes later, the *Epitaph* insisted the fire "would have been hard to control [and] we surely would have lost one of our famous old landmarks, the Bird Cage Theatre."[1] Another close brush with disaster came in 1931, when time and torrential seasonal rains toppled its east wall, "causing the aged theater to crumble in several places." It is fortunate it didn't suffer total structural failure.[2]

The financial security provided by John Sroufe and Hugh McCrum and eventually Charles Cummings protected the building during Tombstone's lean years that saw dozens of other historic landmarks dismantled to save on property tax assessments. Ultimately the Bird Cage was at the mercy of Tombstone's fortunes—for better or worse. The beginning and end of its performance era were dictated by those larger forces. After Tombstone's mining era, the Bird Cage drew in early visitors as the town's must-see landmark for several decades before other historic locations were developed. Throughout the early decades of the twentieth century, dozens and dozens of books, movies, and television shows helped build Tombstone's legend and exposed it to a worldwide audience. More than 140 years after Billy Hutchinson's hard-fought dream became a reality, the Bird Cage is as celebrated as ever, and the future outlook looks strong.

As for the people who were a part of its storied period, their endings weren't always quite as fortunate. After Frank Broad, Oliver Trevillian, and William Sprague ended their joint partnership in the summer of 1885, they each went their separate ways. Frank carried on as a saloon man, operating at a number of different locations in the neighborhood of the Bird Cage. In 1889, while Joe Bignon still packed the theater, Frank ran a saloon directly next door.[3] In tandem with his saloons he served Tombstone and the vicinity

Under the arrow are signs of bracing and repairs made after a portion of the east wall collapsed in 1931. Author's collection.

as a city constable—a position he earned through his many supporters in the city elections.[4] His years as constable were marked with an impeccable record of daring and honorable service, executing everything from serving papers to tracking hardened criminals across the county. In many ways he more completely embodied the clean and heroic version of Wyatt Earp than Wyatt Earp himself. Frank's capable reputation also earned him a position as an officer in the local fire department and county livestock inspector.[5] Throughout town he was known as an affable businessman and an incredible athlete who participated in foot races, bare-knuckle fights, and even wrestling matches at the Oriental.[6] He and his wife made a cozy home and added three children before suffering the loss of their youngest in 1893.[7]

Further tragedy awaited the Broad family. In the spring of 1895, Frank's tuberculosis worsened, and he was sent to Tucson for monitoring and treatment. For two weeks he was laid up, unable to eat full meals.[8] The local newspaper noted Frank "must be held in a high esteem by his fellow townsmen as there was a delegation to see him."[9] In following months Frank saw some improvement and was observed "gaining health and strength," but it didn't last.[10] On July 24, 1895, he died at the age of 37. His funeral was conducted under the auspices of the Tombstone fire department and was largely attended. A long procession of carriages escorted his remains to the city cemetery (not Boothill) accompanied by all three fire companies in full uniform. At the graveside service, Tombstone's notable lawyer Allen English made a speech "extolling the virtues" of Frank and closed with "a fitting and impressive eulogy." Frank's casket was covered in an array of floral arrangements, lowered into the grave, and covered. The *Epitaph* solemnly noted, "Thus ends the worldly career of one who lived among us, was known to all of us, and will be missed."[11] Even Tucson newspapers recognized "he was greatly esteemed."[12] His death was reported in Bisbee as well. "Frank Broad's friends [in Bisbee]—and they are not few—were much grieved to learn of his death. They all speak in the highest terms of his many noble and generous qualities."[13]

Half a world away from his birthplace in Cornwall, England, Frank Broad rests in an unmarked grave in Tombstone Cemetery.[14] The life he lived seems to be forgotten along with his stint as Bird Cage proprietor despite the large mark he left on those who knew him. With the absence of a headstone, only the Bird Cage remains to landmark his life in Tombstone.

It was an even more tragic end for his former partner and fellow Cornwall native Oliver Trevillian. After the Bird Cage, Oliver stayed extremely active in Tombstone. His younger brother Frederick joined him, and together they became "well known musicians" who played countless socials, weddings, gatherings and parties.[15] The *Epitaph* acknowledged, "Their sweet music has enlivened many social entertainments in the city."[16] For years Oliver hosted dancing classes and orchestrated social dances in the Mining Exchange building in the Gird Block, now an empty parking lot across the street from Schieffelin Hall.[17] Hosting these events retained his popularity with every social goer in Tombstone and afforded him many continuing friendships. Like his former partner Frank Broad, he also looked to serve the community. With a legion of supporters behind him, he ran for city treasurer and won.[18] By 1886 he also married and had a baby boy.[19]

Unfortunately, like both of his former Bird Cage partners, Oliver was also consumptive—a condition one report claimed he had suffered from "for many years." As his condition worsened he became bedridden. His inability to work and provide for his family took a heavy toll on his spirit and heart. By early 1890 the pain and indignity became so bad he openly expressed his will to die. Still his wife and son remained by his side and had done "everything possible to make his life bearable."[20] On March 2, 1890, his wife offered to make him dinner, but he declined and asked her only for some quiet and privacy. An hour later she walked past his room and caught a glimpse of a ghastly scene. Oliver had taken a razor and gashed his wrists and his throat. He made a determined effort to sever his windpipe, but blood loss depleted his strength, so he had resorted to "[tearing] his wind pipe open with his hands." Amazingly he not only survived but also remained conscious and was "perfectly rational." Dr. Goodfellow was one of two physicians rushed to his aid to sew up the wounds. Despite their best efforts, he was not given a good prognosis, and a day later Oliver died. He was only 33 years old. The official cause of death was listed by the county coroner as "suicide and consumption."[21] Mere steps away from Frank Broad's grave, Oliver was buried in Tombstone Cemetery less than five years removed from running the Bird Cage. His grave remains unmarked today just like Frank Broad's.[22]

After Joe Bignon relinquished efforts to rejuvenate the Bird Cage, he sat tight in Tombstone, never losing his confidence that the town would rise again. He even told the public he was going to "wait [in] Tombstone for the boom."[23] His patience paid off in 1894 when a considerable silver strike just twenty miles away gave rise to the new community of Pearce. On June 26, 1895, he and his wife, Tillie, disassembled the wood-frame house they were married in, loaded it on Joe McPherson's freight wagon, and relocated to Pearce. Almost immediately Joe made mining claims that quickly produced "some excellent ore." His move to Pearce was so quick he was referred to as "the pioneer of Pearce, having built the first house in that camp."[24] Mesmerized by the first great opportunities he'd seen in years, he didn't bother to sell his homesite lots in Tombstone or pay his property taxes at year's end.[25]

In coming years Pearce mines produced a quarter of a billion dollars in today's money, and Joe rode the wave all the way to the end of his life. He ran a number of businesses there, including a saloon, hotel, and a dry-goods store.[26] For a number of years, at least until 1921, he even ran a motion picture theater called the Idle Hour Theater, but he never again operated a live performance venue.[27] With the same drive and energy from his theater endeavors, Joe doggedly pursued mines and mining property for the last forty years of his life. Perhaps he was motived by the mining and real estate prowess of Sroufe and McCrum, who owned the Bird Cage building while he operated it. Perhaps he had just run his course on the live entertainment business. Whatever his reasons, Joe changed his entire focus. Before he left Tombstone, he started exploring the mountains of southeast Arizona, making several claims of promising outlook. By 1909 he had a formal company called the Bignon Group, which employed as many as one hundred men in the development of his mines.[28] He also became director of the Courtland Copper Company in the neighboring community of Courtland (now a ghost town).[29] In all, Joe's mining and real estate activities are too numerous to list. He tackled them in typical tenacious and tireless Joe Bignon style. His mine portfolio included locations across Cochise County, including Bisbee, Douglas, the Chiricahua Mountains, and Tombstone, just to name a few. Despite all of these ventures, he considered himself humbly a "saloon proprietor" in the 1910 census.

With growing confidence in Pearce's potential, Joe also claimed a 160-acre parcel through the Homestead Act that flanked the western edge of the town. He named it the "Bignon Addition." To help encourage its growth, he sold many lots for one dollar on the promise that the buyer would build and improve. Other lots were sold for twenty-five dollars, depending on the location.[30] Joe named two of the principal thoroughfares Bignon Street and Tombstone Avenue.[31]

Joe's life played out comfortably among the 1,500 close-knit inhabitants of Pearce, and he became well known. But it was not without downtimes. On August 4, 1900, just as life was aligning for Joe, Tillie died after several months of suffering through uterine tumor complications.[32] In a casket purchased by a friend near their old home in Tombstone, she was laid to rest in the Pearce cemetery two days later.[33] She was only 48 years old. True to his nature, Joe picked up and moved on in stride and met Ellen McGrogan, an Irish dressmaker eighteen years his junior who had been living in Pearce with her sister's family. They were married in Tucson four months after Tillie passed.[34] Unlike his first forty years of restless wandering, he remained in Pearce and southeastern Arizona for the rest of his life, with Ellen by his side till the end.

After a five-month battle with bacterial meningitis, Joe died at 4:00 p.m. on December 6, 1925.[35] A special era of Tombstone and the American West went to the grave with him. The nineteenth-century flavored entertainment and adventures of his youth had passed forever. Notice of his death found its way into the columns of papers across the country that identified him as the notable operator of the Bird Cage.[36] He was a man of great energy, irrepressible resilience, a sense of civic contribution, and character far beyond the common mythologized stories told today. He left the comfort of home and Canada while still a boy, found his American Dream, and single-handedly doubled the performance era of the Bird Cage. Alongside both his wives, Tillie and Ellen (who died in 1935), Joe lays at rest in the open flat of Pearce cemetery, surrounded once by a vibrant town but now nearly devoid of buildings with no sounds other than those of the dust-laden winds.[37] An 1888 biographical profile published in Tombstone may have summed up Joe bet. "There are few . . . who are more enterprising and successful than Joe

The tall marker on the left is Joe Bignon's headstone. In the center foreground is the grave of his first wife, Matilda Quigley. The small iron cross on the right is Joe's second wife, Ellen McGrogan. They lie together in the Pearce cemetery. Photo by author.

Bignon, and the fallacy of saying 'that a rolling stone gathers no moss' never better shown than in his case."[38] He did a lot with his 80 years, and his legacy is forever etched in the Bird Cage.

As for Billy and Lottie Hutchinson, who started it all, their post–Bird Cage life is as obscured as their life before Tombstone. After Billy officially closed up the Bird Cage and served his five days in jail for public drunkenness in August of 1883, the Crystal Palace was opened as a variety theater by one of his former entertainers, Alphonse King. Surprisingly, Billy took no part in the endeavor.[39] Instead it was rumored that he planned to take over Tucson's Park Theater, where dozens of his performers and musicians were employed. That plan never materialized.[40] After a short trip to Galveston, Texas, Billy returned and became the foreman of Tombstone's Engine Company No. 1—the very company that he and Lottie supported for many years.[41] They remained in Tombstone until February 1884. Until his final days in Tombstone, Billy remained active in at least one of his mines, hinting that he may not have been entirely committed to leaving.[42]

After a short stint in Tucson, the Hutchinsons moved on to San Francisco.[43] The power couple that was very active in town matters and were so deeply woven into Tombstone's social fabric that surprisingly don't appear in the forefront of other communities' doings. Years later, in 1892, Billy wrote to one of his friends in Tombstone, William D. Monmonier. The letter indicated he was living in Chicago and was curious about the business prospects of Tombstone.[44] Although the letter may have shown his interest in returning, he never did. Monmonier, the recipient of Billy's letter, was one of many Tombstone citizens who relocated to Pearce with the likes of Joe Bignon in the late 1890s. He became the justice of the peace and signed Joe's death certificate. (Monmonier and Joe are buried a few plots apart in Pearce.) He was in a unique position to know both Billy and Joe well, but to date nothing from Monmonier has been found to shed light on either of the men or the Bird Cage.

Ultimately the fate of Billy and Lottie Hutchinson remains unknown. There is strong evidence that suggests they participated in the Alaska gold rush passing through Skagway and Nome in the late 1890s.[45] In those same years a William J. Hutchinson who was living in Seattle, Washington, made a number of trips by steamer back and forth between Alaska.[46] The possibility that this is Billy is made stronger by the fact that many former Tombstone residents chased fortunes in Alaska at the same time. That list includes former mayor John Clum, Bird Cage performers John Mulligan and Carrie Linton, legendary Tombstone businesswoman Nellie Cashman, Wyatt Earp, and many others.[47] It is no stretch to think a man clearly infatuated with mining in Tombstone would be found in Alaskan gold fields. As late as 1911, a Mrs. W. J. Hutchinson ran a boardinghouse in Port Hadlock north of Seattle, though positively identifying her as Lottie has remained elusive.[48] These small hints hardly dignify their life stories, and many unanswered questions remain. It may have been beyond Billy's imagination to think that more than 140 years after opening the Bird Cage it would become one of the most storied landmarks of the American West. In addition to representing several hundred performers and the bygone era of global entertainment, the Bird Cage also stands as a monument representing Billy and Lottie Hutchinson, whose lives are not memorialized in any other way found thus far.

If Billy was in fact living in Seattle in 1896, he may have caught newspaper reports about his former nemesis, Ed Field. After Field's timely victories in the territorial court system in 1881, he amassed a fortune by cashing in on the demand for Tombstone property at peak values. His elevated status earned him the moniker "Duke Field" and "the Duke of Tombstone." One Tombstone local recalled he earned the nickname "on account of the gorgeous manner in which he carried on his establishment [and he] assumed a mode of life that made him the most conspicuous character in the West." The meaning behind his curious phrasing is up for interpretation. As a symbol of his wealth, rumors persisted that he "took three baths a day when water cost five cents a gallon."[49] Understanding the scarcity of water in early Tombstone helps punctuate the opulence of such a claim.

Field collected exorbitant rents and sold properties for inflated prices, taking advantage of many who had already paid for their lots from previous owners and established homes and businesses on them. He paraded around town "behind a pair of horses that were a sensation" and wore highly recognizable white flannel suits, which he changed "whenever the smallest blemish in the way of dust was noticeable."[50] This was a bold sign of wealth in a dusty mining town where complaints about dirt freely blowing around town regularly made the newspapers. Grandstanding his wealth would have sat poorly with Billy Hutchinson and many who were unjustly forced to pay him for lots they already owned.

Perhaps no man in Tombstone cashed in like Ed Field did in 1881. Even after Billy and many others gave into his demands, Field sued them repeatedly for damages and unpaid rents during their legal standoff. It was bitter and ugly, but in the end Ed Field walked away with more money than nearly every merchant and miner that ever came through Tombstone. Later reports noted he sold his Gilded Age mine for $600,000.[51] County mining records do not dispute or confirm this figure, but even the rents and proceeds from lot sales alone (which are on record) amount to more than most working people made in a lifetime. It is certain that Field got rich at the expense of people like Billy Hutchinson.

So naturally Billy may have been amused and shocked to read reports out of Chicago about Field's fall from grace in 1896. The Chicago newspaper that broke the story simply titled it, "From Riches to Poverty." The details proved to be so shocking and irresistible that it was reprinted in dozens of newspapers from coast to coast. If Billy read it he may have found satisfaction or even pleasure in the justice of Field's demise. The column read:

Edward Field, once wealthy is now in dire distress. Field, at one time a millionaire mine owner, was removed from a cheap looking lodging house at 68 Thirteenth street last night by the police station ambulance and taken to the county hospital. Today he will probably be removed to the county poorhouse at Dunning, where he will spend his few remaining days.

Field, who was then in the prime of life, went to Tombstone, Arizona. . . . From a poor man he suddenly became rich and the owner of what was known as the Gilded Age mine. His wealth and his ability to spend it gained form his sobriquet of the "Duke of Tombstone." The far west was too dull for Field with his possession of riches, and he removed to St. Louis. In the Missouri town Field fitted up and establishment in elegant style and maintained a stable of fast horses. He began operating on the Board of Trade and his wealth gave evidence of fading away. Not content with dabbling on the St. Louis market, he took a flier on the Chicago wheat pit and lost heavily.

Having lost over $1,000,000 of his fortune, the tide turned again and the "Duke of Tombstone" began to win back some of the money he had lost. He was a [habitual] gambler however, and determined to either win an enormous sum of money or lose the remaining hundreds of thousands. He invested in the grain and stock markets heavily. He awoke one morning to find himself penniless, with his fine house and fast horses the property of another.

With the aid of friends who had known him in the zenith of his prosperity he managed to scrape together a few hundred dollars and with this sum came to Chicago. For four or five years he has made this city his home and few knew how he lived. Several months ago he drifted in to the lodging house at 68 Thirteenth street and has since made that place his home. He never tired of telling the landlord and his fellow lodgers the story of his life and of the day when he was the original and sole owner of the famous Gilded Age mine.

Some time ago Field was stricken with consumption and has failed so rapidly that his time is now short. Yesterday he became so ill that it was decided to have him removed to the county hospital, and the police were notified. Field refused to accompany them. A doctor's certificate, stating that [he] was of unsound mind was secured, and with this the officers forcibly removed the former millionaire. Today he will probably be transferred to the poorhouse.[52]

Part of Field's downfall came from gambling in Chicago's bucket shops. Bucket shops were establishments that took bets on the stock market and price of commodities without actually buying and selling them directly. It was literally gambling on prices as they went up or down. Field was hit hard, and the losses took a toll on his psyche, lifestyle, and appearance. Joseph Greer, a former Tombstone pharmacist who knew Ed Field in the

town's early days, relocated to Chicago and had a chance run-in with Field as
he hit rock bottom. Greer described him as "seedy looking" and was shocked
to find out he had gone bust. He claimed Field told him he "squandered a
cool million dollars" and was working in a retail store in Chicago's Southern
Hotel for a measly fourteen dollars a month. It was quite a change for a man
who wore fine white linen, patrolled Tombstone with the finest bay horses
in town, was serviced by his own personal valet, and was "the most talked
of man in the country."[53] The same greed that acquired his fortune cost him
the same.

The rise and fall of Ed Field may have been poetic justice to Billy
Hutchinson if he did in fact read the reports. In a way, Field's boom and
bust was parallel to that of Tombstone itself. The Ed Field/Gilded Age saga
is often overlooked when discussing early Tombstone, and it's completely
omitted from Bird Cage discussions despite being a controlling factor
over its very existence. Field's greed and stubbornness brewed violence
and uncertainty as the scramble for Tombstone wealth was in full flight.
His actions dictated how and when the Bird Cage came to be and likely
played a role in how Billy Hutchinson's finances became critically low in
1883, forcing him to lose the business. Field's persona in early Tombstone
was controversial. Today he can be remembered for his major role in the
story of the Bird Cage and Tombstone's most colorful period.

Ten years of researching the Bird Cage has revealed many previously
unknown and unused resources, now gathered in this book. Their combined
value has revealed truths that have been ignored and buried under decades
of hastily crafted myths. Taking measure of it all reveals two undeniable
conclusions: One is that there is so much more to find. Many new leads
were available at the time of writing. However these deeper answers cannot
be found if the fictionalized version of the Bird Cage is assumed to be real.
Secondly, and most importantly, is that the Bird Cage truly is a national
treasure worth all the effort required to properly excavate its true history
and the stories of those that contributed to it. Tombstone's most iconic
original building has waited a long time to have its day. May this be the
rising curtain to a new era of realizing its authentic legacy.

Appendix A
A Concise Bird Cage Timeline

This timeline has been compiled from the text of this book to serve as a reference and quick overview of all the new information presented. While citations have not been included here, all of the dates and information come directly from the book and have been cited throughout.

1880

July 28—Billy Hutchinson purchases the eventual Bird Cage lot from Henry Fry and Jerome Ackerson for $600. The lot contains a modest frame cabin with an adobe chimney on a lot surrounded by an ocotillo-limb fence (lot 9, block 5, on the Tombstone townsite plot map).

October 14—Billy Hutchinson and William Ritchie open the second floor of Ritchie's Hall as a gambling establishment. The interior is lavishly decorated with black walnut, marble, and the best liquors and cigars. Billy deals faro to the gambling fraternity of Tombstone and becomes warmly known as "Hutch." Some of the games are favorably reported in the local newspapers with as much as $1,200 won and lost on a turn.

October 28—Village marshal Fred White is shot by "Curly Bill" Brocius behind the frame cabin on Billy Hutchinson's lot. Wyatt Earp is directly involved in the unfolding events. His friend Fred Dodge claims that he and Wyatt's younger brother Morgan Earp are living in the cabin at the time.

November 13—Billy Hutchinson purchases the future Bird Cage lot a second time from the Townsite Company for $465 to avoid legal dispute over ownership. To fund this purchase, he receives a $315 loan from lawyer Ben Goodrich. The loan is to be paid back in ninety days with 1 percent interest. Instead of paying Goodrich back, Billy puts up $500 for Doc Holliday's bond in the OK Corral hearing a year later. Goodrich is ironically part of the prosecution team. Infuriated, he immediately takes Billy to court.

November 29–December 15—Nellie Boyd's troupe overwhelms Ritchie's Hall with professional theatrical performances. Just above the crowded hall on the second floor, Billy Hutchinson continues to deal faro, acutely aware of the financial success of the show below.

1881

March—In letters written decades later to Wyatt Earp's biographer Stuart Lake, Fred Dodge claims he and Morgan Earp are still living in the cabin on the future Bird Cage lot and are joined by Wyatt Earp. The story is repeated in Wyatt Earp's biography, *Wyatt Earp: Frontier Marshal*.

April 10—Tombstone town council passes Ordinance 10, establishing legal boundaries for conducting and soliciting prostitution. The lot where the Bird Cage is eventually built is not inside the legal boundary.

April 14—Mine owner Ed Field scores a victory in the Territorial Supreme Court, giving him surface rights to his Gilded Age mining claim, which covers the east portion of the Tombstone townsite. This ruling forces Billy Hutchinson to pay for the lot a third time. However, he and approximately sixty other lot owners refuse to pay Field and take him to court.

Late April—Johnny Behan forcibly ejects lot occupants on the Gilded Age mining claim who have not paid Ed Field. At the same time, Billy Hutchinson and approximately sixty other lot owners band together in an organization called the Gilded Age Protective League and prepare to battle Ed Field in courts. Billy contributes significant funds to the cause while in default of the Ben Goodrich loan from November 13, 1880. More than one hundred lawsuits stem from the feud, and courts are bogged down, unable to get through them.

June 22—A massive fire guts the east portion of Tombstone's business district, including the historic frame cabin on Hutchinson's lot where Fred Dodge, Morgan Earp, and, for a short period, Wyatt Earp had stayed.

June 25—Billy Hutchinson erects a small frame cabin on the eventual Bird Cage lot to deter lot jumpers and Ed Field from seizing it.

July 19—Billy Hutchinson gives up his legal fight with Ed Field over legal lot ownership and secures a loan of $650 to pay him for the eventual Bird Cage lot. It's the third time Billy pays for the lot. Adding to the ridiculousness of the situation, Billy puts up the lot he is paying for as collateral to secure the final mortgage.

August 30—Billy Hutchinson asks the town council for permission to move into the street the small frame cabin he rebuilt on the Bird Cage lot after the fire. The council approves the request, and the construction of the Bird Cage begins shortly after.

Early September—Building of the Bird Cage progresses. The local newspaper reports it is nearing completion and will be opened as a "first class saloon."

Early October—The *Epitaph* projects that Billy's Bird Cage building is complete.

October 26—The gunfight near the OK Corral rocks Tombstone.

October 30—The *Nugget* reports that Billy Hutchinson puts up $500 bond for Doc Holliday. He is one of eight who come to the financial aid of Holliday to keep him out of jail during the OK Corral court hearing. Ben Goodrich, one of the lawyers for the prosecution, becomes irate because Billy is more than nine months overdue in paying back a loan he gave him. Days later Goodrich sends Billy a summons. It is served by Johnny Behan's deputy, Billy Breakenridge.

November 19—Lottie Hutchinson is made an honorary member of Engine Company No. 1 in a public ceremony where she is gifted an elegant membership certificate. Among fellow honorary members is Wyatt Earp. She is the only known woman to receive the honor.

December 15—Tombstone's newspapers report that Billy is in San Francisco recruiting performers for the Bird Cage grand opening. He visits two of San Francisco's leading venues, the Bella Union and Woodward's Gardens, and successfully persuades a number of their top performers to come to Arizona.

December 18, 5:00 p.m.—Billy Hutchinson and his recruited performers pass Fresno, California, on a train headed for Arizona.

December 19—Billy and his performance company pass through Colton, California.

December 20—After getting off the train in Benson, Billy Hutchinson, sixteen performers, and one toddler arrive in Tombstone via stagecoach during a snowstorm. The *Epitaph* reports that finishing touches to the Bird Cage are being put on.

December 22—Billy Hutchinson's San Francisco performers put on their first show in Tombstone. Instead of the Bird Cage, it takes place in Schieffelin Hall, possibly because of its increased capacity and because Bird Cage finishing touches were not complete. Billy names his wife, Lottie, as the performance beneficiary. Her popularity and involvement in community charity helps pack Schieffelin Hall.

December 24—The Bird Cage Grand Opening. This also marks the first day that the building is referred to as the Bird Cage by name in newspapers. Admission is set at fifty cents, but there are no box prices. The theater opened without boxes, which were not installed until early 1882.

December 25—Billy's trusted and experienced stage manager Harry Lorraine
dies of an unnamed illness just hours after the first Bird Cage performances are given the night before. After less than five days in town,
Harry is buried in Tombstone. His wife is a performer, and she continues
to appear at the Bird Cage for several months while taking care of her
fatherless daughter.

1882

Early winter through spring—Regular reports in both the *Epitaph* and the
Nugget state that the Bird Cage is crowded every night with quality
performances.

February 8—The Hutchinsons host a benefit performance at the Bird Cage
for a local man who can't afford travel expenses needed to seek medical
attention in Hot Springs, Arkansas. They donate all the theater's door
admissions, which amount to $170. Given the price of admissions, the
event reveals that roughly 160–200 people visited the theater that night,
suggesting how busy the Bird Cage was. It also sheds light on how much
revenue was being generated. This figure does not include drink sales,
which was where variety theaters made the majority of their money.

March 5—To accommodate overwhelming crowds and capitalize on
increased revenue potential, Billy Hutchinson advertises the first
matinee performance at the Bird Cage.

March 8—Billy hosts the first social ball at the Bird Cage. The feature
becomes a weekly event that is highly popular among patrons, talked
about in newspapers, and recalled years later by former customers.

March 13—After nearly three months of reportedly packed houses and large
nightly crowds, Billy Hutchinson inexplicably mortgages the Bird Cage
and the lot for $2,500 to San Francisco liquor merchants John Sroufe
and Hugh McCrum. The loan is to be paid back in six months. Seventeen
months later (and eleven months overdue) Billy only repays $262.50.

June 13—Ed Field wins a significant judgment for legal fees and unpaid rents
from the Gilded Age holdout a year prior, totaling more than $12,000.
The bill falls in the lap of Billy Hutchinson and others in the Gilded Age
Protective league who put up a resistance in the summer of 1881.

July—By this time Billy formally changes the name from the Bird Cage
Theater to Bird Cage Opera House. Other venues across the country do
the same to remove negative stigma associated with variety theaters. Billy
also cuts general admission in half, from fifty cents to twenty-five cents.

August 19—Billy is in Denver recruiting more performers. Apparently successful in his efforts, he writes a letter to Tombstone stating, "[I] will start home Tuesday morning, with some good people to make Tombstoners laugh."

August 25—Billy gives a promotional parade with his cast of Bird Cage performers and musicians. The spectacle is led through Tombstone's main streets and includes two wagons led by Billy himself mounted on a "dashing charger."

September 13—The deadline to repay John Sroufe and Hugh McCrum from the March 13 mortgage passes. Billy has only made one payment of $162.50, well short of the $2,500 plus interest he owes.

September 15—A benefit at the Bird Cage is put on for popular performer Lola Cory, a young mother of two who is dealing with a chronic health issues.

Mid-October—A sizable addition is placed on the back of the Bird Cage, extending auditorium seating twenty feet and enlarging the stage. It brings the building to its present-day dimensions. Prior to that the back of the building had three openings—one being used as a back entrance and two others for staircases that led directly to boxes above general admission seating.

December—A mini theater boom in Tucson lures away more than a dozen of Billy Hutchinson's performers. The *Epitaph* notes "what is lacked in quantity is made up in quality." At the same time Billy makes another recruiting trip to restock his troupe. The Bird Cage is still noted as being crowded nightly.

1883

January 1—Billy fails to pay his 1882 property tax bill of $143.00 for the Bird Cage and another lot on Fremont Street that likely serves as his residence. County records indicate the bill was never paid.

March 27—Billy arrives in San Francisco for unknown reasons. He may be recruiting more talent or meeting with Sroufe and McCrum to negotiate the overdue mortgage.

April 16—More than seven months overdue on the $2,500 loan from John Sroufe and Hugh McCrum, Billy has made only two payments for a total of $262.50. He is served a summons and a foreclosure notice on the Bird Cage. The court date is set for May 14, 1883.

April 25—With the court date fast approaching, Billy desperately mortgages all of the Bird Cage contents, including chairs, tables, scenery, silverware,

light fixtures, the safe, glasses from behind the bar, and more for $500. It
is another loan he fails to repay, and he loses all of the items necessary to
operate the Bird Cage six weeks later.

May—Billy and Lottie attempt to host a ladies' night at the Bird Cage, but the
event fails for undisclosed reasons.

May 14—Billy fails to appear in court for the defaulted mortgage from
John Sroufe and Hugh McCrum, putting the Bird Cage in dire risk.

July 2—Billy agrees to sell the Bird Cage and the lot to John Sroufe and
Hugh McCrum for $4,350. Records do not indicate whether this value
is in consideration of the $2,237.50 still owed from the original mort-
gage or not. What began as a simple six-month loan to Billy Hutchinson
resulted in ownership of the building for twenty years for Sroufe and
McCrum.

July 4—Billy still operates the Bird Cage. He plans a promotional parade, but
it is canceled by torrential rains and violent storms.

July 6—Billy still continues operation of the Bird Cage and returns from
Tucson, where he recruited three performers. All three eventually end up
working at the Crystal Palace during its run as a variety theater.

July 14—Rumors in Tucson suggest Billy is planning on taking over the Park
Theater, a venue that shared dozens of performers and employees with
the Bird Cage. The rumors come to nothing.

August 16—Billy Hutchinson publicly announces he is closing the Bird
Cage. He cites "dull times" as the reason. In reality his financial negli-
gence is to blame. On the same day he is also arrested for being drunk
and disorderly. After being found guilty he is given an option to pay a
five dollar fine or take five days in jail. He takes the five days in jail,
perhaps showing how bad his financial state was.

August 18—One of Billy's former performers, Alphonse King, leases the
Crystal Palace (the same location as the Crystal Palace in Tombstone
today) as a genuine variety theater. It has an orchestra pit and boxes
common to many theaters. Several former Bird Cage entertainers
perform there. Billy Hutchinson is not a part of this enterprise.

1884

March 22—World champion boxer John L. Sullivan visits Tombstone. A local
resident recalled Sullivan came to the Bird Cage and was of particular
interest to many of the women working there. This is the first account of
the Bird Cage being reopened after Billy Hutchinson closed it.

April—Advertisements in the *Epitaph* note that the Bird Cage is open under the proprietorship of William Sprague, a young, likable local from Cornwall, England, who, as a miner and saloon man, experienced many western boomtowns before Tombstone.

October—Cole's Circus travels along the Southern Pacific Railroad and stops to play in Benson. Among their featured performers are English-born aerialists Rose and Aimee Austin. Promotional lithographs advertising their Human Fly act are placed around Benson and are left behind when the circus pushes on toward New Mexico. Two of the lithographs end up in the Bird Cage, where today they are promoted as show bills for the last Bird Cage performance even through the Austin sisters were never in Tombstone.

1885

June 27—William Sprague takes on two partners in running the Bird Cage. They are fellow Cornwall natives and local saloon men Frank Broad and Oliver Trevillian. After an extensive renovation, they reopen the building and plan to run it in tandem with their other business pursuits. Sprague's health problems force him to seek treatment in Hot Springs, Arkansas.

September—With Billy Sprague's health continuing to falter, the partnership with Frank Broad and Oliver Trevillian ends. All three men pursue other business ventures in Tombstone and Bisbee. For a time Frank Broad operates a music saloon right next door to the Bird Cage.

December 31—After losing in an upset and breaking his collarbone in a wrestling match at Schieffelin Hall, Lucien Marc Christol is thrown a benefit at the Bird Cage. Impressed with the Bird Cage and the response from the public at the benefit, Christol announces interest in opening the Bird Cage as a sporting hall.

1886

January 16—Fearless wanderer, entertainer, and entrepreneur Joe Bignon reopens the Bird Cage after extensively renovating the interior. He operates it as the Elite, but many locals still refer to it as the Bird Cage. His opening act is the Frush Oriental Circus, a financially unstable circus that he had traveled with down from Idaho in the latter part of 1885.

February 6—The first wrestling match is held at the Bird Cage. Joe Bignon chooses Dr. George Goodfellow as the referee. Among other things,

Goodfellow is famously known as the attending physician who operated on Virgil Earp after his assassination attempt in December 1881.

May 3—A 7.2-magnitude earthquake rocks southern Arizona, northern Mexico, and patrons at the Bird Cage. The news reverberates all the way to New York, where the nation's leading entertainment journal reported, "The earthquake shook the [Bird Cage] theatre and audiences up badly last week, but business is now picking up."[1]

May 8—Joe Bignon schedules a six-hour walking match inside the Bird Cage. It is conducted on a track around the perimeter of the auditorium and commences at the same time as performances so patrons can observe two forms of simultaneous entertainment.

July 4—Joe Bignon plans a big Independence Day celebration, including a 2:00 p.m. matinee at the Bird Cage, fireworks display, and huge balloon ascension out front at 6:00 p.m. The celebration is a success except for the balloon, which catches fire during inflation.

August 29—Joe Bignon opens the Kingston Opera House in the mining boomtown of Kingston, New Mexico, 230 miles east of Tombstone.

Early to late September—Joe Bignon closes the Bird Cage to extensively renovate.

1887

January 29—Joe Bignon reopens the Kingston Opera House in Kingston, New Mexico, after an unreported amount of downtime. For a period he closes the Bird Cage in Tombstone. It remains closed until mid- to late March.

1888

July 15–August 11—Joe Bignon again closes the Bird Cage to extensively renovate.

December 8—Joe Bignon returns from San Francisco on another performer recruiting trip. He brings with him a group of performing monkeys and gorillas. On the trip he met and recruited Tillie Bouton, a widowed performer from England.

1889

May 5—Joe Bignon marries Matilda Quigley (professionally known as Tillie Bouton) at his Tombstone home on Sixth Street. The marriage occurs more than three years after Joe had been operating the Bird Cage, and the couple are often found performing together.

May 11—Joe Bignon leaves Tombstone right after his marriage to Tillie and opens the People's Theater in Phoenix, Arizona.

Late August to early September—Joe Bignon closes the Bird Cage "for a few weeks" and is reportedly taking a company to Phoenix to perform. The Bird Cage remains closed until Joe returns with performers in January 1890.

1890

January 17—Joe Bignon arrives in Tombstone from Phoenix with two stage-coaches filled with performers. After a performance at Schieffelin Hall, they perform at the Bird Cage through late February.

February 8—Tough times in Tombstone prompt Joe Bignon to petition the city council for a reduction in the licensing fee he is required to pay.

February 23—Joe Bignon closes the Bird Cage "for a short season" because of "dull times."

July 10—Joe Bignon starts a two-year lease on the Crystal Palace and operates it as a genuine variety theater. He assumes control of the theater and the bar.

1891

January 15—Joe Bignon opens another venue in Phoenix called the Elite, just like the name he uses for the Bird Cage. He operates it simultaneously with the Crystal Palace in Tombstone.

February 18–26—After a month of successful operations of his Elite theater in Phoenix, the Salt River floods to epic proportions. Joe's performers put on a benefit performance to aid the early sufferers. Days later the river continues to swell and overtakes the theater, leaving the charitable performers stranded and in distress. Ultimately Joe sells the building for less money than was donated by the charity performance.

December 12—The Bird Cage reopens as the Olympic. It is unclear how long it remains open, and it is uncertain whether Joe Bignon is behind the endeavor.

1892

July—Joe Bignon's lease on the Crystal Palace in Tombstone ends.

August 6—Joe Bignon opens a variety theater in Albuquerque, New Mexico, called the Horse Shoe Club. To fund the endeavor, he mortgages his and

Tillie's personal possessions in Tombstone, including beddings, pots, pans, photographs, rugs, furniture, and more, indicating his years operating the Bird Cage did not afford him a financial cushion.

November 30—After weeks of successful operations in Albuquerque, local police close Joe's Horse Shoe Club down on a licensing technicality and throw him in jail. The action may have been politically motivated by the community's division over variety theaters. Joe returns to Tombstone intent on waiting for the next boom but does not reopen the Bird Cage. This officially ends the Bird Cage performance era.

1897

Alfred Henry Lewis publishes his first Wolfville Book. The commercial success prompts Lewis to add five more books in the next sixteen years. Although they are works of fiction, he draws on many elements in and around Tombstone, often assigning made-up names to locations. One of the few real-world names he uses is the Bird Cage, which becomes a recurring setting throughout the series. Twenty years after the first book, early movie giant Vitagraph produces a series of at least fifteen films based on Wolfville stories. Over the next forty years the book's influence brings many people to Tombstone specifically to visit the Bird Cage.

1902

June 27—Hugh McCrum dies. His estate (which includes half ownership of the Bird Cage) is controlled by his widow, who jointly owns the building with John Sroufe.

1903

February 12—Hugh McCrum's widow and John Sroufe sell the Bird Cage to longtime Tombstone businessman Joseph Tasker for $1,000. Shortly after, Tasker announces a physical culture exhibition at the Bird Cage, but the event is moved to Schieffelin Hall at the last minute.

March 11—Less than a month after buying the Bird Cage, Joseph Tasker sells the Bird Cage to local rancher Edward Jacklin for $1,500, scoring a quick $500 profit.

1906

December 14—Edward Jacklin sells the Bird Cage and thirty-seven other properties to his ranching partner Charles L. Cummings. Charles continuously collects Tombstone properties and becomes one of the largest volume lot owners. His portfolio includes the majority of Tombstone's most historic properties. Arriving in Tombstone in 1880, he was once a customer of the Bird Cage and took great pride in owning the building. His love for the Bird Cage and his secure financial state will result in preservation efforts and promotional endeavors until his death in 1930.

1910–1929

Charles Cummings recognizes tourists are magnetically fascinated with the Bird Cage, and he gives hundreds of personal tours through the building, offering memories of things he witnessed inside as a young man.

1914

May 23—The Bird Cage almost burns to the ground when a fire starts in the adjoining building. A local police officer who happens to pass by alerts the fire company as strong winds fan the flames. The Bird Cage narrowly escapes.

1920

June 6—After countless tourists come to Tombstone looking for the Bird Cage mentioned in Alfred Henry Lewis's Wolfville books, Charles Cummings places a sign on the building that reads "Birdcage Theatre of Wolfville Tales by Alfred Henry Lewis." The building is the main draw before other points of interest that are popular today are developed.

1921

November—The highway through Tombstone, which turned off at Fifth Street, is officially moved one block to Sixth Street by Arlington Gardner so that people pass by the Bird Cage.

1922

Journalist Frederick Bechdolt publishes his book *When the West Was Young*. In the research phase he came to Tombstone and rubbed elbows with Bird Cage lovers Arlington Gardner and Charles Cummings. The book's success introduces the Bird Cage and Tombstone's legend to many nonfiction readers.

February—Locals recognize the value and deteriorating condition of the Bird Cage and call to form a preservation group. Early ideas include using the building to house a museum showcasing Tombstone's history. Charles Cummings is supportive and contributes to preservation efforts.

1923

October—The crumbling adobe facade on the Bird Cage is removed and is replaced with cement blocks. Across the top of the façade, "Bird Cage Theatre" is painted in large letters for the first time to make it easily identifiable to tourists. That look continues today, and many incorrectly assume it represents the theater's appearance in the 1880s.

1926

February—Tucson's rodeo features a rebuilt Wolfville town based on Alfred Henry Lewis's books. Included in the town is a replica Bird Cage, complete with drop curtains actually used at the Bird Cage and donated by Joe Bignon. He also donates a punch bowl used at the Bird Cage to serve refreshments at the rodeo. Professional performers are hired, one of whom (George A. Bird of the Parker Brothers) was an actual former Bird Cage performer who appeared under Joe Bignon in 1886.

November—The Broadway of American, the country's southern transcontinental highway, is connected through southern Arizona. Through the guidance of Arlington Gardner (the Broadway of America's vice president, responsible for the western section), the road passes through Tombstone and right past the Bird Cage, bringing an influx of tourists.

1927

Author Walter Noble Burns publishes the landmark book *Tombstone: An Iliad of the Southwest*—the first book dedicated entirely to Tombstone's history and cast of characters. He includes a lot of information on the

Bird Cage and credits Charles Cummings and other longtime locals as the source of some of it. The book becomes the basis of a movie called *Tombstone: The Town Too Tough to Die* fifteen years later. Many of the movie's scenes take place inside a movie-set version of the Bird Cage, and several performance numbers are performed nearly uncut.

1929

October 24–27—Tombstone's first Helldorado celebrates Tombstone's colorful history and the town's fiftieth anniversary. As part of the festivities the Bird Cage is reopened. Performers are contracted through the Los Angels–based talent agency Fanchon and Marco. Shows run all afternoon and evening. Former Mayor John Clum attends one of the shows in a box near the stage.

1930

October 16–19—Tombstone's second Helldorado features more Bird Cage performances. Among the performers is Cal Cohn, who was advertised as having appeared at the Bird Cage when the Hutchinsons owned the building.

November 30—Charles Cummings passes away. He is buried in Tombstone Cemetery. His widow honors his love of the building and continues to offer it for Helldorado performances.

1931

October—After Charles's death, his widow, Margaret, opens a storefront at Fifth and Allen to display his collection of items formerly stored in the Bird Cage. These items (such as the *Almeh* painting fictitiously referred to as "Fatima" and "Little Egypt") were returned in part to the Bird Cage throughout the 1930s and in whole in 1941 after the Bird Cage Coffee Shoppe closed for good. Many of those items are seen inside the Bird Cage today.

1931–1932

Performances continue to be held at the Bird Cage for the annual Helldorado celebration each October. Admission for performances in 1932 are forty cents, which is ten cents less than Billy Hutchinson charged the day he opened the building fifty years earlier.

1933

Annie Ashley, the last known active Bird Cage performer, retires after more than fifty years onstage.

1934

June 9—The Bird Cage Coffee Shoppe opens. Charles Cummings's widow conceives the idea to take advantage of growing tourism by opening a food and drink bar. Local friend Nettie Lavalley and her husband, who is a licensed contractor, help renovate the building. Among other improvements they add a room off the east wall and use it as a kitchen. Other improvements include reinstallation of a bar, which had been absent from its present location in the front entrance.

1936

January 31—Amelia Earhart visits the Bird Cage Coffee Shoppe. Sixteen months later she disappears between Australia and Hawaii in an attempted flight around the world.

April—Bird Cage Coffee Shoppe operator Margaret Ewing reveals plans to revive the Bird Cage as a performance venue. She communicates with contacts in Hollywood, but the plans never materialize.

1941

Late September—The Bird Cage Coffee Shoppe era ends when the hostess Margaret Ewing follows her husband to California. Margaret Cummings decides to honor her dead husband Charles's love for the building by opening it as a museum. On display are many of the items related to local and regional history that Charles had collected. Many of those items are on display today and fill the theater auditorium.

1942

Author C. L. Sonnichsen publishes the recollections of an old-time Tombstone saloon man titled *Billy King's Tombstone*. Billy King knew Bird Cage proprietors Frank Broad and Joe Bignon personally and offered extensive recollections about both men, the Bird Cage, and many other Tombstone topics. His memories range from fairly accurate to wildly fallacious.

1945

Actor-turned-author Lynton Wright Brent publishes the first novel dedicated to the Bird Cage. In an effort to draw on reality, he moved to Tombstone for six months and interviewed longtime locals who gave him a foggy version of the town's history.

1951

January 30—Melville Frush, the last known living Bird Cage performer, dies in Bisbee, Arizona.

1970s–1990s

Many fictitious elements of the Bird Cage are creatively added to its lore, such as murders, operation as a brothel, the longest poker game, and the backstory given to the *Almeh* painting by Charles Vaccari falsely identified as "Fatima" and "Little Egypt." Many of these stories were created to explain things that were not fully understood while at the same time sensationalizing the Bird Cage's identity for publicity. When the stories were created, the period resources that could prove them false were not known to exist.

1993

The major motion picture *Tombstone* depicts a lengthy scene inside the Bird Cage. Its portrayal includes many correct and incorrect elements, which influences what many think the Bird Cage was really like.

Appendix B
Index to Bird Cage Myths

Endnotes

Notes for Chapter 1

1. Leavitt, *Fifty Years in Theatrical Management*, 209.
2. *Washington Standard* (Olympia, WA), October 17, 1879.
3. Carolyn Grattan Eichin, *From San Francisco Eastward: Victorian Theater in the American West* (Reno: University of Nevada Press, 2020), 6.
4. *Pioneer Times* (Deadwood, SD), January 1, 1882.
5. *Tombstone Epitaph*, April 24, 1882.
6. *Dodge City* (KS) *Globe*, September 16, 1879.
7. *Black Range* (Socorro, NM), January 11, 1884.
8. *San Antonio Light*, December 22, 23, 1884, January 16, 1885.
9. *Black Hills* (SD) *Weekly Pioneer*, May 19, 1877.
10. *New York Clipper*, July 13, 1878.
11. *Butte Miner*, May 9, 1885.
12. *Butte Miner*, May 6, 1885.
13. *Daily Alta California* (San Francisco), April 26, 1877.
14. *Detroit Free Press*, February 12, 1881.
15. X. Beidler, "The Vigilante Committee Takes Care of Slade, c. January 1864," in *Eyewitness to the Old West: Firsthand Accounts of Exploration, Adventure and Peril*, ed. Richard Scott (Lanham, MD: Taylor Trade Publishing, 2004), 181. "Slade" was the notorious local stagecoach robber Jack Slade who was lynched by local vigilantes less than a year later.
16. *Coffeyville* (KS) *Weekly Journal*, March 22, 1879.
17. Deadwood *Daily Pioneer Times*, December 20, 1899.
18. Rosemary P. Gibson, *The History of Tucson Theatre before 1906* (thesis, University of Arizona, 1967), 42–54; Thomas Fitch, *Western Carpetbagger: The Extraordinary Memoirs of "Senator" Thomas Fitch* (Reno: University of Nevada Press, 1978).
19. *New York Clipper*, April 27, 1889; *San Francisco Examiner*, February 25, 1890.
20. Leavitt, *Fifty Years in Theatrical Management*, 223.
21. *Tombstone Epitaph*, January 15, 1886; *New York Clipper*, January 23, 1886; John Mulligan biographical file in author's collection.
22. Nine years earlier Tom Wade was a Bird Cage performer.

23. *Detroit Free Press*, February 12, 1881.

24. *Galveston Daily News*, January 10, 1885.

25. *Butte* (MT) *Daily Post*, March 1, 1887.

26. *San Francisco Examiner*, January 25, 1877.

27. *Louisville* (KY) *Courier Journal*, May 25, 1891.

28. *San Francisco Examiner*, August 6, 1892.

29. *Seattle Post Intelligencer*, February 20, 1889.

30. *San Francisco Chronicle*, April 29, 1893.

31. *Marshall* (TX) *Messenger*, November 21, 1879.

32. *Denver Rocky Mountain News*, November 15, 1887. See also various reports across the country that carried the story.

33. *Atlanta Constitution*, October 7, 1886.

34. *Chicago Inter Ocean*, January 14, 1882.

35. Letter to the *New York Sun* from Leadville, published in *Emporia* (KS) *Ledger*, May 10, 1877.

36. *Cheyenne Daily Leader*, July 10, 1872.

37. *New York Clipper*, Aug 28, 1880.

38. *San Antonio Light*, January 19, 1885.

39. *Tombstone Epitaph*, November 11, 1881.

40. *Dallas Daily Herald*, May 3, 1881.

41. Eddie Foy and Alvin Harlow, *Clowning through Life* (New York: E. P. Dutton, 1928), 166.

42. *Detroit Free Press*, February 12, 1881.

43. *Butte Weekly Miner*, June 3, 1885.

44. *Arizona Daily Star*, June 24, 1884.

Notes for Chapter 2

1. *Report of the Sonora Exploring and Mining Company Made to the Stockholders, 1856–1860* (Cincinnati: Railroad Record Print, 1856).

2. Robert A. Lewis and Charles Morgan Wood, "Reminiscences of an Arizona Pioneer: Personal Experiences of Robert Alpheus Lewis" (unpublished manuscript, n.d.), 6, Arizona Historical Society, Tucson.

3. *Arizona Daily Star*, January 14, 1879.

4. Letter from Tombstone dated June 17, 1879, published in the *Arizona Daily Star*, June 25 1879; "William Ohnesorgen Reminiscences" (unpublished manuscript, n.d.), Arizona Historical Society.

5. William N. Miller, "First Impressions of Tombstone," ed. Roy B. Young, in *Cochise County Cowboy War: A Cast of Characters*, ed. Roy B. Young (Apache, OK: Young & Sons Enterprises, 1999), 165.

6. Solon Allis, Tombstone townsite survey map, March 5, 1879, Cochise County Recorder's office, Bisbee, AZ.

7. Lewis and Wood, "Reminiscences of an Arizona Pioneer," 6; *Arizona Weekly Star*, April 11, 1878; Pima County, Miscellaneous Records Book 1, p. 526.

8. 1881 Arizona Gazetteer Business Directory, author's collection; *Tombstone Epitaph*, September 15, 1880; Miller, "First Impressions of Tombstone"; 1882 Sanborn Fire Insurance Map, author's collection.

9. *Weekly Nugget*, April 1, 15, 1880; *Tombstone Epitaph*, August 29 and December 13, 1880.

10. *Nugget*, February 9, 1882; *Tombstone Epitaph*, March 29, 1882.

11. See incoming passenger reports in the *Tombstone Epitaph*, July 21 and September 15, 1880, and the *Nugget*, December 3, 4, and 5, 1880.

12. *Topeka Weekly Times*, March 24, 1882.

13. Act No 39: To incorporate the City of Tombstone, February 21, 1881. The original signed copy is in the Law Collection at Arizona State Library and Archives.

14. William N. Miller Recollections.

15. *Chicago Tribune*, February 7, 1880.

16. *Tucson Citizen*, July 9, 1879.

17. D. S. Chamberlain, "Early Day Happenings in Tombstone, Arizona from the autobiography of DS Chamberlain" (unpublished manuscript, n.d.), 2, Arizona Historical Society. A marker for Hicks is in Boothill, but that burial ground wasn't established until two years after he was killed. Boothill wasn't surveyed or approved by the mayor and council until the summer of 1881.

18. *Arizona Daily Star*, September 17, 1879. County transactions note Danner and Owens was on lot 10 block 4; see Cochise County Deeds of Real Estate, book 1, pp. 566–68, Deeds of Real Estate, Grantor and Grantee, Cochise County Recorder's Office.

19. D. S. Chamberlain, "Tombstone in 1879, the Lighter Side" (unpublished manuscript, n.d.), Arizona Historical Society.

20. *Weekly Nugget*, June 10, 1880.

21. *Arizona Daily Star*, July 20, 1880.

22. *Tombstone Epitaph*, September 8, 1880.

23. *Tombstone Epitaph*, August 15 and September 14, 1880; *Arizona Daily Star*, October 14, 1880.

24. *Tombstone Epitaph*, September 10, 1880.

25. *Nugget*, October 20, 23, 1880.

26. *Nugget*, October 22, 1880; Gary L. Roberts, "Wyatt Earp: The Search for Order on the Last Frontier," in *A Wyatt Earp Anthology: Long May His Story Be Told*, ed. Roy B. Young, Gary L. Roberts, and Casey Tefertiller (Denton: University North Texas Press, 2019), 8.

27. John Boessenecker, *Ride the Devil's Herd: Wyatt Earp's Epic Battle against the West's Biggest Outlaw Gang* (New York: Hanover Square Press, 2020), 110.

28. *Arizona Weekly Citizen* (Tucson), January 1, 1881.

29. *Nugget*, November 4, 1880; *Arizona Daily Star*, November 14, 1880.

30. Cochise County Deeds of Real Estate, book 1, pp. 556–57.

31. Cochise County Great Register, 1881, Cochise County Recorder's Office; *Tombstone Epitaph*, May 8, 1881. Fontana's sale of the lot is noted in the *Epitaph*, November 19, 1881.

32. *Tombstone Epitaph*, October 21, 1880

33. One example is Kitty Wilson, who was noted as having performed at the Sixth Street Opera House in the November 16, 1880, *Tombstone Epitaph* and later at the Bird Cage in the July 22, 1882, *Tombstone Epitaph*. Joe Bignon performed at the Sixth Street Opera House, as reported in the *Tombstone Epitaph*, November 13, 1880, and then assumed proprietorship of the Bird Cage starting in January 1886.

34. *Tombstone Epitaph*, October 24, 26 1880; *Nugget*, March 26, 1880; *Carson City* (NV) *Daily Appeal*, April 22, 1880.

35. *Tombstone Epitaph*, June 24 and July 1, 1881.

36. *Tombstone Epitaph*, November 19, 1881.

37. *Weekly Yuma Sentinel*, March 7, 1879; *Arizona Weekly Citizen*, March 14, 1879; *Tombstone Epitaph*, November 15, 1881; Fontana sells the Sixth Street Opera House lot per *Tombstone Epitaph*, November 19, 1881.

38. *Nugget*, April 20, 1882; *Tombstone Epitaph*, November 11, 1881; 1883 Tombstone Tax Plot Map, Arizona Historical Society.

39. *Tombstone Epitaph*, April 4, 1924.

40. *Weekly Nugget*, April 15, 1880; Cochise County Deeds of Real Estate, transcribed from Pima County, book 1, pp. 199–202, 499–501.

41. Cochise County Great Register, 1881 and 1884.

42. Cochise County Deeds of Real Estate, book 1, pp. 497–98.

43. *Tombstone Epitaph*, August 14, 1880; *Tombstone Epitaph*, September 18, 1880.

44. Among many other examples, see: *Tombstone Epitaph*, September 12, 26, 1880.

45. *Tombstone Epitaph*, December 2, 16, 1880.

46. *Nugget*, October 15, 1880; *Tombstone Epitaph*, October 15, 1880.
47. *Nugget*, October 15, 1880; *Tombstone Epitaph*, October 15, 1880.
48. *Tombstone Epitaph*, October 15, 1880.
49. *Tombstone Epitaph*, May 27, 1882.
50. *Tombstone Epitaph*, June 27, 1882.
51. *Tombstone Epitaph*, July 28, 1882.
52. *Daily Tombstone*, November 3, 1886.
53. Arizona Death Records, 1887–1960, Ancestry.com.
54. *Tombstone Epitaph*, March 10, 1881.
55. *Tombstone Epitaph*, September 23, 28, 1880.
56. *Nugget*, October 26, 1880.
57. *Tombstone Epitaph*, December 13, 1880; *Nugget*, December 15, 1880.
58. *Tombstone Epitaph*, March 11, 1881.
59. *Tombstone Epitaph*, March 10, 1881.
60. *Tombstone Epitaph*, March 11, August 13, 1881; Original Turnverein Dance Card, McCubbin Collection; the McCubbin Collection was sold at auction through Brian Label's Old West Events in February 2019, and the item was retrieved through the auction house catalog.
61. *Tombstone Epitaph*, August 16, 1881.
62. Clara Spalding Brown, *Tombstone from a Woman's Point of View: The Correspondence of Clara Spalding Brown, July 7, 1880, to November 14, 1882*, comp. and ed. Lynn Bailey (Tucson: Westernlore Press, 2001), 71.
63. *Tombstone Epitaph*, March 16, 1881; *Arizona Weekly Citizen*, March 20, 1881.
64. *Tombstone Epitaph*, March 23, 26, April 17, 1881.
65. *Tombstone Epitaph*, March 23, 1881.
66. *Tombstone Epitaph*, September 24, 1881; *Nugget*, September 25, 1881.
67. *Tombstone Epitaph*, April 30, 1881.
68. *Nugget*, October 31, November 2, 1880.
69. *Tombstone Epitaph*, December 3, 10, and 17, 1887.
70. For one example see the *Tombstone Prospector*, February 12, 1903.
71. *Tombstone Epitaph*, December 2, 1881; *Nugget*, January 21, 1882.
72. *Nugget*, May 9, 20, 1882.
73. *Tombstone Epitaph*, February 4, 1882.
74. *Tombstone Epitaph*, January 14, 1882.
75. *Tombstone Epitaph*, May 8, 1882.
76. *Tombstone Republican*, July 7, 1883; *Tombstone Epitaph*, October 12, 1881.
77. *Tombstone Epitaph*, February 3, 1886.
78. Brown, *Tombstone from a Woman's Point of View*, 22.

79. The Crystal Palace was first called so in the summer of 1882.
80. *Tombstone Epitaph*, November 13, 1881.
81. A full description of the interior is given in the testimony for the John Mulligan trial, August 1883; see George W. Chambers Papers, MS1079, Box 2, f.32, Arizona Historical Society, Tucson, AZ.
82. *Nugget*, January 3, 1882.
83. *Tombstone Epitaph*, August 19, 1881.
84. *Tombstone Epitaph*, May 6, 1880.
85. *Nugget*, October 15, 17, 1880; *Tombstone Epitaph*, October 19, 1880.
86. *Tombstone Epitaph*, September 14, 16, 1880.
87. *Tombstone Epitaph*, September 30, 1880.
88. *Tombstone Epitaph*, October 7, 1880.
89. *Tombstone Epitaph*, October 28, 1882.
90. *Record Epitaph*, August 20, 1885.
91. *Daily Tombstone*, August 19, 1885.
92. *Phoenix Weekly Republican*, March 23, 1882.
93. *Weekly Nugget*, May 6, 1880; *Tombstone Epitaph*, May 8, 1880.

Notes for Chapter 3

1. Pauline Markham, *The Life of Pauline Markham, Written by Herself* (New York: n.p., 1871), 6.
2. *Police Gazette*, April 23, 1881.
3. Copy of advertisement cards in author's collection.
4. *Wilkes-Barre News*, October 28, 1897.
5. Markham, *Life of Pauline Markham*, 10–11.
6. *Wilkes-Barre News*, October 28, 1879.
7. Markham, *Life of Pauline Markham*, 13.
8. Those familiar with Kevin Costner's *Wyatt Earp* movie from 1994 may recall the scene where Wyatt first sees Josie on a stage performing in Dodge City. The play and music Josie is performing to is the opening of *HMS Pinafore*. Lawrence Kasden, dir., *Wyatt Earp* (Burbank, CA: Warner Bros., 1994).
9. *Tucson Citizen*, November 4, 1879.
10. *Arizona Weekly Citizen*, November 1, 1879.
11. *Arizona Daily Star*, November 25, 26, 1879.
12. *Arizona Daily Star*, November 29, 1879.
13. *Arizona Daily Star*, December 2, 1879.
14. *Tombstone Weekly Nugget*, December 4, 1879.

15. *Arizona Weekly Citizen*, December 6, 1879; *Prescott* (AZ) *Weekly Miner*, December 12, 1879.
16. *Tucson Citizen*, January 19, 1880; *New York Clipper*, February 28, 1880.
17. *Arizona Daily Star*, April 20, 1880.
18. *Tucson Citizen*, April 15, 19, 1880.
19. *Arizona Daily Star*, April 20, 21 1880.
20. *New York Clipper*, October 18, 1873; *New York Clipper*, December 26, 1874, *New York Clipper*, August 11, 1894.
21. *Omaha Daily Bee*, November 19, 1880; Lotta refers to Lotta Crabtree, whose name is being used as a standard measure of the best abilities.
22. *Tucson Citizen*, May 7, 1880.
23. *Tombstone Epitaph*, May 8, 1880.
24. *Tucson Citizen*, May 6, 1880.
25. *Weekly Nugget*, May 6, 1880.
26. *Weekly Nugget*, May 6, 1880.
27. *Weekly Nugget*, May 20, 1880.
28. *Weekly Nugget*, May 13, 1880.
29. *Weekly Nugget*, May 6, 1880.
30. *Weekly Nugget*, May 13, 1880.
31. George Whitwell Parsons, *A Tenderfoot in Tombstone: The Turbulent Years, 1880–1882*, vol. 1 of *The Private Journal of George Whitwell Parsons*, ed. Lynn Bailey (Tucson: Westernlore Press, 1996), May 11, 1881, entry, 46–47. Ed Schieffelin took the same passenger train from Tucson to Pantano as Patti Rosa and company days earlier and may have noticed or even met them at that time. See May 3, 1880, *Tucson Citizen* and May 13, 1880, *Weekly Nugget*.
32. *Arizona Daily Star*, May 21, 1880. She also inspired the naming of an entire mining company in Colorado Springs, Colorado, in 1896 that incorporated as "The Patti Rosa Gold Mining Company."
33. *Weekly Nugget*, May 13, 1880.
34. *Ogden* (UT) *Standard*, December 8, 1882.
35. *Tombstone Epitaph*, April 6, 1881.
36. *Fort Collins* (CO) *Daily Express*, January 20, 1883.
37. *Manford's New Monthly Magazine*, July 1887, 386–89; *New York Clipper*, April 7, 1877; *San Francisco Chronicle*, April 17, 1887; H. J. Burlingame, *Leaves from Conjurers' Scrap Books; or, Modern magicians and their works* (Chicago: Donohue, Henneberry & Co., 1891), 14–33.
38. *Ogden Standard*, December 8, 1882.

39. *Tombstone Epitaph*, April 6, 1881.
40. T. Allston Brown, *A History of the American Stage* (New York: Dick & Fitzgerald, 1870), 231.
41. *Tombstone Epitaph*, April 3, 1881.
42. *Tombstone Epitaph*, April 17, 1881.
43. *Tombstone Epitaph*, April 19, 1881.
44. *Pomona* (CA) *Progress*, March 5, 1913; *Buffalo Times*, March 8, 1913.
45. Of the many advertisements and reviews in newspapers, see the September 21, 1912, *Coshocton* (OH) *Tribune* for a photograph of the Pastime Theater featuring a *Rip Van Winkle* movie lithograph.
46. See the Society of American Magician Hall of Fame, www.samhalloffame.com/members/, accessed August 20, 2024; SAM Hall of Fame certificate in Taylor family collections as printed in E. Cooper Taylor III, *A Few Moments from the Career of Prof E. Cooper Taylor, 1852–1927* (repr., Tuckahoe, NY: self-published, 1990).
47. *Tombstone Epitaph*, April 29, May 2 and 3, 1881.
48. *New York Clipper*, August 25, 1883. This is in reference to well-known French magician Jean-Eugène Robert-Houdini.
49. *Tombstone Epitaph*, April 30, May 8, 1881; *New York Clipper*, August 25, 1883.
50. *Tombstone Epitaph*, May 6, 1881; see also the account in the January 2, 1881, *Sacramento Daily Bee*.
51. *Tombstone Epitaph*, May 6, 1881.
52. *Napa Valley Register*, January 24, 1880; *Tombstone Epitaph*, May 6, 1881; Taylor, *Moments from the Career of Prof E. Cooper Taylor*, 1990.
53. *Tombstone Epitaph*, April 30, 1881; *Tombstone Epitaph*, May 6, 8, 1881; Parsons, *Tenderfoot in Tombstone*, May 5, 1881, entry.
54. *Tombstone Epitaph*, May 4, 1881.
55. *Tombstone Epitaph*, May 6, 1881.
56. *Girard* (KS) *Press*, January 1, 1880.
57. *Tombstone Epitaph*, September 21–26, 1880.
58. See daily reports in the *Epitaph* and *Nugget* from November 27 to December 16, 1880.
59. *Fresno* (CA) *Morning Republican*, November 14, 1909.
60. *Tombstone Nugget*, December 9, 1880.
61. *Tombstone Nugget*, December 5, 1880.
62. Parsons, *Tenderfoot in Tombstone*, December 10, 1880, entry.
63. Parsons, *Tenderfoot in Tombstone*, December 4, 1880, entry, 107.
64. *Tombstone Epitaph*, November 30, 1880.
65. *Tombstone Epitaph*, December 4, 1880.

66. *Tombstone Nugget*, December 4, 1880.

67. *Tombstone Epitaph*, December 8, 1880.

68. *Tombstone Nugget*, December 9, 1880.

69. In December 1881 Nellie Boyd returned and played Schieffelin Hall and again in September 1883. See the *Tombstone Nugget*, December 8, 1881; and George Whitwell Parsons, *The Devil Has Foreclosed: The Concluding Arizona Years, 1882–1887*, vol. 2 of *The Private Journal of George Whitwell Parsons*, ed. Lynn Bailey (Tucson: Westernlore Press, 1997), September 4, 1883, entry.

70. *Tombstone Nugget*, December 8, 1881.

71. Thomas H. Peterson Jr., *The Stagecoach Lines, 1878–1903: A Study in Frontier Transportation* (thesis, University of Arizona, 1968), 74.

72. Cochise County Deeds of Mines, book 7, 571.

73. Cochise County Location of Mines, book 4, 214–15, Cochise County Recorder's Office.

74. *Tombstone Nugget*, December 5, 1880.

Notes for Chapter 4

1. *Arizona Daily Star*, January 15, 1879.

2. Cochise County Deeds of Mines transcribed from Pima County book 2, 157–58.

3. 1850 US Census, Ancestry.com; 1879 Tombstone Village Census, author's collection; 1881 and 1882 Cochise County Great Register, Cochise County Recorder's Office; 1882 Cochise County Census, author's collection.

4. Lloyd DeWitt Bockstruck, *Revolutionary War Bounty Land Grants: Awarded by State Governments* (Baltimore: Genealogical Publishing, 2006), 257; the Reconstructed 1790 Census of Georgia, 63, and Georgia Tax Index, 1789–1700, both from Ancestry.com.

5. War of 1812 Service Records, 1812–1815, and US Marshal's Returns of Enemy Aliens and Prisoners of War, 1812–15, part 1, both from Ancestry.com.

6. Many advertisements include the *Augusta Chronicle and Gazette of the State*, April 11, 1795, and June 16, 1798.

7. *Georgia Constitutionalist* (Augusta), December 21, 1833; Horace S. Foote, ed., Pen Pictures from the Garden of the World . . . (Santa Clara County, CA: Lewis Publishing, 1888), 326; Estate of James G. Hutchinson, Probate Records Book C, 436–51, Harris County Clerk's Office, Houston, TX.

8. *Houston Morning Star*, June 27, 1839, in Marilyn Hoye, "The Houston Morning Star," *Texas State Genealogical Society Quarterly* 35, no. 4 (December 1995): 39.

9. Certificates Issued by Harris County Board of Land, and Land Grant Abstract 147, Texas General Land Office Records, Austin, TX (hereafter cited as TXGLO).

10. Harris County Map, 1847, 1884, and 1893, book 2, p. 362, TXGLO.

11. 1850 and 1860 US Federal Censes.

12. Texas County Marriage Records, 1837–1965, familysearch.org.

13. 1860 and 1870 US Population Censes.

14. 1860 US Population Census; *Fort Worth Star Telegram*, December 12, 1936; Ella A. Rundle death certificate, Texas Death Certificates 1903–1982, Ancestry.com.

15. Batting Game Log, July 13, 1901, retrieved June 2022, www.baseball-reference.com/boxes/DET/DET190107130.shtml, accessed August 20, 2024.

16. 1850 US Population Census.

17. 1860 US Population Census; 1860 Products of Industry Census.

18. William D. Hutchinson Probate, Galveston, TX, Bonds and Letters of Administration, vol 1–4, 1848–1879, case 759, Texas State Library and Archives Commission, Austin, TX.

19. 1870 US Population Census.

20. Texas Select County Marriage Index, 1837–1965; 1880 US Population Census.

21. W. A. Fayman and T. W. Reilly, eds., *Galveston City Directory for 1875–6* (Galveston: Strickland & Clarke, 1875); John H. Heller, comp., *Galveston City Directory, 1876–7* (Galveston: John H. Heller, 1876); Tarrant County, Texas, Marriage Records, Tarrant County Clerk's Office, Fort Worth, TX; 1880 US Population Census.

22. *Arizona Daily Star*, November 19, 1882.

23. *New York Clipper*, November 9, 1878; *Galveston Daily News*, December 31, 1878.

24. *New York Clipper*, December 22, 1877.

25. *Galveston Daily News*, August 1, 1874; *Galveston Daily News*, June 9, 1877.

26. 1879 Tombstone Village Census; 1882 Cochise County Census.

27. *Tombstone Epitaph*, March 23, 1881.

28. *Nugget*, December 15, 1880.

29. *Nugget*, December 9, 1880.

30. Cochise County Deeds of Mines, book 5, 593.

31. *Weekly Nugget*, October 2, 1879; 1880 US Population Census.

32. Cochise County Deeds of Mines, book 2, 265–66.

33. Cochise County Deeds of Mines, book 5, 435–36; Cochise County Records of Mines, book 7, 160–61.

34. Lot 18, Block 29, Delinquent Tax Roll of Cochise County, 1882, Cochise County Tax Assessor's Office.

35. *BJ's Tombstone History Discussion Forum*, posted Dec 29, 2011, retrieved June 2022.

36. Deeds of Mines, Pima County transcribed for Cochise County, book 5, 593; Cochise County Deeds of Real Estate, book 2, 41–43, Cochise County Recorder's Office. Both men were involved in private loans from John Sroufe and Hugh McCrum on March 13, 1882. Le Van repaid the loan. Billy did not, which started the downfall of the Bird Cage under his management.

37. *Tombstone Epitaph*, October 9, 1880.

38. Many examples exist in both the *Epitaph* and *Nugget*. Among others, see *Tombstone Epitaph*, September 28, October 20, November 30, 1880.

39. *Tombstone Epitaph*, October 15, 1880; *Nugget*, October 15, 1880; *Arizona Daily Star*, March 4, 1883.

40. *Nugget*, October 30, 1881.

41. C. L. Sonnichsen, *Billy King's Tombstone* (Caldwell, ID: Caxton, 1942), 162.

42. *Ben Goodrich v. W. J. Hutchinson*, case 304, and Cochise County Criminal Register of Actions, Arizona State Library and Archives, Phoenix.

43. See various membership announcements in the *Tombstone Epitaph* in September and October 1880.

44. *Tombstone Epitaph*, September 8, 15, 1880.

45. *Tombstone Epitaph*, October 28, November 27, 1880.

46. *Tombstone Epitaph*, October 2, 1880; *Nugget*, November 24, 1880.

47. *Tombstone Epitaph*, March 23, 1881.

48. Examples include *Tombstone Epitaph*, November 27, 1880, and *Tombstone Epitaph*, July 15, 1881.

49. *Tombstone Epitaph*, February 20, 1884; *Tombstone Republican*, February 24, 1884.

50. *Tombstone Epitaph*, June 1, 1882.

51. *Tombstone Epitaph*, December 15, 1880; *Tombstone Epitaph*, September 16, 1881.

52. *Tombstone Epitaph*, May 6, 1881.
53. *Tombstone Epitaph*, February 5, 1882; *Nugget*, February 7, 1882.
54. *Tombstone Epitaph*, November 19, 26, 1881.
55. *Tombstone Epitaph*, January 5, 1881.
56. *Nugget*, November 19, 1881.
57. *Tombstone Epitaph*, November 19, 1881; Cochise County Deeds of Mines, book 5, 435–36. Billy was also McAllister's power of attorney per Cochise County Power of Attorney, book 1, 346–48, Cochise County Recorder's Office.
58. *Tombstone Epitaph*, May 1, 1882.
59. 1883–1884 Tombstone Business Directory, author's collection.
60. *Tombstone Epitaph*, August 26, 27, 1880.
61. *Tombstone Epitaph*, March 23, 1881; *Tombstone Epitaph*, October 14, 1880.

Notes for Chapter 5

1. Memoirs of Charles Gordes, Works Progress Administration (WPA), Federal Writer's Project Interviews, copy in author's collection; also available at "Charles Gordes," *Cochise County AZGenWeb*, accessed August 14, 2024, https://azgenwebcochise.com/firstfamilies/gordesc_wpa.html.
2. Solon Allis, official survey map of Tombstone, March 5, 1879, Cochise County Recorder's Office.
3. Miller, "First Impressions of Tombstone," 166. This recollection is supported by the fact that many of Tombstone's initial lot owners did not have deeds recorded with the county, but there are records showing they sold those lots.
4. *AZ Daily Star*, February 4, 1880; *Nugget*, November 2, 1880; 1880 US Population Census.
5. *Weekly Nugget*, Oct 2, 1879; 1880 US Population Census.
6. 1880 US Population Census; Carleton Watkins photograph 1313, author's collection.
7. Deeds of Real Estate, Cochise County, book 3, 231–33.
8. Hutchinson's four lots are mentioned in District Court, Case 304, Cochise County, District Court Civil Cases, Arizona State Library and Archives; see also Register of Actions, First District Court, Cochise County Recorder's Office, book 1, 304. See also Deeds of Real Estate, Cochise County.

9. Fred Dodge, *Under Cover for Wells Fargo: The Unvarnished Recollections of Fred Dodge*, ed. Carolyn Lake (Norman: University of Oklahoma Press, 1999), 9–10.

10. Letter from Fred Dodge to Stuart Lake, October 8, 1928, and September 30, 1929, in Dodge, *Under Cover for Wells Fargo*, 234, 241.

11. *Arizona Weekly Citizen*, January 1, 1881.

12. Letter from Fred Dodge to Stuart Lake, October 8, in Dodge, *Under Cover for Wells Fargo*, 236.

13. *Tombstone Epitaph*, October 29, 1880; *Nugget*, October 30, 31, 1880.

14. *Tombstone Epitaph*, October 29, 1880; *Arizona Daily Star*, November 4, 1880.

15. *Nugget*, November 2, 1880; *Weekly Citizen*, November 6, 1880.

16. *Nugget*, November 2, 1880; *Weekly Citizen*, November 6, 1880.

17. *Tombstone Epitaph*, October 29, 31, 1880.

18. Dodge, *Under Cover for Wells Fargo*, 24–25.

19. Stuart Lake, *Wyatt Earp: Frontier Marshal* (New York: Pocket Books, 1994), 245.

20. Letter from Tombstone to the *Yuma Sentinel* dated December 13, 1879, and published on December 27, 1879.

21. *Arizona Daily Star*, August 7, 1880.

22. Parsons, *Tenderfoot in Tombstone*, December 4, 1880, journal entry, 107.

23. *Tombstone Epitaph*, November 10, 1880.

24. *Epitaph*, November 15, 1880.

25. *Goodrich v. Hutchinson*; First District Court Register of Actions, book 1, 304; Deeds of Real Estate, Cochise County, Book 1, 4–5.

26. Deeds of Mines, book 2, 589–91, Cochise County Recorder's Office.

27. *Nugget*, October 30, 1881; *Goodrich v. Hutchinson*.

28. *Arizona Sentinel* (Yuma), April 3, 1880.

29. *Weekly Star*, April 21, 1881.

30. John Plesent Gray, *When All Roads Led to Tombstone: A Memoir of John Plesent Gray*, ed. and annotated, W. Lane Rogers (Boise, ID: Tamarack Books, 1998), 22–23.

31. See US Mining Law, approved May 10, 1872.

32. *Arizona Daily Star*, September 17, 1879.

33. Palmquist, "Justice in Tombstone," in Young, Roberts, and Tefertiller, *Wyatt Earp Anthology*, 454.

34. *Arizona Daily Star*, September 11, 1879.

35. Paul L. Johnson, *The McLaurys in Tombstone, Arizona: An OK Corral Obituary* (Denton: University of North Texas Press, 2012), 110.
36. *Weekly Star*, April 21, 1881.
37. *Tombstone Epitaph*, November 17, 1880; *Nugget*, November 19, 1880.
38. *Weekly Star*, September 11, 1879.
39. *Tombstone Epitaph*, July 28, 1882.
40. *Boston Globe*, August 10, 1881.
41. Johnson, *McLaury's in Tombstone*, 94.
42. *Tombstone Epitaph*, April 19, 1881.
43. *Tombstone Epitaph*, April 18, 1881.
44. *Weekly Star*, April 21, 1881.
45. Cochise County Leases, book 1, 86–89; *Epitaph*, June 5, 1881.
46. Parsons, *Tenderfoot in Tombstone*, April 25–27, 1881, entries.
47. *Boston Globe*, August 10, 1881.
48. The name of the organization is in the May 28, 1881, *Epitaph*.
49. *Tombstone Epitaph*, April 23, 1881.
50. Deeds of Real Estate, Cochise County, book 1, 601–7; *Tombstone Epitaph*, July 22, 1881. Records show Hutchinson first leased the property from Field for $175 on July 15; noted in Leases of Cochise County, book 1, 173–75, Cochise County Recorder's Office. Their final arrangement was an outright transfer of ownership. This suggests they had some back-and-forth negotiations. Bad blood may have played a role.
51. See the *Tombstone Epitaph* of July 29, 1882, for local report on the Supreme Court ruling.
52. *Tombstone Republican*, October 27, 1883.
53. *Arizona Sentinel*, July 2, 1881.
54. *Tombstone* Epitaph, June 25, 1881.
55. *Tombstone Epitaph*, March 15, 16, 1881.
56. Tombstone City Council Minutes, 1880–1882, Tombstone City Archives.
57. *Tombstone Epitaph*, October 4, 1881.
58. *Tombstone Epitaph*, September 8, 1881.
59. *Tombstone Epitaph*, September 8, 1881; see also Giuseppe Fontana's Stone Corner building next to the Bird Cage being built at the same time per the September 21, 1881, *Epitaph* and finished by the November 11, 1881, *Epitaph*.
60. Revenue generated from saloon operations possibly funded the interior additions ahead of the theater's grand opening at the end of December.
61. *Tombstone Epitaph*, December 24, 31, 1881.
62. *Nugget*, July 10, 1881.

63. *Weekly Echo* (Lake Charles, LA), July 8, 1875; *Dallas Daily Herald*, April 8, 1884; *Parsons* (KS) *Daily Eclipse*, September 23, 1879.

64. *Dallas Daily Herald*, May 3, 1881.

65. *New York Clipper*, August 24, 1921.

66. *Pascagoula* (MS) *Democrat*, December 3, 1886; *Sea Coast Echo* (Bay St. Louis, MS), August 20, 1892.

67. *Cincinnati Enquirer*, November 30, 1924.

68. *Bisbee* (AZ) *Daily Review*, April 1, 1903.

69. *Arizona Republic*, December 25, 1927.

70. Bernard Sobel, *Burleycue: An Underground History of Burlesque Days* (New York: Farrar & Rinehart, 1931), 58.

71. *Galveston Daily News*, August 1, 1874; 1877 Galveston City Directory; *Galveston Daily News*, June 9, 1877.

72. *Tombstone Epitaph*, December 19, 1881.

73. *Tombstone Epitaph*, December 15, 1881.

74. Hutchinson, performer biographical files, author's collection.

75. *Tucson Citizen*, April 26, 1924.

76. Millie De Granville, Harry and Clara Lorraine, John Burns, and Matt Trayers biographical files, author's collection.

77. *Tombstone Epitaph*, December 19, 1881; *Los Angeles Herald*, December 20, 1881.

78. *Tombstone Epitaph*, December 23, 1881.

79. *Nugget*, December 21, 1881.

80. *Tombstone Epitaph*, December 22, 1881.

81. *Tombstone Epitaph*, December 20, 1881; *Nugget*, December 21, 1881.

82. *Nugget*, December 22, 1881.

83. *Weekly Epitaph*, December 26, 1881.

84. *Nugget*, December 23, 1881.

Notes for Chapter 6

1. *Tombstone Epitaph*, December 20, 1881.

2. Many incorrect opening dates for the Bird Cage have been published. The correct date comes from two sources. Billy placed advertisements for the grand opening in the *Nugget*, December 22–24, 1881, and submitted a formal city license application. That original document notes an opening date of December 24, 1881, and is in the collections of the Tombstone Western Heritage Museum.

3. *San Francisco Examiner*, December 28, 1881; Harry Lorraine biographical file, in author's collection.

4. *Tombstone Epitaph*, December 28, 1881.

5. Press dispatch from Tombstone printed in the *Los Angeles Times*, December 27, 1881, and the *Los Angeles Herald*, December 27, 1881.

6. *Nugget*, December 28, 1881; Clara Lorraine biographical file, author's collection.

7. *Tombstone Epitaph*, December 28, 1881.

8. *Tombstone Epitaph*, December 28, 1881; *Los Angeles Herald*, December 27, 1881; Bird Cage performer biographical files, in author's collection.

9. *Arizona Daily Star*, February 10, 1929.

10. *Nugget*, December 31, 1881; other examples include the *Nugget*, February 4, March 4, 1882.

11. *Nugget*, February 5, 8, 10, 1882.

12. *Nugget*, February 22, 1882.

13. *Arizona Daily Star*, October 22, 1882. This math is corroborated by a letter published in the *Exhibitors Herald and Moving Picture World* on March 24, 1928, which noted the capacity was "about 200, not counting the room occupied by the bar." John Clum, mayor of Tombstone when the Bird Cage opened, later claimed the building "accommodated only about 250 patrons" after the building's sizable addition was put on eight months after the benefit. During the benefit, 200 people would have been absolute capacity, and that was achieved based on door receipt totals. See John H. Clum, "Helldorado, 1879–1929," *Tombstone History Archives*, http://tombstonehistoryarchives.com/helldorado-1879-1929.html, accessed August 20, 2024.

14. *Nugget*, December 31, 1881.

15. *Tombstone Epitaph*, July 18, 1882.

16. *Arizona Daily Star*, November 19, 1882.

17. Code of Ordinance, Tombstone City Archives; 1880–1882 City Council Minutes, Tombstone City Archives.

18. *Nugget*, February 22 to March 2, 1882; *Nugget*, April 13, 1882.

19. See numerous fashion advertisements that ran from January 13 to March 13, 1883, in the *Arizona Daily Star*.

20. *Arizona Daily Star*, February 10, 1929.

21. *Butte Miner*, April 22, 1885.

22. *Butte Miner*, June 2, 1885.

23. *Arizona Daily Star*, October 28, 1882.

24. Carlisle Stewart Abbott, *Recollections of a California Pioneer* (New York: Neale Publishing, 1917), 208. By the time of Carlisle's 1888 account, Tombstone had changed culturally and economically from the early days of the Hutchinsons' operation of the Bird Cage.

25. *Nugget*, December 31, 1881.

26. *Nugget*, March 3, 1882.

27. *Nugget*, February 14, March 22, 1882.

28. *Tombstone Epitaph*, July 25, 1882.

29. *Nugget*, March 15, 1882.

30. *Arizona Daily Star*, October 22, 1882.

31. *Tombstone Epitaph*, July 26, 1882.

32. *Arizona Daily Star*, February 10, 1929.

33. *Arizona Daily Star*, October 22, 1882. See also the testimony of Billy Hutchinson summarized in the *Weekly Epitaph*, March 13, 1882.

34. *Weekly Epitaph*, September 16, 1882.

35. *Tombstone Epitaph*, July 16, 1882. The Delinquent Tax Roll of Cochise County for 1882 notes the official name as "Bird Cage Opera House." Cochise County Chattel Mortgages, book 1, 84, also notes official name as "Bird Cage Opera House." Formal ads placed by Billy though the March 9, 1883, *Tombstone Republican* all noted the name as "Bird Cage Opera House," whereas his ads prior to July 1882 used "Bird Cage Theater".

36. Eichin, *From San Francisco Eastward*, 81.

37. Several examples include the *Weekly Epitaph*, December 19, 1882, and *Sacramento Daily Record*, March 27, 1883.

38. *Tombstone Epitaph*, August 19, 1882.

39. Hutchinson performer biographical files, author's collection.

40. Cochise County, Deed of Mines, book 2, 157–58.

41. *Tombstone Epitaph*, May 1, 1882.

42. *Tombstone Epitaph*, July 17, 1882.

43. Harry K. Morton Scrapbook, 11, New York Public Library. The clipping is likely taken from the *Tombstone Epitaph* of August 26, 1882, of which there are no known surviving copies.

44. *Tombstone Epitaph*, February 5, 7, 1882.

45. Letter from Tombstone published in the *Arizona Daily Star*, October 19, 1882.

46. *Stockton* (CA) *Mail*, August 20, 1881.

47. Foy and Harlow, *Clowning through Life*, 165–66; Buckley's was praised by the *Stockton Mail* newspaper on August 20, 1881: "Next to the Bella Union, the Adelphi is the leading theater of San Francisco." The Bella Union was the source of many of Hutchinson's performers.

48. *Nugget*, December 31, 1881.

49. *Tucson Citizen*, April 26, 1924.

50. William M. Breakenridge, *Helldorado: Bringing the Law to the Mesquite*, ed. and with an introduction by Richard Maxwell Brown (Lincoln, NE: Bison Books, 1992), 268.

51. *Tucson Citizen*, February 16, 1926.
52. *Tombstone Epitaph*, July 15, 1882; Tombstone City Recorder's Docket, 203, Tombstone City Archives.
53. Deposition of Robert Hatch, inquest on Morgan Earp, March 22, 1882, author's collection; *Nugget*, March 18, 1882.
54. *Tombstone Epitaph*, March 17, 1882.
55. *New York Clipper*, August 22, 29, 1882.
56. *Nugget*, May 23, 25, 1882.
57. *Tombstone Epitaph*, July 22, 1882; *Kansas City Times*, July 26, 1882.
58. *Tombstone Epitaph*, July 16, 1882; Harry K. Morton and Annie Duncan biographical files, in author's collection.

Notes for Chapter 7

1. *Tombstone Epitaph*, January 11, 1882.
2. *Tombstone Epitaph*, February 4, 1882.
3. Original mortgage document, District Court case 695, Arizona State Library and Archives.
4. John Sroufe death certificate, copy in author's collection.
5. *Sonoma County* (CA) *Journal*, July 17, 1857.
6. 1870 US Population Census.
7. *Petaluma* (CA) *Daily Morning Courier*, July 18, 1904.
8. *Petaluma Argus*, August 27, 1875.
9. Varying birthdays are indicated in numerous California Voting Registers, the California death records, and his published obituary. No official birth or death record has been located.
10. New York, US, Irish Immigrant Arrival Records, 1846–1851, Ancestry.com.
11. 1860 and 1870 US Population Censes.
12. *Prescott Weekly Journal Miner*, July 2, 1902.
13. *Weekly Arizona Miner*, March 2, 1872.
14. *Los Angeles Star*, reprinted in the *Weekly Arizona Miner*, March 2, 1872.
15. *Weekly Citizen*, March 2, 1872.
16. *Arizona Daily Star*, March 14, 1902.
17. *San Francisco Examiner*, June 29, 1902.
18. *San Francisco Call*, March 20, 1895. McCrum's wife, Emma, filed for divorce on two occasions, the first time noting "habitual intemperance and extreme cruelty." See the *San Francisco Examiner*, August 21, 1874.
19. *Nevada State Journal* (Reno), July 22, 1882.

20. *Prescott Weekly Journal Miner*, July 2, 1902.
21. Many ads note their available products, such those printed in the *Weekly Nugget*, June 24, 1880, and the *Tucson Citizen*, January 1, 1895.
22. *Petaluma Weekly Argus*, August 27, 1875; Cochise County Deeds of Real Estate, book 19, 190–10.
23. *Prescott Weekly Miner*, July 2, 1902.
24. *Arizona Daily Star*, July 3, 1902; *Arizona Daily Star*, February 24, 1886; *Prescott Weekly Journal Miner*, July 2, 1902; *Arizona Champion* (Peach Springs), July 12, 1884; Cochise County Deeds of Real Estate, books 8 and 9; Cochise County Reverse Index to Deeds of Mines, grantee book 1.
25. *Tombstone Epitaph*, September 13, 1889, and *Arizona Daily Star*, October 10, 1902.
26. See collected travel notices from Tombstone and Tucson newspapers from August 1, 1879, to October 25, 1891. There is no record that John Sroufe ever came to Arizona. Hugh McCrum was also heavily interested in the Prescott, Arizona, area. He owned a stock farm and several notable mines, including the McCabe mine, which was valued at $750,000. Following his deep investments, he made many prolonged trips to the area.
27. *Weekly Nugget*, April 1, 1880.
28. *Tombstone Epitaph*, March 11, 1882.
29. Arizona District Court Case 695, Exhibit "A," and Mortgage Indenture, Arizona State Library and Archives.
30. Summary of Plaintiff District Court case 695, *Sroufe v. Hutchison*, Arizona State Library and Archives.
31. Original letter archived by Heritage Auctions, June 11, 2016.
32. 1882 Delinquent Tax Roll of Cochise County.
33. Weekly Epitaph, December 9, 1882.
34. Parsons, Devil Has Foreclosed, 39, entry for November 18, 1882.
35. Parsons, Devil Has Foreclosed, 40, entry for November 27, 1882.
36. Weekly Epitaph, December 9, 1882.
37. Summary of Sroufe v. Hutchison.
38. Original summons, Sroufe v. Hutchison.
39. Chattel Mortgages, Cochise County, book 1, 83–86.
40. Default, Sro*ufe v. Hutchison*.
41. Recorder's Docket, 318, Tombstone City Archives.
42. Cochise County Bill of Sale, book 1, 142.
43. *Tombstone Republican*, February 24, 1883.

44. *Tombstone Republican*, July 7, 1883.
45. Brown, *Tombstone from a Woman's Point of View*, 73.
46. *Arizona Daily Star*, May 29, 1884.
47. *Tombstone Republican*, July 7, 1883.
48. *Arizona Daily Star*, May 22, 1883.
49. Cochise County Deeds of Real Estate, book 5, 520–21.
50. Cochise County Deeds of Real Estate records, 1881–1906; Cochise County Probate Orders, book 7, 166–68; Cochise County Docket 230, pp. 588, 590.
51. *Weekly Citizen*, August 18, 1883.
52. Recorder's Docket, 383, Tombstone City Archives.
53. Cochise County District Court, case 463, Arizona State Library and Archives.

Notes for Chapter 8

1. *Arizona Daily Star*, August 2, 1884; *Daily Tombstone*, July 20, 1885.
2. *Arizona Daily Star*, May 29, 1884.
3. *Phoenix Weekly Republican*, June 26, 1884.
4. 1861 England Census, Ancestry.com; 1884 Cochise County Great Register; *Reno* (NV) *Journal Gazette*, June 7, 1879; 1880 US Population Census.
5. *Daily Tombstone*, September 20, 1886.
6. *Daily Tombstone*, September 8, 1886.
7. If a lease agreement was made, no formal paperwork was filed with Cochise County.
8. *Tombstone Epitaph*, April 27, 1884.
9. *Tucson Weekly Citizen*, March 22, 1884; *Arizona Daily Star*, March 22, 1884.
10. *Arizona Daily Star*, April 6, 1882.
11. *Tombstone Epitaph*, April 5, 1882.
12. *Weekly Epitaph*, April 10, 1882.
13. James G. Wolf, WPA Interview recorded by Richard J. Kelley, *Cochise County AZGenWeb*, accessed August 15, 2024, https://azgenweb-cochise.com/firstfamilies/wolfj_wpa.html. Helen Yonge Lind recalled a story about her father, who was 7 years old when Sullivan came to town: "John L. Sullivan visited Tombstone once. Mr. Yonge (her grandfather) took his children to see the fighter at the home of a friend, and the little Duke Yonge [her father] sat on Sullivan's lap"; Charles Morgan Wood Manuscripts, MS 1159, Arizona Historical Society, Tucson, AZ.

14. *Tucson Citizen*, March 22, 1884.

15. *Tombstone Epitaph*, April 27, 29, 1884.

16. *Tombstone Epitaph*, April 27, 1884.

17. *Brooklyn Daily Eagle*, March 23, 1938; Brent E. Walker, *Mack Sennett's Fun Factory: A History and Filmography of His Studio and His Keystone and Mack Sennett Comedies, with Biographies of Players and Personnel* (Jefferson, NC: McFarland, 2009).

18. *Los Angeles Times*, March 23, 1938.

19. *Fort Worth Star Telegram*, March 23, 1938.

20. *Tombstone Epitaph*, April 27, 1884.

21. *National Police Gazette*, November 15, 1885.

22. *Daily Tombstone*, August 5, 1885.

23. *Daily Tombstone*, August 5, 1885; *Record Epitaph* (Tombstone), August 26, 1885; *Tucson Citizen*, September 12, 1885.

24. On May 8, 1885, Billy Sprague also paid for a county license for a saloon in Bisbee. See Cochise County License Logs at the Tombstone Courthouse State Park, Tombstone, AZ.

25. *Daily Tombstone*, March 21 to August 15, 1885.

26. 1861 England Census.

27. *Nevada State Journal*, June 22, 1877; *Carson City Daily Appeal*, June 22, 1877.

28. *Nevada State Journal*, June 22, 1877; *Carson City Daily Appeal*, June 22, 1877.

29. *New York Clipper*, April 8, 1876.

30. *Eureka* (NV) *Daily Sentinel*, June 19, 1877; 1884 Cochise County Great Register.

31. *Tombstone Epitaph*, March 16, 1886.

32. *Tombstone Epitaph*, March 3, 17, 24, 1888; *Weekly Epitaph*, December 17, 1887.

33. *Tombstone Prospector*, January 6, 1889.

34. John P. Clum, "Nellie Cashman," *Arizona Historical Review* 3, no. 4 (January 1931): 9–35; *Pioche* (NV) *Record*, January 10, 1873; Peter Brand, *Doc Holliday's Nemesis: The Story of Johnny Tyler & Tombstone's Gamblers' War* (self-published, 2018).

35. 1879 Tombstone village census; 1880 US Population Census; 1881 and 1882 Cochise County Great Register.

36. *Tombstone Nugget*, January 1, February 24, 1882.

37. *Weekly Epitaph*, November 8, 1891; *Tombstone Epitaph*, June 27, 1889.

38. *Daily Tombstone*, September 11, 1886.

39. *Tombstone Prospector*, November 5, 1890.
40. *Weekly Epitaph*, May 10, 1891; *Tombstone Epitaph*, February 3, 1886; *Tombstone Epitaph*, October 17, 1889.
41. *Weekly Epitaph*, September 4, 1892.
42. *Weekly Epitaph*, October 30, November 9, 1892.
43. *Daily Tombstone*, July 20, 1885.
44. *Daily Tombstone*, June 23, 1885.
45. *Daily Tombstone*, June 27, July 3, 1885.
46. *Daily* Tombstone, July 6, 1885.
47. Mark and Ida Grayson biographical file, in author's collection.
48. Jefferson De Angelis and Alvin F. Harlow, *A Vagabond Trouper* (New York: Harcourt, Brace, 1931), 49–50.
49. *New York Clipper*, July 18, 1885.
50. *Daily Tombstone*, July 3, 1885.
51. *Daily Tombstone*, August 5, 1885.
52. *Daily Tombstone*, September 12, 1885.
53. *Daily Tombstone*, November 28, 1885; *Arizona Daily Star*, January 17, 1889. Sprague also moved to Butte, Montana, for a time.
54. *Daily Tombstone*, August 5, September 11, 1885.
55. *Tombstone Epitaph*, May 5, 1889.
56. *Daily Tombstone*, October 30, 1885; *Daily Tombstone*, August 20, 1889.
57. *Tombstone Epitaph*, December 22, 1885.
58. *Daily Tombstone*, December 26, 1885. Goodfellow also refereed a match held at the Bird Cage a few months later, as noted in the following chapter.
59. *Tucson Citizen*, February 11, 1926; *Tombstone Epitaph*, January 3, 1886.
60. *Tombstone Epitaph*, January 3, 1886.
61. *Tombstone Epitaph*, January 3, 1886.
62. Parsons, *Devil Has Foreclosed*, see December 21 and 24, 1885.

Notes for Chapter 9

1. 1918 Cochise County Great Register; Billy Hattich measure book for men's suits, 1889–1891, William Hattitch Papers, MS 0337, Arizona Historical Society.
2. US Naturalization Records, Arizona Index to Certificates of Citizenship, www.familysearch.org; Cochise County Great Register, 1888 and 1914; US Federal Census, 1900, 1910 and 1920.

3. C. E. Willson, "From Variety Theater to Coffee Shoppe," *Arizona Historical Review* 6, no. 2 (April 1935): 10–11.

4. *History of Manistee County, Michigan with Illustrations and Biographical Sketches of Some of Its Men and Pioneers* (Chicago, H. R. Page, 1882).

5. Cochise County Great Register, 1888, 1890.

6. *New York Clipper*, April 14, 28, 1877; *Weekly Tombstone Prospector*, January 15, 1889.

7. *Manitoba Free Press*, July 6, 1878.

8. For a well-researched background on Dwyer and the circus failures, see Bruce Cherney, "Circus Comes to Town," *Winnipeg Regional Real Estate News*, July 2013.

9. Augustus Ellis, Muster Roll Abstracts of NY State Volunteers, www.fold3.com; *New York Clipper*, January 5, 1877; *Bismarck Tribune*, December 9, 1878.

10. *Bismarck Tribune*, March 1, 1879.

11. *Bismarck Weekly Tribune*, September 25, 1878.

12. *Los Angeles Times*, December 11, 1925.

13. *New York Clipper*, December 20, 1879; Gary L. Roberts, *Doc Holliday: The Life and Legend* (New York: Wiley & Sons, 2007), 108–14.

14. *Santa Fe New Mexican*, April 2, 1880.

15. *Weekly Santa Fe New Mexican*, March 15, 1880.

16. One example is Harry Collins. See: *New York Clipper*, January 10, 1880.

17. *Arizona Daily Star*, September 2, 1879.

18. *Tombstone Epitaph*, November 13, 1880.

19. *Tombstone Epitaph*, November 21, 1880.

20. *Tombstone Epitaph*, November 20, 1880.

21. 1880 Federal Census.

22. *Tombstone Epitaph*, November 28, 1880.

23. *Arizona Daily Star*, November 21, 1882.

24. *Arizona Daily Star*, November 14, 1882.

25. *Arizona Daily Star*, December 14, 1882.

26. *Arizona Daily Star*, December 2, 1882.

27. See unclaimed mail noted in the May 7, 1882, *Nugget*.

28. Billy King recalled the Hutchinsons hired Joe. See Sonnichsen, *Billy King's Tombstone*, 110. In 1879 and 1880, Joe traveled with Dick and Mollie Durand, two performers the Hutchinsons hired in 1882. The web of connections among these performers was extensive.

29. *Tulare* (CA) *Advance Register*, September 19, 1884; *Eureka Daily Sentinel*, December 17, 1884.

30. *Arizona Daily Star*, November 16, 1882.

31. *Lyon County Times* (Silver City, NM), June 27, 1885; *Weekly Tombstone Prospector*, January 15, 1889. See also Cushing's Ocean to Ocean Circus fiasco in the *Idaho Semi Weekly World* (Idaho City) and the *Wood River Times* (Hailey, ID) of July and August 1885.

32. *Idaho Semi Weekly World*, July 17, 1885.

33. *Sacramento Daily Bee*, June 25, 1885; *Idaho Semi Weekly World*, July 21, 1885.

34. *Idaho Semi Weekly World*, July 21, 1885.

35. *Wood River Times*, August 14, 1884.

36. *Wood River Times*, July 29, 1885.

37. *Wood River Times*, August 14, 1885.

38. *Wood River Times*, August 15, 1885.

39. *Wood River Times*, August 18, 19, 1885.

40. 1870 and 1880 US Federal Census.

41. *New York Clipper*, September 16, 1882; *Lewiston* (ID) *Daily Teller*, October 11, 1883; *Deseret Evening News* (Salt Lake City), July 1, 1884.

42. *Salt Lake Evening Democrat*, August 26, 1885.

43. *Phoenix Weekly Republican*, June 26, 1908.

44. *Tucson Citizen*, December 19, 1885.

45. *Tucson Citizen*, December 19, 1885.

46. *Tombstone Epitaph*, January 3, 1886.

47. *Daily Tombstone*, January 16, 1886.

48. *Tombstone Epitaph*, January 3, 1886; *Daily Tombstone*, January 15, February 24, 1886; *New York Clipper*, February 6, 1886.

49. *Daily Tombstone*, January 12, 16, 18, 1886.

50. For years the building would continue to be referred to as the Bird Cage by locals and the newspaper, much like modern well-known landmarks that retain their former monikers after name changes. The first time "Elite" was used is February 15, 1886, almost a month after Joe reopened it. It's unknown if Joe opened as the Elite from day one or if he renamed it after the fact.

51. Sonnichsen, *Billy King's Tombstone*, 110.

52. *Daily Tombstone*, July 1, 1886; see also *Daily Tombstone*, July 15, 1886, which made note of "all the fair ladies who have left Tombstone for California and other points to spend the summer."

53. See the *Weekly Epitaph*, December 10, 1887; *Prospector*, November 28, 1888.

54. *Chicago Inter Ocean*, March 17, 1895; William and Frank Miehle biographical file, author's collection.
55. Dan Creelan biographical file, author's collection.
56. Keene worked there from opening in early 1886 until January 1890.
57. *Tombstone Epitaph*, April 7, 1887; *Prospector*, November 5, 1890.
58. *Prospector*, February 22, 1888.
59. *Tombstone Epitaph*, August 2, 1889.
60. *Tombstone Epitaph*, February 7, 1886.
61. Sonnichsen, *Billy King's Tombstone*, 191–92.
62. *Buffalo Courier*, May 25, 1878.
63. *Daily Tombstone*, May 3, 1886.
64. *Daily Tombstone*, May 24, 1886; *New York Clipper*, June 5, 1886.
65. *Tombstone Epitaph,* December 8, 1888.
66. *Daily Tombstone*, May 27, 1886.
67. Ordinance 60, passed April 7, 1887, Tombstone City Archives.
68. *Prospector*, January 11, 1890.
69. Parsons, *Devil Has Foreclosed*, entry for July 24, 1886.
70. *Weekly Epitaph*, September 17, 1887.
71. *Tombstone Epitaph*, July 30, 1889.
72. Susan M. DuBois and Ann W. Smith, *The 1887 Earthquake in San Bernardino Valley, Sonora: Historic Accounts and Intensity Patterns in Arizona*, State of Arizona Bureau of Geology and Mineral Technology Special Paper no. 3 (Tucson: University of Arizona, 1980). Interestingly, Dr. George Goodfellow was part of the field study group sent to investigate the earthquake's effects.
73. *New York Clipper*, May 28, 1887.
74. *Daily Tombstone*, September 8, 1886.
75. *New York Clipper*, July 21, 1886.
76. *New York Clipper*, July 10, 1886.
77. *Tombstone Epitaph*, July 24, 1889.
78. *Weekly Tombstone Prospector*, January 15, 1889.
79. Parsons, *Devil Has Foreclosed*, entry for July 24, 1886.
80. *Daily Tombstone*, August 5, 1886.
81. Copy of August 16, 1886, Deed in author's collection, with special thanks to Barbara Lovell, Kingston School House Museum, Kingston, NM; *El Paso Times*, August 28, 1886; *New York Clipper*, September 4, 1886.
82. *Sierra County Advocate* (NM), February 8, 1901.
83. *Tombstone Epitaph*, May 5, 1889; *New York Clipper*, June 1, 1889; *Phoenix Republican*, January 14, 1891; *Weekly Epitaph*, July 19, 1890;

New York Clipper, January 31, 1891; *Tombstone Epitaph*, June 12, 1892; *Weekly Epitaph*, August 6, 1892.

84. Original Elite/Bird Cage handbill, author's collection.

85. *Phoenix Republican*, January 14, 1891.

86. *Prospector*, January 24, 1891.

87. *Phoenix Republican*, February 20, 1891.

88. *Phoenix Republican*, February 22, 1891.

89. *New York Clipper*, March 28, 1891.

90. Andrew M. Honker, "'A Terrible Calamity Has Fallen Upon Phoenix': The 1891 Flood and Salt River Valley Reclamation," Journal of Arizona History 43, no. 2 (Summer 2002): 109–32.

91. *Tombstone Epitaph*, July 19, 1891.

92. Cochise County Deeds of Real Estate, book 10, 397–98.

93. *Tombstone Epitaph*, January 6, 1889.

94. 1900 Federal Census; Pearce, AZ, Cemetery records, http://files.usgwar-chives.net/az/cochise/cemeteries/pearce.txt, accessed August 21, 2024.

95. Account of her performance specialties are mentioned in a number of period clippings including, *New York Clipper,* July 13, 1878.

96. Dozens of examples of her advertised performances exist. Some examples include *New York Clipper,* February 4, 1873; *St. Louis Post Dispatch*, March 3, 1874; *New York Clipper*, April 7, 1877, and *New York Clipper*, January 19, 1889.

97. David B. Gould, comp., *Gould's St. Louis Directory for 1875* (St. Louis: David B. Gould, 1875).

98. Missouri Death Records, 1850–1931, Missouri State Archives, Jefferson City, MO; *The Era* (London), October 22, 1876.

99. Her movements are recorded in dozens of *New York Clipper* notices. Some examples include: *New York Clipper*, January 26, 1878; *New York Clipper*, March 30, 1878 NY; *New York Clipper*, February 21, 1885.

100. *New York Clipper*, July 13, 1878.

101. *Leadville* (CO) *Daily Herald*, December 5, 1882.

102. *New York Clipper*, July 28, August 25, 1888.

103. *Prospector*, November 28, 1888.

104. *New York Clipper*, December 8, 1888.

105. Cochise County Deeds of Real Estate, book 10, 397–98.

106. United States Western States Marriage Index, vol, 2, 295, familysearch. org; Arizona, County Marriages, 1871–1964; marriage certificate copy, author's collection.

107. *New York Clipper*, January 19, 1889; *New York Clipper*, May 7, 1891; *Phoenix Republican*, January 14, 1891.

108. Sonnichsen, *Billy King's Tombstone*, p. 110.

109. *Tombstone Epitaph*, May 5, 1889.

110. *Prospector*, May 11, 1889.

111. *Prospector*, May 11, 1889.

112. *Prospector*, May 11, 1889; *Tombstone Epitaph*, May 12, 1889.

113. *Prospector*, May 11, 1889.

114. *Tombstone Epitaph*, May 12, 1889.

115. Sonnichsen, *Billy King's Tombstone*, 109–10.

116. Sonnichsen, *Billy King's Tombstone*, 109.

117. *Tombstone Epitaph*, January 18, 1890.

118. *Tombstone Epitaph*, February 1, 1890.

119. *Tombstone Epitaph*, January 25, 1890.

120. *Tombstone Epitaph*, February 8, 1890.

121. *Prospector*, January 27, 1890.

122. *Prospector*, January 23, 1890.

123. *Prospector*, January 28, 1890.

124. *Tombstone Epitaph*, February 1, 1890; *Prospector*, February 1, 1890; *Brooklyn Times Union*, February 14, 1890; *New York Clipper*, February 15, 1890.

125. *Prospector*, February 3, 1890.

126. *Tombstone Epitaph*, February 22, 1890.

127. *Tombstone Prospector*, July 11, 12, 1890.

128. Sonnichsen, *Billy King's Tombstone*, 111.

129. Sonnichsen, *Billy King's Tombstone*, 190–91.

130. *Tombstone Epitaph*, December 12, 1891.

131. *Sierra County Advocate*, April 28, 1888; *Tombstone Epitaph*, February 8, 1890.

132. Cochise County Deeds of Real Estate, book 9, 629. See also Cochise County Separate Property of Married Women book 1, p. 7, Cochise County Recorder's Office.

133. Chattel Mortgages, Cochise County book 1, 429–31.

134. *Tombstone Epitaph*, June 12, 1890.

135. *Albuquerque Journal*, August 7, 1892.

136. *Tombstone Epitaph*, August 6, 1892.

137. *Tombstone Epitaph*, July 17, 1892.

138. *Santa Fe Daily New Mexican*, November 30, 1892.

139. *Albuquerque* Journal, December 2, 1892.

140. *Tombstone Epitaph*, November 30, 1892.
141. *Tombstone Epitaph*, Dec 7, 1892.
142. *New York Clipper*, June 5, 1886; *Tombstone Epitaph*, July 21, 1888; *Tombstone Epitaph*, August 27, 1889.
143. *Daily Tombstone*, May 17, 1886.

Notes for Chapter 10

1. *Omaha Daily Bee*, February 20, 1888.
2. *St. Paul Globe*, April 8, 1894.
3. *Boston Globe*, December 5, 1896.
4. In one instance, a journalist interviewed Virgil Earp's daughter and took the liberty of describing the famous gunfight in Tombstone. Instead of the lot near the OK Corral, he insisted it happened in the Bird Cage and described the carnage. See: *Morning Oregonian* (Portland), July 21, 1900.
5. Retrieved from the Bird Cage official website: "Self-Guided Tours Inside the Bird Cage Theater," TombstoneBirdCage.com, https://tombstonebirdcage.com/tours.html, accessed June 2022.
6. Search inquiry of https://timesmachine.nytimes.com and email exchanges with *New York Times* personnel, August 2018, in author's collection.
7. This conclusion is derived from hundreds of period materials gathered for and published in this book and is further supported by early twentieth-century reports from several former Bird Cage customers. Of many examples see the *Epitaph*, September 12, 1929. See also the *Windsor Beacon*, February 11, 1937, for the account of a visitor of the Bird Cage in 1937 who was simply told it was a saloon and variety theater. For more on all Bird Cage myths, see the Index, "myths about the Bird Cage."
8. Pamphlets handed out to tourists at the time of this writing cite sixteen gunfights, while a book published in 2010 and sold by the Bird Cage cites twenty-six killed; Charles William Edelman, *The Bird Cage Theatre: A Guide to Legends, Artifacts and Ghosts* (self-published, 2010).
9. Breakenridge, *Helldorado*, 268.
10. S. J. Reidhead, *A Church for Helldorado: The 1882 Tombstone Diary of Endicott Peabody and the Building of St. Paul's Episcopal Church* (Roswell, NM: Jinglebob Press, 2006), 17.
11. *Weekly Nugget*, April 15, 1880.
12. Immediately after the shooting of Fred White, notices were physically posted around town and city law officers were instructed to enforce the laws "at all hazards" per the *Tombstone Epitaph*, October 30, 1880.

13. For notes of renovations see the following clippings: *Arizona Daily Star*, October 19, 1882; *Daily Tombstone*, June 15, 1885; *Tombstone Epitaph*, January 16, September 8, 1886; *New York Clipper*, July 21, 1888; *Tombstone Epitaph*, August 11, 1888.

14. Tombstone Code of Ordinance, 17–20, Tombstone City Archives; Ordinances 10, 14, and 35, Tombstone City Archives; see also *Nugget*, October 22, 1880; *Tombstone Epitaph*, April 24, May 3, 1881.

15. *Tombstone Prospector*, November 5, 1890.

16. Sonnichsen, *Billy King's Tombstone*, 101.

17. Recorder's Docket, Tombstone City Archives.

18. *Tombstone Epitaph*, September 17, 1931.

19. *Tombstone Epitaph*, July 25, 1882.

20. Walter Noble Burns, *Tombstone: An Iliad of the Southwest* (New York: Grosset & Dunlap, 1929), 380. Performer names and time of appearance at the Bird Cage were confirmed with engagement notices printed in numerous editions of the *New York Clipper*. There was also another account of seeing performer signatures published in the *Abilene* (TX) *Reporter News*, December 22, 1929.

21. Original Bird Cage pamphlet, collected from the Bird Cage in 2021, author's collection.

22. Chattel Mortgages, Cochise County, book 1, 84–86; Cochise County Bill of Sale, book 1, 142.

23. Recorder's Docket, 383, Tombstone City Archives.

24. Cochise County Chattel Mortgages, book 1, 429–31.

25. As outlined and cited in chap. 8.

26. *Arizona Daily Star*, October 22, 1882; *Daily Tombstone*, June 15, 1885; *Tombstone Epitaph*, January 16, September 6, 1886; *New York Clipper*, July 21, 1888; *Tombstone Epitaph*, September 3, 1889.

27. *Boston Globe*, August 10, 1881.

28. *Tombstone Epitaph*, July 19, 1882.

29. *Tombstone Epitaph*, June 16, 1882.

30. *Daily Tombstone*, June 10, 1886.

31. Among many examples see *Weekly Epitaph*, October 28, 1882.

32. Henrietta Herring biographical file, Arizona Historical Society; *Tucson Citizen*, March 21, 1963.

33. Robin L. Andrews, "Belle of Tombstone," *Wild West Magazine*, August 2007.

34. The Lotta Crabtree Will Case, Historical and Special Collections, Harvard Law School Library.

35. Cochise County Deeds of Real Estate, book 36, 521.

36. *Arizona Daily Star*, February 10, 1929. In fact two Bird Cage performers did retire from performing and marry local Tombstone men. One moved to Phoenix and lived in the shadows of the capitol, operated a local business, and hobnobbed with the territory's social and political elite, including several governors.

37. *Los Angeles Times*, March 6, 1927.

38. *Bisbee Daily Review*, August 26, 1934, *Tombstone Epitaph*, December 9, 1926; *Arizona Daily Star*, February 10, 1929. Author Alfred Henry Lewis took the story and modified it, claiming it was Ike Clanton who shot the heel from the boot of a man named "Nixon." For that account see the *Butte Miner*, December 21, 1896.

39. *Tombstone Epitaph*, November 19, 1931.

40. "Reminiscences of William Ohnesorgen," (unpublished manuscript, October 22, 1929), 1–4, Arizona Historical Society.

41. "Reminiscences of William Ohnesorgen," 7.

42. *Epitaph*, November 16, 1881; *Arizona Weekly Citizen*, November 20, 1881.

43. Breakenridge, *Helldorado*, 261.

44. *Tucson Citizen*, April 26, 1924.

45. Breakenridge, *Helldorado*, 261.

46. Sobel, *Burleycue*, 59–60.

47. Account of Mrs. J. C. Coyler in Boessenecker, *Ride the Devil's Herd*, 205.

48. *Harper's New Monthly Magazine*, December 1882 to May 1883, 500.

49. Sobel, *Burleycue*, 60.

50. *Tombstone Epitaph*, June 9, 1882.

51. Sobel, *Burleycue*, 76.

52. Sonnichsen, *Billy King's Tombstone*, 98.

53. Recorder's Docket, 207–8, Tombstone City Archives.

54. *Weekly Epitaph*, September 16, 1882; Tombstone City Recorder's Docket, 227.

55. *Tucson Citizen*, April 26, 1924.

56. *Tombstone Epitaph*, February 4, 1882; *Los Angeles Herald*, February 8, 1882; *New York Clipper*, March 3, 1882.

57. *New York Clipper*, April 8, 1882.

58. The "chap" refused to give his name and was recorded as "John Doe" in the City Recorder's Docket, 172, Tombstone City Archives.

59. 1880 US Federal Census; see also various entries in the Recorder's Docket, Tombstone City Archives.

60. Recorder's Docket, 203, Tombstone City Archives
61. Recorder's Docket, 208–9, Tombstone City Archives
62. *Weekly Republican*, August 18, 1882.
63. *Tombstone Epitaph*, February 18, 1888.
64. *Tombstone Epitaph*, July 21, 1888.
65. *Tombstone Prospector*, January 5, 1889.
66. *Nugget*, January 1, 1882.
67. *Tombstone Epitaph*, December 9, 1881.
68. See *Arizona Daily Star*, April 13, 1889, for public notice of Act 13 and its particulars.

Notes for Chapter 11

1. WPA interview EA Wittig, 1940, Arizona Historical Society.
2. *Variety*, December 12, 1908.
3. *New York Clipper*, December 8, 1878; *New York Clipper*, November 13, 1880; *Pueblo Daily Chieftain*, April 26, 1882; *Chicago Inter Ocean*, January 27, 1884; *New York Clipper*, February 9, 1884.
4. Among many examples, see: *Pueblo Daily Chieftain*, January 5, 1884; *New York Clipper*, July 7, 1888; 1888 Leadville City Directory; *New York Clipper*, April 20, 1889; *Ballenger & Richards Twenty-First Annual Denver City Directory* (Denver: Ballenger & Richards, 1893).
5. Muster Roll Abstracts of NY State Volunteers; *Brooklyn Daily Eagle*, October 25, 1865; *New York Clipper*, November 22, 1879.
6. *Tombstone Prospector*, February 1, 1890; *Brooklyn Times Union*, February 14, 1890; Tombstone Cemetery map, in author's collection.
7. *Tombstone Epitaph*, July 27, 1882; Harry K. Morton scrapbook, New York Public Library; *Daily Tombstone*, March 1, May 5, 1886.
8. Wittig interview, Arizona Historical Society.
9. Wittig Family Biographical file, author's collection.
10. *Arizona Daily Star*, October 19, November 19, 1882.
11. *Nugget*, March 23, 1882.
12. *Tombstone Epitaph*, July 19, 1882; City Recorder's Docket, 207–8.
13. *Washington National Tribune*, March 29, 1883.
14. *Winfield Daily Courier*, October 7, 1887.
15. *Tombstone Prospector*, February 8, 1888.
16. Letter from George H. Kelly to A. H. Gardner, January 25, 1927, in author's collection; *Exhibitors Herald*, September 17, 1927; *El Paso Herald*, September 21, 1927.
17. *London Illustrated Sporting Dramatic News*, July 28, 1900; *Brooklyn Life*, October 13, 1900; *New York Clipper*, December 29, 1900.

18. Clair Eugene Willson, *Mimes and Miners: A Historical Study of the Theater in Tombstone* (Tucson: University of Arizona, 1935), 22.

19. *Chicago Inter Ocean*, November 29, 1903.

20. Foy and Harlow, *Clowning through Life*, 157.

21. *New York Clipper*, October 29, 1881; *San Francisco Chronicle*, November 1, 1881; *San Francisco Examiner*, November 3, 5, 1881; see also weekly newspaper advertisements and performance reviews from January 27, 1881, to July 25, 1881, in the *Denver Rocky Mountain News* and the *Great West*.

22. *Sacramento Record Union*, October 27, 1881.

23. See Mike Mihaljevich, "Eddie Foy: Clowning through Lies?," *Wild West History Association Journal* 15, no. 1 (March 2022), for a complete look at Eddie's movements.

24. Armond Fields, *Eddie Foy: A Biography of the Early Popular Stage Comedian*, illustrated ed. (Jefferson, NC: McFarland, 2009), 42.

25. Information provided from description card on display at the Bird Cage, pamphlets distributed by the Bird Cage, and the verbal script dictated to theater visitors.

26. *Tombstone Epitaph*, June 10, 1882.

27. *Weekly Epitaph*, November 11, 1882. Much of the in-depth research on Moore's background, his original painting, and the location in the Alhambra Palace was researched by Nancy Sosa, who published a groundbreaking five-part essay on the "Fatima" painting on her History Raider's Facebook page, posted between May 1 and 13, 2016, www.facebook.com/historyraiders.

28. *Tombstone Epitaph*, October 9, 1931.

29. *Almeh* postcards in author's collection; *Life Magazine*, May 1, 1946; *Detroit Free Press*, May 4, 1947; *Tombstone Epitaph*, June 7, 1934.

30. *New York Clipper*, December 19, 1885.

31. *Arizona Daily Star*, September 27, October 1, 1884.

32. *Arizona Daily Star*, July 9, September 27, 1884.

33. *Arizona Daily Star*, February 10, 1929.

34. Future research will likely reveal more.

35. For the complete story of this wild affair, see Peter Brand's *Perry Mallon: The Conman Who Arrested Doc Holliday*, 2nd ed. (self-published, 2022).

36. *Billboard*, October 11, 1913.

37. Pearl Ardine biographical file, author's collection.

38. Annie Ashley biographical file, author's collection.

39. Tom Nawn biographical file, author's collection.

40. Annie Ashley biographical fie, author's collection.

41. *Courier Journal* (Louisville, KY), September 13, 1907; *Tombstone Republican*, January 24, February 23, 1883.

42. *Arizona Daily Star*, February 11, 1883; Charles H. Duncan sheet music, 1879, author's collection.

43. Duncan sheet music.

44. *Epitaph*, December 2, 1882; *Tombstone Republican*, January 24, 1883.

45. *Galena Miner*, August 25, 1877.

46. *New York Clipper*, January 8, 1881.

47. Millie de Granville biographical file, author's collection.

48. *Andrew County Republican* (Savannah, MO), July 31, 1874.

49. *Fort Scott* (KS) *Daily Monitor*, September 22, 1874.

50. *Salt Lake Herald*, July 15, 1882; *Sunday Herald* (Waterbury, CT), January 5, 1890.

51. Interview with Joe Adams (who was hired by Joe Bignon in January 1891), *Variety*, December 12, 1910.

52. *Variety*, December 12, 1908; *San Francisco Examiner*, August 26, 1881; *Butte Weekly Miner*, September 9, 1885.

53. *Anaconda* (MT) *Standard*, May 8, 1914.

54. *Tombstone Epitaph*, February 13, 1886.

55. Code of Ordinance, p. 2, Tombstone City Archives. City positions were paid monthly. Weekly salaries were calculated off of those monthly figures.

56. Henry Dixon recollections in Sobel, *Burleycue*, 132.

57. Sobel, *Burleycue*, 190.

58. Mark Hellinger recollections, in Sobel, *Burleycue*, 192.

59. *Indianapolis People*, May 26, 1877; *Stockton Mail*, March 7, 1881; *Pueblo* (CO) *Daily Chieftain*, April 8, 1882; *Wood River Times*, August 15, 1885; *Stockton Mail*, August 3, 1895.

60. *Tucson Citizen*, April 26, 1924.

61. Sobel, *Burleycue*, 59.

62. *Arizona Daily Star*, June 22, 1884.

63. *Denver Rocky Mountain News*, November 18, 1887.

64. *Arizona Daily Star*, October 19, 1882.

65. *Variety*, December 12, 1908.

66. J. C. Hancock, "Notes by Judge JC Hancock on Walter Noble Burns' Book Tombstone" (unpublished manuscript), James Covington Hancock Papers, Arizona Historical Society.

67. Sobel, *Burleycue*, 60.

68. Foy and Harlow, *Clowning through Life*, 106.

69. Recollections of Casmore, in Sobel, *Burleycue*, 76.

70. Sonnichsen, *Billy King's Tombstone*, 98–99.
71. *Arizona Daily Star*, February 10, 1929.
72. *Arizona Range News*, May 10, 1907.
73. *Arizona Republic*, February 1, 1891.
74. *Los Angeles Herald*, May 24, 1884.
75. *San Antonio Light*, March 4, 1885.
76. *Leadville Daily Chronicle*, February 1, 1894.
77. *Denver Rocky Mountain News*, December 6, 1887.
78. Sobel, *Burleycue*, 74.
79. Sobel, *Burleycue*, 73.
80. *Los Angeles Times*, February 26, 1934.
81. Bird Cage performer biographical files, author's collection.
82. *Butte Weekly Miner*, June 3, 1885.
83. *Arizona Daily Star*, November 19, 1882.

Notes for Chapter 12

1. Chattel Mortgages, Cochise County, book 1, 429–31; *Tombstone Epitaph*, July 17, 1892; *Albuquerque Journal*, August 7, 1892.
2. Letter from Owen Wister to his mother dated June 25, 1894, and journal entry of that same day, published in *Owen Wister Out West: His Journals and Letters* (Chicago: University of Chicago Press, 1979), 212.
3. Cochise County Tax Assessor Records, 1882–1900.
4. Lewis used the pen name Dan Quin in his early writing career.
5. Flournoy D. Manzo, "Alfred Henry Lewis: Western Storyteller," *Arizona and the West* 10, no. 1 (Spring 1968): 5–24; *New York Times*, December 24, 1914.
6. *Topeka Daily Capital*, January 3, 1915.
7. *Kansas City Times*, December 7, 1896; *Butte Miner*, December 21, 1896.
8. *Kansas City Times*, April 29, 1889.
9. James G. Wolf, WPA Interview, recorded by Richard J. Kelley, in authors collection.
10. *Arizona Republic*, January 11, 1940.
11. *Tombstone Epitaph*, June 13, 1920.
12. World Cat, Alfred Henry Lewis overview.
13. *Champaign* (IL) *Daily Gazette*, August 3, 1918.
14. *Tombstone Prospector*, October 24, 1908.
15. *Tombstone Epitaph*, June 6, 1920.
16. *Los Angeles Times*, February 27, 1927; *Tombstone Epitaph*, June 7, 1934.

17. *Arizona Republic*, December 25, 1927.

18. *Tombstone Prospector*, January 2, 1908.

19. *Los Angeles Times*, February 27, 1927.

20. See the *Tombstone Epitaph*, August 27, 1922, for discussion of the most notable attractions at that time.

21. *Tucson Citizen*, February 19, 1926, printed that day only as the *Wolfville Citizen*.

22. *Tombstone Epitaph*, January 3, 1886; *Daily Tombstone*, March 6, 1886; *Tucson Citizen*, February 11, 1926.

23. *Tucson Citizen*, February 11, 1926; *Tucson Citizen*, February 19, 1926.

24. Copy of Joe Bignon death certificate, in author's collection.

25. *Casper* (WY) *Star Tribune*, June 14, 1928.

26. *Tombstone Epitaph*, October 11, 1931.

Notes for Chapter 13

1. Gambling: *Weekly Epitaph*, January 19, 1908; Prostitution: *Weekly Epitaph*, February 24, 1918.

2. Burns, *Tombstone*, 380.

3. California, San Francisco County Birth, Marriage, and Death Records, 1849–1980, Ancestry.com; *San Francisco Call*, June 28, 1902.

4. *Arizona Daily Star*, July 2, 1902; *Tucson Citizen*, July 28, 1902.

5. Hugh McCrum, Helen Lakeman marriage certificate in California, Select Marriages, 1850–1945; Cochise County Deeds of Real Estate, book 19, 109–10.

6. *Tombstone Prospector*, February 24, 1903; *Arizona Daily Star*, February 26, 1903.

7. *Tombstone Prospector*, March 2, 1903.

8. Cochise County Deeds of Real Estate, book 19, 260–61.

9. Cochise County Deeds of Real Estate Index; Cochise County Deeds of Real Estate, book 36, 521–25.

10. Cochise County Probate Orders, book 7, 166-168; Cochise County Deeds of Real Estate Index; *Bisbee Daily Review*, Oct 21, 1917.

11. *Portrait and Biographical Record of Arizona* (Chicago: Chapman Publishing, 1901), 851–52

12. *Winslow* (AZ) *Mail*, July 2, 1926.

13. *Portrait and Biographical Record of Arizona*, 851–52; Jo Conners, *Who's Who in Arizona* (Tucson: Arizona Daily Star Press, 1913), 693.

14. *Tombstone Epitaph*, May 9, 1929; Burns, *Tombstone*, 84. Similar shootings from Charleston were also reported in the March 23, 1881,

Epitaph, which carried the story of a 15-year-old boy who was shot at while searching for his stray mules outside of town.

15. *Weekly Epitaph*, March 1, 1891; *Tombstone Prospector*, September 1, 1897; *Tombstone Epitaph*, June 5, 1910; *Tombstone Epitaph*, September 1, 1912; *Tombstone Epitaph*, December 2, 1922, notes his location opposite Schieffelin Hall. See also Billy Hattich's *Tombstone, In History, Romance and Wealth* (repr., Norman: University of Oklahoma Press, 1981), which spotlights Charles Cummings. Hattich even published a personal copy for Charles with his name embossed on the front cover per Kevin Mulkins Collection, Tucson, AZ.

16. *Clifton (AZ) Copper Era*, November 18, 1910; *Tombstone Epitaph*, January 29, 1922.

17. *Tombstone Epitaph*, January 29, 1922; *Graham Guardian* (Safford, AZ), February 7, 1922.

18. *Tombstone Epitaph*, February 12, 1911. Eventually the county seat would be relocated to Bisbee in 1929, shortly before Charles died.

19. *Arizona Daily Star*, December 1, 1930; *Tombstone Epitaph*, December 4, 1930; *Portrait and Biographical Record of Arizona*, 851–52.

20. *Arizona Business Directory, 1909–1910* (Denver: Gazetteer, 1909); *Tombstone Epitaph*, August 15, 1915; *Bisbee Daily Review*, January 15, 1918; *Phoenix Tribune*, December 6, 1919.

21. George H. Kelly, *Legislative History of Arizona, 1864–1912* (Phoenix: Manufacturing Stationers, 1926).

22. See: Tombstone's Rose Tree Museum for ephemera noting Charles as a member.

23. *Portrait and Biographical Record of Arizona*, 851–52.

24. *Bisbee Daily Review*, November 4, 1920.

25. *Clifton Copper Era*, November 18, 1910.

26. *Tombstone Epitaph*, December 4, 1930.

27. Several examples include the Washington, DC, *Morning Star*, December 1, 1930; *Rapid City (SD) Journal*, December 2, 1930; and *Spokane Spokesman Review*, December 2, 1930.

28. See interview in the *Arizona Daily Star*, February 11, 1929.

29. *Graham Guardian*, February 7, 1922.

30. *Tombstone Epitaph*, January 29, 1922. See also the *Los Angeles Times*, February 27, 1927, for notes of restoration.

31. *Tombstone Epitaph*, September 9, 23, 1923.

32. *Tombstone Epitaph*, April 4, 1924.

33. *New York Clipper*, October 1, 1904. See also Willson, *Mimes and Miners*, 94n234.

34. *Arizona Highways*, 1926, retrieved from St. Mary's University Louis J. Blume Library. See http://library.stmarytx.edu/ost/roadway/OSTAZ2.html.

35. *Los Angeles Times*, March 6, 1927; *Arizona Daily Star*, October 23, 1942.

36. *Los Angeles Times*, March 6, 1927; *Arizona Daily Star*, October 23, 1942; see also June 7, 1934, *Epitaph* for additional diamond signs being installed.

37. Most lots in the original Tombstone plat map measured thirty feet in width.

38. *Los Angeles Times*, February 27, 1927; *Tombstone Epitaph*, June 7, 1934. Interestingly, prior to Arlington's involvement, the proper location was known. The January 23, 1906, *Epitaph* talked about the gunfight occurring "in front of Mrs. Fly's photograph gallery," proving at least someone in town at the turn of the century knew the proper location. In 1906 the OK Corral was still owned and operated by the same John Montgomery who owned it the day of the gunfight.

39. *Arizona Republic*, April 19, 1934.

40. See *Tombstone Epitaph*, May 18, 1933, for some of his questionable findings.

41. *Exhibitors Herald and Moving Picture World*, September 17, 1927; *El Paso Times*, September 21, 1927; January 25, 1927, letter from state historian George H. Kelly to Arlington Gardner, in author's collection.

42. *Exhibitors Herald*, September 17, 1927; *El Paso Times*, September 21, 1927.

43. In the *El Paso Times* of December 11, 1934, Arlington asked readers who may have had connections for help.

44. *Arizona Daily Star*, October 23, 1942.

45. *Tombstone Prospector*, August 6, 1919.

46. *Tombstone Prospector*, June 8, 1908.

47. See *Arizona Republic*, August 29, 1926, for the Automobile Club of Arizona.

48. See *Los Angeles Times*, March 6, 1927, "Automobile" section.

49. *Tombstone Prospector*, July 23, 1919. For one interesting sample of Arlington's columns as the Highway Publicist, see the October 29, 1931, *Epitaph*.

50. The Lotta Crabtree Will Case, 1870–1928, Langdell Hall, Harvard Law School Library.

51. Among many examples see the February 6, 1936, *Epitaph* and a traffic count in the January 23, 1936, *Epitaph* noting 21,111 tourists passed through in December 1935.

52. *Tombstone Epitaph*, February 21, 1929.

53. *Tombstone Epitaph*, May 16, 1929.
54. *Tombstone Epitaph*, June 11, 1931.
55. *Tucson Citizen*, June 6, 1926.
56. *Tombstone Epitaph*, February 20, 1925.
57. *Exhibitors Herald and Moving Picture World*, March 24, 1928; *El Paso Herald*, March 12, 1929; *Arizona Republic*, April 19, 1934.
58. *El Paso Herald*, March 12, 1929.
59. *Arizona Daily Star*, February 10, 1929.
60. *Tombstone Epitaph*, December 9, 1926. As discussed in chap. 10, the crowds' reaction to the single gunshot in this scenario is consistent with many period examples provided. A gun going off in the Bird Cage and Tombstone in general was a big deal and drew strong reactions from people in the area, police, and newspapers. It was not tolerated.
61. *Bisbee Daily Review*, August 26, 1934. Emil Marks was partnered in a barber shop with the son of Ed Wittig who was one of the leaders of the orchestra of the Bird Cage.
62. *Tombstone Epitaph*, November 19, 1931. Charles's story continued to be told after his death. From his account the upper left-hand box in the auditorium was identified as the place where it happened. See *Windsor Beacon*, February 11, 1937.
63. *Tombstone Epitaph*, August 8, 1915.
64. *Weekly Epitaph*, July 28, 1895.
65. Cochise County Bills of Sale, book 4, page 409; see also the September 19, 1935, *Epitaph* for English's law library being given to Nettie Lavalley's son.
66. Cochise County Bill of Sale, book 6, 36–37.
67. Charles took over Montgomery's estate. See *Tombstone Epitaph*, February 5, 1910. John Montgomery death certificate, Arizona, US, Death Records, 1887–1960, Arizona Department of Health Services, Phoenix.
68. *Tombstone Epitaph*, August 22, 1935; *Tombstone Epitaph*, February 6, 1936; Frasher's original postcard of John Heath saddle inside the Bird Cage, author's collection; *Tombstone Epitaph*, October 9, 1931; Cochise County Bill of Sale, book 5, 259.
69. *El Paso Times*, September 18, 1929.
70. *Tombstone Epitaph*, October 9, 1931.
71. *Tombstone Epitaph*, June 5, 1910.
72. 1929 Helldorado Collection, University of Arizona Special Collections Department, Tucson.

73. John P. Clum, "Tombstone's Semi-Centennial," *Arizona Historical Review* 2, no. 4 (January 1930): 29.
74. *Tucson Citizen*, August 9, 1929.
75. *Arizona Highways*, October 1929, p. 7.
76. *Springfield* (MO) *Press*, October 23, 1929.
77. *Arizona Highways*, October 1929, 6–7.
78. *Pomona Progress Bulletin*, August 29, 1929; *Springfield Press*, October 23, 1929; Harry K. Morton Scrapbook, page 27 and page 78; New York City Municipal Deaths, 1795–1949, www.familysearch.org.
79. R. W. McGowan to William H. Kelly, October 12, 1929, 1929, Helldorado file, University of Arizona Special Collections Department.
80. Fanchon and Marco contracts and Helldorado committee communication, 1929 Helldorado file, University of Arizona Special Collections Department.
81. Clum, "Tombstone's Semi-Centennial," 29.
82. Transcript of radio address reprinted in the *Tombstone Epitaph*, July 24, 1930.
83. Bird Cage ephemera, Arizona Historical Society.
84. No Cal Cohn shows up at the Bird Cage in the early 1880s; however, there was a comedy team of Mulligan and Cohan as well as a Mickey Cohan that were engaged there under Billy Hutchinson.
85. *Tombstone Epitaph*, December 4, 1930.
86. *Tombstone Epitaph*, October 11, 1931.

Notes for Chapter 14

1. *Reading Times*, December 6, 1929.
2. *Tombstone Epitaph*, June 7, 1934.
3. *Tombstone Epitaph*, November 13, 1921.
4. Cochise County Probate Orders, book 7, 166–68.
5. Arizona, US, Death Records, 1887–1960.
6. 1920 Federal Census; *Tombstone Epitaph*, September 8, 1932.
7. *Tombstone Epitaph*, September 8, 1932.
8. *Phoenix Republic*, August 13, June 7, 1933; *Arizona Daily Star*, October 5, 1933; *Arizona Daily Star*, January 24, 1934; September 20, 1934, *Arizona Daily Star*.
9. *Arizona Daily Star*, December 7, 1933.
10. *Arizona Daily Star*, August 3, 1933; *Arizona Daily Star*, April 19, 1934.
11. *Arizona Daily Star*, January 17, 1935.
12. *Tombstone Epitaph*, June 14, 1934.

13. *Tombstone Epitaph*, June 7, 1934.
14. *Tombstone Epitaph*, June 7, 1934.
15. The bar was also absent for a period prior to 1929 Helldorado performances. See *Tombstone Epitaph*, June 7, 1934.
16. *Tombstone Epitaph*, June 7, 1934.
17. *Tombstone Epitaph*, August 16, 1934. Joe Lavalley was also awarded the contract for making repairs to Tombstone's historic city hall which still serves the municipality on Fremont. See the *Phoenix Republican*, October 16, 1937.
18. *Tombstone Epitaph*, August 16, 1934.
19. *Tombstone Epitaph*, June 14, 1934.
20. *Arizona Daily Star*, June 7, 1934.
21. *Tombstone Epitaph*, June 14, 1934.
22. *Tombstone Epitaph*, June 7, 1934.
23. *Arizona Daily Star*, June 7, 1934.
24. *El Paso Times*, December 11, 1934.
25. Original Bird Cage Coffee Shoppe menu, author's collection.
26. *Arizona Daily Star*, August 23, 1934.
27. *Tombstone Epitaph*, June 7, 1934.
28. *Tombstone Epitaph*, June 14, 1934; *Arizona Daily Star*, June 21, 1934.
29. *Tombstone Epitaph*, June 14, 1934.
30. *Arizona Daily Star*, April 11, 1935.
31. *Arizona Daily Star*, April 4, 1935.
32. *Lansing* (MI) *State Journal*, June 5, 1930; *Arizona Daily Star*, September 19, 1935.
33. 1920 and 1930 Federal Census; Arizona, US, Death Records, 1887–1960; *Arizona Daily Star*, August 15, 1935.
34. *Arizona Daily Star*, June 7, 1935.
35. *Arizona Daily Star*, August 29, 1935.
36. 1940 Federal Census; *Phoenix Republic*, June 28, 1941.
37. *Washington DC Evening Star*, April 29, 1936.
38. *Tombstone Epitaph*, September 27, 1928.
39. Arizona, US, Death Records, 1887–1960.
40. *Arizona Daily Star*, September 27, 1941.
41. *Tombstone Epitaph*, June 13, 1920.
42. *Arizona Daily Star*, February 10, 1929.
43. *Arizona Daily Star*, September 27, 1941.
44. Original booklet titled *Souvenir of the Birdcage Theatre*, in author's collection.

Notes for Chapter 15

1. Frederick R. Bechdolt, *When the West Was Young* (New York: Century, 1922), 82.

2. *Tombstone Prospector*, August 6, 1919.

3. Letter from Wyatt Earp to William S. Hart, September 6, 1926; letter from William S. Hart to Wyatt Earp February 26, 1927, retrieved 2022, http://tombstonehistoryarchives.com/letters-between-wyatt-earp---william-s.-hart.html.

4. James Covington Hancock reminiscences, 1911–1935, Arizona Historical Society, Tucson.

5. In a letter from Frank J. Wilstach of the Motion Picture Producers and Distributors of America in New York to William S. Hart on March 23, 1928, Wilstach wrote, "I understand Wyatt and Burns are in a row over royalties. Wyatt claims, as I understand it, that he should be paid for the information furnished." See www.tombstonehistoryarchives.com/letters-between-wyatt-earp---william-s.-hart-2.html, accessed August 21, 2024.

6. Original Bird Cage Coffee Shoppe menu, author's collection.

7. Burns, *Tombstone*, 31, 149.

8. Burns, *Tombstone*, 146–64; *Tucson Citizen*, November 13, 1881.

9. *Arizona Champion*, November 3, 1883; *Nugget*, February 22, 1882; *Tombstone Epitaph*, July 18, 1882; *Arizona Daily Star*, November 19, 1882.

10. Liberty Magazine Historical Archive, 1924–1950, www.gale.com/c/liberty-magazine-historical-archive, accessed August 21, 2024.

11. *Tucson Citizen*, April 22–30, 1924.

12. Breakenridge, *Helldorado*, 261, 268.

13. Lynton Wright Brent, *The Bird Cage: Tombstone, Arizona Territory* (Pittsburgh: Dorrance & Company, 1945), inside cover dust jacket.

14. *Arizona Daily Star*, July 30, 1945.

15. See also: Lela Nunnelley, *Boothill Grave Yard: A Descriptive List*, which has been handed out to tourists since the early 1950s. This pamphlet includes dozens of fictionalized graves and is the basis of many prevailing historical errors.

16. *Tombstone Epitaph*, November 19, 1931.

17. *Montreal Gazette*, February 7, 1947.

18. *The Film Daily*, July 8, 1940.

19. *Tombstone Republican*, February 23, 1883.

20. *The Life and Legend of Wyatt Earp*, season 6, ep. 19, "Johnny Behan Falls in Love," directed by Paul Landres, written by Frederick Hazlitt

Brennan, featuring Hugh O'Brian, Morgan Woodward, and Steve Brodie, aired February 14, 1961, on ABC.

21. *Santa Ana Register*, May 13, 1935.
22. Larry Booth and Jane Booth, "Do You Want an Exposition? San Diego's 1935 Fair in Photographs," *Journal of San Diego History* 31, no. 4 (Fall 1985): 292.
23. *Santa Ana Register,* May 13, 1935.
24. *Californian* (Salinas), April 19, 1935.
25. *Themed Entertainment Association Index*, 2018, p. 3, author's collection.
26. *Whittier* (CA) *East Review*, July 15, 29, 1954; Jeff Heimbuch, "History of Melodramas At Knott's Berry Farm's Bird Cage Theatre," *Knott's Berry Farm*, March 12, 2018, https://www.knotts.com/blog/2018/march/3-12-2018-history-of-the-bird-cage-theatre.
27. *Reno Gazette Journal*, October 25, 1948; *Billboard*, April 2, 1949; *Hollywood Reporter*, August 18, 1949.
28. *Billboard*, April 2, 1949.
29. *Los Angeles Times*, November 7, 1948; *Billboard*, April 2, 1949.
30. *Hollywood Reporter,* August 18, November 3, 1949.
31. *Signal*, May 5, 1949.
32. *Signal*, July 7, 1949.
33. *Signal*, June 29, July 6, 1950.
34. "History of Lincoln's Children's Zoo," *Lincoln Zoo*, retrieved June 2022, www.lincolnzoo.org/about.
35. *Lincoln Star*, November 27, 1960.
36. *Lincoln Star*, March 13, 1983.
37. *Tucson Daily Citizen*, October 13, 1949.

Notes for Epilogue

1. *Tombstone Epitaph*, May 24, 1914.
2. *Tombstone Epitaph*, September 17, 1931; *San Bernardino County* (CA) *Sun*, September 18, 1931.
3. *Tombstone Epitaph*, May 5, 1889.
4. *Tombstone Prospector*, November 5, 1890, *Weekly Epitaph*, November 1, 1894.
5. *Weekly Epitaph*, September 27, 1893; *Weekly Epitaph*, April 8, 1894.
6. *Tombstone Epitaph*, February 3, 1886; *Tombstone Epitaph*, October 17, 1889; *Weekly Epitaph*, May 10, 1891.
7. *Weekly Epitaph*, January 25, 1893; Arizona, US, County Coroner and Death Records, 1881–1971.

8. *Weekly Epitaph*, May 12, 1895.
9. *Arizona Daily Star*, April 20, 1895.
10. *Weekly Epitaph*, May 26, 1895.
11. *Weekly Epitaph*, July 28, 1895.
12. *Arizona Daily Star*, July 26, 1895.
13. *Weekly Epitaph*, August 4, 1895.
14. Tombstone Cemetery plot map, author's collection.
15. *Daily Tombstone*, March 22, 1886.
16. *Tombstone Epitaph*, March 16, 1886.
17. Among many examples see *Weekly Epitaph*, December 17, 1887; *Tombstone Epitaph*, February 4, 1888; *Tombstone Prospector*, January 5, 1890; *Tombstone Epitaph*, June 1, September 27, 1890.
18. *Tombstone Prospector*, January 6, 1889.
19. *Daily Tombstone*, October 1, 1886; *Tucson Citizen*, March 6, 1890.
20. *Tucson Citizen*, March 6, 1890.
21. Arizona County Coroner and Death Records; Cochise County Coroner and Death Records.
22. Tombstone Cemetery plot map, author's collection.
23. *Tombstone Epitaph*, November 30, 1892.
24. *Tombstone Prospector*, June 26, 1895; *Tombstone Epitaph*, October 6, 1895; *Bisbee Daily Review*, May 28, 1905.
25. *Tombstone Epitaph*, December 15, 1895.
26. July 1898–January 1899 IRS Tax Assessment List, Ancestry.com; *Arizona Weekly Citizen*, January 25, 26 1896; *Tombstone Epitaph*; *Phoenix Republican*, March 29, 1896; 1911–1915 Arizona Business Directory; 1920 Federal Census.
27. Arizona Business Directories, 1915–1920.
28. *Bisbee Daily Review*, March 7, 1906.
29. *Arizona Daily Star*, October 1, 1909; *Tombstone Epitaph*, April 19, 1914.
30. *Weekly Epitaph*, January 16, 1910; see also Cochise County Deeds of Real Estate, book 14, 634.
31. Cochise County Declarations of Homesteads, book 1, 73; Bignon Tract map, Pearce Addition, Cochise County Recorder's Office and author's collection. Footnote: Joe also made a similar 160-acre claim on the Gila and Salt Rivers the year prior. See US Homestead Records, 1863–1908, certificate number 1020, Cochise County Recorders Office.
32. Matilda Bignon Death Certificate, State of Arizona Register of Deaths.
33. *Weekly Epitaph*, August 5, 1900.
34. 1900 US Census; *Arizona Daily Star*, December 2, 1900; *Cochise Review*, December 8, 1900.

35. Joe Bignon Death Certificate, State of Arizona Register of Deaths.
36. (Examples include *Salt Lake City Tribune*, December 9, 1925; *Madison* (WI) *Capital Times*, December 10, 1925; *Los Angeles Times*, December 11, 1915; *Arizona Daily Star*, December 13, 1925.
37. Ellen Bignon Death Certificate, State of Arizona Register of Deaths.
38. *University of Arizona Bulletin* 6, no. 7 (October 1, 1935): 24.
39. *Tucson Weekly Citizen*, August 18, 1883; August 18, 1883, *Epitaph*; August 18, 1883, *Tombstone Republican*.
40. *Tucson Weekly Citizen*, July 14, 1883.
41. *Galveston Daily News*, October 23, 1883; 1883–1884 Tombstone City Directory.
42. Cochise County Records of Mines, book 7, 160–61.
43. *San Francisco Examiner*, June 22, 1884; *Tucson Weekly Citizen*, July 5, 1884.
44. *Tombstone Epitaph*, October 11, 1893.
45. *Tacoma Daily Ledger*, August 5, 10, 1897; *Seattle Post Intelligencer*, August 15, 1900.
46. 1898, 1899, and 1900 Polk's Seattle City Directory; *Tacoma Daily Ledger*, July 6, 1899; 1900 Federal Census.
47. *New York Clipper*, March 15, 1902; *New York Clipper*, June 4, 1904.
48. *Seattle Daily Times*, April 9, 1911.
49. *Sacramento Pacific Bee*, February 12, 1896.
50. *Sacramento Pacific Bee*, February 12, 1896.
51. *Chicago Chronicle*, January 11, 1896; *Sacramento Pacific Bee*, February 12, 1896.
52. *Chicago Chronicle*, January 11, 1896.
53. *Sacramento Pacific Bee*, February 12, 1896.

Note for Appendix

1. *New York Clipper*, May 28, 1887.

Bibliography

Abbott, Carlisle S. *Recollections of a California Pioneer.* New York: Neale, 1917.

Arizona Business Directory, 1909–1910. Denver: Gazetteer, 1909.

Ballenger & Richards Twenty-First Annual Denver City Directory. Denver: Ballenger & Richards, 1893.

Bechdolt, Frederick R. *When the West Was Young.* New York: Century, 1922.

Beidler, X. "The Vigilante Committee Takes Care of Slade, c. January 1864." In *Eyewitness to the Old West: Firsthand Accounts of Exploration, Adventure and Peril,* edited by Richard Scott, 181–83. Lanham, MD: Taylor Trade, 2004.

Bishop, William Henry. *Old Mexico and Her Lost Provinces: A Journey in Mexico, Southern California, and Arizona by Way of Cuba.* New York: Harper & Brothers, 1883.

Bockstruck, Lloyd DeWitt. *Revolutionary War Bounty Land Grants: Awarded by State Governments.* Baltimore: Genealogical Publishing, 2006.

Boessenecker, John. *Ride the Devil's Herd: Wyatt Earp's Epic Battle against the West's Biggest Outlaw Gang.* New York: Hanover Square Press, 2020.

Booth, Larry, and Jane Booth. "Do You Want an Exposition? San Diego's 1935 Fair in Photographs." *Journal of San Diego History* 31, no. 4 (Fall 1985): 282–97.

Brady, Donald V. *The Theatre in Early El Paso, 1881–1905.* El Paso: Texas Western College Press, 1966.

Brand, Peter. *Doc Holliday's Nemesis: The Story of Johnny Tyler & Tombstone's Gambler's War.* Self-published, 2018.

Brand, Peter. *Perry Mallon: The Conman Who Arrested Doc Holliday.* 2nd ed. Self-published, 2022.

Breakenridge, William M. *Helldorado: Bringing the Law to the Mesquite.* Edited and with an introduction by Richard Maxwell Brown. Lincoln, NE: Bison Books, 1992.

Brent, Lynton Wright. *The Bird Cage: Tombstone, Arizona Territory.* Pittsburgh: Dorrance, 1945.

Brown, Clara Spalding. *Tombstone from a Woman's Point of View: The Correspondence of Clara Spalding Brown, July 7, 1880, to November 14, 1882.* Compiled and edited by Lynn Bailey. Tucson: Westernlore Press, 1998.

Brown, T. Allston. *A History of the American Stage*. New York: Dick & Fitzgerald, 1870.

Brown, T. Allston. *A History of the New York Stage*. 3 vols. New York: Dodd, Mead, 1903.

Browne, Walter, and E. De Roy Koch, eds. *Who's Who on the Stage, 1908*. New York: B. W. Dodge, 1908.

Burlingame, H. J. *Leaves from Conjurers' Scrap Books; or, Modern magicians and their works*. Chicago: Donohue, Henneberry, 1891.

Burns, Walter Noble. *Tombstone: An Iliad of the Southwest*. New York: Grosset & Dunlap, 1929.

Carr, John. *Pioneer Days in California*. Eureka, CA: Times, 1891.

Cherney, Bruce. "Circus Comes to Town." *Winnipeg Regional Real Estate News*, July 2013.

Clum, John P. "It All Happened in Tombstone." *Arizona Historical Review* 2, no. 3 (October 1929): 46–72.

Clum, John P. "Nellie Cashman." *Arizona Historical Review* 3, no. 4 (January 1931): 9–35.

Clum, John P. "Tombstone's Semi-Centennial." *Arizona Historical Review* 2, no. 4 (January 1930): 28–30.

Conners, Jo. *Who's Who in Arizona*. Tucson: Arizona Daily Star Press, 1913.

Cunningham, Florence R. *Saratoga's First Hundred Years*. Fresno: Valley, 1967.

De Angelis, Jefferson, and Alvin F. Harlow. *A Vagabond Trouper*. New York: Harcourt, Brace, 1931.

Dodge, Fred. *Undercover for Wells Fargo: The Unvarnished Recollections of Fred Dodge*. Edited by Carolyn Lake. Norman: University of Oklahoma Press, 1999.

DuBois, Susan M., and Ann W. Smith. *The 1887 Earthquake in San Bernardino Valley, Sonora: Historic Accounts and Intensity Patterns in Arizona*. State of Arizona Bureau of Geology and Mineral Technology Special Paper no. 3. Tucson: University of Arizona, 1980.

Dyer, Frederick H. *A Compendium of the War of the Rebellion*. Des Moines, IA: Dyer, 1908.

Edelman, Charles William. *The Bird Cage Theatre: A Guide to Legends, Artifacts and Ghosts*. Self-published, 2010.

Eichin, Carolyn Grattan. *From San Francisco Eastward: Victorian Theater in the American West*. Reno: University of Nevada Press, 2020.

Ellington, George. *The Women of New York or the Underworld of the Great City*. New York: New York Book Company, 1869.

Fayman, W. A., and T. W. Reilly, eds. *Galveston City Directory for 1875–6.* Galveston: Strickland & Clarke, 1875.

Fields, Armond. *Eddie Foy: A Biography of the Early Popular Stage Comedian.* Illustrated ed. Jefferson, NC: McFarland, 2009.

Fitch, Thomas. *Western Carpetbagger: The Extraordinary Memoirs of "Senator" Thomas Fitch.* Reno: University of Nevada Press, 1978.

Foote, Horace S., ed. *Pen Pictures from the Garden of the World, Or, Santa Clara County, California, Illustrated, Containing a History of the County of Santa Clara from the Earliest Period of Its Occupancy to the Present Time . . . and Biographical Mention of Many of Its Pioneers and Also of Prominent Citizens of Today.* Santa Clara County, CA: Lewis Publishing, 1888.

Foster, Lois M. *Annals of the San Francisco Stage, 1850–1880.* 2 vols. San Francisco: Federal Theatre Project, 1936.

Foy, Eddie, and Alvin F. Harlow. *Clowning through Life.* New York: E. P. Dutton, 1928.

Gipson, Rosemary P. "A History of Tucson Theatre before 1906." Thesis, University of Arizona, 1967.

Gird, Richard. "True Story of the Discovery of Tombstone." *Out West,* July 1907, 39–49.

Gould, David B., comp. *Gould's St. Louis Directory for 1875.* St. Louis: David B. Gould, 1875.

Gray, John Plesent. *When All Roads Led to Tombstone: A Memoir of John Plesent Gray.* Edited and annotated by W. Lane Rogers. Boise, ID: Tamarack Books, 1998.

Greene, Charles W., ed. *A Sketch of Kingston and Its Surroundings.* Kingston, MN: Tribune Office, 1883.

Guinn, J. M. *A History of California and the Extended History of its Southern Coast Counties.* 2 vols. Los Angeles: Historic Record Company, 1907.

Hamilton, Patrick. *The Resources of Arizona.* San Francisco: A. L. Bancroft, 1884.

Hattich, William. *Tombstone.* Reprint. Norman: University of Oklahoma Press, 1981.

Heller, John H., comp. *Galveston City Directory, 1876–7.* Galveston: John H. Heller, 1876.

History of Arizona Territory with Illustrations, 1884. San Francisco: Wallace W. Elliott, 1884.

A Historical and Biographical Record of the Territory of Arizona. Chicago: McFarland & Poole, 1896,

Historical Review of South-East Texas. Chicago: Lewis, 1910.

History of Manistee County, Michigan with Illustrations and Biographical Sketches of Some of Its Men and Pioneers. Chicago: H. R. Page, 1882.

History of Nevada, 1881 with Illustrations. Berkeley: Howell, North, 1958.

History of Texas Together with a Biographical History of the Cities of Houston and Galveston. Chicago: Lewis, 1895.

Honker, Andrew M. "'A Terrible Calamity Has Fallen Upon Phoenix': The 1891 Flood and Salt River Valley Reclamation." *Journal of Arizona History* 43, no. 2 (Summer 2002): 109–32.

Hoye, Marilyn. "The Houston Morning Star." *Texas State Genealogical Society Quarterly* 35, no. 4 (December 1995): 39–61.

Johnson, Paul Lee. *The McLaurys in Tombstone, Arizona: An OK Corral Obituary.* Denton: University of North Texas Press, 2012.

Kasden, Lawrence, dir. *Wyatt Earp.* Burbank, CA: Warner Bros., 1994.

Kelly, George H. *Legislative History of Arizona, 1864–1912.* Phoenix: Manufacturing Stationers, 1926.

Lake, Stuart N. *Wyatt Earp: Frontier Marshal.* New York: Pocket Books, 1994.

Leavitt, M. B. *Fifty Years in Theatrical Management, 1859–1909.* New York: Broadway, 1912.

The Life and Legend of Wyatt Earp. Season 6, ep. 19, "Johnny Behan Falls in Love." Directed by Paul Landres, written by Frederick Hazlitt Brennan, featuring Hugh O'Brian, Morgan Woodward, and Steve Brodie. Aired February 14, 1961, on ABC.

Locke, Harry. *Arizona Good Roads Association Illustrated Road Maps and Tour Book.* Los Angeles: Frank E. Company, 1913.

Manry, Joe Edgar. "A History of Theatre in Austin, Texas, 1839–1905: From Minstrels to Moving Pictures." Dissertation, University of Texas at Austin, 1979.

Manzo, Flournoy D. "Alfred Henry Lewis: Western Storyteller." *Arizona and the West* 10, no. 1 (Spring 1968): 5–24.

Marion, J. H. *Notes of Travel through the Territory of Arizona.* Prescott: Arizona Miner, 1870.

Markham, Pauline. *The Life of Pauline Markham, Written by Herself.* New York, n.p., 1871.

Mihaljevich, Mike. "Eddie Foy: Clowning through Lies?" *Wild West History Association Journal* 15, no. 1 (March 2022).

Miller, William N. "First Impressions of Tombstone." Edited by Roy B. Young. In *Cochise County Cowboy War: A Cast of Characters*, ed. Roy B. Young, 165–68. Apache, OK: Young & Sons Enterprises, 1999.

Myrick, David F. *Arizona Railroads*. Berkley: Howell North Books, 1975.

O'Neill, M. J. *How He Does It: Sam T. Jack, Twenty Years a King in the Realm of Burlesque*. Chicago: M. J. O'Neill, 1895.

Palmquist, Bob. "Justice in Tombstone." In Young, Roberts, and Tefertiller, *Wyatt Earp Anthology*, 451–56.

Parsons, George Whitwell. *A Tenderfoot in Tombstone: The Turbulent Years, 1880–1882*. Vol. 1 of *The Private Journal of George Whitwell Parsons*, edited by Lynn R. Bailey. Tucson: Westernlore Press, 1996.

Parsons, George Whitwell. *The Devil Has Foreclosed: The Concluding Arizona Years, 1882–1887*. Vol. 2 of *The Private Journal of George Whitwell Parsons*, edited by Lynn Bailey. Tucson: Westernlore Press, 1997.

Peterson, Thomas H., Jr. "The Stagecoach Lines, 1878–1903: A Study in Frontier Transportation." Thesis, University of Arizona, 1968.

Porter, Esther. "A Compilation of Materials for a Study of The Early Theatres of Montana, 1864–1880." Dissertation, State University of Montana, 1938.

Portrait and Biographical Record of Arizona. Chicago: Chapman, 1901.

Reidhead, S. J. *A Church for Helldorado: The 1882 Tombstone Diary of Endicott Peabody and the Building of St. Paul's Episcopal Church*. Roswell, NM: Jinglebob Press, 2006.

Report of the Sonora Exploring and Mining Company Made to the Stockholders, 1856–1860. Cincinnati: Railroad Record Print, 1856.

Rice, Edward Le Roy. *Monarch of Minstrelsy, From Daddy Rice to Date*. New York: Kenny Publishing Company, 1911.

Roberts, Gary L. *Doc Holliday: The Life and Legend*. New York: J. Wiley & Sons, 2007.

Roberts, Gary L. "Wyatt Earp: The Search for Order on the Last Frontier." In Young, Roberts, and Tefertiller, *A Wyatt Earp Anthology*, 2–25.

Rockfellow, John A. *Log of an Arizona Trail Blazer*. Tucson: Acme Printing, 1933.

Schillingberg, William B. *Tombstone, A.T.: A History of Early Mining, Milling and Mayhem*. Seattle: Arthur H. Clark, 1999.

Scanlon, Gretchen. *A History of Leadville Theater*. Charleston, SC: History Press, 2012.

Sobel, Bernard. *Burleycue: An Underground History of Burlesque Days*. New York: Farrar & Rinehart, 1931.

Soldene, Emily. *My Theatrical and Musical Recollections*. London: Downey, 1898.

Sonnichsen, C. L. *Billy King's Tombstone*. Caldwell, ID: Caxton, 1942.

Strahorn, Carrie Adell. *Fifteen Thousand Miles by Stage*. 2 vols. University of Nebraska Press, 1988.

Stinson, H. C., and W. N. Carter, eds. and compilers. *Arizona, a Review of its Resources*. Tucson: Compliers, 1891.

Taylor, E. Cooper, III. *A Few Moments from the Career of Prof. E. Cooper Taylor, 1852–1927*. Reprint, Tuckahoe, NY: self-published, 1990.

Tefertiller, Casey. *Wyatt Earp: The Life Behind the Legend*. New York: J. Wiley & Sons, 1997.

Theobald, John, and Lillian Theobald. *Arizona Territory Post Offices and Postmasters*. Phoenix: Arizona Historical Foundation, 1961.

Theobald, John, and Lillian Theobald. *Wells Fargo in Arizona Territory*. Tempe: Arizona Historical Foundation, 1978.

Turner, Alford E. *The OK Corral Inquest*. College Station, TX: Creative, 1981.

A Twentieth Century History of Southwest Texas. 2 vols. Chicago: Lewis, 1907.

Underhill, Lonnie E. *The Bird Cage Theatre, Tombstone, Arizona*. Gilbert, AZ: Roan Horse Press, 2016.

Walker, Brent E. *Mack Sennett's Fun Factory: A History and Filmography of His Studio and His Keystone and Mack Sennett Comedies, with Biographies of Players and Personnel*. Jefferson, NC: McFarland, 2009.

Walker, Phillip Nathaniel. "A History of Theatrical Activity in Fresno, California from Its Beginnings in 1872 to the Opening of the White Theatre in 1914." Dissertation, University of Southern California, 1972.

Willson, C. E. "From Variety Theater to Coffee Shoppe." *Arizona Historical Review* 6, no. 2 (April 1935): 10–11.

Willson, Clair Eugene. *Mimes and Miners: A Historical Study of the Theater in Tombstone*. Tucson: University of Arizona, 1935.

Wister, Owen. *Owen Wister Out West: His Journals and Letters*. Chicago: University of Chicago Press, 1979.

Young, Roy B. *Cochise County Cowboy War: A Cast of Characters*. Apache, OK: Young & Sons Enterprises, 1999.

Young, Roy B., Gary L. Roberts, and Casey Tefertiller. *A Wyatt Earp Anthology: Long May His Story Be Told*. Denton: University of North Texas Press, 2019.

Zweers, John U. "E. Cooper Taylor, Jr., Magician of the Month." *MUM*, July 1973.

Newspapers and Magazines

Abilene (TX) *Reporter News*
Albuquerque Journal
Anaconda (MT) *Standard*
Andrew County Republican (Savannah, MO)
Arizona Champion (Peach Springs)
Arizona Citizen (Tucson)
Arizona Daily Star (Tucson)
Arizona Quarterly Illustrated (Tucson)
Arizona Republican (Phoenix)
Arizona Sentinel (Yuma)
Arizona Weekly Citizen (Tucson)
Arizona Weekly Star (Tucson)
Arkansas Democrat (Little Rock)
Arkansas Gazette
Aspen Daily Chronicle
Aspen Daily Times
Atlanta Constitution
Augusta (GA) *Chronicle and Gazette of the State*
Austin American Statesman
Bakersfield (CA) *Morning Echo*
Baltimore Sun
Belfast News Letter (Northern Ireland)
Billboard
Bisbee (AZ) *Daily Review*
Bismarck Tribune
Bismarck Weekly Tribune
Black Hills (SD) *Daily Times*
Black Hills (SD) *Weekly Pioneer*
Black Range (Socorro, NM)
Boston Globe
Bozeman Avan Courier
Brooklyn Citizen
Brooklyn Daily Eagle
Brooklyn Times Union
Buffalo Courier
Buffalo Express
Buffalo Times

Burlington (VT) *Daily Free Press*
Butte (MT) *Daily Post*
Butte (MT) *Miner*
Butte Weekly Miner
Cairo Bulletin
Californian (Salinas)
Carson City (NV) *Daily Appeal*
Casper (WY) *Star Tribune*
Champaign (IL) *Daily Gazette*
Cherokee (KS) *Index*
Cheyenne (KS) *Daily Leader*
Cheyenne (KS) *Daily News*
Chicago Inter Ocean
Chicago Tribune
Cincinnati Daily Star
Cincinnati Enquirer
Clifton(AZ) *Clarion*
Clifton (AZ) *Copper Era*
Cochise Review
Coffeyville (KS) *Journal*
Coffeyville (KS) *Weekly Journal*
Colorado Chieftain (Pueblo)
Colorado Miner (Georgetown)
Columbus (OH) *Courier*
Columbus (OH) *Dispatch*
Columbus (OH) *Vidette*
Commercial Advertiser (Tombstone)
Coshocton (OH) *Tribune*
Council Grove (KS) *Republican*
Courier Journal (Louisville, KY)
Daily Alta California (San Francisco)
Daily Appeal (Carson City, NV)
Daily Enterprise (Livingston, MT)
Daily Inter Ocean (Chicago, IL)
Daily Journal of Commerce (Kansas City)
Daily New Mexican (Santa Fe, NM)
Daily Nonpareli (Council Bluffs, IA)
Daily Ohio Statesman (Columbus)
Daily Tombstone

Dallas Daily Herald
Dayton (OH) *Herald*
Defiance (OH) *Democrat*
Denver Republican
Denver Rocky Mountain News
Deseret Evening News (Salt Lake City)
Detroit Free Press
Dodge City (KS) *Globe*
Duluth (MN) *New Tribune*
El Paso Times
Elk County Advocate (PA)
Empire City (KS) *Echo*
Emporia (KS) *Ledger*
Enterprise (Virginia City, NV)
Era (London)
Eureka (NV) *Daily Sentinel*
Exhibitors Herald and Moving Picture World
Fall River (MA) *Daily Herald*
Feather River Bulletin (Quincy, CA)
Ford County Globe (KS)
Fort Benton (MT) *Weekly Record*
Fort Collins (CO) *Daily Express*
Fort Scott (KS) *Daily Monitor*
Fort Wayne (IN) *Daily Gazette*
Fort Wayne Sentinel
Fort Worth Daily Democrat
Fort Worth Daily Gazette
Fort Worth Star Telegram
Frank Leslie's Illustrated
Freedman's Journal (Dublin, Ireland)
Fresno (CA) *Expositor*
Fresno (CA) *Morning Republican*
Galena (KS) *Miner*
Galena (KS) *Weekly Republican*
Galveston Daily News
Galveston Evening Tribune
Georgia Constitutionalist (Augusta)
Girard (KS) *Press*
Globe Arizona Silver Belt

Gold Hill (NV) *Daily News*
Graham Guardian (Safford, AZ)
Great Falls (MT) *Tribune*
Great West (Denver)
Guardian (London)
Gunnison (CO) *Free Press*
Gunnison (CO) *Review*
Harper's New Monthly Magazine
Hartford (CT) *Courant*
Helena Independent
Houston Morning Star
Houston Telegraph
Idaho Semi Weekly World (Idaho City)
Idaho Weekly Keystone (Ketchum, ID)
Independent (Hutchinson, KS)
Indianapolis Star
Kansas City Journal
Kansas City Star
Kansas City Times
Kansas Democrat (Oswego)
Kansas Herald of Freedom (Wakarusa)
Knoxville Evening Sentinel
Labor Enquirer (Denver)
Lansing (MI) *State Journal*
La Plata Miner (Silverton, CO)
Las Vegas (NM) *Gazette*
Leadville (CO) *Daily Herald*
Leadville (CO) *Democrat*
Leavenworth (KS) *Bulletin*
Leavenworth (KS) *Post*
Lewiston (ID) *Daily Teller*
Los Angeles Herald
Los Angeles Times
Louisville (KY) *Courier Journal*
Luzerne Union (Wilkes Barre, PA)
Lyon County Times (Silver City, NM)
Mail (Stockton, CA)
Manford's New Monthly Magazine
Manitoba Free Press

Marshall (TX) *Messenger*
Memphis Daily Appeal
Memphis Public Ledger
Milwaukee Journal
Missoulian (Missoula, MT)
Mohave County (AZ) *Miner*
Montreal Gazette
Morning News (Wilmington, DE)
Morning Oregonian (Portland)
Morning Star (Washington, DC)
Napa (CA) *Journal*
Napa Valley Register
National Police Gazette
National Republican (Washington, DC)
Nevada State Journal (Reno)
New Century (Fort Scott, KS)
New Orleans Bulletin
New York Clipper
New York Dramatic Mirror
New York Evening World
New York Times
New York Tribune
Norwalk (CT) *Gazette*
Oakland Times
Oakland Tribune
Ogden (UT) *Daily Commercial*
Ogden (UT) *Standard*
Ohio State Journal (Columbus)
Omaha Daily Bee
Oregon Statesman (Salem, OR)
Otago Witness (New Zealand)
Owensboro (KY) *Messenger*
Pantagraph (Bloomington, IL)
Pall Gazette (London)
Parson (KS) *Daily Eclipse*
Pascagoula (MS) *Democrat*
Penny Illustrated (London)
Petaluma (CA) *Argus*
Petaluma (CA) *Daily Morning Courier*

Philadelphia Inquirer
Phoenix Tribute
Phoenix Weekly Republican Pioche (NV) *Record*
Pioneer Times (Deadwood, SD)
Pitkin (CO) *Independent*
Pittsburgh Commercial
Pittsburgh Dispatch
Placer Herald (Rocklin, CA)
Police Gazette
Pomona (CA) *Progress*
Prescott (AZ) *Weekly Miner*
Pueblo (CO) *Daily Chieftain*
Quad City Times (IA)
Racine (WI) *Journal Times*
Radio Doings Magazine (Southern California)
Rapid City (SD) *Journal*
Record Epitaph (Tombstone)
Redondo (CA) *Reflex*
Reno (NV) *Evening Gazette*
Reno (NV) *Journal Gazette*
Richmond (IN) *Item*
Richmond (VA) *Times Dispatch*
River Press (Fort Benton, MT)
Rocky Mountain News (Denver)
Rocky Mountain Sun (Aspen, CO)
Sacramento Daily Bee
Sacramento Daily Union
Sacramento Record-Union
Saint Paul (MN) *Globe*
Salt Lake City Tribune
Salt Lake Evening Democrat
Salt Lake Times
San Antonio Light
San Bernardino County (CA) *Sun*
San Francisco Call
San Francisco Chronicle
San Francisco Examiner
San Jose Daily Evening News
Santa Fe New Mexican

Sea Coast Echo (Bay St. Louis, MS)
Seattle Daily Times
Seattle Post Intelligencer
Show World
Sierra County Advocate (NM)
Silver World (Lake City, CO)
Sioux City (IA) *Journal*
Sonoma County (CA) *Journal*
Springfield (MO) *Press*
St. Johns (AZ) *Herald*
St. Joseph (MO) *Herald*
St. Louis Post Dispatch
St. Paul Globe
Stanford (KY) *Interior Journal*
Sterling (KS) *Bulletin*
Sterling (KS) *Gazette*
Stockton (CA) *Mail*
Sunday Herald (Waterbury, CT)
Sun River (MT) *Sun*
Sydney (Australia) *Morning Herald*
Tacoma (WA) *Daily Ledger*
Tacoma (WA) *News Tribune*
Temple (TX) *Times*
Terre Haute (IN) *Journal*
Times (Philadelphia)
Times Democrat (New Orleans)
Tombstone
Tombstone Epitaph
Tombstone Nugget
Tombstone Prospector
Tombstone Republican
Tombstone Weekly Nugget
Topeka State Journal
Tucson Citizen
Tulare (CA) *Advance Register*
Vancouver Sun
Variety
Victoria (British Columbia) *Daily Times*
Wabash Express (Terre Haute, IN)

Washington Standard (Olympia, WA)
Washington (DC) *Times*
Weekly Echo (Lake Charles, LA)
Weekly Santa Fe New Mexican
Weekly Standard and Express (Blackburn, England)
Weekly Yuma Sentinel
Western Liberal (Lordsburg, NM)
Western Mail (Cardiff, Wales)
White Pine News (Treasure City, NV)
Whittier (CA) *East Review*
Wichita Beacon
Wichita Daily Eagle
Wichita Star
Wilkes-Barre News
Wilmington (DE) *Evening Journal*
Windsor Beacon
Winslow (AZ) *Mail*
Wisconsin State Journal (Madison)
Wood River Times (Hailey, ID)
Yellowstone Journal (Miles City, MT)
Yerington (NV) *Times*
Yuma Sentinel

Archives, Collections, and Records

Arizona Historical Society, Tucson, AZ.
   George W. Chambers Papers
   James Covington Hancock Papers
Arizona State Library and Archives, Phoenix, AZ.
   Chattel Mortgages
   Criminal Register of Actions
   District Court Civil Cases
   Law Collection
   Superior Court Civil Cases
Cochise County Recorder's Office, Bisbee, AZ.
   Bills of Sale
   Chattel Mortgages
   County Coroner and Death Records
   Declarations of Homesteads

   Deeds of Mines, Grantor and Grantee
   Deeds of Real Estate, Grantor and Grantee
   Great Register, 1881–1931
   Leases
   Locations of Mines
   Power of Attorney
   Probate Orders
   Records of Mines
   Register of Actions
   Separate Property of Married Women
Cochise County Tax Assessor's Office, Bisbee, AZ.
   Delinquent Tax Roll
   Tax Roll, 1881–1931
Harris County Clerk's Office, Houston, TX.
   Probate Records
Harvard Law School Library, Cambridge, MA.
   Historical and Special Collections
   Langdell Hall
Kevin Mulkins Collection, Tucson, AZ.
Kingston School House Museum, Kingston, NM.
Missouri State Archives, Jefferson City, MO.
   Missouri Death Records, 1850–1931
New York Public Library, New York, NY.
Pima County, AZ
   Miscellaneous Records Book
Tarrant County Clerk's Office, Fort Worth, TX
   Marriage Records
Texas General Land Office Records, Austin, TX.
   Land Grant Abstracts
Texas State Library and Archives Commission, Austin, TX.
Tombstone City Archives, Tombstone, AZ.
   City Council Minutes, 1880–1882
   Code of Ordinance
   Recorder's Docket, 1881–1891.
Tombstone Courthouse State Park, Tombstone, AZ.
   Cochise County License Logs
Tombstone Western Heritage Museum, Tombstone, AZ.
University of Arizona, Tucson, AZ.
   Special Collections Department

US Department of the Interior, Bureau of Land Management, General Land
    Office Records. glorecords.blm.gov.
    Arizona Mineral Surveys
Western Heritage Museum, Tombstone, AZ.
    Elliott Collection
Works Progress Administration, Manuscript Division, Library of Congress,
    Washington, DC.
    Federal Writer's Project interviews

Index